Praise for *The River Wife*

"Fascinating . . . Agee is a gifted storyteller. Life is difficult, but never dull in the house that Jacques built."
—*USA Today*

"Epic in scope, covering a series of generations and bursting with entwined layers of plot tension, sex, violence and intrigue. . . . The writing through-out is lush, as the author examines the addictive allure of risk, along with the blessings and curses of family ties."
—*Los Angles Times*

"Engaging . . . Just as the ghost in Toni Morrison's *Beloved* is an infant and the narrator of Alice Sebold's *The Lovely Bones* is a murdered girl, Annie, al-though twice abandoned, is given immortality."
—*The Washington Post*

"Atmospheric . . . a savory gumbo of melodrama and beautiful writing."
—*The Christian Science Monitor*

"A historical novel that rewrites the rules with a unique gothic elegance . . . [Agee's] Southern gothic prose is raw and graceful."
—*The San Diego Union-Tribune*

"What a grand and gorgeous novel this is: passionate, stirring, filled with action, intrigue, romance, and surprise. Glorious."
—RON HANSEN, author of *Mariette in Ecstasy*

"Agee is a marvelous storyteller, and *The River Wife* is a complex and irresistible saga in the tradition of classic Southern fiction."
—SUSAN VREELAND, author of *Girl in Hyacinth Blue*

"Make sandwiches and turn off the phone, because *The River Wife* is a novel you won't put down. With her mythic vision, Agee has created a whole new version of family out of catastrophe, passion, treachery and blood."
—SANDRA SCOFIELD, author of *Occasions of Sin*

"In the tradition of Faulkner's *Absalom, Absalom!* . . . This story of secrets, ghosts, courage, and family will grab hold of you from the first page and hold you to the gorgeous and haunting end."
—LEE MARTIN, author of *The Bright Forever*

ALSO BY JONIS AGEE

Pretend We've Never Met

Bend This Heart

A .38 Special and a Broken Heart

Taking the Wall

Acts of Love on Indigo Road

Sweet Eyes

Strange Angels

South of Resurrection

The Weight of Dreams

THE
RIVER
WIFE

THE
RIVER
WIFE

a novel

JONIS AGEE

RANDOM HOUSE TRADE PAPERBACKS
NEW YORK

2008 Random House Trade Paperback Edition

Copyright © 2007 by Jonis Agee
Reading group guide copyright © 2008 by Random House, Inc.

Published in the United States by Random House Trade Paperbacks, an imprint of The Random House Publishing Group, a division of Random House, Inc., New York.

RANDOM HOUSE TRADE PAPERBACKS and colophon are trademarks of Random House, Inc.
RANDOM HOUSE READER'S CIRCLE and colophon are trademarks of Random House, Inc.

Originally published in hardcover in the United States by Random House, an imprint of The Random House Publishing Group, a division of Random House, Inc., in 2007.

Library of Congress Cataloging-in-Publication Data
Agee, Jonis.
The river wife: a novel / Jonis Agee.
p. cm.
ISBN 978-0-8129-7719-6
1. Women—Missouri—Fiction. 2. Domestic fiction. I. Title.
PS3551.G4R58 2007
813'.54—dc22
2006051046

Printed in the United States of America

www.randomhousereaderscircle.com

2 4 6 8 9 7 5 3

Book design by Susan Turner

For Brent Spencer

There is no evil angel but Love.

—*Love's Labour's Lost*

THE
RIVER
WIFE

PROLOGUE

HEDIE RAILS DUCHARME

THE TREES WERE SO VERTICAL—THAT'S THE FIRST THING I NOTICED, EVEN before the river. And the land that rolled carpet flat away from the eye. As I stepped from the coupe in front of the courthouse in Jacques' Landing, Missouri, just above New Madrid, the only shiver I felt was a slight vertigo. I held on to the door of the coupe for a moment, and Clement Ducharme must have thought I was reconsidering, because he put his hand under my free arm and lifted me away. I was taller than him by a good two inches, and it seemed to make him proud. He insisted I wear my high heels whenever we were in public. Over the next few weeks, he would buy me pair after pair of shoes, all high heels, open toed, many with tiny straps and coy little rhinestone buttons. I was too young in love to question then.

In the street, tired farmers came and went, worrying about taxes, fore-closures, money they didn't have. It was 1930, the Great Depression, and everybody was poor but us, and nobody stopped to talk.

Cotton fibers floated in the air, rising and settling again, as if on an in-visible tide rinsing over the town. They caught in the screens of doors and windows, settled over uncovered dishes of beans and cornbread and fresh tomatoes, and clung to your tongue when you tried to talk, so you constantly found yourself licking every syllable as if it were part of a filthy word as you scraped your tongue against your front teeth and swallowed.

We climbed the worn flagstones, each with a small trough from eighty-some years of feet, up the cupped gray granite steps, and into the round green marble atrium. Clement pointed up at the green stained-glass rose that domed the roof three stories above us, and made me squint to see the repaired glass on the right side.

"Cannon fire from the Yankee bombardment," he said.

In fact, I would discover later that it was Billy Shut, the Confederate raider, whose rifle went off during a brief skirmish not long after the town was taken.

The light from the dome was green and slightly milky, and I wondered if I needed to slip on my glasses for a moment. It was the only secret I kept from him in the beginning—my weak eyes that wouldn't let me decipher words and details up close.

But I saw the drifts of dust in the shafts of green light, saw the cotton lint on the shoulder of his gray suit jacket. Harvest was early, the yield poor in the relentless heat, and he'd left a puny, half-full wagon in the farmyard to take me to town. There was still a slice on his chin where he'd cut himself shaving at the last minute. Do I have to explain everything? My mother had made me leave. I was seventeen. My sisters had stood aside. I would not be welcome back in the family for ten more years, but by then it would be too late.

My soon-to-be husband stood patient, red faced and freckled from the sun, his orange-red hair slicked down with oil, with a part along the right side that looked like it was made with a razor, the scalp bright red in the groove. Somehow he had managed to get a haircut that did not rise so far above the ears that you could see a rind of moon white where his lobe ended. Even farming, he was a neat man, clean, almost prissy with his scrubbed nails. He cleaned his teeth nightly with salt and a slick of river-willow bark he would slide between each of the small pegged points. You have child's teeth, I would tell him a few weeks after the wedding.

Although I would later return to the courthouse to retrace my path into the peculiar destiny I had chosen, family history wasn't what I was thinking about that day as I followed the path of Billy Shut's horse up the steps and felt the places where the iron shoes scored the marble floor as he began to collapse. The soles of my shoes were the thinnest leather, and in the other part of my mind, I would be registering the gouges with my toes as we stood there in the atrium waiting for Clement's uncle Keaton to come witness for us.

"Is your uncle coming?" I finally asked. He looked at the clock over the entrance to the courtroom, then at his wrist where he had on a gold Hamilton watch with a brown alligator band that stank a little when he sweated too much.

"Did you tell him we had to do it before the courthouse closes?" I asked. It wasn't only that, and he knew it. I couldn't go back home. I'd spent all my money on the bus ticket down here and a present for him—a cat's-eye ring for his little finger. It was the only size they had at Johnson's Jewelry in Resurrection when I left that morning, and I couldn't come empty handed, with nothing but a cardboard suitcase my mother begrudged me.

My feet began to ache after a while, and when I shifted my weight so I could lean against one of the columns, my heel caught in a chip from the horseshoe, and I started to go down. He caught me, though, and held me briefly, his ear against my chest, as if he could hear the double heartbeat through the good linen of my white suit. It was the last white suit I ever owned.

"Do you think—" I started to say again, but he put his fingers to my lips. His hands smelled of tobacco and the soft lavender scent he ordered from the barbershop twice a year. As much as anything, it was the scent of him that made my stomach pull hard with want. I was so young and there was a mystery unraveling, a door opening to the other side where the whole business you watch as a child suddenly becomes your own. You're grown up and now the world throbs with something bright the color of blood.

At four o'clock, Clement turned to me and nodded, his jaw clamped shut, lips thinned. It wasn't a face I wanted to see on my wedding day, but it was all I had, so I took his arm and we walked in a straight line through the atrium to the judge's chambers. When it came time to slip the ring on my finger, he pulled out a platinum band with a large round yellow diamond embedded in the middle. It was so big I had to squeeze my other fingers around it to keep it from sliding off.

When it came time to kiss, he whispered in my ear, "Get that ring fixed so it don't ever come off, hear?"

I was thrilled that he wanted to so thoroughly claim me, and after he paid the judge, we walked proudly arm in arm through the hot milky green light out into the late afternoon.

That was my wedding day. His uncle Keaton Shut waited three months to come to visit and by then the damage had been done. We didn't care though, we were happy. And almost nothing can dent that kind of joy. We were going to have the baby at home, where children of his family had always been born. I wasn't even afraid. And he was a good husband to me, bringing me flowers, feeding me ice cream, a spoonful at a time in the panting heat after dark when the river swished against the banks and the bullfrogs' deep bass rode the low notes below the peepers' high throbbing. Afterward, he would make love to me, sucking my swollen nipples until I felt an urgency, a burning so shrill I wanted him to tear me open, empty me and refill me with himself. I tore at his skin, and my own, trying to put us closer and closer still, as if the blood mingling could do that. We spent our days napping in the cool of the fan blowing over a cake of ice, and our nights loving, as we waited for the baby. I didn't care if another soul ever came to the door in those days. In fact, I didn't want them to . . .

This is love, I kept saying to myself as he sponged cool water over my shoulders and face while I lay in the tub, this is love, the yellow diamond ring wedged so tightly on my swollen finger that it sat between two ridges of flesh. And this is love as the light in the room darkened with an afternoon storm, and we stood out on the second-story porch, naked in the green rain, watching the tree limbs along the river flatten and spread horizontal in the wind while the phone in the hallway behind us rang and rang and rang.

"Clement," I said, looking out across the flat land shimmering in the heat, "this isn't a land to love, is it?"

He shook his head. "The Bootheel is a different kind of country altogether."

Jacques' Landing sits west of New Madrid, above the water in the table-flat bottomland spread between the foothills of the Ozarks, a distant shadow to the west, and the Mississippi to the east. St. Louis is only 165 miles north. Hanging between Kentucky and Tennessee to the east and Arkansas to the west, it's as if the whole state of Missouri has been trying to shake it off for years, like a vestigial tail.

I missed the Ozarks—the deep hollows and iron-colored streams of the woods, the crying birds running from tree to tree overhead as my sisters and I plunged through the underbrush, looking for purple pawpaws and ripe persimmons, then resting on the granite outcropping of the natural bridge we thought only our family knew about, peeling the fruit we'd found and sucking the sloppy sweet juice. I missed the dense scent of moist bark and pine needles, that heavy spice that filled your head like smoke until you were dizzy and falling into the wet leaves and wild grass. When you stood still and listened, the woods ticked and rustled around you. Always it seemed wet there, just after rain, just before rain, even in the fall, something primordial and damp, dirt being made beneath your feet, the slick silver trails of snails across the dead branches and dried leaves, the moist undersides of rocks soaking the air of the woods. I was never afraid as a girl. It took Clement to teach me fear.

"You're just tired with waiting," Clement said. "Come lie down now." He led me from the second-story porch where I'd been lying in a white wicker lounge with a pillow tucked in the small of my back, which ached so I couldn't ever sleep for long. The baby rolled and kicked inside me every time I tried to turn until I felt oddly battered and could not stand to be touched anymore, as if Clement's hands would bruise me.

I read magazines, *Harper's* and *National Geographic* and *Scribner's*, anything old because I could not stand the present or the future anymore. It was all I could do to last through another hot day, I did not want to imagine all that living outside this house. I began to stay up all night, holding my belly like a water-filled melon between my legs, panting in the heat on the balcony, wetting towels to lay across my chest, while Clement slept on until the telephone rang.

"Who is calling here every night?" I asked him.

"Just sleep," he said. "I'll be back before morning."

I watched the lights of his car bob against the willows across the road, then slash from one side to the other as the driveway turned into the road, pocked with holes and ruts after the recent rain, and the purr of the big Packard engine was soaked up by the wet air and replaced by the high grating rasp of the cicadas. If I had a torch, I'd set fire to every living thing tonight, I thought. A barge chugged up the river, its lanterns lit so I could see the men on deck passing a jug of moonshine and laughing, even their curses oddly clear. Someone began to play a fiddle and another joined in with harmonica, and two of the men stood and began to dance side by side in the clogging style so familiar in the hills. I tried to let it soothe me. I tried to think of the warm brown water slopping in its big basin, but I was seventeen and the doctor would only promise that I wouldn't remember a thing when the baby came. They'd give me a shot and I'd wake up a new mama.

I put on a thin cotton nightgown and went downstairs to the library with the dark forest-green walls, heavy mahogany furniture, and brightly colored Tiffany lamps and sank into the cool whisper of the Moroccan leather chair, lifting my feet to the footstool and finding relief from the heat at last. Determined to wait up for Clement, I gazed at the walls of books around me, thinking to find a title that would take me through the night. When I got to the bottom shelf on the wall to my right, I noticed a row of identical brown leather-bound books without titles on their spines, the sort of thing people used as diaries or journals or sketchbooks. I got up and awkwardly knelt down, pulling out the first. It had been there a long time apparently, for at first it seemed stuck to its neighbor, until the leather let go with a sticky tearing sound and the book eased into my hand. Inside the water-spotted cover was written:

ANNIE LARK DUCHARME, 1811–1821, Volume I.

The roses so red
And the lilies so fair—
The myrtle so bright
With the emerald dew—
He taught me to love him
And called me his flower
That was blooming to cheer him
Through life's dreary hour—

A Wildwood Flower

Was this his great-grandmother? Clement had never mentioned her. And what an odd name. I thumbed the pages, noting the drawings of insects, birds, butterflies, and flowers. It was probably one of those naturalist field books that would prove boringly exact, but with narrative passages in the neat penmanship of a previous age, I thought it looked varied enough to keep me awake.

Actually, it began with a curious passage, noting that what followed was a true account, a witness of death and resurrection following "the great New Madrid Shaking." My first impulse was to put the book away. I was in no mood for a religious tract of some sort, having heard of the "earthquake Christians," fanatics and Holy Rollers who abounded here in the Bootheel since the disaster. But her next sentences caught me, seeming almost familiar . . .

And so it was that the women of the old house on Jacques' Landing began to tell me their stories, and went on telling me over the years I've lived here. Sometimes I read the words they had written, sometimes they visited me in dreams; on many occasions they spoke outright, out loud to me, and I've never told a soul—until now. What follows is a true account, in their words and mine, the only wonder that we are so separate when the years are as a veil of dust put to dancing each time one of us moves through the rooms of the house One-Armed Jacques Ducharme built.

Part One

ANNIE LARK
DUCHARME

· · ·

"Numberless are the World's Wonders."

I

ER NARROW IRON BED, WITH ITS LOVELY WHITE SCROLLWORK—A LUXURY somehow accorded a girl of sixteen though her father was against it from the beginning—slid back and forth behind the partition as if they were on the river, the roar so loud it was like a thousand beasts from the apocalypse set loose upon the land, just as her father had predicted. Then the partition hastily erected for her privacy crashed to the floor. The cabin walls shook so, her bed heaving like a boat on rough waters. The stone chimney toppled, narrowly missing her brothers, who had leapt awake at the first rumbling and run outside in their nightshirts.

"Mother!" she cried, for hers was the last face the girl wished to see on this earth if this were truly Judgment. "Mother!" knowing she was too old to be held like a babe at breast, but wanting it anyway, "Mother!" and the ancient oaks to the south of the cabin groaned and began to crash with mighty concussion and the horses and cows bellowed. She clung to the tiny boat of her bed, and therein lay her mistake. "Mother!"

But her mother was busy with the young ones, rushing them in their bedclothes outside the cabin to join her father and brothers, who were on their knees praying while the ancient cypress shook like an angry god overhead, and the birds swarmed in screaming flocks, and the ground opened up. She could smell it, the cabin floor a fissure that stank of boiling sand and muck.

There was a terrific hammering and squealing as nails popped from wood, planks pulled apart, and the roof split in two. "Oh my mighty Lord," she prayed, "take me to your bosom where I shall not want."

Just then, as if in response, there was a deep rumbling, followed by a loud grating overhead as the roof beam pulled away from the walls with a sudden sigh and crashed down across her legs, numbing them with the sudden unbearable weight and pinning her to her grave.

She tried pushing at the beam, but it was too thick and heavy. Still she pushed and clawed, tearing her nails bloody, hammered with her fists, tried to lift her legs and kick out, but they were helpless, unable to move at all against the weight that kept pushing her down, past the point where she could stand it. She screamed until she was hoarse, unable to make herself heard over the chaos.

When the shaking subsided, her father appeared in the doorway holding a lantern, her brothers standing just behind, looking so frightened she almost felt sorry for them.

"Annie? Annie Lark?" he called into the darkness full of dust and soot from the collapsed chimney. The ground shivered and she could hear her brothers pushing away.

"She's dead!" the older brother cried. "Leave her—" They never could abide each other, and now he would consign her to hell.

"I'm in here," she called. "The roof beam has trapped me." She was certain that her father would rescue her then.

"Here—" Something flew through the air and thudded on the floor beside her. Although she stretched her arm, she could not possibly reach it, and the movement cost her a terrible tearing pain across her thighs.

"Father!" she called as another shiver brought another section of roof crashing down halfway to the door.

"Pray for strength, dear Annie, read the Scripture in the Bible and pray. He will deliver you!" Her father's voice began to grow distant as he backed away from the collapsing cabin.

She called out again, "Help me! Mother, please!"

The cabin groaned in a chorus with the falling trees and screaming birds. Then her father drew close again to the cabin door.

"I can't dislodge the beam, Annie, there's no time. Your brothers, the horses, nothing will come near to help. Please let us go." His voice was no longer deep and confident, full of authority. It had taken on the pleading softness of her younger brother, a child full of fear and want.

The beam was some two feet thick and twenty feet long, its displacement impossible to calculate amid the frantic animals and crying children and their own fearful hearts.

She wondered that they did not shoot her like a cow or horse with a broken leg. The roof groaned, spilling dust that appeared to be filled with the brittle leavings of tiny broken stars in the sudden moonlight.

"Give me a betty lamp and candle," she said. "And blankets, I'm so cold." She did not mention the pain radiating its terrible burning rays down her legs and up her back.

It took her father a moment to collect his courage to enter the cabin, find and light the lamp, and gather several candles and sulphurs. He placed only a single deerskin over her feet, which had begun to turn icy in the weight of the cold. He must take the other blankets to the family, she understood. When he tugged her own quilts up to her chin and kissed her forehead, his body was quaking.

"Farewell, dear girl"—his voice grew raspy—"we shall meet on the far shore, clothed in His bright joy."

The roof groaned again. His eyes went wild and he took a step back, almost stumbling over the log across her legs, and having to balance himself on the beam, pressing down, which caused a surge of pain that made her cry out. He whirled away and grabbed up guns, powder, and what provisions he could before running out the door into the darkness. She had so much to say that she clamped her lips closed, sealed them from cursing him forever as he hurried away. That was the last she ever saw of her family.

The pain came in waves rising up from her legs, clenching her stomach, spreading through her arms and bursting into her head. She panted and cried out in a rhythm as if giving birth, alone, to this terrible night.

There was a small window in the wall to her right, and as she lay there waiting for the Beasts of the Apocalypse to devour her, the waters of the damned to swirl about and swallow her, the mighty breath of God Himself to blow her into pieces that would never see salvation, she saw the distant fires devouring houses, heard the unnatural roar and rush as trees along the riverbank collapsed taking great chunks of earth with them, felt the wet hot air escaping from hell itself as the seams of the earth split and the damned cried forth, their breath the foul hissing steam that invaded the world.

At first she prayed in between the spasms of pain, but it was a dry excuse. Then she pushed at the beam, tried to dig her fingers into the shuck mattress, hollow a hole to drop through, but to no avail. She tried turning on her side, no, tried dragging herself upwards, no, tried edging out at an angle, no, tried pushing herself down beneath it, out the foot of the bed, no. She was panting and cold in her sweat-soaked gown, longing for a sip of water, which she had forgotten to ask for. We are always more interested in light than anything else, she discovered that night. If we could only see our predicament, then it would be somehow possible to imagine escaping it. In the darkness nothing is possible except terrible occurrences, so she lit the betty lamp.

Then in spite of her thirst, she had to relieve herself. Ashamed, she afforded herself the small pleasure despite the hours it meant afterward, lying in the wet. It was hers, not a younger brother's or sister's, and that made a difference. Oh, she was paying for the pride of this bed, she thought, and watched the dawn arrive, first gray coated, then blue and bright through the small window. She fell into a fitful half sleep. So ended the first day.

When she awoke, the sun was shining, and she could see for certain the devastation and solitude that was her world. Her legs were merely a heavy aching numbness now. The betty lamp had died, and she wondered that her father could not spare the oil to give comfort to a dying daughter. Looking around the cabin, though, she knew with certainty that they would never return. With the partition down, there was one large room, and she could see the fireplace near the doorway. When the chimney tumbled, some of the large stones had fallen onto the hearth, where her brothers slept in cold weather. In summer, they slept outside on the porch, wrapped in hot blankets against the insects. The large black stew pot had tumbled into the room. A wonder her father had not bothered to pick it up. Her mother would miss the pot, which had served faithfully every day of their lives. Along the wall to her left, the pallet where her younger sisters slept, next to her parents' bed, was strewn with broken crockery and jars of pears her mother had preserved from the first crop of their new trees. How the children loved those pears, so sweet when ripe that the juice ran between their fingers!

Her mother must have hastily snatched the few pieces of clothing they owned, for there was nothing of value that she could see. Her father had indeed taken all the blankets. The crock of oil she so desperately needed was broken and spilled across the dirt floor. She was lucky the shaking occurred in the night when no candles or lamps were burning, and the fire in the hearth had so burned down that it was gray empty ash now. The crude wooden rocking horse she had constructed for the baby was on its side but intact beside her parents' bed. He'd never know how his sister had loved him. In the middle of the room, the rough oak table her father had made was crushed by the other end of the beam that imprisoned her legs. The benches too were crushed. Only her mother's rocking chair remained in the corner of the room, miraculously unscathed, its black lacquer finish glowing dully in the dusky light. She had rocked all her babes in that chair, but the carved lion faces with their jaws agape and fierce, enraged eyes had always frightened the girl enough that she never envied the other children given permission to sit in it. Now she imagined the eyes glaring at her, triumphant, and she couldn't even look in that dark corner by the door that hung half off its leather hinges.

The hellish smell in the air was gone, replaced by what she surmised to be the dense odor of earth released when the huge trees with the deepest roots were upturned like twigs. It was oddly comforting, the scent of fresh split wood, the dense musk of dirt overriding the sharp stink of piss and the salt rime of her fear.

She thought of all the days when she had wanted only to lie abed, dreaming, and now she was cursed to die here, in a growing thirst, her tongue swelling, her throat so parched she had difficulty swallowing. This would be a slow death. Her father was right, she must have been the worst of sinners. What good came of a life such as hers? She tried to make amends in prayer. She begged for release. She promised herself to God. She would be handmaiden pure, and rejoice only in His glory. But nothing worked. And so she began to curse, trying to thrash, to move herself, to tear her legs from under the crushing weight of the beam. Yes, now she could feel it: The numbness was turning again to unbearable pain as her legs began to die. She screamed, hoping some passerby would hear, come to her rescue, but only the wind replied, rattling the broken world, sifting a few snowflakes from the roof. She held her mouth open trying to collect enough to satiate her thirst, but they disappeared on her tongue too quickly.

It was well after noon that second day when she heard a knocking at the front of the cabin, and a voice she recognized called her name. It was Matthieu, a boy she had once danced and flirted with at a social, whose family lived in the town of New Madrid.

"I'm here!" she cried. "In here—"

He came hesitantly, like a deer picking its way into a meadow, stopping every few steps to look for danger. He was a tall, thin boy, with white blond hair and a narrow face that made him look sensitive—sympathetic watery blue eyes, thin nose, and a rather full wide mouth that would be more appealing on a girl perhaps, though she had liked it enough to let him kiss her quickly on the lips. He had tasted of anise.

Stopping a few feet away as if to maintain propriety—she was, after all, a girl in a bed—he snatched off his red knit hat and tucked his hands under his arms and inquired as to her health. He didn't look so well either, with dark sleepless circles under his blue eyes, scrapes on both cheeks, blood matting his hair, and coat torn and stuck with burs and dried grass.

Still she felt ashamed of the damp she was lying in, the acrid smell, and the full brown head of hair that had been her pride, now tangled like a madwoman's around her face. She could not drive him off, she told herself, she must charm and cajole him, convince him to help her.

"Matthieu," she said. "Can you move this log, please?" She was proud of herself, so polite and ladylike. If he came any closer she'd snatch his face and bloody it raw with her nails. *Hurry! For God's sake, hurry!* she wanted to scream. There had been five big shakes and twenty small ones since last night. She'd been counting. She could hear the river sucking close by. Soon the outer walls would come down.

He frowned and looked around the cabin in wonder, his mouth opening and closing in questions that answered themselves. He frowned some more when he glanced up at the open roof, the sagging shingles and boards.

"Where is the river now?" she asked. He clambered over the beam, pushing down with his hand inadvertently as his leg caught. She could have killed him, but bit her lip against the painful surge, and smiled as her crushed legs throbbed anew. Her lips were chapped raw and bloody, a fitting color for seduction.

"I'm thirsty," she said, her voice croaking at the end.

He looked up startled and glanced out the door. She hadn't meant to send him away.

"No," she said, "don't leave me."

"I'll have to check the well," he said. "It might have been split open, but I have my canteen. It's right outside—"

"Don't leave," she pleaded.

"I'll just get the water," he said, his voice soft and comforting, his lips quivering.

She saw in his eyes that she was dying. That he would give her the mercy of water, the hour of comfort, but that he could do nothing to free her. They would not speak of it, then. It would not do to make him feel a failure. She knew about men, knew them from her father and brothers, and now this bitter bitter lesson.

The roof beam had taken six men, five horses, and a pair of oxen to raise—how could one boy, not full grown, manage to move it? Her father had been right. It was wedged just so between the walls. It would take too long to chop it into segments small enough to move, and perhaps even that was impossible since the wood was old oak, like iron, and would dull the ax blade down too quickly.

Matthieu returned with his canteen, the water tasting tinny but cold as it trickled down her throat.

"Keep it," he said. "But drink slowly. The well's filled with sand." He looked toward the hearth and empty shelves along the far wall. "I'll find you something to eat."

She spied the pan of field peas from supper lying on its side under what was left of the table kneeling in the center of the room, and pointed it out. He retrieved the pan and a spoon and apologized for something that was unclear to her so she grabbed the spoon and stuffed her mouth with the cold gritty paste, unmindful of how she looked. Matthieu drew up a log stool and sat down beside her. When she had finished several spoonfuls, she put the pan aside. It must last, she suddenly realized.

"Tell me of the others," she said, laying her hand on his, now clasped on his knees like the best boy in church. "My family—"

There was a slight tremor of the earth and more snow and dirt sifted onto the bed from the roof as the cabin walls groaned. The stew pot rolled hard against a chimney stone and clanked. They both jumped and she tightened her hand on his while his face paled and he bit his lip. He was a braver boy than most.

"All of the townspeople have fled inland." He glanced outside and she knew then. "It was a hellish night—we were all certain that the morrow would bring naught but Judgment Day. Most folks have left their worldly goods and begun to pray. The minister and priest are with us, having abandoned their churches that were anyway knocked apart. They say it is a great sign of God's disapproval and we must abandon what God has put asunder. The river will take it." He chanced a look at her face and she tried to smile some encouragement, as if she were not included in what God and the river planned.

"My family?" She rubbed his skinned knuckles with her thumb. To have him here was almost more than she could bear now, knowing that he must leave.

"Your mother wept and pleaded with your father and brothers, then with anyone who would listen, that someone return to seek news of you." His voice softened and his eyes filled. He bit his lower lip and looked at the beam and her trapped legs and shook his head. What news he would bring would be more awful than the girl's death. He bent his head to their hands, his back shaking. She could feel the tears soaking her fingers, and would have cried if her own tears had not dried hours ago in the long night.

"The river is close, isn't it?" she asked. By dawn she had begun to hear its peculiar talk, the murmurings and chasing questions of the many streams that fed it, swirling, resisting, courting and escaping, the fish-thick muddy water such a grave.

He lifted his head, wiping his eyes on his coat sleeve, and looked in her eyes for a moment, as if that were all he could risk. "There was a packet boat, two paddlers, several flatboats and barges when it began. They've disappeared. The fur trappers who dig into the banks above town, the Indian village—Shawnee or Osage I believe, just south of us—all gone. Word kept arriving all night as stragglers stumbled in, exhausted and terrified. This is a fearful place now. We are all waiting for the Resurrection, which the minister and priest claim will be coming any day." He looked at her legs one last time and stood.

"No." She tried to clasp his hand in hers, to forbid its escape, but he backed away.

"I'm sorry, Annie Lark. I had hoped—" He took another step back and pulled on his red knit hat, so joyful a color among the ruins. If only she could convince him to stay, to be with her until—

"Don't leave me! Matthieu, please, I'm afraid!" Her eyes flooded with tears as he swam backward, as if time were retrieving itself back into the womb of its birth.

"I'm sorry, Annie, I thought we'd be married." His face twisted with anguish.

"Yes," she cried. "We will, help me, we will, Matthieu."

He continued as if she hadn't spoken, caught up only in his own failure and shame. "I thought—oh, I can't! I can't help you anymore!" The cabin walls shook and rolled softly and he turned and fled. She could hear him struggling with his frantic horse, shouting at it, then finally mounting apparently, because the last sound was the hooves hitting the frozen churned dirt, then nothing but the burst of birds screaming in the remaining trees outside, and what she took to be the whisper of river cinching its way to her door.

She threw the pan of peas across the room, likewise the water, and vowed to outrace the river's claim. Then she closed her eyes and slipped into sleep, waking only for the renewed shaking and uproar as the world continued to come apart around her. She could feel a fever coming on, chills followed by soaking sweats, and sounds hurt her head fiercely, and daylight when it came was a spike in her skull. The pain in her legs reduced to numbness again and rose to her waist, then her arms, finally her chest, so she was pinioned to the bed, half-dead. In her delirium she saw her mother again, bade farewell to her with the youngest in her arms, would not speak to the father or brothers she could see running away to the west, so affrighted they abandoned the family altogether.

"NO!" SHE SHOUTED HERSELF AWAKE. IT WAS THE THIRD DAY, HER THROAT SO closed she could hardly breathe, her eyes hurt to open more than a squint. Yet it was enough to see the water beginning to finger its way across the floor of the cabin, hesitant, darting, puddling in depressions like milk poured into a bowl of flour. She could not die fast enough, it seemed.

She was burning up amid a cold snow falling through the ceiling, her tongue swollen so far she could only groan like an animal. The last human words her own denial, and the sun would not set, would not take its light out of her face—she struck out at it—

"*Doucement, ma chère, doucement.*" The gruff voice was French. God was French? Impossible! The voice was a tablespoon pushing between her teeth, and something soothing trickling into her mouth, down her throat. She bit down for more but the spoon disappeared. "*Bien sûr,*" he said, and the spoon again, water and something smoky and burning that made her open her eyes.

"Brandy. Ward off pain, no?" He spooned another draught of the mixture into her mouth. Then he offered to let her sip from the metal cup, lifting her head and shoulders easily with one arm that smelled of burnt animal fat and lavender. Lavender? After a few more sips, her throat opened enough that she could breathe again without choking. She had not realized how she had begun to pant in shallow gulps.

He was clad in a buckskin jacket beaded with flowers, a white ermine hat perched on his ears, and buckskin trousers, darkened and shiny with grease. Around his neck in jaunty style was tied a bright blue silk lady's scarf—ah, the lavender, he had been courting in this catastrophe! His deer-hide mittens, fur inside, lay carelessly thrown on her stomach. One of the French fur trappers her father had warned her about. A scavenger who took Indian wives, spawned countless half-breed children, and abandoned all for the next new territory. Disease ridden and godless. A woman touched by one of those men might just as well kill herself, her father had announced. The French! He spat when he said it. For once her mother had kept quiet.

"Here's more, drink it all." He filled the cup with brandy only slightly diluted by water now. As she drank, he watched her as if making up his mind about something. Then his eyes slid down her body and back to her face. He nodded as if she had met with his approval, despite her filthy condition.

"Pretty!" he murmured, then picked up her hands, turning the palms up and rubbing the thick calluses with his thumb. "Work hard!"

She nodded. It didn't matter what he did to her now.

"I must move *ce petit bâton*." He tapped a thick, long finger on the log as if it were a mere sapling.

She watched him slopping through the ankle-deep water on the floor. She couldn't let him leave her alone, that was all, whatever he really wanted, she would not let him go. Even if she had to grab his knife or gun and hold him prisoner, she was not going to die alone, damn it! Then she noticed the pile of their household goods by the door. So he was a scavenger. He wouldn't leave her. She was a rich find—a young woman abandoned by her family, a girl who could cook and clean and—

She shivered. It was up to her to make him like her, to make him want to save and care for her while her legs healed. She made up her mind at that moment, if he helped her, she would—

Then he surprised her by reappearing with a length of heavy chain. Wrapping it around the beam, he dragged the other end outside and began yelling, cursing in French, shouting at what she later discovered was a yoke of oxen and a couple of saddle horses he had found wandering confused and frightened, owners fled.

At first the huge beam only shifted an inch, enough to awaken the shattered bones in her legs so she thought she would faint. But she drank long and deep from the cup and felt the pain move away, perch merely on the edge of her mind, not in the center. The man yelled again, then she heard the sound of a leather strap hitting the broad flanks of the oxen. In her mind she saw the arm rise and fall, and urged it to hit harder, her own arm aching with the force of the blow, and the beam slid another few inches, shifting so its end hung just over her head, threatening to decapitate her. He won't move it, a voice tempted, nothing can save you, you know that. But he yelled, cajoled, and beat the animals, and the log inched toward her head, forcing her to turn and cling to the far side to give it room, and then her right leg was free, and the log ground as it pivoted and slid off her left and she cried out.

The man came running with an odd spraddling gait as if he were astride rolling logs in the water, because another shaking had commenced. "*Espérez*," he said, in his broken French-English, but she knew what he meant.

She tried to lift her crushed legs, but could not. He saw and quickly collected her in his arms, pressing her face against the lovely red and white beaded flowers, abrading her cheek, for which she had never been more grateful. She clasped her arms around his neck, ignoring the pain that fought to take her into its black embrace, and allowed herself to be released from her watery tomb.

Outside, the devastation stretched for as far as she could see. Capricious this God, leaving some trees standing, smashing others, ripping open the earth, turning good red soil yellow with sand, heaving bones and coal from the deep, then closing the door as if cleaning a room after death. The river was wider and haphazard now, the banks moved back or gone in places. The little town of New Madrid, so scientifically laid out in neat squares, now looked as if a giant wolf had swiped it apart with his paw. Houses tumbled, some half-burnt, others with walls askew, roads erupted, the river already surrounding and covering the site. And silence, except for the water slopping, not even wind, as if the final days had come and emptied the world of what was good, and in the aftermath, there was only this . . .

She closed her eyes to the destruction and bodily pain as he placed her in the back of a high wheeled cart on a bed of clothing and goods he must have scavenged from other cabins. He tucked her in as lovingly as her own mother, and she could hear him pushing the oxen into the shafts and tying the horses to the back of the cart, hurrying through the water that was surging toward them.

"The wooden horse—inside, take it!" she yelled as loudly as she could, hoping he would hear her despite her worn-out voice. Because she must have something from this life, she thought, one thing for the world she would enter next, where she would never be known again as daughter and sister. In a moment he shoved the toy into the makeshift bed beside her, and she stroked the soaked wood, thanking him over and over as the cart bounced briefly with his weight climbing in and then lurched forward through the rising waters. She would not know until later that among the several goods, he had also taken the iron stew pot and the rocking chair, whose faces mocked her in the days to come.

. . .

I closed the volume of Annie's story as my eyes flooded with tears of relief for her rescue. I let myself have a good, long cry, as if I were Annie, the trapped girl, in need of help. When I was done, I dried my eyes with the hem of my loose cotton gown. Just as I turned the journal page, I saw something shift in the dark shadow of the doorway.

Clement was home! I started to clamber out of the chair, but when I called his name, there was no answer. No one was there. I sat back, listening, but there was only the wind shushing the trees, fluttering the brocade drapes at the open windows. It must have been my imagination, I assured myself with one last look around the dark edges of the room. I thought of going to bed, but wasn't sleepy yet, so I opened the book again, despite the chill across my shoulders that made me tuck my legs up and draw the light silk shawl from the back of the chair around me.

2

THAT EVENING, LIKE EVERY EVENING WHEN THEY LAY DOWN BESIDE THE fire, her legs, which had healed as bent twigs and troubled to bear her weight, ached so terrifically that Jacques had to conjure every form of diversion to halt the tears she could not control. He sang and played the little squeezebox, and though he filled their little cabin with an ungodly squeal, it brought laughter from deep within her. She was so grateful for the rough Frenchman. He sang the bawdy tunes of rivermen and fur trappers, such as "Ride the White Swan," but he sang with such sincerity that they took on the air of love songs, which she knew them to be in his fashion. For he did love her. Though she felt herself a burden—a cripple, forever needing him—he shouldered it willingly. When they closed their eyes and fell asleep, it was as if she were a perfect blue robin's egg he cupped easily in his hand.

For five years they had wandered far from what was left of Annie's home. They followed the weather, the game, killing what they ate, trading pelts when they could. For the sixth winter, they had returned to this cabin in the Ozarks. Here game was plentiful, and they could avoid the worst of the northern cold, staying near hot, healing springs the Indians had told Jacques about, where Annie could ease her body.

Now that they had finally arrived, she would spend days lying in a mound of old deer hides. Each morning, he left their tiny cabin to check the traps and hunt for meat. The cabin was tucked into the trees against a rocky hill, and what little light filtered through by late morning was full of shadow and smoke from the fireplace and disappeared altogether by midafternoon.

Annie had not spent the past four winters growing weaker and unhappier by the hour. The first winter she'd concentrated on healing, the second, she'd tried and failed to learn to cook as well as Jacques. The third, she'd tried her hand at beadwork and quillwork in the fashion of the Indians they met and traded with. The fourth, she'd spent reading and rereading the few books he'd found. Now, in her fifth winter with Jacques, what would she do those dark months besides sleep? She thought about it all night.

The following morning she dragged herself to the fireplace a few feet away, took up the fleshing knife, and began on the deer hide Jacques had worked last night, being careful to use the concave underside for scraping as she'd seen him do. It took most of the day for her to gain enough of the smooth motion necessary to scrape the two-handled knife along the hide more than an inch or two at a time. The hide was hung over a wide piece of log raised at one end by short legs to create a slope. It made the work easier than spreading it on the dirt floor, but her shoulders and back ached mightily from bending over at the waist and drawing the knife toward her. For hours she stopped only to feed a log into the fire for light and warmth, and when the cabin door burst open, she was startled to see that it was dark outside, so intent had she been.

At first Jacques stared, the small frown lodged between his dark eyes, his wide, generous mouth a straight line. Then he raised his eyebrows, threw back his head and laughed.

"My little wife!" he said. "And where is the supper?" He waved at her mother's stew pot and scowled. She tossed the fleshing knife at his feet, and he hopped up and down pretending that she had cut him.

"Now I must beat you, my little robin!" When he bent down to gather her up, she pulled on his shoulders and he lost his balance, sprawling on the floor against her. She held his cold grizzled face in her two hands and kissed his mouth as he had taught her, soft then firm, waiting for his tongue to seek her lips. There was a splash of dried blood on his cheek, and he stank of wood smoke and blood and body, and his leather coat and trousers were stiff with cold, but it mattered not. When he held her, working the lacings of her buckskin shirt open, she would have become anything he wanted. He had saved her life, and he had taught her how a man and woman can love, and no matter what anyone might say, they were husband and wife in every sense. When her shoulders were free of the shirt he caressed her breasts, kissing her nipples, suckling until she was wild, pulling the lacing of his buckskin breeches to free his "monster" as they called it, and then he mounted her, carefully holding his weight so as not to hurt her legs or back, though it would not have mattered at that moment when pain and pleasure became one surging wave washing them down and together.

That night he showed her how to use the other edge of the fleshing knife for trimming, how to improve her stroke for long, smooth scrapes that left the hide intact. They ate venison stew and held each other in bed, watching the flames while the wind howled outside the tiny cabin, thrusting down the chimney as if it wanted to put out the fire protecting them from the bitter cold.

The next afternoon he brought in a brace of red fox, an ermine, and a rabbit. She was to learn on the rabbit while he peeled and slid the skin from the others. He laid the limp gray and white body on the hearth, the long ears so delicate it seemed that the firelight shone through their pale length. There was something so utterly still about the animal, it reminded her of the way rabbits froze in the presence of danger, and she immediately wanted to draw its form. It could have been stretched out sleeping, caught by drowsiness in midleap.

"We can eat your mistakes," Jacques said. "As long as you finish before the body stiffens. Remember," he held her with his rich brown eyes, "if the hind legs are rigid, you may still eat, but if the joint becomes loose, throw it away." He pushed a long strand of brown hair off his face, tucking it behind his ear.

There were things she didn't understand about him at all, such as why he insisted on the many small vanities of his oiled hair, which he tied back with a buckskin strip instead of cutting it shorter as her father and brothers had, and why twice a year he handed her his big bowie knife to cut the length to his shoulder again. That was another thing. Jacques never let any-one else touch the knife he kept in the beaded sheath at his side, where it slipped out so smoothly and quietly that it was almost more dangerous than a gun. When she'd asked for her own knife, he'd laughed and said that his pretty little wife had no need for such things. She was determined to change his mind.

She took the rabbit without hesitation, ignoring the droplets of blood clinging to the gray fur along the belly gash where he had emptied out the guts.

"Look, *ma chère*." He lifted the rabbit's head and thumbed the cleft in the lip. "Young, fresh rabbit, narrow cleft, and this—" He took a paw between his forefinger and thumb and pressed, spreading the claws. "Smooth, sharp." He turned the claws sideways. "In the old, they crack."

He held out the rabbit's ear, rubbing it gently. "Feel."

It was soft and bent easily.

"Always the young ones make the best eating. Don't let fur touch the meat though." He made a sour face and shook his head. Her brothers and father had done all the hunting and skinning of the animals that her mother and she cooked, and they were often blamed for the poor taste that resulted. Now she knew why.

"Save the blood for—how you say—to make *boudin* and soup." He held up a stoppered gourd. When she didn't seem grateful, he shrugged and set it aside. "Also *le coeur*." He put his fingers to his heart. "And the liver." These he loved to fry and eat so hot they burned his fingers and mouth.

He rose to his knees, picking the fox up by the long leather loop binding the hind legs together and hanging it from a nail on the split-log mantelpiece. With his big knife he sliced down the front legs, then repeated the incision on the hind legs, slicing from the anus to the throat in one long stroke. He was constantly sharpening the knife.

He looked expectantly at her and watched as she picked up the butcher knife in one hand and pulled the rabbit toward her with the other.

"Cut." He pointed to the front leg joint of the rabbit and made a sawing motion with his knife. When she poked at it with the tip of the knife, he snorted and made a clean slice through the leg as if it were butter. She had to hack a bit on the other leg, but managed and then watched as he began to peel the skin off the fox as if he were turning a glove inside out, using the knife on any connecting tissue that resisted only a moment before releasing. When he reached the head, he left the skin hanging and looked down at her.

The rabbit skin seemed harder to pull than his fox, and she ended up gouging the flesh in several places and tearing holes in the fur as the knife slid out of her control. When she reached the head she flung the knife and skin down on the wounded red flesh, angry and discouraged.

He nodded and took up the fox head, slipping the blade under the chin and loosening the skin carefully so that the face seemed to lift and slide off like a garment, leaving the naked flesh and clouded eyes so whole it was possible to observe the musculature stretched tautly over the skull. There was a terrible beauty in the demarcations of those fine bones and exposed parts. While he worked to reverse the skin and prepared to flesh it, she could not keep her eyes from the striations that seemed to hold the jaws in place, teeth bared at the last of its luck.

When she went back to her rabbit, she saw that she had worked against the body, jabbing and forcing pieces of skin away. Jacques made a sound of disapproval with his tongue, picked up what was left of the rabbit and sliced the head away. From the neck down, the body lay tender red as one of mother's lost babies, back curved and legs curled into its body. Despite her poor work, she could make out the muscles of the powerful hind legs and back and again felt that awful wonder. Of all that passed that winter in the cabin, this moment was the awakening of a powerful curiosity, one that would change both of them forever.

Within a fortnight she had learned to hone her knife, although the blade was inferior to Jacques' and would not hold the sharpness long. She learned to skin fox, ermine, beaver, raccoon, opossum, muskrat, otter, coyote, mink, skunk, weasel, lynx, bobcat, badger, bear, and of course, rabbit.

Later that winter she would carefully boil rabbits whole to release the disguising flesh from the bones so she could study the construction of the animal, see how the hind legs were built to spring and speed away. The body seemed composed of the same parts as their own: skull, neck, backbone, ribs, feet, shoulder and hip, leg, but such variety! At first Jacques was amused at her wonder, and claimed to relish the boiled meat in daily soup or stew. Then as she began to boil the other animals to work on, he helped her separate the clean bones and reassemble them like a child's wooden puzzle. She delighted in the fineness of the bones surrounding the eye sockets, bones sometimes so thin the light shone through, and the heavy jaws in contrast. The teeth varied by use, she discovered: the large front teeth of the rabbit for gnawing vegetable matter, the sharp teeth of the mink and ermine for tearing meat. With the white skeletons of animals hanging around the cabin like ghosts, she felt the same wonder as before, but also frustration. She knew each bone had a name, but she was ignorant of it, ignorant of all that others knew. It disgusted her, and she vowed that she would no longer take the lives of things she was so ignorant of. If they were to live in this fashion, she would learn the particulars. She wasn't blind, her legs were crippled, but she could see and taste and hear and smell and touch. She would never know the broad world—she realized that—but she would know its infinite details, and she would write them down and not forget them. If she could learn all she had this winter, she could learn more.

THE FIRST SPRING RAIN CAME DURING THE NIGHT WITH A SUDDEN WARM WIND from the south, and Annie left the cabin door open all morning to watch as the snow and ice disappeared from the hillside, releasing a rich scent of dirt and rock. The dark wet branches of the trees seemed to fatten before her eyes, the buds growing large and visible as if plumping with the softly falling rain. She rubbed her arms and stretched in the good air, too restless to draw or work on her hides. She had a surprise for Jacques, something that made the day so delicious, even the water dripping off the roof seemed to clean the air, sharpen the edges. She was standing in the doorway now, waiting, when she caught a glimpse of motion amongst the trees to the left. She stepped back without taking her eyes off the woods, groping for the gun they kept beside the door, but instead of grasping it, she knocked it down. Oh, there it was again—something large, brown, a bear? Her chest tightened and she began to pant. They ran so fast, if she took her eyes off it, would it charge before she had the gun up, prepared to fire? If she closed the door, it could smash it down. The animal stepped out of the trees, reared up on its hind legs, and sniffed the air hungrily. Without taking her eyes from the figure, she eased down, braced on her crutch, and found the gun, an old flintlock. But the bear must have caught her motion, because it swung the massive head toward her, sniffing for her scent, which she prayed the wet was keeping to ground. She waited, motionless, though her thighs cried for relief and her hips ached. The bear seemed puzzled, lifting its nose higher to catch her scent, finally sighing, dropping to all fours and shuffling hurriedly past their clearing, leaving a rank, decayed scent and paw impressions so deep in the mud that the claws filled with silver water and hadn't washed away by the time Jacques returned at twilight.

Although she was eager to relate the tale of her encounter, Jacques immediately made her close her eyes and hold out her hands. There was a strange squawk and Jacques cursed in French, but she kept her eyes shut until she felt the warmth and feathery weight in her hands. A crow! Trying to balance on one leg, holding up the other with a twig splint, the agitated crow struggled to keep upright. She closed her hands gently and could feel its bone structure—why, it was starving!

The bright intelligent eye stared back haughtily, almost as if the creature expected her to wait on him. She laughed and lifted her face to Jacques' for a kiss, which prompted the crow to squawk. How could she not love a man who would save a bird like this? While Jacques held the body still, she bound the snapped leg with deerhide strips and began to offer pieces of the rabbit stew she had just made. At first the crow hesitated, examining her with its dark glittery eye, and then the beak stabbed at her fingers and plucked away the morsel. Holding the food in its beak, the bird tilted its head and studied her again for a sign of some malice or trick, then gulped the meat. She fed him several more scraps, as well as a few kernels of their precious dried corn, and finally held up the tin drinking cup of water, dipping her fingers in it to show the clear liquid. Again he watched her for a moment before he thrust in his beak, filled it, then tipped his head back to swallow. When he had his fill, he shook the water from his beak, scraped one side of his beak against the lip of the cup, then the other, as if sharpening, and for the first time took a look at the repaired leg, holding it out as a young girl would admire a new bracelet.

Jacques and Annie laughed and moved the crow to the pile of furs at the side of the fireplace where she usually rested and worked. She scooped stew onto two tin plates, along with her poor attempt at biscuits from breakfast, and sat back to eat. The crow watched them through the whole meal, trying to balance on the good leg, finally nestling down in the fur, eyes closed, firelight glistening on the oily black feathers.

"Let's call him Carl," she said. "For my brother who disappeared on the river. I still miss him." Her voice caught and Jacques hugged her, stroking her head while her eyes filled as they did every time she was reminded of her lost family.

"I'm your family, *chérie*." His breathing hurried as he held her, his fingers unlacing the front of her deerhide top.

"I just want to see it again," she whispered as he pulled the bottom of her shirt up her thighs. "I miss the river."

"Soon as the woods are green, it will be time to take the hides. It's been a good season, *ma chère*, we will have enough to begin building." He slipped his hand between her legs. "I make you a proper bed, eh?"

She forgot all about the bear until the morning, when Jacques found the footprints, each claw a frozen slash. She wanted him to see her bravery, but he made her go through another shooting lesson instead and fashioned a gun rest at her height beside the door. Scolding her for having the door open, he marched off in possession of righteous anger, and she waited until she was sure he was gone before she eased the door open to welcome in another day of spring rain. "I'm not going to be a prisoner," she told the crow, who gave a deep chortle and hopped one-legged to the breakfast scraps on her plate. "When we get home, it will all be different."

"JACQUES, JACQUES. JACQUES, JACQUES." CARL'S SUDDEN CRY CARRIED JUST THE note Annie used. She turned around in time to see Jacques throw his head back and roar with laughter. The crow imitated him, ending with a raucous caw that scattered the flock of sparrows out of the trees behind them. At the sudden rush of wings Carl flapped and stepped forward as if to follow them, but then stopped and looked at Annie.

"He is healed, yes?" Jacques asked. He reclined by the small fire they had built for the noon repast, knowing they'd be too tired to make much of a meal by nightfall.

"Yes, but he doesn't seem to know it."

"He prefers the company of a pretty girl, eh? I understand." He laughed. She had shaved him for the journey and where the beard had shielded his flesh from the cold his face looked too pale and somewhat weak. She had just cut his hair too and insisted they wash it with the harsh lye soap she'd made from ashes and bear fat. She had hidden the grease he used to keep it stuck firmly in place, and now it shone a rich dark brown. There was nothing she could do about their buckskin clothes soaked in smoke and grease.

Carl picked his way around the fire and stood in front of her, eyeing the half-eaten biscuit on the ground.

"All right." She broke off a bit and he took it cunningly from her fingers. Then she fed him jerky, which he gulped in one bite.

"He must remember to feed himself, *ma chère*," Jacques gently reminded her.

"Not yet." She reached out to stroke the black glistening back, scratching delicately behind the head as he liked. Carl rolled his head like a tiny man and moved closer, pressing his beak into her chest. She could feel the warm hurried breath on her bare skin between the lacings of her shirt. Lately her clothes had become too restrictive, and she could barely fasten the skirt across her bulging stomach. Her breasts were too tender for any but the lightest of Jacques' touches, let alone a crow's sharp beak and pointy claws. She hurriedly lifted the black body off and set him on the ground. He stood for a moment, considering the development, then gave her hand a quick jab and marched a few paces away, muttering.

Jacques watched, the curious expression on his face quickly replaced by recognition. "Ah," he exhaled, "*bien sûr*, of course."

She felt the pink spread up her neck and across her cheeks.

"How long?" Jacques said.

"In the fall," she said.

"We must hurry then. My child must be born on my own land." He leapt up, knocking over the pan of tea he had boiled as well as his cup, and gave a deep oath.

Annie laughed and Carl flapped farther away from the commotion. "It's months away, Jacques." They were beside a placid stream of sweet cold water so clear that if she lay on her side she could see the slices of small silver fish dart about the gravelly bottom. When she dipped her hand in they scattered wildly, but she left it there and they soon gained courage and came back to nibble at it curiously. Their tiny bites felt like the pecks of miniature birds.

He looked at her, then across the little stream to the dark green woods on the other side. "There is much to build now. Come."

They loaded their cart, yoked the oxen, and tied the horses to the back. They had so many furs this time that by necessity they loaded the rest on the backs of the two horses, who rolled their eyes and would have objected more strenuously but for Jacques' firm tug on their halters. Annie rode in the cart, seated as comfortably as possible in the furs on top of their few household goods. Carl the crow alternately rode on her shoulder, her head, or on top of the horse's packs, chattering words they'd taught him and repeating snatches of Jacques' bawdy songs, while Jacques walked.

"You can't walk all the way to Les Petites Cotes," Annie had protested at the first noon break for dry biscuits and jerky. Although they could have easily consumed the repast while continuing forward, Jacques insisted that they stop to build a fire and boil water, brewing more of the black tea he had recently traded two good beaver skins for. She knew he was doing this for her. Alone he would have driven the animals and himself without pause. Every day for the rest of the long journey he pushed the animals until they were exhausted, then insisted that Annie rest for too long, then hurried them all again. Carl took to flying up into the trees as they went, following them, dropping back, catching up. He had begun to feed, and perhaps to worry that he was leaving his home. Each evening he reappeared when Annie called his name, and nestled against her, cooing the words she had been teaching him. Her name, and the name of the baby girl she knew now lived within her: Jula.

By the time they reached the river and followed it north, stopping just before the New Madrid site, they were all exhausted. Jacques hobbled the horses and oxen, and spilled furs on the ground for the two of them, and they slept without bothering with a fire, the river turning restlessly beside them.

Waking at dawn, Annie heard the soft murmuring of the river, the first tentative calls of birds, and opened her eyes to the gray fog dripping off the trees. "We're home, my husband," she whispered, and curled against Jacques' strong back, feeling the baby kick alive for the first time.

Later that first morning of their return, Jacques and Annie stood looking into the river for any glimpse of the village of New Madrid, but the old channel remained averted and clogged with decapitated trees and debris, while the new expanse flowed where the town had once stood. In places the once-fertile fields were now two and three feet deep with sand. Dangerous new pools of water were churning from below where formerly the land was whole, and everywhere there were bottomless sand-filled craters. Where there had been magnificent old trees reaching high to shade the land, now there were new saplings among the ragged stumps and devastation. Rivers, streams, and bayous had new channels, and some that formerly flowed into the river simply ended abruptly where the land heaved upward.

"Next spring, eh? We build our house. See, the boats return now." Jacques raised his chin toward the small flatboat bucking in the current. Annie shaded her eyes, biting back a comment. She had learned that a man needed his plans for the future, no matter how improbable or difficult.

"We'll be the first," she said.

"*Très bien*," he laughed. "You will have rooms and rooms, each with a huge fireplace to keep you warm. And dresses, a dress for each day, and servants to cook and care for you."

"And you," she murmured. Wrapped in his arms, tucked against his bare chest, the hairs prickling her cheek in a most pleasant manner, she could hardly imagine feeling safer or warmer.

But then she thought of their world suddenly crowded with others, and said, "But Jacques, I want always to be the one to care for you. I don't want another person shaving or bathing or cooking for you, we're enough. We're enough together, the two of us."

He laughed and hugged her closer, and she buried her nose in his chest and licked the smoky skin.

"As queen of the house, you may do as you wish with me—I will be your servant then!"

"I don't care for that, Jacques." Now that they had reached the river, they would finally take off their deer hide, maybe for good, if Jacques' promise was true. She had already begun to long for a dress she could wash and hang in the sun to dry and gather the smell of the wind.

He grew serious. "We must take you to see the doctors in St. Louis, *chérie*, and that will take more money than you know. I have a plan. You'll see. Then we will make you well!" He pulled her down on top of him and surprised her with his ferocious lovemaking, the monster out of its cave once again.

Those days she was trapped under the roof beam with her legs shattered, she had longed for the release of Death, had courted him as a reluctant suitor. But now she was not afraid of anything. They would build their house, and raise their children, in the curving shelter of the great river, and call it Jacques' Landing. She could see the house Jacques would build, the rooms full of airy light, the love that would live in them like another person, one who only meant good to them, who fed them and kept them kindly to each other, their bellies full and their hearts satisfied. It would not matter that in days to come Carl would abandon them for life among his own kind.

. . .

My body filled with a rush of warmth as I read Annie's words. I was living in a house built with love for Jacques' bride and baby—our stories were exactly alike! Suddenly, and for the first time, I felt as if I belonged here, as if I were going to share all the luck of those lives despite having lost my own family. I wondered if Clement had ever read Annie's story. Somehow I doubted it. He wasn't much of a reader, and seemed like most of the boys I'd known at home, to lack much curiosity about the past. It was the present and the future that sent them dreaming. Just like Jacques, I realized. For them the past was a piece of discarded clothing, something I would find and immediately try on.

3

BY THE SPRING OF 1817 THEIR CLEARING ON THE RIVER HAD BECOME A gathering place for those men who had been dispossessed during the great quakes, men who stayed after the fur trade began to move west, and those from the river who tired of its brown monotonous journeying. They hunted game for the stew pot kept by the fire for any who were hungry; they rested from their travels telling stories of the families they had left or lost; and they helped Jacques build. The Indians mainly shunned the place. This was because of "Tecumseh's prophecy," or so they were told by Jacques' friend, the French trapper known as Chabot, the morning after he arrived in the company of a Creek wife, her brother, and two small children. The Indians disappeared by first light, leaving Chabot behind. A large hearty man with a ruddy face, big nose, and rosebud mouth that belonged on a small boy's face, he laughed and shook his fists at the ground beneath his feet.

"I am always losing the wife, Jacques, how does a man hang on to such a pretty one as this Annie?"

Jacques spread his arms wide. "It is the way of it these days, my friend.

Horses, cattle, pigs in the woods, those geese and chickens, dogs, and see, even the cats, all seek my company now." He reached for the mug of coffee Annie was holding out. "Like these animals who grow fat and lazy in our presence, Chabot, my Annie does nothing but sit and talk all day while I build for her."

Jacques sipped the coffee they had bartered from a downriver flatboat trader yesterday, along with the undyed flax shirt he wore. Rubbing her belly lightly, he smiled at no one in particular.

"I'd be happy with a woman like Annie," Chabot said, taking off his hat and bowing slightly. Annie handed him a mug of coffee.

"When you two are done discussing my worth, maybe you can plant my garden so we don't starve this winter, without furs to trade."

One of the men by the river shouted and Jacques and Chabot quickly clambered to their feet, peering at the wide brown expanse.

"Boat coming," Jacques said, pulling off the new shirt and laying it carefully over the branch of a tree. He had lost his winter pallor, his skin baked to a rich acorn brown. As he reached for his old buckskin shirt, his broad shoulders tightened with sinewy muscles. He was a man confident in his physical strength, lacking self-consciousness of his power. The knife scar on his left shoulder glistened red as he stood looking out across the river. Then he pulled on his shirt.

"They're coming ashore. Help me, Chabot! We must get what we can for my sweet girl." He kissed Annie on the top of her head and jumped up. "This *dégringolade*—this fall from status—will not be long. Soon I will have everything!"

Annie felt a flush of shame as Chabot glanced at her, his blue eyes thoughtful as he took in the soiled dress, the muddy bare feet, and the dirt-streaked arms.

She said, "I wasn't rich before, Jacques. My family worked hard. You saw that." Her cheeks glowed deep red beneath the tan and freckles. Her eyes darted at Chabot, who gave an encouraging smile and shrugged slightly.

"I work hard, too, Ann-nee." Jacques spun back to gaze at the approaching boat, doing the arithmetic on his long fingers as he counted men, animals, and barrels.

"When I finish building the inn, we will have the trade to make our fortune. You'll see." Jacques spoke without taking his eyes off the new arrivals. Annie shook her head, eyes downcast.

"But how can I cook and clean for so many?"

"We will find a way." Jacques reached the tenth finger and closed his hands into fists.

Annie looked around the disheveled campsite strewn with garbage, animals, rags of bedding and clothing, cooking and hunting tools. Most of the men who stayed with them carried enough personal belongings to crowd their packhorses—even useless, sentimental items such as a hair comb, a piece of china plate or cup missing a handle, a violin bow with no strings, a schoolboy's wooden ruler, a book of poems the owner could not read. She'd seen all this and more, plus the dogs and cats that daily slunk out of the swamp that had overtaken parts of the woods to the west or the devastated land to the north and south. There was so much draining and clearing to do. She couldn't see how they'd manage to order the quake damage enough in one season to survive the winter. She remembered her family's struggles those first years without enough food and clothing, and it sent a shiver through her.

"Jacques, maybe we'd do better moving upriver to one of the settlements there. We could—" The expression on his face made her stumble to a halt.

He turned to face her, his eyes gleaming. "This is mine, *ma chère*. What do I own elsewhere? What can I claim? *This* is mine, for my son, for *you, ma chère!*" He knelt in front of her, laying his cheek on her breast.

Her face softened, the worry fleeing from her eyes as she stroked his head. Chabot smiled, quietly delighted that his friend had finally succumbed to a female. The inn was a fine idea, too, a place to lay up when he grew tired of hunting and his wives, a place where a man might drink in comfort. Little Annie would never interfere with such pleasures.

"Your boat is landed," Chabot announced. "Let's see what good thieves we are today." Jacques laughed at Annie's big eyes. "With the trade, *chérie*, the barter, Chabot is famous for his skills. He once traded a blind horse for two milk cows and a crate of china doorknobs."

Chabot held up a hand. "Every woman in a hundred miles wears one now."

"A china doorknob?" Annie asked.

The men burst out laughing, slapped each other on the back, and started down the path to the boat landing.

When they reached the clearing, the boat crew was already unloading goods and talking with the men gathered onshore to meet it. Amongst the cargo stood three black Africans, chained together by the ankles, dressed in roughly sewn garments dyed brown-yellow, two men and a woman so huge with child she had to stand with her legs slightly apart and lean back to balance the weight.

At first Annie was going to follow the two men, but she didn't want to expose herself to the eyes of strangers. Since the pregnancy had swollen her figure, she had ceased wearing anything but a shift under her dress and often found it necessary to confine her movement or work when in the company of others. Now, she cursed her body as she watched Jacques engage in conversation with the four white men from the boat, who gestured repeatedly toward the slaves and waved to the encampment. Finally, there was a shaking of hands and the entire company began marching up from the river's edge, including the Africans, who were being prodded by a man with a cane stick, as if they were slow-witted cattle.

Annie stiffened her body with resolve, prepared to stop whatever evil agreement these men had entered together. But Jacques waved his hand once and gave a quick shake of his head, his lips forming the word *no* as he approached, so she waited.

When the pregnant African stumbled, the men hurried to help her before she pitched forward, each taking an arm though it meant an awkward, even painful shuffling dance to keep the chain from tangling their feet together. When they neared the oxen pen, the man with the cane pointed to the muddy, trampled earth beneath the trees.

"No." Annie hobbled toward them. When Jacques tried to dissuade her with his arm, she shook him off.

"Sir," she said boldly, "since the woman is imminent with child, perhaps she would be safer out of the way of hooves."

The man looked at Annie for the first time, taking in her homespun clothing not much better than that of his slaves. He was clad in tan doeskin breeches, brown boots that laced up the front and rose up his thick legs almost to his knees, a filthy white shirt and yellow waistcoat, all a degree too small, so it appeared that his flesh might at any moment burst forth, shed its casing, and emerge as a new, larger man than before. He considered for a moment, making a sucking noise between his front teeth, then took his straw planter's hat off, revealing a pink bald pate. He wiped his brow on his sleeve and shrugged.

"Can't unhook her, though. She won't have it." He gave an ambiguous smile.

"Bring them to the fire," Jacques said. With a glance at Annie, he led the way to the fire pit under the makeshift canvas shelter built to keep the weather out when she cooked or needed to work out of the sun.

Again, without touching them, with the almost formal courtesy some men reserved for horses, dogs, and servants, the man pointed to a position that placed them at the farthest distance from the fire yet allowed them to avail themselves of the canvas roof. The two men assisted the woman in lowering herself to the ground, and when it became obvious that she would be unable to sit upright without support, so great was the size of her belly, the two men positioned themselves behind her, facing outward, so that she might lean against their backs as in a chair. All three immediately collapsed into sleep, the exhaustion falling like deadweight on their faces and limbs. Although the woman was large with child, her face was sunken with hunger. In fact, the arms and legs of the three seemed mere bones loosely wrapped with the thinnest of skin the shade of wet elm bark.

"It's something, isn't it?" The man shook his head.

Annie started to move toward them, but this time Jacques put his hand on her shoulder and she stopped.

"They're a fierce people, ma'am." This time the man sounded almost respectful. "They was bought in Jamaica. Pretty wild there, I reckon." He made that snicking noise through his front teeth again. "Not your American-bred field hands. These two won't give trouble 'less a person tries to put a hand to the woman. Then, watch out."

"They're hungry," Annie said.

"Expect so, ma'am." This time he sounded regretful, and she had to look more closely at the bland full face to make sure that he was not some sort of actor who could shape-shift at a moment's notice. He had small blue eyes that could widen or narrow and in so doing change the entire aspect of his face from the picture of broad innocence to the fleshy epitome of cruelty and disgust. His face was curious in that it seemed composed almost entirely of flesh devoid of the structuring bones beneath. Even his nose seemed to rise like a shapely continuation of the molding flesh on all sides. His hair was so fine and fair it hung limply along his face, despite his effort to tie its length back with a ragged black ribbon. His brows and lashes were so yellow and fine they created the illusion that he was indeed a hairless man, beardless and entirely lacking any necessity to shave.

"Haven't they been fed?" Jacques asked.

The man shrugged. "I tried."

"*Mon dieu!*" Jacques stomped to the fire pit, knelt, and began filling trenchers with venison stew and biscuits. But when he tried to present the food, the three Africans shook their heads and looked at the ground, despite the way their throats worked at the rich smells.

Jacques looked on the verge of dumping the food in frustration when Annie approached.

"Let me." She lowered herself to the ground near the woman, and laying the crutches down signaled to Jacques to put the trenchers down in front of her.

"Bring water and milk," she said. Jacques nodded.

The woman's ankles were chafed raw from the iron manacle, flayed almost to the bone in places. The flesh shone pink and festering, and although the flies were working both wounds, she was either too tired and weak or too despairing to brush them away. So Annie did.

The woman started at the touch, drawing herself up and gripping her long, narrow arms around her stomach protectively.

"Is it soon?" Annie pointed to the woman's stomach, then back at her own. "In the fall, when the leaves turn," she started to explain, then realized it might not mean anything to a Negro from Jamaica. She had no idea where Jamaica was, but assumed it was a warmer place than here. She held up five fingers for five months and pointed again at her own belly, then back at the woman's, who watched Annie the whole time, the suffering on her long, narrow face easing slightly as she began to understand. She had dark brown eyes, the color of Jacques', but hers turned up slightly at the corners, giving her face an aspect of grace, emphasizing her long narrow nose and her full lips, which also turned up at the corners as if they were used to wearing a constant smile until recently. She wore her tightly curled hair cropped around the oblong skull, and her long ears, shaped like young pear leaves, came almost to a point at the top. In each lobe she wore braided horsehair knotted with tiny yellow and red beads.

Annie held a finger to her own empty lobe, then pointed to the woman's, and said, "Pretty." The woman grimaced in an apparent attempt to smile, then gave up and simply stared. Annie stared back.

"Here." Jacques set down a bucket of water with a dipper, and a cup of the precious milk from the cow, which they had recently acquired from a family fleeing the frontier to return to the safety of the East. He dropped to his knees and looked more closely at the wounds on her ankles, then cursed and quickly rose to his feet.

"I'll heat water and get the tools to take those off." And he was gone again.

"Now see here!" the slaver shouted.

"The baby needs food," Annie said. Breaking off a small piece of biscuit, she touched it to her own belly and put it in her mouth, chewing elaborately. The woman watched Annie closely, and as soon as she swallowed, the woman picked up the biscuit and took a bite. Her throat was apparently so dry that she choked and Annie tried to hand her the cup of milk, but despite her agony, she refused until Annie sipped and swallowed; then she grabbed the cup and emptied it. Patting the base of her throat when she was done, she handed the cup back and gave the fleetest of smiles.

The slaver watched the proceedings with a cocked head and a disdainful twist to his mouth.

Using a crude wooden spoon, Annie repeated her food-testing with the trencher of stew, until using her fingers to scoop the food, the woman fell to eating so swiftly Annie feared she would choke again. When she was finished, she herself tested the other trenchers and gave them to the men, who groaned as their bellies began to fill. The food was washed down by water until the bucket was empty.

It was then that Jacques returned with hot water, poultice, and strips of cloth for bandages. Chabot, the half-breed, followed with tools and quickly removed the trio's leg irons. Jacques was so gentle in his ministrations that he might have been caring for his wife. After he finished wrapping the woman's ankles, he turned to the men, whose legs also held festering wounds.

When the task was completed, the woman surprised them all by murmuring something in the strange guttural language of her people.

The corpulent slaver inspecting his charges, however, was less pleased with the turn of events. "How am I supposed to keep these men from running off now? They's a nice commission for these three. I don't intend to lose it." At that he took out a large knife, and the woman gasped.

Jacques raised a heel and drew a finger across it, whispering, "He will slice the tendons to keep them from fleeing."

"No," Annie hissed and began to step forward, but Jacques stopped her with a look.

The slaver was standing before the woman now. But before he could raise his knife, the woman from Jamaica spoke in a low voice. "They won't run away," she said. "They're sworn to protect me." She looked up at the man, her voice laced with disdain. "You'll be paid, Mr. Sullans."

He stared at her for a long moment, cocked his head, then abruptly nodded, sheathed the knife, turned and left.

The remainder of the day they rested as best they could on the hard ground while the encampment continued its work on the inn, which was to be both their future home and place of business. While Annie worked at preparing the evening meal of roast venison and boiled wild greens, the wind picked up and the sky began to darken with huge purple-bottomed clouds quickly advancing from the west. She glanced at the poles and ropes holding the canvas overhead, and they appeared tight, but she needed more firewood brought in before the soaking. The men, however, were busy scurrying about covering supplies and securing animals.

Then the two African men sprang up, moving awkwardly at first, as if they still wore the leg irons. Before the first drops, a large stack of wood rested where it would remain dry. The men seemed to relish the work, not resentful or defeated in the manner of slaves she had observed in Les Petites Cotes.

"Please move closer to the fire," she said when they were done. "You'll get soaked sitting there."

With great effort and the two men aiding her, the woman rose and came to settle near Annie, a brother on either side of her, once again providing a resting place for her back.

After much thunder and some lightning, the rain began to pour in earnest, and the men helping Jacques resigned themselves to the shelter of nearby trees or their own tents or lean-tos. Jacques returned with Chabot, leaving the slaver Sullans standing uninvited outside getting soaked.

"He should return to his boat," Jacques said with a shrug.

"He won't leave us here unguarded," the woman said.

"Mr. Ducharme?" Sullans ducked his head under the canvas and peered in. "May I join you, and my merchandise?" Water ran in rivulets off his head and shoulders.

Jacques glanced at Annie, his dark eyes filled with humor. He would never turn a person away, but he was enjoying Sullans standing out there getting soaked.

"Come in, Mr. Sullans," she called. "You can sit over there—" She nodded to the place where the Africans had first rested. Once inside with water streaming from his clothing, he hesitated, but finally took his place, as far from the fire as possible, where he'd no doubt grow chilled.

The little enclosure was smoky from the fire, but it was definitely an improvement on the wild scene outside where the sheets of rain obscured both the encampment and the river. They could hear the tossing trees overhead, but could not see them for the rain that arrived in thick waves. Annie made hot tea and passed the cups to all, and they sat there, cozy indeed despite the downpour. As soon as Mr. Sullans began to shake with the chill, she invited him nearer the fire and he hastily joined them. Since he seemed to lack the aversion to the dark skin of his charges that was in evidence in other slavers, Annie grew curious. Leaning back with her head in Jacques' lap, she watched the four newcomers until her lids grew heavy and her heart slowed to the steady sound of the rain.

. . .

The wing of flame in my lamp began to stutter and shift as if the wind had insinuated itself into the house. I heard a thump in the hallway, as if someone had dropped a heavy boot or a piece of firewood. My heart banged against my chest, and I put my hand over the top of my swollen breast. "Clement?" I called softly, knowing he wasn't really there. This house was full of noises I'd had to get used to. Or at least I was used to most of them. That thought was followed by the thing I dreaded—footsteps on the stairs. One after another, slow, measured, lifted and put down with great effort, they mounted to the second floor. I knew better than to go out there and peer up those stairs. I'd done that enough to know that sometimes it's more frightening to look and see nothing. So I sat and waited until the sound reached the top and trudged down the hallway to the last bedroom before the bachelor's ell, with its warren of small rooms just large enough to accommodate a bed and a dresser and a straight-back chair.

Once the steps stopped, I waited for the last sound, imagining someone outside the locked door, palm on the knob, fingers slipping around the figured brass, gripping, turning slowly, listening for the click that never comes. I'd seen the doorknob turn, felt the heaviness in the air outside the door, the held breath. It was my room, you see, the one I went to when I couldn't sleep and didn't want to awaken Clement.

After it had been quiet for a few minutes, I went back to reading, my heart still pounding.

WHEN SHE AWOKE, IT WAS DARK, AND THOUGH IT WAS STILL RAINING, THE intensity had lessened, and it was possible to see the other little campfires glowing dimly around them. Men had already come and taken a share of the venison haunch, and from the trenchers beside their guests, everyone had eaten while she slept. She had not known she was so tired, but attributed it to the baby. Her body surprised her constantly now.

"You eat." The dark-skinned woman placed a trencher of food in front of her. The meat, greens, and biscuit were artfully arranged, not heaped in the manner she was accustomed to serving.

Thanking her, Annie ate quickly, more hungry than she usually was. Of course, she had missed the noon meal, and only eaten lightly at dawn when they arose. No wonder she was tired and hungry! Jacques leaned on one elbow, smoking his pipe, watching the fire, but with an eye on the Africans as Sullans related a story in a quiet voice. Annie could catch a word or two of it, but not enough to make sense of the whole. There was a flagon of whiskey on the ground between them, and she noted that Sullans was drinking more often than Jacques, who had given up drinking almost entirely.

Annie wiped up the last of the juices with the biscuit and put it in her mouth. The woman was lying on her side, holding her belly like a giant gourd in her arms. Jacques had given her a folded deer hide for her head. She glanced at the two young men sitting across from her. They lay stretched out, staring at the sagging canvas beaded with water.

The African woman looked at Sullans, whose shirtfront was wet with spilled whiskey, and shook her head. A spasm of motion rippled across her belly, which she followed with her hand, like a caress. She lifted her hands, the lovely long fingers curving to the empty shells of her palms, as if she had been helpless to do anything but receive the gift of her baby's beauty.

Jacques watched Sullans get drunk, taking a small sip for every one of Sullans's greedy swallows.

The woman scrubbed her face and rubbed her scalp hard, digging into the thick wool with her fingernails as if she meant to hurt herself.

Her belly rippled again. This time she tapped her fingers on the humped outline and spoke in African, words that took shape in the back of her throat. The protrusion disappeared, the belly smoothed out.

Sullans made a snorting noise, like a rooting pig, and they looked over in time to see him fall face-first to the ground, the drool from his open mouth forming a muddy mixture on his tongue. He had lost consciousness from the homemade whiskey. Jacques carefully picked the flagon out of Sullans's grasp and held it to the fire to see if there were shadows of remaining liquor. He shook the bottle, put it to his lips, and took the last few drops on his tongue, swishing it around, then swallowing as if he were drinking the French wine he was able to purchase at Les Petites Cotes when they had sold the furs in the spring.

When he noticed the women watching him, he winked and smiled. Carefully rising, he tiptoed around the unconscious Sullans without disturbing him. Squatting, he said, "It's time to go."

The African woman blinked and nodded.

While the two brothers helped their sister stand, Jacques looked at Annie and put his finger to his lips. His dark eyes were full of liquid light reflected from the fire and he held a hatchet in his hand. For a wild moment, Annie thought he was going to harm them.

"Go to the boat wreck and wait with Chabot." He pointed downriver. "You'll be safe there." Chabot stepped into the light, a large knife in his hand, although he appeared sober.

"Jacques?" Annie said, trying to keep her voice low, but across the fire Sullans stirred, opened his eyes, blinked as if unsure where he was, and suddenly started. Sitting up, he held his head, still trying to focus on the figures before him. Tightening his grip on the hatchet, Jacques turned to face the slaver. Sullans stared for a moment, then comprehending, slid his hand inside his shirt.

"My gold," he said.

Jacques nodded and put his finger to his lips, lifting the hatchet. Sullans stared at him, his eyes wide, mouth opening to shout an alarm, but by then the hatchet had embedded itself in his chest with such force that he toppled backward with a disappointed sigh.

For once she could not feel the pain in her legs, numbness having struck her as the hatchet fell. There was nothing but the river's urgent slapping on the bank and the flowing wound in Sullans's chest.

Jacques yanked the shirt out of Sullans's britches and used his knife to cut the money belt, pulling it free like offal from a gutted deer. A few coins fell clinking into the mud. Jacques scrambled after them. "Go!" he whispered to the Africans and pointed toward the river again, his hard features savage.

Chabot gestured with his knife. The three Africans exchanged terrified looks but stood like horses confused by an open gate. They glanced at Sullans, despair filling their faces as they realized they'd be blamed for the murder—then back at Annie, who was trying to wave them on without making sounds that would awaken the sleeping men around them. Who knew how many had already seen too much.

"Thank you," the woman whispered, then said something in her foreign tongue and pointed to Annie's belly and hers. Annie tried to smile and nodded, wanting only to be rid of them and the body of Sullans before they were all discovered by the men from the boat.

At that, the three followed Chabot and melted into the darkness without a sound, although she listened hard for anything that would give away their escape. Jacques meanwhile bound the body with rope. He looked at her across the fire, bloody to his elbows, his eyes dark and furious, his long face almost cadaverous.

Annie got up and hobbled after his slow progress into the brush, where the body caught on bushes and wedged itself between saplings as if, even in death, the man was going to deny Jacques what he wanted and needed. At the river, Jacques tore off Sullans's clothing and buried it, then tied the naked body to bait ropes for the huge river snappers. By morning, he would be gone.

When they returned to the fire, Annie drew Jacques to her and wound her arms around him. There was a desperation in her grip, as if she could pull him back from that savage moment and the hatchet's glinting arc. She told herself that Sullans had to die. Jacques was only saving the Africans from a life of suffering and early death. Now they were safe. That was all that mattered. They would have a new home, new lives, and the baby would be born and thrive. Then Chabot appeared on the other side of the dying fire.

"They got away," he whispered with a shrug.

Jacques sat up, wiping his face with a big hand and looking around for the water jug. "What do you mean?"

"One minute they are there, in front of me, roped together as we agreed, next minute, they are not there. Gone. Poof. I looked all over, but didn't want to raise an alarm. I'm sorry."

"You let them go. I should keep your share of the gold, Chabot." Jacques spoke in a low whisper.

Chabot's face flushed with anger. "Monsieur, you are not in a right mind tonight. I will see you in the morning." He rose, hand on the knife at his belt, and disappeared into the darkness.

"How am I to build without those Africans?" Jacques said in a whisper so loud that several sleepers muttered and rolled over in their blankets. Jacques scowled into the dark.

All night Annie kept seeing the bright blood bubbling around the blade, the filthy white shirt filling with blood, the stream of blood flooding the ground, running toward the fire, hissing in the heat, the bloody steam filling the air with a red mist that rose and flattened along the sagging canvas roof over their heads, then returned in droplets that rained down on them as if the air itself were bleeding. In the dream she kept asking, "When will that thing stop bleeding? Couldn't you have killed him someplace else?"

When she woke up, she was angry at all men.

At first light, Jacques told the men from the boat that Sullans had taken the Africans inland. He was stealing them to sell himself, rather than returning them for the commission. The men wanted to raise a general alarm for Sullans along the river, but Jacques persuaded them that it would be better to keep silent. It would only mean trouble for all of them, should anyone say a word. It was an easily believable story, and the men cast off that morning with few grumbles. She made an extra batch of biscuits and tucked pieces of the previous night's roast venison in the middle and the men from the boat took them gratefully. No one was going to miss Sullans or his human cargo. Most of the river traders and settlers lacked the resources to own slaves, or abhorred slavery on religious grounds as her family had, so the presence of the Africans had brought a profound unease to the camp that was now released.

It was almost too easy, she was discovering, to dispatch another person and relieve them of their property. In this land, they were all dispensable. Was this what Jacques and Chabot meant by bartering and trading? Maybe Sullans deserved to die. She wasn't sure. As she watched the flat boat pole itself upriver, minus Sullans and his three captives, she could not stop stealing glances downriver, hoping that the Africans were well hidden until darkness.

4

HE NEXT DAY, JACQUES AND THE MEN RETURNED TO THE BUILDING OF the inn that was to be their home and livelihood. The men had already cut and hauled trees until there was a massive pile of logs at the edge of the clearing, which supplied the walls and roof beams of the nearly completed inn. As he did every morning, Jacques asked Annie about the way he was sitting the inn—was it close enough to the river so boats would see it, close enough to the proposed stables? Had he left enough room to build a house on the small hill to the west once they had accumulated the money? He asked her to walk with him around the vegetable garden, the orchard they would begin to plant in the fall, the smokehouse, the granary, the still for making beer, wine, and whiskey, and the summer kitchen they would use until the bitter cold. In addition, he paced off the four small cabins some distance from the inn, which he said this morning were for the Africans he would need to buy now that Sullans had opened his eyes.

Annie kept silent, praying that Jacques would change his mind when he became a father. The man who had saved a young girl and an injured crow couldn't turn slaver. She examined his face carefully: He appeared calm today, despite the dark sleepless circles around his eyes. His lean body was quick, filled with purpose as he pulled up and pounded the stakes back in for the slave cabins. She'd just have to convince him of the wrongness as soon as they were alone. He was almost a different person when they were alone, she realized, more the man she loved and respected, and now feared a little too.

Annie's spirits were lifted somewhat when Heral Wells, the peddler who had been thrown from a flatboat for cheating at cards, slipped in mud created by horse urine and fell to his hands and knees. Heral was a round-faced man who would cheat a widow of her pittance if a game of chance were involved, but otherwise was softhearted and helpful around the camp, taking special care of Annie's needs, so she waited to join in the laughter until she saw that his face was suffused with smiles also. Jacques pretended to offer him a hand, then jerked it away as soon as the stink of mud lifted toward him. The men laughed heartily until Heral climbed to his feet on his own and shook his hands in midair, catching the bystanders with gouts of mud. To their cries of dismay, he responded by scraping the mud from his knees and flinging it also. A mêlée would have followed if Jacques had not stepped in, grabbing Heral by the hair and dragging him without ceremony to the wash bucket. The men went back to work after that.

From that spring of 1817, Jacques' dream grew. First, the log house was accomplished with maul, mortise ax, and saw. Jacques and Chabot showed the ten other men in camp how to square the logs so the outside walls would be flat, not rounded as Annie's father had left them in their own cabin. He had been hasty in his building as in all things. The sight of the huge roof beams rising in the air made her shiver, and she busied herself at the cook-fire to keep from crying out while her legs shook with waves of remembered pain.

Erecting the walls, they made square corner pieces that locked into each other, notches fashioned neatly with the ax by a man called Skaggs (they never learned his given name), who had learned his trade as a settler in Ohio and Kentucky. There were two Foley cousins, Frank and McCord, who were large and strong enough to lift and balance several planks four inches thick and eight feet long on their shoulders. Also building walls were Forrest Clinch, who had lost his wife during the first night of the quakes, and Pilcher Wyre, a lean, morose man of middle age who had been living with Indians encamped along the river until the quake wiped out his village.

They carried planks between them and worked at a steady pace that took them through the day, as if shared grief had made them comrades.

The other men in camp included three Burtram brothers, Nicholas, Mitchell, and Ashland, ages sixteen to twenty, who had arrived from Virginia, which they claimed was too civilized, and were looking for more adventure. They spent each evening around the fire arguing about going west or north to the "real" frontier. They were willing to help until they decided on a direction. Jacques put them to work building sturdy wood fencing for the livestock, far enough from the clearing that only an occasional word or shout could be heard.

Since the building was to be an inn for travelers and rivermen, as well as for their own use, it had a long narrow shape with a large room at either end, and the hallway between was lined with small sleeping rooms. Little Dickie Sawtell and Judah Quick built narrow beds one atop the other in the marked-off rooms, while Annie was occupied making mattresses, stuffing them with leaves, moss, bulrushes, cotton from the massive cottonwood trees along the shore, and dried grasses, whatever could be gathered from surrounding fields and woods. They would be welcome under weary bodies no matter what they contained. Their own bed, which the men made larger than the others, she piled with the crudely tanned furs she had worked on the previous winter, the ones that wouldn't bring money, and covered with quilts Jacques had bought from a man fleeing the frontier, where he'd lost both his wife and children to pneumonia in one month. Annie washed the quilts carefully in a pot of boiling water and lye soap and had Dickie hang them on a makeshift line to let the sun and wind beat the disease from them. When they were gathered, they were scented spicy with flowers and leaves and bark. It was the most luxurious bed she could imagine, including the musky smell of wood smoke and animal, which never quite disappeared from the hides.

Dickie Sawtell and Judah Quick watched with longing on their faces as Jacques picked her up in his sweaty arms speckled with sawdust and laid her in the center of their bed, and the three of them stood there as she sank into the fur luxury, protesting for the work she had left undone. Seeing the expressions on those faces made her wish that there were wives for all of the men in camp. What a difference to have other women to talk to these days, but she schooled herself to keep silent and be grateful. She had so nearly died, every day of her life was a miracle she could not question. When

Jacques lifted her out of the bed, she vowed to speak to him about finding women to work with them. Perhaps they could live in those little cabins he was building.

The inn took another two weeks to complete, then the men went on to the stables while Dickie Sawtell and Judah Quick helped Annie with the inside comforts. They placed the small wooden horse she had made for her baby brother on the stone mantel above the large fireplace in their room, and hung her mother's stew pot on an iron pothook that could swing over the fire. Jacques had already begun to trade for the pots and utensils necessary for the customers of the inn, and these they arranged on shelves on either side of the fireplace in the great room at the other end. Dickie and Judah carved new wooden trenchers and spoons for the guests. They covered the small windows cut into the walls with oil-soaked parchment that let in light. Having spent those long winters in the cabin alone while Jacques was trapping, she was grateful for those windows, especially now that she would be caring for a little one.

Her belly grew as the buildings took shape, as if the babe knew to wait until its cradle was carved and there was a good roof over its head. Jacques was careful of her those days, a pleased smile on his face as he built a three-sided shelter against one wall of the inn for cooking in the hot months, while the men raised the walls of stables and small cabins. The men treated her with respect and even tenderness, bringing her the ripest mulberries and raspberries from the woods, and bouquets of wildflowers half-crushed in their hands. Annie began to mend their clothing and listen to their stories as they poured out their hearts after a long day of labor. Her status as wife and mother lent her respect, which she did not discourage. It felt good to be the center of their attention, and even Jacques seemed to enjoy the spectacle of the men sprawled at her feet, drinking in the homely picture of her fingers plying the needle on a torn sleeve or trousers.

As soon as the other buildings were nearing completion in midsummer, Jacques went to work on fashioning a dock for the boats that would ferry goods and men out to the keelboats and flatboats. It was difficult to round the bend going upstream where they were, there being both upstream and downstream currents, so the boats had to make a circle following the inner shore to the tip of the point, then row across the river. It sometimes took an hour for such a careful maneuver, and Jacques often stopped work to watch in case a boat got into trouble when the wind and waves were strong. His growing reputation was beginning to draw customers to their little enterprise. Sometimes Jacques' men had to help the crew tow a flatboat or keelboat up the stream, a practice called "cordelling" after the name of the rope. Mostly it was flatboats that poled the cargo on the river, and Annie so looked forward to their arrival, which meant the possibility of news and goods from St. Louis or New Orleans.

Several times a day, no matter how heavy the work, Jacques would appear at her side, often with a present, something he had found that might delight her: a newly hatched box turtle, legs scrambling helplessly as he held it between forefinger and thumb, a piece of rock with a shell embedded in it, a five-leaf clover, a precisely chipped arrowhead, an ancient jawbone with huge teeth much larger than those of any animal they knew, a clay marble some settler child had apparently lost, a bright red feather, a root in the shape of a heart, and finally a puppy from the litter of one of the half-wild dogs that hung around the fringes of the camp, dogs abandoned during the quakes, some driven mad by fear and grief. The puppy was white with black ears and a spot on his back in the shape of a squirrel. From the size of his paws, he was going to be small and wiry, just the right size to grow up with the baby. She named him Pie for piebald.

Annie was happy during those hot summer days as her time grew near. From the river travelers she learned that the War of 1812 was over, boats driven by steam were coming to the river, the state of Mississippi was going to be admitted to the Union, someone had invented a machine that knitted and another device, a thing called a camera, that made an image of a person you could hold forever. But what intrigued her more was the way the greens of the cypress and oak leaves grew richer, almost edible in their dense glow. And every creature, from red and black spotted ladybird bugs to the long-tailed butterfly striped yellow and black like a tiger, seemed in concert with one another, and with her also as she worked in the shade of the cypress trees. She was in a drowsy heat those days, half-awake. One afternoon in late summer, she was lying on a quilt, and saw something pushing up crumbles of dirt at the foot of the tree. Soon a tiny dark head appeared, followed by the cylinder of body, some two inches in length. Wet and disoriented, it paused only a moment or two before staggering onward into a splotch of sunlight, where it spread its wings, so thin they resembled those of a dragonfly, to dry. As soon as it began producing the shrill, ear-piercing sound that it might play for several hours without intermission, she recognized the cicada. Capturing and carefully pinning it between two fingers, she discovered a pair of horny plates on the underside of the body, just behind the last pair of legs. Carefully, she pulled the plates back to uncover two drumlike membranes and a set of powerful muscles—the source of the noise! On that day she began to take note of such discoveries in a book of blank pages Jacques had procured for her amusement from the latest trading boat. After drawing the creature, both front and back, and listing her discoveries, she set him loose, only to find that her exploration had taken its life. She burst into tears. When Jacques discovered the source of her misery, having rushed over at the sound of her moaning, he laughed and tried to comfort her, saying that he would capture a barrel full of the noisy creatures if that would stop her wailing.

She could not bear to take life just then, but of course she smiled and brushed his offer aside, as he used her skirt hem to dry her tears. When the baby shifted restlessly at his weight, he murmured "*espérez*" and patted her stomach, leaving sawdust on her deep indigo skirt. He had been acquiring clothing for the baby and Annie the past month, although she was never certain how he paid. Perhaps it was by trading for the dried meat and berries or fresh bird eggs and honey the men found in the woods. Yesterday he had led another cow off a visiting flatboat and penned it in a little corral, then carried off a crate of chickens she was sure the foxes would eat. But he was right. They needed such animals to supply the inn with good food. Weary travelers would be much gratified by such a repast.

And so the summer months flew by, the only disagreeableness the occasional trembling of the earth, which gave her nightmares, or the pricking of her finger with the needle as she sewed a gown for the baby, spotting the cloth with a drop of blood that would not be washed out and could only be covered with needlework flowers and bees. Her body seemed to swell with the heat, her breasts a size that amazed Jacques and made her shoulders ache. Sometimes she thought of the young African woman and her two brothers, praying they had made it to safety, that her child was healthy, that he would only wonder about the scars on his mother's ankles, never know the source for himself. On nights the wind blew rain in, she thought of the murder of Sullans and their escape, and felt grateful that her own child had not been born yet, had not witnessed her father's violence.

IT WAS AN UNUSUALLY LONG FALL, LASTING UNTIL MID-NOVEMBER, BUT THE cold finally arrived in one afternoon on a strong wind that first blew hot enough to wither any grass or flower that had so far resisted. Then about midafternoon, the wind shifted its perspective and bore a coolness along its edges that grew colder and colder until at dark there was a skim of ice in the water trough, and for the first time since they'd built their abode, she had to sit close to the fire to keep her body warm. The wind raged all night, pulling at the wood shingles of the roof, flapping the oiled parchment windows so they produced a sound like a blacksmith's bellows, throwing tin cups left outside rattling and clanking against the walls of the inn, and swinging the huge cypress and oaks as if they were twigs. With the great moaning and creaking, it seemed a miracle that limbs were not flung off to come crashing through the roof of their shelter. She lay nearest the fire in their private quarters, belly too large to sit comfortably, and certainly too heavy for her poor legs to support for more than a few staggering steps with the aid of her homely crutches. Although Jacques kept trying to move her to the bed in the corner, she was insistent on staying where she was, close to warmth like any common animal. Her back ached terrifically, and she was so thirsty Jacques finally placed a bucket and dipper beside her, although sitting up was becoming more and more difficult. Finally, she stuck her fingers in the water and sucked the drops from them while Jacques tended the men at the other end of the hall. Even with their door closed, she could hear the riot of laughter and loud talk over the storm outside, and for the first time wished for the silence of those long winter nights of their fur-trapping years again.

When Jacques finally reappeared bearing a bowl of venison stew and a thick piece of dense bread, she could not stomach the smell of wild game, and told him to leave it within her reach. He brought another quilt from the bed and tucked it around her feet, which he had already covered in thick woolen socks and a pair of Indian moccasins that Chabot had traded for his food and lodging before he left for the winter's trapping. With Chabot gone, Jacques would be lonely for someone to speak a few phrases of his native tongue with, and there had been a sad longing in his eyes as the other man departed, packhorse loaded down with traps and provisions. As soon as Annie and Jacques had seen the last of Chabot's packhorse round the bend and disappear into the trees, Jacques surveyed all he had built and clapped his hands together once, bringing the puppy Pie barking from the hole he was digging beside the bench next to the doorway.

"Mon petit joujou!" Jacques picked him up, giving him a loving shake, and received a lick on the face for his mock scolding. The puppy was devoted to Jacques, though he constantly threatened to make dog soup or roast a haunch every time the dog got underfoot or stole a boot and dragged

it in large circles outside, drawing the other dogs in chase. Only the three half-wild dogs that had recently arrived stayed on the fringes of the camp, refusing play or companionship, raising hackles and baring teeth when anyone passed too near. There was speculation that they had arrived with a sullen man named Ford Jones who never looked anyone in the eye and kept himself as separate as the dogs.

That morning, when Jacques had been trading with a flatboat from New Orleans for flour and ammunition, the dogs had been skulking so close to the supplies that he had shot his pistol over their heads to drive them off. Later, he'd warned Ford Jones that the dogs would have to be killed. When Jacques was cutting meat for the supper stew from a freshly killed deer hung from a tree by the cooking shed, the dogs lurked too closely again, growling, and Jacques pulled his pistol and surely would have shot them had he not glanced at Annie first, and thought better of it. Instead, he ordered Jones to chain the dogs. The man had started to argue about the fact that the other dogs in camp were free to roam, but he must have realized that Jacques' stiff shoulders and tight jaw meant an end to discussion. Jones promised to leave with the dogs in the next day or two, so their peace would soon return.

Now Annie could hear the men drinking the corn liquor they'd made from the newly harvested patch and singing at the other end of the hallway, and it infuriated her to have no company but the fire and the thumping windows and moaning trees. Then the dogs set up outside, snarling and howling, as if they were fighting for the last morsel on earth. She tried calling Jacques to make them stop, but he couldn't hear her through the closed doors, long hallway, and roaring wind. Eventually, she fell into a feverish sleep, the sort where you believe you are still awake, though your eyes will not open. She saw the dogs leap through the parchment window, one after another, and begin to circle her, their jaws slavering, hot tongues lolling with hunger as they eyed her baby—she had her baby! Annie didn't remember having her, but there she was, a perfect bundle in her arms, and the dogs were circling, starting to lunge so closely that she could see the quiver in their throat muscles. The beasts were going to kill them! She shouted for help—

And awakened to the flood of liquid beneath her. She had been with her mother during four childbirths and knew what this signaled. Sure enough, the waves of pain soon followed, gradually building to crescendos, then relaxing. She tried to call for help betweentimes, but the men were still too noisy. At first the pain wasn't so bad. A relief, after the months of waiting. She was just so thirsty, but when she tried to sit up to drink, she could not manage the dipper without spilling the water and drenching herself on top, and she was already lying in wet. She threw back the quilts and struggled to remove her skirt between the waves of contractions. When her body was free of restriction, she lay back, panting and waiting for what was to come. The fire was burning low, and she struggled to grasp a log and push it toward the flame, hoping that the end that still lay on the stone hearth would not ignite the cypress floor. In the process, she tipped over the bowl of stew and suffered the sickening odor of greasy meat, corn, and onions in the thick brown gravy congealing on the floor like vomit, so close she feared her head would roll into the mess.

The waves of pain came leisurely for several hours, rolling up her body, cramping her legs, tightening her chest until she felt she could not breathe, but then gradually letting go. Betweentimes she slipped in and out of a light slumber, unmindful of the soaked mattress, awakened and talked to the babe, telling her to be of ease, that the wind outside was nothing to be afraid of, her father and mother would protect her. She said all this though she could not escape the terror of the dream every time the dogs howled or came sniffing along the cabin wall, scratching at the door to come in, as if they smelled the bloody birthing.

Sometime in the night Jacques finally stumbled down the hall, drunk, crashed the door against the wall, and flung himself on the floor by her side. He lay there for a few minutes until his senses returned and he recognized that something was amiss. Sitting up, he gazed at the soaked quilts and naked stomach for a moment before he understood.

He leaned over and put his fingertips on her cheek. "*Ça va?*" How goes it? he asked, his sour liquored breath making her gag.

Despite that, she was so relieved he had finally arrived that she began sobbing.

"*Chérie, chérie,*" he murmured and tried to gather her into his arms, but a contraction began and she pushed him away with a quick curse. He sat back stunned, watched as she braced and fought the pain, finally gasping at its peak. Even in the semidarkness she could see how stricken he was, face pale and pasty as if he were about to faint. As the pain subsided, she laughed, but it was a brutal, harsh sound. She bit her tongue to stop herself from mocking him. He looked around desperately, then sprang up and began feeding logs to the fire. When it was roaring, he mopped up the spilled stew, and began to ease the soaked bedding and clothes from around her. Though she fought him to leave her be, in truth, the soft dry mattress he moved her to felt infinitely better. It was as if there were two of her now, and the furious one prevailed, while the gentle one looked on helplessly. She wanted to tell him about the dream, but another wave came, harsher than before, and clamped down and would not release for a very long time. It was as if that disastrous roof beam were severing the lower half of her body again, slowly, inch by inch. She wanted to pound her belly, tell her to stop, to let go, but Jacques held her arms, tears running down his face as she screamed curses at him. When it finally released, she collapsed into a semisleep, fettered by the horror of the dogs waiting just on the other side.

This struggle went on into the next morning, past afternoon, and into the following evening, by which time she was too exhausted to lift her head. She could remember snatches of what her mother had said about birthings that lasted too long, that killed the mother and babe alike, or so wore the woman down that she was not the same later. Jacques was distressed beyond any power of utterance, and seemed to enter a catatonic state rocking by the fire betweentimes.

At some point the wind died, and a cold silence took hold, until she realized that he had let the fire die down. It took her several minutes to muster the strength to force the words from a thickened throat and swollen tongue. At her sound, he lifted his head and gazed at her, stricken as any dumb animal until she repeated the request and managed to point at the fire. He leapt up and worked the flame alive again, and warmth spread across her exhausted body like a much-needed shawl. Having made a positive good, he propped her head under his arm and offered her water, tucked quilts around her, and stood looking around the room as if to vouch for his good conduct.

There was a knocking on the door, the first she could remember, and he hastened to answer. Amid the pigeon-soft murmurings that followed, she slept again, barely waking for a contraction that seemed to hold on so long her body grew numb, and it wasn't until it subsided that she realized what had happened. When next she opened her eyes, Chabot was kneeling beside her, holding a cup of warm liquid to her lips.

"You came back," Annie tried to say, but it didn't sound right.

"Forgot my new traps." He smiled, a round full face, marked by a long mustache that he was very vain about, combing it with his fingers while he calmly talked of his wife and her birthings out in the wilderness before she was killed.

"Not the worst I've seen. She's young, that's all. The young ones don't want to give it up at first." His tone was kindly despite the words. "Be better if she could squat or sit." He glanced at the roof beams, then down at her withered legs and shrugged. "Some folks wouldn't move into a new cabin without tying a bird's nest on the beam. Brings luck"—he stroked his mustache—"and easy birthing." He tugged at the scarf wrapped around his neck and glanced at the roaring fire. "Hot water and rags to wash the young one?" He nodded toward the kettle. While Jacques sprang into action, Chabot knelt beside her.

"I'm just needing to see how this little one's thinking of coming out into the world." He ran his rough palms over her naked belly, but she was too exhausted to care. She'd seen cows when the calf was lying wrong or already dead and knew she wore the same resignation on her face.

"Is it dead?" she asked, her voice a tiny chirruping sparrow.

"Just resting like its mama." He examined her face carefully. "Jacques, we need to get this girl of yours some relief. She's worn down to a nubbin."

Annie closed her eyes against the tears that suddenly welled, surprising her. She had thought she was too dried out to cry anymore, had gone beyond the point where tears meant anything. She dozed again, and woke to a bitter liquid on her tongue that first she thought to spit out, but heard Chabot's voice urging her to swallow. It was corn liquor!

"Damn you!" she said in a hoarse whisper, convinced they'd burned her throat with their nonsense. Immediately Chabot put the cup to her lips and poured a mouthful into her, which she had no choice but to swallow if she wasn't to choke. And choked anyway. When she regained her voice, she cursed them again.

"Now we're going to sit you up here. Jacques's holding you, feel him? Next time that baby pushes, you push back, hear?" Chabot was peering between her legs, but modesty was so long forgotten she doubted she would care again in this lifetime, if she survived.

As soon as she started to relax against Jacques—and it did feel better, she hadn't realized how sore she was from lying on the hard floor for a day and a half—a huge wave of pain contracted up her belly.

"Push, Annie, bear down!" Chabot yelled, and instead of fighting the pain, she pushed until a new violent tearing came from below, and she howled.

"Here it comes, here, here it comes—" Jacques leaned over her shoulder and watched as the slippery red thing slid out onto the quilts.

Chabot scooped it up, cut the cord with his big knife, and spanked its bottom until it cried out.

"Baby girl," he said with a triumphant grin. "Let me clean her up." Quickly and efficiently he wiped the baby down with a wet rag and wrapped her in a blanket. As soon as he put her in Annie's arms, she felt the sudden rush of Jacques' tears on her cheek. They were a family full of joy, with the griefs that would follow held at a distance for this brief hour.

5

THE MILD WINTER MOVED COMFORTABLY INTO 1818 WITH SOFT SNOWS THAT soon melted, brief icy rains that gave them beautiful glittery mornings but didn't break trees apart, winds that blew softly around the corners of the inn without frightening the baby or the men who slept soundly the sleep of the just, while dreams embedded their secrets like mica in the rocky landscapes of the dark. Each morning Annie awoke to wonder at the baby Jula cradled at her breast, while Jacques slept in front of the fire to keep a steady warmth in the room. He shunned liquor that winter, spending every spare hour with his family, despite the noisy laughter at the other end of the hall.

The men's labor was over. The inn built solid and true, the barn raised just in time to shelter the cows and horses in its lee and protect the summer grass they had cut and dried for hay. The corn was heaped in the slatted shed where it would keep from molding, and the firewood was piled high as the roof of the inn. Each day's work required only the splitting of logs and chopping of kindling for the fires. It was a season of good feeling, one Annie treasured for the rest of her days. Though she sometimes worried that they were living on the borrowed goodness of the future, and like borrowed salt, it could never be returned without bad luck.

Jula was a quiet, smiling baby, adored by her father and mother, and by all the men who came to see her as their own in some way, as if the inn, the barns and fences had all been built to shelter their one progeny. When Chabot left after the baby was born, it was with tears in his eyes and trembling lips that would not shape into words as he raised a big mittened hand in farewell.

The temperature dropped that day, bringing in the kind of frozen stillness that turns the air into shimmering particles of silver that brush your face and the backs of your hands like a ghost hurrying past. The heart gone out of them, they stayed indoors the whole day, watching the fire burn into crumbles, only to be built up again, until finally Skaggs, who was as good with a knife as an ax, grabbed a thick chunk of cypress from the stack beside the fireplace and began to whittle. As he bent over the task, his gray-streaked brown hair fell in thick clumps around his face, while his strong, blunt-fingered hands worked a shape from the wood. Soon a head emerged, then the features: the soft rounded features of a child. When that was complete, he laid it aside and began on the torso, arms, hands, legs, and feet, each piece a lifelike reminder of a young child.

When the body was complete, he began to carve and shape the joints, until he had fashioned curious wooden hinges so that the figure could move. But Annie was distracted by the head lying on the hearth beside him. What manner of doll was this? she wondered.

At last, Skaggs laid the pieces down with the tenderness of a man handling small birds, rose and went down the hall to the room he shared with seven other men. When he returned, he began to fasten the doll limbs with pieces of sinew stretched thin as string. He attached the head to the body with sinew so that it would bob and turn like a real child's. He continued his construction all afternoon, pausing only for a cup of sassafras tea, which he let cool on the hearth.

By then the Burtram brothers had abandoned their never-ending card game laced with argument and moved close enough to observe Skaggs's every move. Nicholas, the oldest, was the first to unsheathe his knife and begin to whittle and carve on a stick of wood. Mitchell soon followed, then Ashland, the youngest, each boy struggling clumsily while glancing at the beautifully carved limbs and expression of the doll in front of them. Finally Ashland threw down his stick in disgust, nursing a sliced thumb. He was on the verge of uttering a deep oath, but a sharp look from Nicholas stopped him. Instead, he sat sulking like a spoiled child.

The carving went on to dark, until the candles were lit and the carvers collected closer to the fire for light. Little Dickie Sawtell was already adept enough to shape an old man with crooked back and bent arms. He'd been carving since he was just a boy, he bragged, brushing the shock of red hair out of his eyes and looking all of fourteen. Judah Quick, it turned out, had a knack for painting the bodies of the animals and people. He made several different-sized brushes from horsehair tied with thread to the ends of small sticks, and began to paint faces. He was especially good at giving the animals expressions that reminded you of people. There was Forrest Clinch's frowning rooster, Heral Wells's flirtatious cow, Frank and McCord Foley's twin pigs who wore the arched brows of the schoolteacher. Dickie's aged man seemed to leer as he peered out from under a thatch of Dickie's own red hair stuck on with glue. Soon everyone was cutting their own hair and applying it to the people and animals they were carving.

In the next few days, the men grew so comfortable with their carving that they began to produce puppets with one another's physiognomies. Heral's round, innocent face was topped with sprouts of wheatgrass hair; little Dickie Sawtell's wide blue-eyed stare and red hair hung braided to the waist of a girl; square-shouldered and broad-headed fathers reminded them of the Burtram brothers; and mothers in checkered dresses and bonnets looked suspiciously like Annie, or Forrest Clinch's description of his wife who had passed in the first night of quakes. It was as if what they were really craving was a family of their own. Only Ford Jones and his three terrible dogs failed to materialize in puppet form. As far as Annie could tell, he spent the weeks hunched in the corner over a jug of liquor on a bench he'd dragged for that purpose. Outside, the chained dogs howled with the wind or the coyotes, whichever was louder. But even that sound could not quench the goodness of those months.

In her short life, Annie had learned that men spent all their time either building or breaking—things, animals, people. Without one to occupy them, they'd turn to the other. And so it was that, by the first of March, the mood changed. The men grew restive. Meat, flour, honey, and corn were running low. They had little of the dried and preserved fruit they had managed to purchase the year before, since their own trees had only just been planted and there had been so many men in camp last summer it was all Annie could do to dry even a few wild berries. With river travel stopped those cold months, they had to rely solely on their own stores and what meat could be hunted. By spring they realized they would have to stretch what little they had even further. As the weather eased, the men began to complain of the greasy, thin hoecakes and watery coffee brewed from wild chicory and walnut meats, though Annie didn't have to remind them more than once that they had used precious corn months ago to make their liquor. The deer that had been plentiful last summer were difficult to find now, and rabbit provided too little meat for grown men to live on. By the time the first boat made its way up the river, they had had to butcher three hogs and one of the two milk cows.

That morning with Jula on her lap, Annie was feeding her dog scraps of gristle and a small wad of fatback from her plate when she became aware of the silence in the room. The Burtram brothers were hunched on the bench across from her, staring with sullen expressions on their faces, while Skaggs shook his head and used the tip of his knife to pry a splinter from the table. When it loosened, he used it to pick his teeth. With plowing and planting still weeks away, the men had too little to do and had begun to find fault with everything around them. She didn't cook enough at meals, Jacques needed to start paying them real wages, the boats would never come, and on and on.

"That dawg should be huntin' his own food," Skaggs said. A quick glance was enough to confirm that the left eyelid, thick with the scar sliced down the side of his face, was twitching. When he was agitated, the eyelid trembled, as if the ruined eye beneath were about to push its way out in righteous anger.

She let the dog lick her fingers with his warm wet tongue, then set the trencher down for him to polish off. He'd had the same lean winter they'd had, and he was gaunt to the point of starvation. Annie had taken to sneaking him some food as often as possible.

"He's too small to hunt, Skaggs," she said, "you know that."

Skaggs dug in his long yellow teeth with the wood sliver, eyeing the dog. "A cur like that, he'd do for mice, rats, might even find himself a rabbit or squirrel. You'll ruin him feeding him table scraps. Dog needs a hungry belly to keep his mind and nose sharp."

"Or we could just roast him, once she's plumped him up nice," McCord Foley said.

Feeling the same vinegar in her blood, Annie said, "Notice you don't give Ford Jones advice about his three dogs. They're fat as ticks out there too. What have they been eating all winter, I wonder."

Skaggs pushed at a clot of mud that had dropped off his boot and muttered under his breath.

Frank Foley chuckled and shoved his empty tin cup at Skaggs. "Ford's looking right plump himself, ain't he?"

Skaggs shot a warning look out of the corner of his eye to Frank, but the younger man ignored him. Pilcher Wyre cleared his throat loudly and swung his legs over the side of the bench and stood.

"Reckon we should head to the river, see if there's any sign of a boat. Good day for it. Might could see a boat today." As he walked across the room to the door, Annie noticed that his leather trousers and wool shirt hung on his lean frame much more loosely than they had last fall. His face was so thin, it appeared skeletal now. She imagined she could see the molars in his jaw through the rough hide. Quickly she glanced around at the other men—all their faces were gaunt, hungry looking, eyes sunken in dark circles, and they moved more carefully now, slower. Good God, they were starving! All except Jones.

"What's Jones eating? Where's he getting food?" she asked Skaggs, but he merely shrugged. She looked at Pilcher, but he held up a hand and pulled open the door.

"Frank?"

He reached out and pulled back his cup, then proceeded to study it as if it were an ancient chalice.

"McCord?"

He turned his back to her.

Then Heral Wells's thin tenor voice spoke out of the shadow of the bed he was keeping to these days since he'd been down with lung congestion the past month. "He takes them dogs hunting. They share whatever they kill. They darn near kilt every living creature in ten miles. While we starve, he and his dogs is dining in high style." He ended his bitter remarks with a coughing fit that sounded harsh enough to break his back in two.

"Why didn't you tell me? Does Jacques know?" Annie pushed the dog off as soon as he began to gnaw on the edge of the wood for the soaked-in juices.

Frank Foley shrugged.

"What did he say?"

"Said to leave him be." Frank turned his cup in his hands, delicately. "So we leave him be."

She snorted and, lifting Jula to her shoulder, stood. "Well, I won't let it be, that's for damn sure!"

Frank's and McCord's heads jerked up at the sound of her oath. The men hardly ever swore in front of her, and she never made a deep oath.

Outside, she found Jacques and Jones shoulder to shoulder looking at the three half-wild beasts that were, upon close inspection, so fat and healthy their coats shone. They examined Annie with glittering eager eyes, panting, the large open mouths exposing long vicious teeth. Jones also looked more prosperous than he had when he'd arrived in camp last summer. In fact, he sported a little belly that he patted proprietarily every few minutes.

Jacques pointed to one of the dogs, said something that made Jones chuckle mirthlessly, then kicked at the animal, stopping his boot just an inch away from the slavering jaws as the dog leapt up and lunged at the men, his body jerked back each time by the thick chain wrapped around a four-foot-wide tree trunk. It seemed more like the Jacques of that bad night than the Jacques she knew. She slipped away to find a better time.

The day turned deceptively warm, the sort that begs you to strip your woolen underwear and slip your shoes by midmorning and plunges you into icy rain by dark. The wind that began as a breeze took such force by noon it nearly blew the New Orleans flatboat into the muddy bank beside the dock. As soon as the boat had been spied as a mere bobbing speck in the distance of the high brown river, the men had quit their mild efforts at work and gathered at the shore, shoving and laughing in horseplay until the boat came close enough to be hallooed.

To their surprise, it looked like Chabot was the first on the plank laid between the boat and dock! Not four months gone, too early for trapping to be done. At least the man resembled Chabot to the degree of having the merry blue eyes that crinkled in amusement at the sight of their ragtag bunch, and those same large, competent hands with the freckled backs she swore she'd never forget as they delivered her baby. But the remaining features were so different, the men spread apart the instant he approached. His face no longer sported a wild brown winter beard or mustache; instead his whiskers were shaved and shaped like those of the gentlemen they glimpsed passing on the decks of boats. His hair was also carefully shaped and tied back in a club, and there was a cloying scent of lavender and lily that rose in small puffs each time he shifted his body or when he raised his hand for the tall black top hat he doffed in greeting to one and all. They stood gaping.

"The new look, *n'est-ce pas?*" He smiled and bowed and they took another step back. It sounded like Chabot all right. But the dandy in the grass-green coat over the tan fitted waistcoat was unlike anything they had ever seen. When he peeled off the tan kid gloves that matched the piping on his coat, flicked the tails draping behind, and pointed his right leg at them, the three Burtram brothers elbowed one another. Instead of trousers, Chabot wore long, tight pantaloons the shade of her grandmother's ivory comb, and low black shoes, revealing white silk stockings under the stirrup of the pantaloon.

"Looks more like a dang green and white rooster than a man," Pilcher Wyre muttered.

But Chabot was much thinner than when he'd left in November, unusually pale skin drawn tight against the bones, dark smudges around his excited blue eyes—he appeared to have climbed out of the sickbed.

Annie stepped forward and touched his arm. "Why Chabot, you've been ill!"

He hesitated, searching her face, then gave a quick shrug and looked over his shoulder toward the boat. Following his gaze, she spied a tall woman dressed in furs despite the heat of the day. A heavy black veil obscured her face, but she waved and gestured excitedly toward the plank to the dock.

"*Mon dieu!*" Chabot took a deep oath and pushed through the men. In a moment he had rushed across the dock and up the plank to help the woman whose gay laughter lifted above their heads into the overhanging cottonwoods and river willows, and they all looked up as if sighting a rare and exotic bird. When they looked back the couple was advancing upon them, the woman's arms filled with a black coat. As soon as they stood before them, she shook the coat and held it out to Chabot.

"Now darling, you must stay warm," she chided with a smile. The wool greatcoat was lined with sheared beaver and would surely roast him on such a warm day, but he put on the coat, although his pale face flushed crimson. Frank and McCord Foley nudged each other and made mocking faces, but fortunately Chabot didn't see them. Skaggs and Forrest Clinch held their grins behind their hands and looked away at the boat. Jacques appeared puzzled at the transformation.

So tall she matched him head to head, the woman adjusted the collar of

Chabot's coat, lifted her veil, and gave him a quick peck on the cheek. Turning to them, her broad face ablaze with happiness and rouge, she said, "Dealie Dare Chabot," and held out a large gloved hand, which Jacques took and brushed with his lips. His sudden courtliness confused Annie so she began a curtsy, but stopped abruptly and glanced at Chabot, who started to laugh. A snicker came from the direction of the three Burtram brothers, and she shot them a quick frown. Dealie gave her such an appraising look with her large sharp brown eyes that Annie's stained and worn blue cotton dress felt unbearably shapeless and shabby, and she curled her bare dirty toes and folded her arms across her milk-filled breasts. Jula, who was taking a nap in her cradle suspended from the limb of an oak on the edge of their clearing, woke up and began to cry hungrily, and Annie felt a sudden wetness against her arms. Face burning, she limped to her baby, hastily unfastened the blankets binding her, and awkwardly hobbled to their dwelling. When Jacques found her, she was huddled in the corner of their bed, nursing with tears streaming down her face, angry at all of them—Jula, Jacques, and especially herself.

"*Chérie, doucement, ma petite poupée,*" he crooned.

"I'm not your little doll!" She shoved him away as he tried to stroke her knotted filthy hair. She'd become an animal like the rest of them. She'd seen it in the woman's eyes, the amused disdain. And to have to hobble away on her ruined legs . . .

"How dare he show up like this!" she began. "Who is she?"

"Shhh," Jacques held his finger to his lips. "They're just down the hall."

The baby choked and coughed, and Annie had to put her over her shoulder and pat her back. Almost immediately she felt the warm curdled milk spill against her neck. It was almost more than she could bear, and tears filled her eyes again. She tried to speak, but a sob caught the words and made her throat swell and ache.

"Chabot brought presents. Soon as she's asleep, you come and see." Jacques patted her arm with two fingers, but she shook her head.

"It's absurd, him bringing her out here, the both of them dressed like that. What's happened to Chabot?" Even to her own ears, her voice sounded pathetic, like a small child denied her pleasure. It made her want to smile, but she wouldn't give over.

"She saved his life! A panther spooked Chabot's horse, threw him, broke his arm and ribs. He lay there for a day, unconscious, before he was found and brought in to a settlement where Madame Dare was lodged on her way home to New Orleans. She nursed him through fever, lung congestion, even set the arm so it healed straight. When he was better, they traveled to New Orleans where she has a house and an import business. Chabot is lucky." Jacques looked at the parchment-covered windows as if he could see through them like glass. "A wealthy widow."

"Maybe you should follow them back. Find a beautiful woman who can dress you in fancy clothing." She yanked his fingers off her arm.

"*Mon Dieu, tu es folle*—don't be a crazy! *Chérie*, you are my beautiful woman." He grabbed her by the shoulders and pulled her hard against him, making the baby gulp and squawk in protest before he let go.

"Look at me!" Annie wailed as she pulled at a clump of her knotted greasy hair, succeeding only in making her scalp ache.

He took his time, looking her over, nodding, clucking, until he smiled. "You're my little wild girl, Annie Lark, the girl I saved from the flood and earthquake. You look just the way you did that day too."

She punched his arm with her fist, and he laughed and rubbed at the spot.

"So you want a piss-covered, half-starved, maddened girl with two maimed legs? What kind of man are you?" This time she hit him in the chest, hard enough that he flinched and clutched her hand before she could strike again.

"Enough," he said. His eyes darkened and his wide mouth thinned and set. "This pity for yourself, *c'est trop bête*, it is ugly, *chérie*." He stood and walked to the fireplace, leaning on the mantel, his back to her. The baby's body began to grow heavy on her shoulder as she slipped into sleep. Annie laid her on the bed, nestled in the quilts, a little smile on her lips. She leaned down and kissed her, the only good thing in her life at that moment.

Outside, the day that had begun warm and bright had darkened, and thunder growled overhead.

"*Merde!* We must tie up the boat!" Jacques rushed out the door and down the hall. If the rain came with a wind, it could sweep the boat against the dock and smash them both to kindling. Then Annie remembered the quilt she had spread outside while she read, and her precious book, a translation of Herodotus left by a traveler just a few weeks ago. Glancing at the sleeping baby one last time, she picked up her cane and hobbled out the door, making certain to close and fasten it against the three half-wild dogs Ford Jones still kept. Despite her protests, they were chained in the trees to the south of the inn. Watchdogs, he claimed when their snarling became

particularly vicious, or the howling set up at night. It's worse than being surrounded by wolves, she told Jacques, but he merely shrugged.

Outside the sky was crowded with black heavy-bellied clouds that
swirled and bumped as new clouds crowded in from the west and south. The
wind picked up and began to gust, and the men at the dock started yelling
to hurry and tie up the boat. The coming rain sent a deep ache into her legs.
Awkwardly braced on the cane, she edged her way down to kneel beside the
quilt spread out under the cradle swing. Stretching off-balance to collect the
book and writing materials, she tumbled forward, wrenching her hip and
landing hard on her knee. The pain jolted her back and she fought off the
tears that stung her eyes. It took a few minutes to pull herself upright and
brace herself on the cane again. Impossible! She would have to leave everything to be soaked, including the precious book. She couldn't pull herself
and the bundle upright at the same moment without further wrenching her
back. She was rising inch by inch when she felt a rough hand jerk her up by
the arm.

Ford Jones bent over the quilt, gathered it all in one swoop under his
arm, and started to pick her up under the other.

"No. I can do it on my own!" she yelled over the rumbling clouds. The
first raindrops splashed against her cheek and she waved him toward the
inn. "Go on, don't let the book get wet!"

He hesitated, his cold dark eyes, the blackness deep underground, and
she felt that shiver of knowledge that comes when you are touched by evil,
true evil, an evil so pure, it can commit an act of kindness without betraying
itself.

The wind gusted hard and a small dead limb clattered down behind
them. He turned and pushed toward the inn against the long sweeping lines
of wind pelting leaves and bits of dirt that stung her arms and face. She
looked up at the boiling black clouds—heavy rain was only a minute or two
away. Fat drops began to plop heavily on her head and back. The black
clouds were darkening the day into twilight. The men on the river continued to shout and curse as the boat bucked against the ropes like a wild horse
and tried to spin out into the quickening current.

Jones had placed her bundle on the hearth, and immediately departed
because Chabot and Dealie were standing over the bed where Jula was gurgling and smiling as if she recognized the man who had helped birth her.
Dealie had taken off her hat and coat to reveal a dark blue wool gown whose
waist rose to just under her ample breasts, the skirt falling straight to the

ankle. When she lifted her hands to smooth her hair, Annie noticed that the sleeves and hem were decorated in swirled black brocade, giving the gown a rich look. Her thick black hair was parted in the middle, with heavy curls hanging on either side of her face; the braid pinned behind her head was coming loose, and the loose strands clung to the damp skin of her neck. She smiled and wiggled her fingers at the baby, and then casting a reassuring glance at Annie, she picked up Jula.

"Why, you're such a pretty one, I'll just have to take you to New Orleans when you grow up. Make you the belle of the ball, would you like that? Dance all night and drink champagne with pretty men like Chabot here?"

Making her way across the room, Dealie swung her arms as if she were the cradle in the trees, and Jula laughed and gurgled. Dealie was handsome rather than beautiful, and she had an underlying strength in her shoulders and back that made the expensive dress seem more costume than part of her, much as Chabot's clothing was. Her big hands looked as if they had done their share of work, her thick wrists and arms muscular despite the fancy dress.

Chabot pulled the rocking chair closer to the fire and when Dealie sat down, he knelt and added wood to the few embers. Annie sat opposite in Jacques' chair. With some coaxing, the fire began to brighten, and Jula caught sight of her and gurgled happily, tiny fingers locked around a gold bangle on Dealie's arm. Dealie glanced at Annie and smiled, slipping the bangle off and holding it up for Jula, who instantly poked it in her mouth and began to chew happily.

"Oh no." Annie lurched forward, but Dealie waved her off.

"She's just teething," she said. "It won't hurt." She had a large face with a square chin and prominent nose that gave an impression of power. Upon closer examination, she was older than Annie had thought, with lines at the corners of her thin lips and large brown eyes. There was a blunt good-nature in her expression, one that said she was satisfied with who and where she was in this life.

How many children did she have? Annie glanced at Chabot, who had straightened and was leaning against the mantel, his own dark eyes filled with admiration for the woman who had saved his life, no matter how she dressed him. He did look so odd that Annie had the urge to chuck a piece of firewood at him, see if he'd scatter and squawk the way the chickens did.

Outside there was a tremendous crack of lightning followed by a long deep roll of thunder that reverberated against the walls and seemed to shake them all as if in an earthquake. A sudden wave of vertigo washed over Annie and she swayed and gripped the chair and uttered a small cry.

"Annie." Chabot knelt and took her hand. "It's only thunder," he said. His palm was so oddly soft, almost like her baby's skin, that she would have laughed but for the vertigo.

"It's been such a stormy spring and the noise reminds me," she whispered.

"Light the lamps," Dealie said in a soft but commanding voice. "Give her a sip of brandy."

Chabot released her hand and rose to obey. As soon as there was some light to dispel the gloom and noise of the storm outside, he pulled a small silver flask from his waistcoat and offered her a sip. When she shook her head, he took a long draught for himself.

Recapping and returning it to his pocket, he smiled at her. "Better than corn liquor."

She shook her head at the idea. She would never have a taste for distilled spirits of any sort, though she was planning on making wine this summer from the fruit they had planted or could gather.

There was another roll of thunder that made the walls seem to shiver, followed by a loud rush of rain that pushed so hard against the parchment-covered windows, it seemed to be on the verge of slashing through. At the far end of the hall there was a sudden burst of noise as the men hurried inside, shouting and laughing, the boat apparently secured.

"I'll see." Chabot nodded toward the noise, and Dealie smiled and looked down at the baby, who was busy chewing the bright metal ring.

"I have three already," she said to Annie's unasked question as soon as Chabot had shut the door. "And another as soon as I can." Despite the matter-of-factness in her words, she watched her face for reaction. Annie nodded.

"I've buried three before him, does that shock you?" She smiled and raised her eyebrows. Annie shrugged.

She leaned down and blew softly in Jula's face, making the baby smile and lean her head against the ample chest. "I've lost more than I kept." She looked at Annie again and smiled. "Babies that is. They slip away so easily, don't they? Like dandelions gone to seed—" There was an edge of sadness and maybe bitterness in her tone as she patted Jula's leg and pulled the yellowed, stained shift down over her plump little knees.

"You never know how long they'll be with you." She glanced at Annie's worn clothing and unkempt hair, considered the fire for a few minutes, then spoke again.

"You're exhausted, aren't you?"

Unable to resist that open, honest face, Annie nodded.

"You need help. You must spend every moment with your baby, Jula, and you can't when you're cooking for those men, washing and mending clothes, taking care of Jacques, and everything else—" She waved her hand at the room. "You need help."

"Jacques and the men help, when they can."

She laughed as if Annie had made a joke, then picked up the hem of Jula's homemade shift again.

"It must be hard to get things clean in the winter here."

Annie's face glowed with shame.

"I'll send you a girl to help." Dealie lifted the baby and settled her back on her lap so she faced Annie while Jula teethed on the gold bangle. "I'll need her back in the fall, should I—" She touched her own stomach. "She's a bit gloomy, but worth every penny I paid."

Annie shook her head.

"Oh the children love her, and you're worn out, Annie."

"We don't use slaves," she said. "Jacques would never agree to it."

Dealie laughed again. "Of course he would! And she's only on loan. A gift for the next few months while you get back on your—" She caught herself and glanced quickly at Annie's legs, which surely she'd noticed or been told about. "Your feet. I'm so sorry, Annie, I didn't mean—"

Her broad face reddened and she looked so stricken that Annie lifted her dirty bare feet and raised her skirt. "It appears that I'm on my feet more than enough." She was relying on two canes now, and it hurt more to push herself up with them. "It's only temporary," she told her. "I'll be strong one day soon. I'll be able to race Jula when she learns to walk."

Dealie hugged the baby and looked at Annie with a serious expression on her face. "I'm good to the slaves, you know. I make sure they eat as well as my family, they have good, clean clothing, and medicine. I never break up a family, and I teach them to read and write and calculate so they can lead useful lives. When they're able, they can even buy their freedom."

Annie didn't know how to argue with her, but she could not imagine anything worse than the uncertain fate of the Africans who had escaped the previous summer.

Dealie took Annie's silence for agreement and continued. "New Orleans is different, a city full of freed slaves, quadroons. The French have bred a beautiful race, a very sophisticated, artistic society. My own business thrives because of the culture, the desire for fine wines, fabrics, dishware, furniture and paintings. I import all of Europe, and soon the taste for such goods will find its way upriver to places such as this even." She spread her arm to include their homely cypress walls and unfinished floor, the raw planks of the ceiling, the stinky mass of furs on the bed in the corner, and her mother's blackened cooking pot sitting on the hearth.

Not knowing why, Annie just shook her head. She didn't want anything to change, didn't want any other house or life, but the shelter of this room, the sound of laughing men down the hall, the rain beating on the roof, the fire eating steadily through the logs burning warmth into the front of her dress, her legs, her arms and face.

The two women sat in silence for a while until Jula began to fuss. Annie lifted her out of Dealie's arms, and their solitude was disrupted by the tramping of the men's boots down the hallway.

Then there was a whimpering and scratching at the door and Dealie rose to open it. Annie's poor little dog scrambled in, soaked and muddy and shaking, apparently caught outside when the storm struck. She couldn't find her cane and didn't know what to do with Jula as the dog slunk over to her chair and pressed against her legs, muddying her skirt.

Dealie leaned down and took Jula, and Annie lifted the little dog to her lap and wrapped him in her skirt, feeling the tremors of his fear and cold against her legs and stomach. There was a gob of mud in one ear, and the white hair on his body was almost all reddish brown from mud. The thunder rolled again and he shrank deeper into her lap, whimpering. Jula began to wail and the hallway door burst open. Jacques and Chabot swaggered in with Jones in tow.

"*Chérie!* We have wine! French wine! Chabot has brought us fine wine and more. Come!" Jacques had already been drinking, and his breath stank, and without warning, he reached down and pulled Annie out of the chair, spilling the terrified dog to the floor.

As soon as Jacques picked him up, the dog yelped, squirmed, and whimpered against the big rough hands, eyes wild with fear. When Jacques tried to stroke its head, the dog growled and tried to sink its small teeth into his fingers.

"Careful." Annie reached for the pup.

"What happened?" Jacques asked, a look of wonder on his face. He'd already had so much wine he couldn't think straight.

"Something spooked him good," Chabot said.

"Been playing with the big dogs," Jones said with a short, mirthless laugh.

"What do you mean?" she asked.

"He comes prancin' by, every day getting closer and closer to where they're chained, just testin' 'em, see. Little mama's boy." He shrugged. "Makes sense they'd grab at him. Lucky he got away. That don't happen very often." He eyed the dog in Jacques' arms as if it owed him something. The dog whimpered and tried to hide its head in Jacques' sleeve.

The way Jones spoke sent a shiver through Annie, followed by a white rage.

"I want you to leave, Mr. Jones. Take your vicious dogs and go. Today, now!" She reached for the dog, who yelped as soon as she got her hand under its belly and started to lift. When he recognized her though, he pressed his head against her chest, his heart pounding so hard she could feel it. Ford glanced quickly at Jacques, then opened the door, stepped into the rain, and banged the door shut behind him.

When Jacques touched her shoulder, the dog growled. *"Ma chère—"*

He had never taken the men's side against her, and she was stung. Ducking under his hand, she turned toward the bench by the door where the water jug and drying cloth sat. Without the aid of her cane, it was difficult to carry the dog and force her legs to support them as she made her way.

"He needs to leave today," she said through gritted teeth.

The dog stayed quiet while Annie sat and dampened the cloth, but as soon as she tried to clean the inside of his muddy ear, he cried out and tried to squirm out of her lap, teeth bared, and she had to settle him again.

"No, *chérie*, Ford's not leaving," Jacques announced. "I need him here." She glared at him and turned her attention back to the dog.

Dealie said, "Well, that's settled," and rose to lay the baby on the bed. Taking Chabot and Jacques by their arms, she said, "Let's see about making a fine supper to go with the wine you men have obviously been enjoying." Her laugh was a little higher than her speaking voice, and the men escorted her to the door as if charmed from their senses.

Then Chabot stopped and turned back. "I can fetch something to calm him, Annie." He glanced at Jacques, who was bending to hear what Dealie was whispering. "Wait for me."

Once the door closed, Annie allowed her tears to flow.

6

HAT NIGHT WHEN THE BABY FRETTED AND JACQUES STIRRED AWAKE TO take her as he often did, Annie stopped him. "You've had too much wine, you'll probably drop her." Instead of arguing, he rolled over and began snoring loudly, filling the air with a damp sour smell that turned her stomach.

"You're disgusting!" she whispered. With Jula fitted into a sling hanging across her shoulder and chest, she could use both canes for support as she made her way across the room and out the door. Despite her anger, it was a lovely damp spring night, with the first of the peepers beginning their song an octave higher than the frogs that would soon start climbing out of the river mud to perch among the new cattails and rushes along the bank.

Through the trees the bronze light undulated on the river as if the moon itself were being jostled by the wind. She looked down at Jula, who was sleepily sucking her tiny fist. She had thought to bring her outside to nurse, but the baby seemed satisfied now.

If the weather held, the men might begin clearing more pasture in the morning, digging drainage ditches for the swamp. The thought of their own horses and cattle grazing in fields around them was comforting.

A few days of warm weather would bring the maple, cottonwood, cypress, elm, redbud, and maybe even the plum into bloom early. They would have to work harder collecting and preserving fruit this year. She made a promise to draw a map of all the plum trees and berry bushes so that she could send someone to pick at the right time. But with Jula here, how would she have time to preserve and dry it all? She thought again of the tempting promise of help Dealie had made.

She was just about to round the corner to the front of the building when she heard a low growl in the brush between her and the river. She stopped, leaning her weight on one cane, prepared to strike out. Should she shout for help?

There was another low growl, which ended abruptly in a grunt with the sound of something hitting flesh.

"It's all right now," a man's voice whispered from the dark. "Just don't try to go down to the river this way."

The voice and growl had come from a thicket of plum and grape vines all tangled together on one side of the path to the dock. She squinted into the dark, but could not make out even an outline of a person.

"You'd best get back inside, Miz Ducharme," the man's voice whispered.

She was about to answer when out of the corner of her eye she caught movement on the river, but just as she turned to look more closely, the growling commenced again, this time louder, almost a snarl.

"You need to go inside," the man whispered louder, more firmly. "Now."

A dark form of a man suddenly took shape only a few feet from her, something glittering in his hand—a knife? She wheeled and hobbled quickly to the back of the inn. Panting hard, she put her hand on the latch, but stopped herself. Who dared tell her what to do! She turned again, peering into the moonlit darkness that seemed denser now, more a black fog, like trying to see through a wool blanket. She put her hand out as if to clear some of it away, and quickly pressed against the log wall. Two men were coming up the path from the docks, laughing and talking loud enough for her to hear despite the hour. A figure stepped in their path, startling them to a halt.

Then she heard the growling again, almost a snarl, and one of Jones's dogs stepped out of the underbrush, directly in front of her. It was a massive creature, with a square, brutish jaw, torn lips revealing fangs, ripped ears flattened against a wedge-shaped head. Pieces of long yellow and brown fur matted with burs and caked with something dark like blood hung from its body, and it stood above her waist, level with Jula's body! She folded her arms protectively around her baby and tried to avoid looking in the creature's eyes, but the growling continued, a deep rumble that shook its sides as it began to inch forward, one cautious stalking step at a time. She was tempted to raise her cane, but afraid of what would happen if it felt threatened—and God forbid, leapt at her. Instead, she forced herself to lift her eyes to meet his—gold-flecked orbs so soaked in blackness they seemed bottomless, absorbing all light into the dark empty skull. Despite the extreme danger, it was fascinating how an animal's eyes could seem so empty and dark at the same time, hypnotizing, like a bottomless pool.

The longer she stared, the slower he moved, as if he were fascinated by the boldness in her eyes. She kept all feeling from her face, demonstrated no fear he could smell, focused instead on drawing herself up tall and sticking her elbows out, as her father had told them to do for the panther, which would hesitate to attack such a sizable creature. She thought of Jones's coldness with the dogs and let it seep into her. The dog hesitated, then stopped, puzzled, his growl softening and rising in pitch until it became a whimper. He cocked his head slightly, gave a final probing look before turning his gaze to the dark underbrush and letting his nose drop to sniff loudly at the ground. At last he raised his leg and pissed on the log wall of the inn, backed up three steps, sniffed the piss spot, and ducked into the brush.

Her legs were shaking so badly, they were on the verge of collapse, and she closed her eyes for a moment as the shaking rose up through her entire body until it subsided. When she opened her eyes again, Jula gurgled, eyes shining brightly. She lifted her tiny fist to Annie, who took it and kissed the fingers that smelled of sweet warm milk. She had no idea if Jula was awake for the whole experience, or if perhaps she was the reason the dog had not attacked.

The sound of a rising voice reminded her of the men, who were now standing so close together that their words were muffled by their bodies. It had to be Jones with the dog on the chain, and she thought about yelling at him for letting one loose, but decided it was more important to see what his business was at this hour. Since her nightdress was dyed indigo, it was easy to blend into the dark shape of the log wall as she crept closer to them.

"We'll bring them up in about a month, then, but we're not paying for this trip, understand? Tell Jacques that we won't come if he's going to charge us again." One of the men stepped out of the tight group, hand resting on his belt at what seemed to be the sheath of a large knife.

Jones shrugged. "Suit yourself." He looked down at the face next to his knee and with an imperceptible sign must have told the animal to attack, because without warning the dog lunged, grabbing the man's elbow, which he had instinctively thrown up. Knocking the man to the ground, the dog began to tighten his grip. The man yelped in pain.

"Stop—there's no problem!" the man cried out.

Jones uttered what sounded like an Indian word and the dog reluctantly released the man's arm and stepped back. She began to worry about where the third dog was. She glanced into the underbrush, but saw nothing. The man on the ground got up, rubbing his arm.

"I didn't mean I wouldn't pay if he asked me to—I never said that," the man whined. "Keep that goddamn beast off me though or next time I'll shoot him."

The other man stood with arms at his side, seemingly distracted by the stars in the sky one moment, and the moonlight on the river the next. He never looked at Jones. He never looked at his companion. And he never so much as glanced at the huge dog.

"We're set then," the man said. When Jones nodded, the man put his arm out and half lifted up his friend.

"My bitch'll tear his balls off!" the man who was attacked said.

"Got two others to finish her then," Jones replied.

"I got a gun says they won't!"

The quiet one shoved his friend ahead of him down the path before Jones could put the dog on him again.

"A month or so," the man said over his shoulder.

Jones watched them until they were on their flatboat, poling away from the dock, and as he stood there Annie slid slowly back along the wall, her bare feet avoiding sticks that might give her away. When her hand was on the leather pull-string of the door latch again, she stopped. With a last glance toward where she had stood, Jones stepped back into the brush, the dog following. Had he seen her?

She stood without moving while the peepers that had been silent during the strangers' visit took up their high throbbing. Jula had fallen asleep again, as if the night sounds were calming. Something rustled in the brush, passing by without stopping. When it had been quiet for some time, Jones's dark figure stepped from the brush and made his way to the front door of the inn. Still she waited until he had been inside for long enough to assure he'd gone to sleep, before she slid inside and put Jula in her cradle. Then, too alert to sleep, she stepped outside again, stopping just on the other side of the door she quietly pulled shut.

The huge brown and yellow dog sidled out of the brush without making a sound, stopping so near her left leg she could feel his hot breath on her hand braced on the cane. Would he tear her fingers off? Why hadn't he warned her this time? Then she felt a hot wetness on her wrist—he was licking her.

She stood very still.

Slowly she lifted her fingers and touched his nose, his big square jaw, up behind his ear and down his neck, burrowing in through the thick hair to the skin. Gradually he bent his head into her hand, and slowly his whole body began to lean against her, the matted tail brushing the back of her dress with the rhythm of wagging. When she hit a bur buried so deeply in his fur that its needle-sharp points were digging into the skin on his neck, he groaned, and she worked it out slowly and let it drop next to the wall. He continued to lick her hand, her arm, her dress, his pink tongue slightly silver with moisture.

"Why you were somebody's baby, weren't you," she crooned. "A good boy like you."

She worked her way to the back of his neck, where he flinched and shied away from her hand, only easing back when she started down the bones of his spine. There were narrow ridges of scar crisscrossing his back and flanks, as if he'd been cruelly beaten, and only his long hair covered the evidence. No wonder he was so mean. Some of the tangles and matted fur were too thick and bound by burs to pull apart. She'd have to use a knife and saw them out in the morning.

She moved back up to his neck and let her fingers sink through the extra-dense fur until they were stopped by what felt like a collar, with spikes every inch or two piercing the thick leather. Circling the collar lightly with her fingers, she searched for the latch, but felt only a solid iron ring. When she managed to slip a finger under the leather, the dog groaned loudly, letting it wind down to a whine. Evidently, the studs were positioned to dig into the dog's neck with any movement. The skin was oozing too, the festering wounds under the studs giving off a stink that made her stomach turn. She had to get the collar off.

"Come on," she whispered to the dog. Behind the inn was a lean-to covering the stack of firewood that was daily replenished from a pile of deadfall, debris from building, and trees cleared last year. Two axes and a hatchet were sunk in the tree stump used as the splitting block. She balanced against the cutting block and used both hands to pull the hatchet out of the wood. It was small, almost like a toy, only a foot long but with a wide handle and flat head like a broadax. Only one side was sharpened, so she could probably control the cut, and the size was perfect.

As soon as the dog saw the hatchet in her hand, he growled and backed away. She dropped the tool, slid to the ground, bracing her back against the stump, and put her empty hands in her lap, palms up. It took a few minutes, but finally the dog began sniffing the ground between them, working his way over. She began gentling him by stroking his legs, then his chest and ribs, and finally when he let out a sigh, she told him to sit.

His hind end dropped without hesitation, followed by his front end, so that the giant dog was straddling her lap. She laughed and gave him a quick hug, careful of his neck, petting him all over his body until his head dropped between his paws. It was odd, but she felt no danger.

Except for squirming when she had to pull or shift the collar to get the correct angle for the hatchet blade, the dog stayed still, panting heavily, but resigned to his fate. While his weight was crushing her legs, reminding her of that fateful night of earthquakes, she had to saw at the thick leather with deliberate slowness. It had to be well past midnight, and clouds were drifting across the moon, dimming the light to shadows, but she was working by feel, her forefinger against the hewing edge to keep it from slipping off the leather or splitting the collar in half before she knew it, since the leather was old and well-cured bullhide, strong as iron.

Suddenly there was a slight give, and the blade sank so quickly, she jerked her whole body to save the poor animal from another cruelty. She put the hatchet down and felt the place she'd been working on. Despite being cut in half, oddly, the collar stayed in place. As soon as she tried to pull it off, the dog whimpered and shifted his front legs, as if preparing to leap away.

"Easy," she whispered. She felt her way from spike to spike, gently pulling the collar away from the neck at each metal post. Apparently, the points had embedded themselves in his flesh, creating sores that could not heal. His flesh had swollen around the metal, trying to embrace and contain the source of the pain. The dog whimpered and squirmed, trying to raise its head against the pain, but she held him down with her elbows. The worst places were on the underside of the neck where the collar was so tangled in hair and burs, and she finally had to use the hatchet blade to cut away the matted fur and ease the collar off.

As soon as the collar was lying on the ground next to them, the dog propped himself on his front legs, yawned, and began to rise. Although the neck wounds needed to be cleaned and something put on the sores, there was nothing more she could do tonight. She picked up the collar and turned it over in the slant of moonlight. The spikes were crusted with blood and hair. She stood and flung it into the brush, letting the anger give her arm extra strength.

The dog leapt up, placing its front paws on her shoulders, jaws open.

"No! Stop!" she shouted, struggling to stay upright.

The dog gazed at her for a long moment, then gave her a big wet swipe across her face.

"What's going on here?"

She whirled around to face Jacques, who was holding a lantern in front of him, his face grotesquely slashed with shadow. In his other hand he held a pistol pointed in their direction. Without thinking she stepped in front of the dog so it was hidden from view.

"Everything is fine."

"Was that a dog I saw?" His words were still slurred with sleep and wine.

"Go to bed, Jacques. You've had too much wine." She couldn't resist the last gibe.

He blinked stupidly and let the pistol fall to his side. He really did look ridiculous, naked except for moccasins on his bare feet. He wasn't the sort of man who was more beautiful with his clothes off, but it was a strong, sinewy body, the only male she'd ever seen aside from her brothers when they were boys. For all she knew, none of them looked glorious once they revealed their flesh, despite what Homer had to say about Achilles and Hector and the ancient heroes of myth.

"Your pup was whimpering so I brought him to bed. Be careful getting in," he said.

"Thank you. Now get some sleep. We'll have a long day tomorrow with the weather holding." She really was grateful. He wasn't a mean man and she did love him with all her heart. It was just that sometimes he wasn't quite himself these days, and she needed to stand up for what was right when he neglected it.

When he turned to go back to bed, his flat buttocks drooped comically, like the stomach on her family's old sow, whose teats dragged in the dirt. There was something endearing about it, and she forgot how angry he'd made her earlier. She decided not to tell him about the events of the night, however, and when she turned to the dog again, he had vanished. In the morning, she vowed, she'd try to talk to Jacques about Jones once more.

The light had changed by the time she nursed Jula and pulled the latch string to their room. Behind her the sky was streaked pale pink and yellow, causing the trees' limbs to turn black, then lighten to gray. The river flowed pink and apricot, then splashed silver blue, before the sun burst out and the water was a rich brown, the color of toasted bread. She was so used to the birdsongs that she had begun to ignore them, but now she listened to the cardinal's loud, slurred whistle, the robin's multiple series of whistled phrases of three or four notes, the raucous *kwrrk* of the woodpecker with its red head.

When she returned to their bed, she wrapped her arms around her husband and pressed her naked breasts against his back, as she had done when they were living in their trapper cabin those winters alone. She wondered that he could continue to sleep so soundly and let her hand slide down between his legs to check—his member stood stiff! Before she could pull her fingers away, Jacques' hand closed on hers and he chuckled deep in his throat.

"My little thief! You are caught!"

They laughed and wrestled until he was on top and they were gasping with pleasure and his sour breath tasted sweet on her tongue and his rough whiskers made the skin of her breasts glow.

"Now you must take your punishment," he whispered as he slowly entered her.

"I'll be naughty all day long," she promised.

7

BY THE END OF APRIL, DEALIE AND CHABOT HAD MOVED IN AND BEGUN to organize much of the cooking and running of the inn while she cared for Jula. In many ways it was a relief, because Jacques was working so hard during the day, and then he stayed up late with Dealie and Chabot drinking rich red wine from his native France and reminiscing. Annie liked being on her own more, coming and going as she pleased—being Jacques' lover when he finally came to bed at night, then getting up for her other night visitor. She was fairly exhausted, sleeping in small pieces. Thankfully Jula was sleeping soundly most of the time.

The dog came back every night, waiting until the men had settled to sleep. Often he gave a single scratch at the door or sniffed loudly once to let her know of his arrival. She would be dozing lightly, Jula snugged into the bed between her and Jacques, who would be snoring, restless with his wine-soaked dreams. Now that the boats were beginning to arrive daily, their food supply was not so uncertain, and she was able to save a good portion for him every day without drawing notice. Only her small dog, Pie, was in danger of giving them away, although recently he had taken to following

Dealie because she cooked for the inn now and would feed him tidbits all day long. He was sleeping at the foot of Dealie's bed most nights.

Then one Friday afternoon in early May the two men she had seen the month before appeared. Jacques greeted them as if they were old acquaintances, and there was much made of their arrival with several other boats. By nightfall, there were so many men at the supper table, they had to eat in shifts and bed down on the floor of the large room. Only her protests kept Jacques from opening the floor of their own room to them also. She feared and probably knew deep in her heart what they were planning as there was a peculiar silence among them when she was near.

"THE MEN WON'T BE CLEARING SWAMP OR DIGGING DITCH TODAY," JACQUES SAID the next morning. He sat slumped at the table with his head between his hands. "Don't bring them lunch."

She watched him pour cream into the coffee that Chabot had brought back from New Orleans, made in a special way that produced a thick black concoction. Something in her resented Jacques' taking the cream when he did nothing to care for the cow, but then she reminded herself that she was merely tired and out of sorts this morning. Caring for Jacques and the baby and then the dog in the middle of the night was beginning to wear her down. She needed to broach the subject with Jacques, but he was too sick from drinking right now.

"You need a cup of willow bark tea," she said in a quiet voice that hinted only of love and concern.

He held up the coffee.

"It will cure your headache." She stood and began to search the jars of teas and medicines on the crude shelves next to the fireplace.

"I don't need your help."

She put the jars back in order. It was no use talking to him in this mood. Instead, she gathered Jula from her cradle, wrapped her in a wool blanket, and laid her on the sling she would wear over her shoulder. As soon as she put on her cloak, a thick wool blanket pattern that was almost too heavy for her small frame, Jacques spoke.

"Where do you think you're going?"

She whirled on him. "Wherever I please."

He was up before she had a chance to collect the baby. Pulling the cloak off her shoulders, he said, "You're staying in today." He put his hands on her shoulders, and kissing the top of her head, glanced outside as if he could see the weather through the parchment-covered windows. "Too much going on." He looked down at her legs. "You and Jula would just be in the way."

Noticing the expression on her face, he added, "For the baby's sake." He ducked his head as he sat down again, picked up his coffee, and held the side of the mug against his forehead.

She wouldn't make him headache tea if his life depended on it now, and she felt like saying so, but instead took off her cloak, unwrapped Jula, and laid her back in her cradle with Dealie's gold bangle to chew on.

"May I fetch some fresh water?" She made her voice subservient, cloying. He waved his hand without looking at her. They both hated to argue, but she wasn't going to give in easily today.

The water was in a barrel just behind the inn, and she used the opportunity to look around for the dog, calling it in a soft whisper, holding out a few crumbs of biscuit. When he failed to appear, it worried her. What if Jones had found him again?

She was just reaching for the door latch when the men trooped out of the front of the inn, stretching in the sun's mildness and horsing around. All except for Jones and the two men from the river. Jones had fetched his two dogs, and was having to use all his strength to keep them from attacking. Apparently the motion of the men was setting them off—and rather than bark or growl in warning, they were lunging silently, raking the air with their teeth, twisting and hitting the end of the chains over and over, sending them into an even deeper frenzy each time the spike collars bit into the already tender flesh of their necks.

At one point the red dog turned on Jones and would have caught his arm but for the pole one of the strangers used to keep dogs at a distance.

By now the men had ceased moving or talking, instead forming a circle around the dogs. The red dog began pacing the perimeter as if waiting for something, his jaws dripping with silver strings of saliva. For some reason, Frank Foley stuck his foot out at the dog and was rewarded by the powerful jaws clamping on his boot, sinking teeth straight through the leather.

"Get him off me!" Frank yelled, held upright by his cousin McCord. "Let go!" He tried kicking his foot, but the dog held fast until Jones wrapped the end of the chain around his head and throat and yanked, choking the dog until it let go. It only took the animal a minute to recover and begin lunging at Frank Foley again, who had the sense now to back up and hide behind the other men.

The men thought this all good fun and would have continued to tor-
ment the animal if Jacques himself hadn't come out and growled some orders that scattered the crowd. Gathering shovels, augers, bucksaws,
adze-hatchet, broadax, and miscellaneous other tools, the men followed
Jacques as he made his way beyond the inn to the small clearing they used
for the cow pasture. She was tempted to follow, but thought to find the dog
while they were occupied.

Using her canes to push away the dried vines, she entered the underbrush where she'd last seen him. Although briars and burs caught at her
skirt, she ignored them. There was a faint trail splitting the dried grasses
and weeds leading toward the river. She hesitated for a moment, cocking
her head to listen for Jula's wail, but hearing nothing she pushed on, and immediately tripped over a fallen limb and sank to her knees with a little cry.
The ground was mucky from spring rains and when she lifted her hands,
they were covered in mud to her wrists. She tried wiping them off on a narrow willow trunk, but to little avail. The handles of her canes were now slippery and she had to concentrate on gripping them hard. She made a low
whistle and click in the side of her mouth, hoping to entice the dog out of
hiding as she continued to follow his trail.

The slope to the riverbank was so gradual that she almost fell in as the
ground stopped abruptly in a brown swirl of water. The river was high and
thick with spring melt, and filled with limbs and brush from flooding above
them. She stepped back and watched the brown water begin to lap at the
toes of her boots. Surely, the dog hadn't gone in the river. She looked
around and spotted the faint trail again, this time leading along the bank
toward the dock.

She hurried as best she could despite the undergrowth, and tripped several times, landing on her hands and knees, having to work her way up
again. Not daring to call the dog now, so close to the dock, she searched
frantically.

As soon as she reached the clearing by the dock, she saw him. He was
staring at a tied-up flatboat on which there were three huge shaggy yellow
tan dogs, chained to rings on an iron bar that stretched the width of the
boat. From the snarling, it was clear that the dogs barely tolerated one another, and certainly not this stranger. The three resembled something bred
from wolves or mountain lions—gaunt, yellow eyed, long fanged. As soon
as they saw her, they set up a vicious snarling and barking that brought a
man scurrying out of the six-by-six cabin on the deck. He tried to wave her

away while he picked up a length of cordwood and pounded the deck to get the dogs' attention, then tossed some raw fish in front of them.

While the dogs ate greedily, the man turned to her and the loose dog.

"Ain't that one of Ford's dogs?" he asked in a voice with a soft drawl to it. He had filthy yellow hair that hung in clumps to his shoulders, and a rough grease-smeared face out of which peered two blue-white eyes so empty they might have been those of a blind man. His face, on the other hand, was etched with lines so deep they might have been cut by a nail in soft clay.

Annie stepped up and put her hand on the dog's back. "No." She buried her fingers in the thick fur. "No, he's not."

The man's face creased into a smile, which somehow made his expression even emptier. "Shore he is. That's the brown bastard took my finger to the knuckle." He held up his left hand to demonstrate the missing little finger. "I'd be careful, I was you." He picked up a length of wood with a wire loop on the end and jumped off his boat onto the dock with the quickness and silence of a cat.

"Stay away from us!" She raised her right cane and the dog started snarling, sounding as mad as those on the boat.

The man nodded in satisfaction and kept coming, his body barely seeming to move as he rapidly advanced, stalking them. She dug her fingers in the fur and tried to get a hold, but as soon as the man was ten feet away, the dog exploded. As the dog sprang into midair, the man turned neatly, like a dancer, filling the wire loop with the animal's head and neck, and quickly twisting the stick so the wire went tight and jerked. The dog fell hard on his side with a grunt and lay still.

"Now I got ya," he said.

"Help! Help me!!" she howled. She could hear men's voices, and Chabot came running, followed by Dealie and Jones.

Chabot ran straight at the man, knocking him over with a blow to his chest, but the man hung onto the stick and wire.

"No. He's hurting my dog—"

Chabot grabbed the stick from the man and eased the noose while Annie knelt beside the prone dog, slipped her fingers under the wire and worked it loose, pulled it over the dog's head, and stroked his head. He gave a little sniff, looked at her as if he'd never seen her in his life, growled and bared his teeth.

Chabot put his arm out to keep Dealie back. "Annie, back up," he said.

Shaking her head, she stroked the dog's side until he raised his head and snapped the air next to her hand. She jerked it away and Dealie gasped.

"He's a sombitch." Jones stepped forward for the first time, taking custody of the stick with the wire. "Wondered where he'd gotten to. This one's sneaky mean. One day he's your friend, next day he's tearing your throat out . . ." He looked at her as if he might know what she'd been doing. "Got him from a family he'd about kilt their little girl. Found him standing over her, teeth marks on her leg. I said I'd take him, put that meanness to work."

"That's a lie!" she yelled.

"Don't do to let a dog think too well of hisself. Woman either."

He looked at her again, his knowing eyes telling her that he had seen her feeding and caring for his dog and had let it play itself out. She hated him. Really hated him. And there was purity in the feeling; it all coalesced in one hard bright spot now. If she were a man with a gun, she would have shot him dead on the spot.

"You can go straight to hell, Ford Jones." She stood and hobbled up the path to the inn, unable to bear seeing the dog taken away, yet uncertain that he wasn't what Jones had described.

"Annie—" Dealie came running after her, but Annie ignored her. They could all go straight to hell. All of them.

Jula was wailing with hunger by the time she got back inside and while the baby fed at her breast, she thought about how to get that dog back.

THAT EVENING THE MEN RETURNED EXHAUSTED BUT BOISTEROUS, SHOVING each other like boys as they washed the mud from their faces and hands. Then they stood in line for their cup of broth, a trencher of venison stew with what Dealie called *sauce espagnole* or brown sauce, plus cornbread and fried apples. The herbs and seasonings Dealie used gave the venison a delicious, if strange, aroma. But nothing could give Annie an appetite. She couldn't stop thinking of the dog.

While the men filled the benches and lined the floor along the walls of the inn eating silently, she sought out her husband, who was not partaking of wine tonight. Instead, he was deep in conversation with Jones and the yellow-haired man with the dogs, but she dared not approach for fear her temper would flare again and she would lash out. By the time the men were finished eating, Jacques drew her aside.

"You didn't listen to me today, and you might have been killed, *ma chère.*" He put his forefinger under her chin and lifted. "Then who will care for the baby Jula?"

She drew her head back and frowned, prepared to answer, but he shook his head, his face softening. "And who would care for your husband Jacques who would die of loneliness?"

He turned the corners of his mouth down and drew the track of a tear on his cheek, and she laughed despite herself.

"I'm glad you're not drinking wine tonight," she said, and instantly regretted it, for his mouth hardened into a line.

"Don't mistake me," he said in a low voice so harsh she wondered that he dared speak to her in such a manner. "Stay here tonight. Stay with Dealie and Jula. If I find out you've disobeyed me—"

He didn't have the opportunity to finish for she turned, snatched the baby from her cradle, and hurried down the hall to their room, slamming the door and barring it so he could not follow her. Then she barred the outside door also, and sank down to the hearth and began piling logs on until the flames were roaring, while Jula watched from her cradle.

It was well past dark when there was a hesitant knock on the door. "Annie? Let me in, Annie." It was Dealie. She thought of pretending she was asleep, but rose instead and unbarred the door.

Dealie had been drinking with the men. Her face was flushed and her eyes overly bright as she swept in with her hands behind her back.

"You must try our wine!" She placed a bottle and two cups on the table with a flourish.

"I don't care for spirits," Annie said as firmly as she could, but Dealie brushed her words aside.

"Everyone loves this wine! It's the best in the world." She poured both cups full and handed her one. Annie tried to demur, but she insisted. "Just a sip, and let the flavor fill your mouth." She giggled drunkenly. "Like a lover's kiss."

The wine did warm and expand with flavor: something of the earth and grape and blackberry and—she could not say, but when she swallowed, the alcohol made her cough. "It's not unpleasant," she managed to choke out. Dealie laughed and took a deep draught from her cup.

"Men must have their games, you know." She smiled and lifted a hand to adjust the knotted mass of hair at the back of her head, which was always on the verge of collapsing. She had given up trying to keep the formal side curls and neatness. As the days had progressed, Dealie's attire had simplified also. Without a maid to help, she was discovering that she could make do with the same plain blue cotton gown every day. There were even a few grease spots on the bodice and skirt tonight. Dealie resembled her now, and it gave Annie a bit of satisfaction.

"Take another sip," Dealie urged. "It's good for the nursing baby."

She drank more this time, and felt her face grow warm and her body relax as the wine spread into her limbs. She smiled.

"Jacques's a good man," Dealie said. "So devoted he'll build a great house and fortune to keep you happy." She smiled and drank, holding the wine in her mouth for a moment before swallowing. Again Annie noticed how powerful Dealie's arms and wrists were. And something else, tonight Dealie was wearing a huge yellow stone on her finger.

Annie drank and felt heady, confident and open, as if her every word were truer than Dealie's. "I don't want that." She looked around the room. "This is perfect, this room, our life, I don't want anything else." She drank again.

Dealie watched her for a moment, then turned her attention to the fire. "A man needs to feel that a woman demands something of him, especially a man like Jacques. He will lose his way unless he believes that he must please you by building more. It's his genius to make money and to create." She nodded her head toward the room.

"You understand him because you're just like him," Annie said, suddenly wise with wine.

Dealie shrugged.

"What about Chabot?"

Dealie laughed. "He's the kind of man you can only afford once you've made a fortune. A wonderful lover, a man who understands women and life, a man who enjoys women and life so much that you want to provide for him and watch such enjoyment. He will work if you require it, but he's at his best when he's not working." Her laugh was rich and suggestive and she stroked the front of her dress, the ring flashing in the firelight.

"Did he give you that ring?"

She held up her hand and studied it, turning the ring this way and that so the light made it brilliant, then shook her head. "No, this was a present from my last husband. A perfect yellow diamond. Very rare. And beautiful. It has a history though." She laughed uneasily and put her hand to her throat. "I'm not superstitious, but it's said to be more a curse of a marriage than a blessing." She drank and swallowed slowly. "My husband died soon after he gave me the diamond. I'm only wearing it now for the first time."

The sound of distant shouting made them pause. Jula woke and gurgled happily, watching them from her cradle. Annie rose, surprised by how much more steady she was on her feet from the wine. When Jula's diapers were changed and she had nursed, Annie put her back in the cradle to sleep, all the while aware of the growing noise the men were making.

"What's going on?" she asked, but Dealie shook her head and continued staring into the fire, a full cup in her hands again. "Where's my little dog?" He had taken to following her everywhere and suddenly he had vanished.

Dealie glanced at her with a guilty expression on her face and shrugged. "I haven't seen him since supper."

"Watch the baby," she said, slipping out the back door and pulling her cloak after her.

"Annie, don't—"

THEY HAD PLACED TORCHES ON THE PERIMETER OF A LOG RING, SOME TWENTY-five feet across, and built a bonfire in the middle while the men stood on or leaned over the waist-high wooden enclosure. They were drunk and wild with something else—the smell of violence, scorched cloth, and rage. Forrest Clinch and Pilcher Wyre were among them. The Burtram brothers were passing a jug of liquor, hooting and yelling at each man to hurry it along. The air was grainy with danger, and she hesitated on the little hillside above the ring. Skaggs had tied a cord around his ax and wore it slung across his body. Where was Jacques? What was it that made the ground so dark in the firelight?

The answer quickly arrived as the yellow-haired stranger from the boat burst out of the dark, one of his dogs on the end of the wire loop and pole. It alternately tried to surge ahead or stay behind since the pole kept it from attacking the man, which it clearly wanted to do. Fangs bared, it snarled and tried to dive at the legs of the men hurriedly clearing a space. The dog flew over the barricade and the man took it in a single stride. There was a great roar as soon as the dog appeared and the yellow-haired man took pride in parading the vicious animal twice around the ring, allowing it to jump and snarl at anyone unlucky enough to lean too far or offer an arm or leg. When it got to Frank Foley, it stopped and glared.

There followed a lull as the men began to bet loudly with one another while Jacques, Chabot, and Heral Wells detached themselves from the crowd and began to circle the barricade taking bets. They wore pistols and knives, and their eyes flashed hungrily at the money offered them—Russian kopecks, Dutch rix-dollars, Spanish reales, English shillings, and silver dollars, halves, quarters, eighths, and sixteenths minted in Mexico and South America. The jumble of currencies often led to confusion in the reckoning of sums in river trade and business at the inn, although barter was still their most common means of exchange. Jacques and Chabot and Heral must have decided on valuation for the various monies because they snatched the coins quickly, dropped them in leather pouches attached at their waists, and kept a running tally, pausing only when a stranger bet two eagles, ten-dollar gold pieces.

As soon as the round of betting was complete, Jones appeared out of the dark with the red dog at his side. When the dog saw the men on the barricade, it went wild, snarling and leaping at them, lashing from side to side with bared teeth. Jones had to half lift the dog over the barricade, so intent was it on attacking the men. If anything, this dog was more ferocious than the yellow dog, and Jones made only one quick circle with it because as soon as it saw the other dog, it locked eyes and paid no attention to anyone or anything as it stood hackles raised, emitting a deep rumbling growl that shook its ribs while the other dog pranced and lunged, its crazed yellow eyes dancing red with reflected flames from the fire.

"Last chance to bet!" Jacques yelled.

There was another quick round of betting until the men grew silent with expectation. Then Jacques climbed into the ring, holding something white, and walked as close as he dared to the strange dog and held it out. Immediately there was a shriek of fear and yelping that sent the huge dog into a frenzy, snapping and lunging to tear the squirming creature from Jacques' hands.

"That worthless piece-of-shit dog gonna take on them two?" a stranger yelled, and the crowd hooted. "I'll take that bet!" he bragged.

As soon as Jacques turned back to Jones, she saw that it was her little dog! Before she could move close enough to be heard, Jacques had teased the red beast also, holding the whimpering pup close enough for the red beast to slash out with bared teeth so close it almost tore Jacques' forearm.

"Jacques!" she yelled. She clubbed at someone's back. "Out of my way!" But the man, a stranger, just turned and sneered.

"Get out of here, lady," he said, grabbing her cane and throwing it into the dark.

She started to push her way to Jacques as he climbed back over the barricade, but was stopped by the unholy noise of the two dogs trying to kill each other. Jacques dropped the little dog, which began to crawl away from the crowd of legs and, despite being stepped on twice, managed to make it into the cover of dark, where his white coat gave him away. As soon as she reached him, he stood and let her pick him up, shivering and whimpering. Poor little Pie. Jacques was crazy tonight—all that money was like a narcotic to his senses.

The men gave a savage howl and burst into shouts as the noise of the dogs ceased. She held her little dog against her bosom, covering him with her cloak so they were both obscured in the shadows on the edge of the clearing.

"Damn you," she yelled. "Goddamn you all."

The men on the barricade parted again as the yellow-haired man lifted his dog over his head and flung him into the weeds near her. He was dead. Blood was pumping from a gaping wound in his throat, and his head flopped unnaturally. Broken neck. The man kicked at the corpse and cursed as he strode past, so close to where she stood that she could see the knife-edge lines of his face speckled with blood. He stank like rotting meat, and the whole front of his shirt and pants was soaked with blood.

Jacques helped Jones lift the red dog over the logs, but as soon as they put the dog down, it collapsed. Jones lifted it in his arms and, staggering under the weight, disappeared into the dark also.

The men drank more, and talked loudly about the fight they'd just witnessed, occasionally looking over their shoulders expectantly. Little Dickie Sawtell was so drunk he swayed, in danger of falling into the ring, and it took Judah Quick and Ashland Burtram to steady him.

The yellow-haired man was the first to appear again, with yet another of his dogs held at the length of the pole. This one came with more dignity, however, like an old warrior. He didn't fight the wire noose or the man at the end of the pole. When they passed the dead animal, he merely sniffed the air, shook himself, and strained for the barricade. This time the men knew to move far enough away so they wouldn't get bitten, but the dog ignored them. Leaping lightly over the fence, he waited for the yellow-haired man, and let himself be paraded without making a fuss. His indifference set the men in motion, betting loudly. Jacques and Chabot and Heral again made their rounds, adding coin to already heavy bags.

Annie didn't see Dealie join the crowd until she appeared at Chabot's side, linking arms and whispering in his ear as she slipped a small pouch of coins into his hand. He laughed and added it to his own bag, then led her to a place on the barricade where she could stand. Even leaning against the log wall, she was so drunk she swayed, and she took a turn at the jug of liquor when it came to her. Surely Jula was asleep, Annie thought; she would only wait until Jones brought the next dog, then she'd take her white dog back and nurse him. It was probably too late to save the other dog now.

But as soon as he appeared and she recognized his square jaw and shaggy coat, she knew she had to stop them. There was fresh blood on the fur around his neck, and his eyes gleamed with hatred as Jones worked him up to the barricade. Unable to get close, the man had to push him with a pole to force him over the wall. Once in the ring, the dog rose on his hind legs and howled in rage, then nearly yanked Jones off his feet as he tried to get away from the other dog, who stood quietly, braced and crouched, jaws parted, ready to spring into battle.

Jacques and Chabot and Heral made their rounds quickly, having to stuff coins inside their shirts because the bags were full. There was no need to tease these dogs into a frenzy.

Suddenly she knew the dog she'd cared for all week wasn't a killer. He was trying to escape, trying to leap the wall while the startled men pushed back and laughed uneasily. She had to stop the fight.

She put the little dog down beside a thick tree trunk and watched for an opportunity. The men too had gone quiet, concentrating on the dogs and the first moment of contact. She had to hurry, it was only a few yards away—

Pushing a space for herself between the men, she called out to the dog. She didn't know why she imagined it would hear her or even listen. She called the name she'd given him, "Sunny." The dog stopped, and while he was looking in her direction, the yellow-haired man let his dog loose. The huge animal locked its jaws around half his head, gouging out the eye, but missing the throat. Sunny reared up, twisted, and fell on the other dog, knocking the jaws loose. Having to keep his head turned so he could see out of the remaining eye, Sunny was at a disadvantage as the other dog tried to come around on the blind side and attack him from behind. Aiming for the back of the neck, it managed to tear some hide off his shoulder. They battled like that, each taking the blow from the other and using quickness and power to push the opponent off, until both dogs were panting with exhaustion while the men stood silently waiting for the end.

In the moment of near silence, she thought she heard Jula wailing, not the plaintive missing-her-mama cry, but her angry, hungry, demanding cry loud enough to peel bark off trees. The stranger's dog perked his ears, bared his teeth, and snarled. Then the dog seemed to make an instant decision, and without hesitation, he hurled himself over the barricade so close she ducked, and streaked toward the inn. The watching men had pulled away from her as the dog sprang, leaving a gap that Sunny instantly filled also, disappearing in the direction of the inn.

It took a few moments for Jacques and the others to realize what she feared. She could already hear the sound of Jula's wailing amid the noise of their battle—a different, more frantic, terrified howl—

There is nothing so terrible. Nothing.

A man falls to his hands and knees, uttering an oath before regaining his feet. Others stumble through the dark, falling, cursing, flailing, while an unholy chorus of the two remaining dogs chained to trees in the dark begin to bark and howl against the pain-filled night, and Dealie is crying, Annie never stops, never, she doesn't know, she doesn't know, she doesn't know, and she curses God and Jacques and Dealie and most of all herself and her legs that won't travel faster so she is the last to enter the room where the two dogs are locked at each other's throats, covered with blood, so much blood, there the baby, silent, bloody, and silent, her head hanging from her torn throat like a rag doll ripped apart. The men shoving into the room are too shocked to move. Even Jacques. It is up to her. She pulls the bowie knife from Jacques' belt and plunges it to the hilt in the yellow dog's chest. He does not even look surprised. Just closes his eyes and sinks down, releasing his hold on Sunny's throat. She pulls the knife out, raises it to bury it in Sunny's chest, but looks into his eyes, sees something that looks like both fear and love. She knows then—he has tried to protect the baby, and for his efforts, he has been killed, because when the dead dog releases his grip, Sunny's throat begins to gush blood all over her, and all she can do is ease the dead dog from his mouth and hold his dying head. If she does this, she will not have to do that—look at her child flung broken and apart at her feet—if she does this, the future they borrowed might not have to be repaid tonight.

After a while, there is a high keening noise, and she thinks it must be the pup who is awake, alone and hurt in the woods on the ground dark with old blood, and she thinks to go to him, save him, and she lets Sunny's head gently down on the blood-soaked floor—she'll never get the stain out, she thinks, they'll live with it for the rest of their days—and she is torn between wanting to scrub the floor and save the dog outside, and the noise is shouting in her ears and she claps her hands over them—and realizes it is she, she is shrieking and cannot stop—

8

HEDIE RAILS DUCHARME

THE END OF VOLUME I. I CLOSED THE BOOK AND WEPT, FALLING ASLEEP IN the Moroccan leather chair, the lamp burning until dawn when I woke and struggled upright. Clement still wasn't home, and the house felt unfriendly, as if it were against me now. There was an odd shadow on the wall in front of me, shaped almost like a man, rising steeply to the ceiling and curving almost over my head . . . almost . . . but I shook it off and stood up, my heart pounding. The baby was restless too, turning in long rolling waves, all sharp elbows and knees this morning. Poor Annie! And that poor baby. I put my arms around my belly to protect it. Dogs. There were so many dangers in the world, how would I be able to keep the baby safe? It was impossible! I simply couldn't have a baby, that was the truth of it. I would have to tell Clement when he came home. I looked around the room lit with rose dawn light. Where was he? Did he have another woman? No, no woman would dare call in the middle of the night like that. It's business, he said, it's always business! What business needed to be done in the middle of the night? Was I safe? Was someone going to come and kill us in our beds? I'd been reading those stories about Prohibition and rumrunners and gangsters. Was Clement doing something illegal? Pictures of bullet-riddled bodies crowded into my worry and I switched off the lamp and shoved the book back on the shelf.

I would not read another word of that woman's terrible story, I vowed, slowly feeling my way through the semidark rooms to the hallway. I peeked out the long narrow window beside the door in hopes of seeing Monte Jean and her husband. There was a black dog sniffing around the front yard, some stray with matted fur and prominent ribs. I knocked on the glass, and immediately regretted it, because when he looked up, his yellow eyes glowed eerily in the rose-colored light.

"You're being silly," I chided myself, and opened the door a crack. The dog watched me carefully as I stuck my head out and said in a loud, firm voice, "You git now, go on, git." He stuck his nose back in the grass, sniffed loudly, swung his small foxy head my way once more, his eyes plain this time, then turned around and trotted back down the driveway to the road. That's what Annie should have done—sent the dogs away, two legged and four legged both.

I looked toward the river beyond the trees and brush, catching a glimpse of the glittering brown water like a living thing, its body so heavy it made a presence even when you couldn't see it. The inn must have been very close to the bank, and those foundations in the field over there must have been the slave quarters. Was that the original barn then? The family graveyard was up there by the fence. Was the baby there? I shivered. The dew had been heavy last night, almost a light frost on the grass as it glistened in the light bursting across the yard. A cow mooed from the barnyard, and an owl that lived in the peak of the bachelor's ell where the roof had rotted *who-whoed* a few times, then shut up. Someone should fix that roof. We didn't need wildlife in the house. I yawned and closed the door, ignoring the shadows and little creakings from the floor above me, too tired to be frightened.

"Everything's going to be fine." I rubbed my belly and began to pull myself up the stairs, using the banister and holding the small of my back, which always twinged when I had to counterbalance the weight in front by leaning away from the steepness. It wasn't good to read such sad stories when I was pregnant, I concluded, pulling the comforter to my chin and closing my eyes. I would look for a happier book next time. But as I fell asleep, Annie's voice kept speaking in my head as if it had become my own, narrating my story as well, and I was to awaken hours later, bathed in sweaty heat, my heart pounding, unable to quite remember the dream.

CLEMENT CAME HOME THAT AFTERNOON, SLEPT A FEW HOURS, GOT UP AND went away after supper. He still refused to tell me where he was going, just patted my shoulder, kissed the top of my head, and adjusted the brim of his fedora so it sat rakishly on his head. There was a bulge under his arm when he hugged me. I hugged him again, slipping my fingers inside his suit jacket. There was leather, and something metal inside it: a gun!

I stepped back, on the verge of asking, but he looked at me with so much tenderness, I didn't. Is it wrong that your heart leaps at love like a dog trained to tricks? He patted my belly, smiled, kissed my lips and lifted his hat in farewell.

With his hand on the doorknob, he put a finger to his lips and then pointed it at me. I hushed. After the baby's born, I am going to get to the bottom of this gun and night business, I vowed.

There was a week where he stayed home after that, and I relaxed, kept Annie's story out of my head and tried to sleep as best I could in little pieces. Being so round meant that I had to get up several times in the night to pee or just relieve the ache in my back. Once I looked for the gun and found it downstairs, hanging in its holster in the back of the coat closet. I remembered my father's pistol, the one he kept from being sheriff. It was huge, heavy, with a long, ornately engraved silver barrel, and ivory grips with his name carved in them. Clement's gun was smaller, snub-nosed and black. It looked more lethal in its impersonality. I didn't know why, but I brought it to my nose and smelled it. Was the scent from being freshly fired? The floor creaked behind me, and I quickly put the gun back and shut the closet door. A woman makes a choice, I realized, between her child and the rest of the world. There was no question about which I had chosen.

THE NEXT DAY I WENT TO WORK ON AN OLD ROCKER I FOUND IN THE PARLOR. I tightened the back spindles with pieces of newspaper jammed in the holes. The black lacquer finish was crackled, the gilt stencils starting to peel, but it was still a good chair, the rocking long and deep and smooth. The carved roaring lion's head on the back reminded me of a picture in my first alphabet book and I took that as a good omen. I found some old Turkish red and gold brocade cushions in one of the parlor rooms downstairs and added them to the back and seat so I could hold the baby there and nurse, as I'd read about in the book the doctor gave me.

About four o'clock Clement moved it up to our bedroom so I wouldn't have to leave at night. He was a good sleeper, solid and innocent and otherly as a child. "You won't have to worry about waking me," he said. "I could sleep through hell and end up in heaven and never know the difference."

He was back to being his old self, funny and bright, and I relaxed into the comfort, letting go of my suspicions. At supper two hours later, he gave me a pair of old-fashioned emerald earrings with ear wires for pierced ears, though mine weren't. He promised to pierce them for me as soon as the baby was born, and we laughed at the idea. I told him I'd have Monte Jean do it. I didn't tell him that my proper Methodist mother would have been scandalized by the idea. Only Gypsies, Negroes, and white trash pierced their ears, she would declare. The idea of flouting her yet again made my feelings for Clement surge. He *was* the right man!

THEN THE TELEPHONE CALL CAME AS SOON AS WE TURNED OUT THE LIGHTS and got in bed that night, and I was so angry, I turned my back to his pleading goodbye. My body rigid, I listened to the closet door as he took out the gun, then the front door, followed by the slam of the car door, the engine catching, and the gravel popping under the tires as he roared away, not bothering with being quiet this time.

Maybe it was because I fell asleep so angry that when I woke up sometime around midnight, I wasn't in myself yet. I sat up quickly, almost as if I had forgotten the extra bulk of my body, swung my legs around, and jumped off the bed. I don't know why I didn't make a wider circle around the rocker. Lately I'd begun to run into things, as if the huge belly had tipped my sense of scale and proportion and size. But my foot caught the runner and I started to fall forward and lurched sideways to grab the foot of the iron bedframe. I still went to my knees and felt the shock rise up my thighs into my stomach, and then there was this sudden wet between my legs, and I was kneeling in water.

"It's too soon!" I whispered because no one was there to help me. Monte Jean always went home with her husband, Roe, after the supper dishes, Clement was gone in the car, and there were only the horses and the wagon and I couldn't harness. I tried standing, but quickly sank back to my knees. I couldn't let go of the iron bedstead because a pain was starting in the front, grabbing me like a fist and yanking, and my back echoed the pain and I didn't think I could stand, but I had to, so I pulled myself up, groaning and cursing, and wishing I'd left a light on instead of all this dark, and trying to think what to do when the cramping fist punched me in the stomach and I knew I had to get to the telephone and call someone, but who?

I staggered into the hallway, naked, dripping, all hell breaking loose below, the baby kicking and rolling, me trying to breathe and not scream out as I picked up the receiver and the operator's sleepy voice said, "Yes?"

HE NEVER TOLD ME WHERE HE WAS THAT NIGHT, HOW THE OPERATOR FOUND him. The baby was born, not as the doctor had promised, painlessly, but on the floor of the downstairs hallway, me naked, alone, screaming at it to leave me alone, stop hurting me, and then waking up as Clement charged through the front door, spilling daylight over us, the bloody mess, the tangled cord around her little neck, the thin blue face, the eyes that never opened, the sealed mouth, the tiny blue fist raised in outrage, utter outrage.

"I am so sorry. Can you hear me, Hedie? I am so sorry, honey. Can you hear me?"

I heard him, but I kept my eyes closed. I already knew. I had closed my eyes, exhausted, for only a minute after I felt her slip out. I thought I had that time, that minute before I had to try to get up and get a knife to cut the cord and clean us both, and make her world right for her.

"I just need a minute to gather myself," I whispered as I closed my eyes and held her little head in the palm of my bloody hand. "Shhh," I said, "shhh—"

And when I opened my eyes, light was coming in the windows beside the front door, and outside a mockingbird had set up in the ancient oak along the side of the house. The house itself was silent, ticking with rising heat already though the rose-colored light said it wasn't even seven yet. I knew then. She hadn't stirred, her skull and my hand had sealed in our blood forever while she struggled silently and died.

You cannot allow yourself to be forgiven for everything you do. At seventeen, I learned that, and no matter what Clement did later, I always felt as guilty as he was.

WE BURIED HER IN THE FAMILY CEMETERY TO THE EAST OF THE HOUSE, UNDER the bur oaks, where the shade covered the grass with a damp cool in summer and the fallen leaves kept the ground warm in the winter. There wasn't enough to say, so we put down the small marker with the shape of a lamb rising out of the top and left it with only the words the stone carver had cut into the border: *This Sweet Lamb of Jesus.*

Then we handled each other like glass, polite as strangers, and wept ourselves to sleep at night. Clement couldn't sleep though, and I couldn't stop sleeping. We were never hungry either. We lost weight as if shedding all that happiness lightened us for the years ahead. I was only eighteen. I'd had a birthday, and already lost a baby and a family. My mother never knew. It wasn't until she died that my sisters tried to contact me again, but by then I wasn't much interested.

LATER I WOULD REALIZE THAT ANNIE LARK HAD BEEN RIGHT ABOUT THAT rocker, and banished it to the bachelor's ell. It would be some time before I took up her book again, so haunted and confused by our similar losses that I began to dream that our babies had suffered the same fate, that I could not save hers or mine when the tale repeated itself night after night. One night I woke up thinking I heard a huge dog pacing the hallway outside our bedroom, his claws so thick and sharp they dug into the cypress floorboards, and all I could do was lie there shivering, alone because Clement had answered the telephone again. He was some kind of gangster, I knew that. In the morning I got down on my hands and knees and saw the tiny commas marching the length of the hall.

I was never going to read another word of Annie Lark's story, I vowed, and climbed back in bed for the day, while Monte Jean kept peering in at me and clucking her tongue as if I were a sulking child. I could hear her complaining to Clement loudly in the front hall that it was time for me to get out of that bed, that it did no good to let a person carry on so. Clement's reply was so quiet I couldn't hear it, but Monte Jean stomped down the hall and left me alone till she brought supper on a tray she put on the dresser by the door because I pretended to be asleep. I was never going to get out of bed again. Or eat.

My resolve disappeared that same night as soon as Clement left again, and the house creaked with the cold north wind, and the river hung sluggish with ice along the banks. I switched on all the lights, put music on the phonograph, turned on the radio to an all-night music station from St. Louis, and built a huge fire in the library to drive out the shadows that hung like clothes on the walls. Suddenly I was hungry, starving in fact, and rummaging in the kitchen, I filled a plate with Monte Jean's biscuits, a slice of ham, some strawberry jam, and as an afterthought, grabbed the dusty bottle of French brandy Clement kept on the pantry shelf. Settling into the leather chair, I pulled out an even more stained and warped book entitled "Annie Lark, Volume II"—prepared, I believed, for what was to come. But now Annie's story came to me in words that flew up from the page, in the shreds of voices carried on the night breeze, and in the skittering claws crossing, endlessly crossing, the hallway above.

9

SHE LOST ALMOST A YEAR TO GRIEF AND LAUDANUM. THERE WERE DAYS
when the puppets the men had carved came to life in a *danse macabre*
as the dogs and cats whined like children. The men drew knives, the children leered. Not an animal was safe from the corruption, and they hung in
corners mocking her until she hid in the deep fur bodies of all the animals
they had trapped and skinned those winters ago. The scent of her baby mingled with theirs and she knew Jula was somewhere in the great heap. She
slid off the bed and went over the covers inch by inch, looking for her baby's
small hidden body, until her fingertips became so sore she could not touch
anything at all, until they cracked and bled, and the blood—hers, hers!
Jacques took the bedding and burned it in haste one day.

Time passed. The wind rose and fell. The trees turned. One morning
Jacques came to her. "I've started our house. Come see!" He flung the covers aside and lifted her, momentarily surprised by the lightness she had become. She'd been hiding food, scraping the plate to the floor for the dog. It
felt better when the door was open, but the green and yellow world was so

far away she couldn't remember how to get there until he carried her into the blinding light, and she had to hide her face in his shirt.

It was early spring, 1819. The sun was fresh and raw as a new-cracked egg, and the air was woven with such smells of cut timber, blooming trees, muddy water, that she was drunk on it. The house, at the top of the hill, was on four-foot-high timbers to keep the river away, and it was so large it looked like they were building something to hold all their sorrow. She looked carefully as he pointed out each space, one for him, one for her, one for—where was the baby's? Where was theirs?

"You'll have a porch downstairs and upstairs both. When it's finished, you'll be better, won't you?" He wanted a promise, his lean face lined with worried hope. He had lost so much weight, she could feel the bones of his shoulders like hardened wings poking through the skin, calcified angels locked out of heaven, she thought to say, or did she say it?

Annie pointed to the three bur oaks below the house, on the riverbank. There, she thought, there was where she should be. Somehow he heard her. She pointed at the tallest and broadest tree, whose long branches almost reached out across the river. He said, "Yes, I know what to do." It was as it was before, she thought, when they thought the same thoughts, said the same words—before the dogs shat and they ate it as if it were the tender, sweet flesh of the deer heart.

THE FIRST DAY GOING UP THE TREE WAS THE MOST DIFFICULT. THE MEN ON THE ropes pulled unevenly and the little platform bucked like an untamed horse. It was unnerving the way the slightest breeze sent her rocking, dizzy, and she thought of Jula's cradle swing, how she loved the gentle swaying, as if she were flying. She began to think of the passage up as a gift Jula had sent her. Perhaps she forgives me after all, she thought, and wanted to say but couldn't. Annie had not spoken a word since that night.

Jacques, she forgives us. She tried to mouth the words at least, but even that had grown impossible, as if her throat had been slit. She grabbed her pad of drawing paper and a charcoal and scrawled the message to him: "She Forgives Us." She folded it and let it go. It sailed like its own ship, fluttering to the ground as if guided by unseen hands.

"What's this?" he said and opened it.

Tears sprang to his eyes as he nodded and smoothed the words with the palm of his hand, smearing them so only the faint outline existed behind the smudge that had become the life between them.

She went up every day for the next week, the land spread out before her like a giant quilt, large enough to canopy the world, hiding all the dead and keeping the living hard at work. She was the only person who was not working, and strangely she was unbothered. Some men clear-cut the woods by the swamp. Some lifted the roof beams into place. Others dug a massive garden and tended the huge field of corn. The air rang with the hammering of iron for horseshoes, barrel staves, and a bell. They were making a bell for the inn, a sound the fogbound boats on the river could follow.

They had so many horses now, more than she could count: browns and bays, blacks and grays, a poem! She watched them breed, the desire, the rich odor of the blackberries and laurel, the dense bloom of river mud, clouds scuttling in the blue spring sky, newly minted leaves, so green even their shadows were bright, and the sun a glorious heat on the nape of her neck, for she had chopped her hair with a knife that morning. She was going to sea and must travel lightly, without husband or babe, without friend or foe. A small wind rocked her boat and sent her handkerchief fluttering. It sailed between branches reaching for it, over the heads of the men with upraised arms, casting a brief shadow over the rushes and short river willows, over the planks of the dock and out to the water where it hesitated, then settled to ride the brown surface out of sight.

"Higher." She pointed upward one morning as if the word had lost some meaning in the time since she'd last spoken. Jacques and the men stopped, amazed at the hoarse sound of her voice, letting the raft slip and start to twist. They caught it before it could slide out of control though, and pulled again. The ropes groaned and her platform rose with a bumpy motion as the four men below strained to hoist her up on the elaborate pulley system Jacques had devised. She held tight to the rope loops attached to the sides and felt the strain of the improvised harness keeping her from falling when one side started to rise a foot higher than the other.

"Level!" Jacques yelled and the platform righted itself. The expression on Jacques' face was both relief and joy as he supervised the tying off of the ropes. He wanted to say something but didn't dare.

She hastily checked the willow baskets holding her notebook, books, tools, drawing materials, canteen, food, and telescope. It was just after breakfast and she wouldn't come down until supper.

Growing out as much as up, the bur oak on the edge of the clearing spread the invitation of its thick limbs out across the bank and river so that she could observe all manner of things. From her vantage point, not even fate could come upon her unawares. Next time, she would not be surprised.

Today the thick corrugations of bark were home to a host of large black ants grinding small tunnels in the deadwood of a section of trunk that constituted a third of the tree. She suspected that they were causing considerable damage, hollowing out the trunk, and that it might topple in a storm this summer. Being on the edge of the clearing, the tree took the full force of the winds that swept in with regularity, the storms seeming almost to follow the river itself. She didn't worry about her little ship in the tree, though. Jacques was a good builder, and he had worked so hard the past year to bring some pleasure back to her life. He had channeled his withheld grief into building. If he could only build tall enough and broad enough, he might build a way past grief.

She found herself more and more fascinated by the ants and their caste system; though most were smaller workers, the queen was large and indolent. Annie spent hours studying the hardy insects, trying different foods for their appetites. These preferred sweets—fruit, sugar, and other insects, unlike the tiny red ants in Dealie's kitchen that collected on greasy spills and dirty pots and plates. With her small knife she poked at the hole in the tree. Wood crumbled away revealing a nest containing the tiny white eggs, larvae, and pupae inside silken cases. They were quite beautiful, contained, sheltered up here from the dangers below. The adults kept other insects away by eating them—such an efficient system. Their real enemies, of course, were the tree-walking birds with their wide-spread toes and beaks pointed for digging into the crevices of bark, the tunnels of ants.

She quickly sketched the black body of an ant, two parts, with a little waist between. If only she knew the names of things!

Antennae on the head, angled with elbows. Eyes large for such a small fellow, less than half the fingernail of her little finger, which she held next to it. The ant bit but didn't hurt. One thing she'd discovered was that these ants did not sting. She only wished to peer into their colony, to shear a section from the tree and watch without being seen.

The light through the trees seemed dusty this morning, particled with damp, hazing over the trees behind hers so her leaves and branches were thrown into sharp relief. Not a leaf fluttered, so complete was the stillness now. The birds huttering from tree to tree, a dove giving its mourning song, the sparrow's buzzy *tsip-tsip-tsip-se-e-e-srr*, then a woodpecker tapping up the tree, pausing only briefly to inspect her little ship before he began to work the ant site she'd exposed. He had visited several times in the past week and was beginning to think her part of the tree.

Her raft of lashed-together planks was six feet by six feet, just large enough to hold her, some supplies, and a thronelike chair Jacques had fashioned from bent willow branches. This eased her hips and legs, which had withered considerably during the past year. It seemed impossible to walk at all now, and Jacques had spent much time and gone to great expense to build several conveyances for her, as if she were a giant baby bird transported from one nest to another. Up there she didn't need to use her voice at all, but she did. Since her first ascension, she had been speaking with the residents of her tree-world. Days had passed since she had spoken aloud, although Jacques was still aglow with what he thought was progress. Twice he had saved her, he believed.

The woodpecker had a barred black-and-white back and was the size of a robin. She drew him again, the tenth time this week, trying to capture him despite his motion. If only he would hold still. When another came with him yesterday, she realized that the more colorful bird had to be the male—red crown and nape—while the female only had a red nape. Both had a rosy patch on the lower abdomen she could see because of her peculiar angle. In between poking the tree for ants, he repeated a loud *churrrr* or *chuck-chuck-chuck*. She wrote all of it down, trying to draw him again.

"Eat them all," she whispered.

She opened the food basket and removed a jar of cold sweet tea and a biscuit. It shamed Dealie that Annie would not eat more of her food. She had grown bitter and remorseful with the guilt, but there were other secrets that singed her face and hands and cast a bruise around each eye.

What Annie had discovered was that once she was out of sight, she was out of mind, as if some odd magic were at work. Some witchery. From her perch, she saw that Jacques had become a trader in all sorts of goods and services. Every day of the week was assigned a particular contest so that Jacques could accumulate his fortune faster. Today it would be cockfighting. Tomorrow horse racing. The next boxing or wrestling or bird shooting or knife fighting. At night now he lay beside her in bed, cataloging the details of his empire so she would know what each part contributed, know how much was in store for her. "You see how much I love you, *ma chère*?" And when she did not reply, "Will you speak to me again when the house is completed?"

The men did not understand his reasoning, especially this morning. "I thought you wanted us laying the cypress floors," Skaggs said. He scratched his gray beard and looked at the huge house Jacques had begun on the small hill above them. The house had been walled and roofed since last fall, but nothing had been done inside. And it lacked glass in the windows, so that birds and animals were already making it home.

Pilcher Wyre picked up a plow plane for groove cuts. "We got the boards cut, ready to be grooved. Leave 'em out much longer, they'll start to warp. No sense wasting good wood like that." He nodded toward the huge stack of planks waiting to be hauled to the house.

Jacques' eye twitched. "Make the barrels first. Use the oak." When Skaggs started to speak, he held up his hand. "I know it was for the doors, but now it's not." He glanced at the house looming on the hill above them. "We need money more than a house right now." The barrels were for the beer Jacques was going to make under the tutelage of the German brewmeister who had arrived yesterday. The man never intended to stay, but by midnight Jacques had won all his money, a bag of clothing, and even the silver buttons off his waistcoat in a game of cards. The man himself he kept under lock and key. "You teach my men to make beer as good as that in your own country, and I will let you go."

Skaggs sighed, with a last glance at the cypress planks. Then he looked down the hill at Annie in her tree, where she seemed to float among the leafy branches of the old oak. He shook his head. "Waste of good wood."

Jacques threw up both arms. "This is what I want! I will have what I want. If I choose to give the inn away and live in the trees, so be it!"

"How many barrels?" Wyre asked.

JACQUES' MEN WERE NOW MORE FEARED THAN RESPECTED, AND HAD BECOME A hardened lot. Although the inn was one of the few such places along the river, it was becoming notorious. It was her fault, she knew, because she had not been a wife and helpmate to Jacques, had not kept him focused on the good he could do for his family, though the very word pained her now.

While Skaggs and Wyre began building the barrels, Jacques took up the river watch on the bench below her tree. She saw something shining on the ground where the men had been standing and picked up the telescope again. It was one of the brewmeister's silver buttons Jacques must have dropped. She thought of calling down to him but didn't. There was something fitting about the oversight, which meant he wouldn't have enough for a new waist-coat, his gain from another man's trouble. She wanted Jacques to go back to the way he was before, to be that man she still loved.

A crow, reminding her of their pet Carl, sailed down to the ground near the stray button. Tipping its glossy head, it peered at the button, the inn, the tree, the button again, and finally Jacques, before walking over and snatching it up in its beak. It stood there a moment before flapping off with the button, and just as it was about to disappear into the trees with it, three sparrows began an uproar, diving and pecking at the crow. Despite its efforts to ignore the three, the crow began to struggle, dropping lower, then flapping upward again, veering right, then left in an attempt to dislodge the attackers. Finally, the crow dropped the button and flew up toward the house on the hill. The bright silver button rolled and winked briefly in the sunlight and disappeared into the underbrush.

When he heard her sigh loudly, Jacques pulled what was left of the brewmeister's silver buttons from the pocket of his waistcoat and tossed them from hand to hand, smiling.

"I am very happy to hear your voice again, *chérie*." He paused in case she wanted to have a conversation, but when it became obvious that she had nothing more to say, he continued talking as he had for the past year when the mood took him. He really didn't need her as more than a listener, she had discovered, and wondered if that had always been so.

"Once when I was a boy—hard to believe I was a child, no?—my *grand-mère* gave me a box of buttons to play with, amuse myself, no? Not like these, but nice. I put them on a string, so pretty a necklace, but my mother would not wear it. No, she was a religious. Huguenot. It is because of her that I am in this new world. But the necklace? It was so beautiful—silver and pearl and the inside of the shell and bone and onyx—every color. So I thought why give up your treasure?"

He stood and looked up, shading his eyes with his hand. "I see your sleeve, *ma chère*. If you must hide from me, you must wear green or brown to match the tree." He put his fingers in the pockets of a black brocade waistcoat he had begun wearing of late. One of Dealie's touches. He sat down and stretched his legs out, slouching on the bench so that she could stare down at his upturned face.

When his jaws worked, she imagined she could see every tendon and sinew, that he was only a knife-slice away from ruin. Some faces needed the padding of flesh so they didn't move too close to the cadaverous. Jacques was such a man. He had escaped age, and now he would escape the bonds of flesh entirely.

"What became of them?" she asked in such a small voice she was surprised he heard her.

He looked at the buttons nestled in the palm of his hand like so many silver mouths he had captured. "The buttons? I buried them, of course." He gave a short mirthless laugh. "No one would have my treasure, I decided."

His thin lips were parted in a slight smile, his brow raised as if inquiring something of her, but in the black, unknowable eyes lingering on her, she could feel the weight of his words. She could never escape. Not even if she wanted to, and that fact alone put a dark seed in Annie's heart. All those remedies, those cures, the salt baths, the potions, the brains and hearts and livers of animals she'd been forced to eat, packed in blankets of ice until she caught cold, lying on stones so hot they blistered her back, tied to posts, tied to the bed, spirits poured down her throat and over her body, leeches placed on every inch of her skin, her face, her shaved head, cupped and bled till she fainted, she bore the scars of all his care, just so he would not lose what was his. His daughter had slipped away, but never his wife. Damn him! She never thought once of leaving him before that moment, but a new rebelliousness rose inside her, shouting: "How dare he!"

She pulled her wedding band from her finger and dropped it over the side. It landed at his feet, sinking into the powdered dirt. Divining her move, he reached to catch it but missed. When he stooped to search for the ring, she emptied a bottle of foul-smelling tonic on him. "Guaranteed to raise her spirits!" the traveling physician had boasted to Jacques with a wink. It was almost pure corn liquor and molasses.

"*Merde!*" he cursed in a low voice so no one could hear him.

"You don't own me, Jacques!" she said loud enough that the nearby dogs raised their heads, ears perked in alarm.

"We will talk of this tonight, Annie, hush." He patted the air with his hands.

The dark seed inside Annie sprouted and filled her with white petulance. "I'm not coming down."

The nights were warm, and it was preferable to sleeping next to Jacques.

"Leave me here for good," she called down. She didn't want to be beholden to him for anything. He thought he owned her! Why, she'd run off with the first peddler or riverman she saw.

He scowled and tried to blot the foul brown liquid from his shirt with a handkerchief. "*Vache*," he muttered. "Cow."

"I know what it means, Jacques, but don't imagine you're the bull to my cow. You're just an old man now, unable to make a child—" She clapped a hand over her mouth, stopped by her own hateful words.

"You go too far." He pushed the handkerchief back into his pocket but refused to look up. His voice had choked at the last word, and he kept his head down so she couldn't see his face. He was right.

"I'm sorry, Jacques, I—" But it was as if in the year of her silence another woman had taken over her speech, one who wasn't afraid to say every bitter word that had been birthed in the dark cave of her heart.

"You were a child when I found you," Jacques said simply. "You grew up to be a shrew." He spread his arms wide to include everything in their clearing. "This is my thanks."

"Your thanks? Your thanks! You—" She heaved a book at him rather than say the next words.

He sidestepped the falling book. "What am I, Annie? What do you have to say to your husband? The husband you've ignored who lost his first child."

"Be a husband." It was out of her mouth before she could stop it, but the words stopped him. He looked at his open hands, closed them, and shook his head and sat down on the bench. She was wrong. She knew she was wrong. He had never stopped being her husband, and yet here she was, driving him away.

She knew then that he might never be a husband again. Suddenly she was filled with fear that they would never make love in the fur-covered bed on a cold night. They would never share another child. The bitterness made her reach out and grab a handful of leaves and stuff them in her mouth, grinding them between her teeth until her tongue ached with the harsh green of regret.

"I'm so sorry," she mouthed, but her throat closed on the words, that dark seed already abloom.

Below her Jacques' shoulders convulsed, though he uttered not a sound, while above him, she held her empty belly to keep the sobbing silent and fell asleep to a small wind rocking the platform.

IT WAS MIDAFTERNOON AND BLAZING HOT WHEN SHE AWOKE TO JACQUES' hailing of a keelboat coming downriver loaded with timber and iron from the north. A flat-bottomed river steamer headed north was already being wooded up while her passengers ate a meal in the inn. Over the past year it had become the job of the three Burtram brothers to maintain the massive stacks of wood needed for the steamers and stern-wheelers that had become common along the river. Helping them were three West Indian slaves Dealie and Chabot had brought with them from New Orleans and Jacques had purchased. Although the slaves appeared in clothing equal to the Burtrams, there was no real equality. The West Indians stayed together in a tiny cabin beyond the woodshed, chained to one another at night, behind a barred door with only tiny slits of windows for ventilation in the sweltering heat.

One of Ford's dogs was chained just outside the door as added insurance. She had had nothing to say on that subject, and since she had just driven Jacques away, she had no power to speak of it now either.

The keelboaters were rough rivermen, a loud-talking, cursing, happy lot who enjoyed the dangers of stopping at Jacques' Landing as much as navigating the snags and pockets and whirlpools of the big river. Tying up on the other side of the dock from the steamboat, the two pushed past Nicholas Burtram, who, with a load of wood on his back, lost his balance and fell into the river. While Mitchell and Ashland especially enjoyed the spectacle of their eldest brother floundering to release the straps from his shoulders to keep from drowning, the keelboaters continued making their way to the shore.

"Jacques!" The first man, with a wide grizzled face, blackened rotting teeth, and bright blue eyes, slapped her husband so hard on the back it almost sent him sprawling. Jacques straightened and shoved the man so hard in the broad chest, he stumbled backward. Then they shook hands.

"McDonough," Jacques said, his eyes on the second man, a stranger dressed in newer clothing, who seemed less at ease.

"This here's Audubon." He paused as if trying to recall the name. "John Audubon. New mate. Just picked him up—Aaron's in jail again." He laughed and gave the man a playful shove on the shoulder, but the man had already braced for it and was only rocked a little. He was a plain, almost homely man in his thirties, with wide-set, large dark staring eyes and an equally large hooked nose. Somewhat high cheekbones and a broad high forehead made his face appear open to study. His mouth had character, with a thin upper lip and curved lower. An interesting face altogether, as seen through Annie's telescope. Neat in stature, he carried a gun and wore a pouch slung over his shoulder as if he were about to go hunting. His jacket and waistcoat and white shirt were counter to the job of keelboatman, and she wondered who he really was. Something about the strong, distinguished face, long brown hair streaked with gray, combed back and hanging to his shoulders, set him apart and made her wonder if he were a man hiding from the world, from his family, or from the authorities. The Landing had always had its share of earthquake Christians, and lost men who recovered their senses after years of wandering to discover that their fevered dreams were nothing without family, and men who were just plain running from their crimes. More of those than any. It was a wonder they hadn't all been murdered in their sleep.

The sun must have caught the brass of her telescope because he suddenly swung his eyes up to the tree and Annie was certain he saw her. Breath quickening, instead of hiding, she kept looking, watching him watching her, hands trembling because at that exact moment, Jacques followed his gaze to her also.

IO

"JOHN JAMES AUDUBON." THE STRANGER BOWED SLIGHTLY, HIS OVERLY large eyes fixed on her face, ignoring the pitiful state of her legs as she was being transported from tree to inn that evening. Jacques shifted her weight in his arms so she was forced to peer over his shoulder at Audubon, who surprised her with a smile. His manners were those of a gentleman, and she wondered how he came to be in his current situation.

"Let me sit with the travelers tonight," she whispered in Jacques' ear, and kissed it.

He hugged her tighter, relieved to be forgiven, and gave a quick nod, tightening his grip on her thighs and back. Crossing the threshold was a large surprise. The room had changed so in the past year. There was glass in the windows, which now swung out to let in the fresh air, and white lace curtains framing them. The walls had been plastered and painted a soft yellow and hung with paintings of horses and animals, and two matching tapestries of royalty in religious procession were draped ceiling to floor on opposite walls. On either side of the fireplace now stood mahogany shelves containing precious books and objects of native use—moccasins, pipes, tools, et cetera, as well as hand-carved animals she recognized as handiwork from the same men who had made the puppets that Christmas. Her throat closed and she had to cough hard to breathe again.

The rough-hewn tables and benches had been replaced by more refined tables with turned legs and chairs with backs, and the room was lit by elaborate oil lamps with etched glass chimneys, not merely crude candles. A huge walnut dish cupboard along the river wall between the windows held stacks of china dishes and crystal salt cellars and pewter steins and glassware and silverware, enough to feed multitudes, it seemed, which was good since the tables would soon be full. The boards of the cypress floor that were visible were scrubbed and waxed, while three large deep red-and-black figured carpets covered most of the room. The hearthstones were clean of soot, and no odors of cooking lingered. In fact, there were no pots at all, only a pair of massive, ornately wrought andirons. All this for the rough river trade? Jacques' ambitions showed plainly.

"Where is the food prepared?" she asked.

"In the next room," Jacques said. "Sit here." He settled her on a soft divan covered in black horsehair beside three armchairs clad in burgundy silk brocade.

As soon as Jacques lifted the long strap of her satchel off his shoulder, and placed it in her lap, then slipped through the door and closed it behind him, Audubon left off studying the paintings and walked directly toward her. Bowing slightly again, he pointed to the chair nearest her. She smiled and he sat down.

"Quite unexpected." He turned his hand to the room and looked about.

"Yes," she said. His eyes were so large it was impossible that he missed any detail.

"And you, Mrs. Ducharme, what do you do in the tree?" His tone, as he brought those large deep eyes to rest on her face, suggested that this was a natural place to find a woman, and she felt the same disturbance she had earlier. She ducked her head so that he might not perceive it. After all, she was a married woman.

"I study." She laid a hand on the satchel.

"I see." He pulled his hunting pouch to his lap and lifted out a black bound sketchbook. Leafing quickly through the pages, he found one and held it up for her to see. It was a bald eagle, head turned defiantly, beak open, eye ablaze, standing on one foot, with the other seeming to reach out for something or to defend itself. The drawing was quite good, full of the bird's haughty grandeur.

"Oh, that's splendid." She reached out to touch the page. "How did you—"

"It became tangled in our fishing line, wounding its leg. They brought it on board and I managed to sketch it before it attacked the captain's dog and the men bashed it to pieces."

When she flinched at the description, he shrugged and shook his head apologetically.

"May I?" She held her hands out and he placed the book in them.

"There are more of the eagle." He leaned forward and she positioned the book on her lap so they could examine it together. Indeed there were several pages of quick sketches from different views of the bird's parts—the head, body, foot, wing—as well as of the bird in motion. On the previous pages there were countless other birds and animals, including hare and vole, deer and snake, fish, butterfly. He was an artist so superior to anything she had seen that she felt humbled and grateful.

"Can you teach me?" she asked, surprising herself with the boldness.

He sat back, templed his long fingers, and looked at her carefully as if he could detect her character or talent from looks alone. Perhaps those eyes could.

"Let me see." He indicated the satchel in her lap, and she fumbled with the clasp and drew out the pages of crude sketching and writing. He took the book and began to examine the contents with nerve-racking slowness.

Around them the noisy conversations of travelers arriving to fill the tables were loud enough to draw her attention, while two unfamiliar slaves with white kerchiefs covering their hair and plain, neat gray gowns quickly laid the plates, silverware, and goblets.

"The Missouri Compromise won't change anything here!" a stout drummer or salesman declared. "It's hard times going to end the slave trade."

The two Negroes eased their work so they could listen, their hands moving so slowly they seemed to be drugged.

"South needs to diversify." The speaker with a European accent was a peddler in motley with long greasy brown hair who'd left his wagon and horse in the stable yard in hopes someone would feed it while he dined. He waved aside the woman setting his place and sat down abruptly. "Manufac-

turing is the key. Follow the Northeast, factories. People want manufac-
tured goods now. Last year's Panic is driving us west, and before we know it,
there won't be anyplace we can't go and sell something."

The stout drummer ran his hand over the baldness on top of his head,
then drifted down to finger the earlock of blond hair on the right side.
"Look at this place. Hog and hominy don't satisfy anymore, and I heard
they're making something called 'ice cream' in Philadelphia at the New
Caveau Hotel, wonder what's next?"

"Don't complain, for God's sake, we could be eatin' beef dodger and
beans."

Jacques' little brewmeister wandered in, wet hair plastered around his
face, looking sodden, followed by Skaggs, Clinch, Wyre, and the Foley
cousins. Chabot appeared and paused in the doorway, scanning the room.
When his gaze came upon Annie, he broke into a huge smile and pushed his
way toward her.

"Annie!" he fairly shouted, and plopped himself on the other end of the
divan. "Little one!" He leaned across her legs, took her hands in his, and
kissed her on both of her glowing cheeks. When he failed to acknowledge
Audubon, she introduced them, noting the formality of two roosters circling a grasshopper.

"You're looking . . . well," she said, at a loss for words. In fact, Chabot
looked poorly: too thin, his face angled with new shadows, more than when
he'd returned that spring after being hurt. His body appeared wasted, as if
some parasite had devoured all the flesh. His color was pale gray, despite the
long hours he and the other men spent toiling outdoors. She hadn't seen
him up close since coming back to herself and ascending the tree. In fact,
she hadn't paid attention to anyone, she realized, she'd been too smothered
by her grief to think anyone else mattered.

"I've been decidedly the opposite, Annie." He glanced at the closed
door. "Ague—though I try not to worry Dealie. The bouts are more frequent these days." He clapped his hands and forced a smile. "Imagine! I'm
keeping Jacques' and Dealie's accounts now! Carefree no more." He smiled
wanly and looked around the room.

"What about New Orleans? Her house and business—" she asked.

He shrugged. "She says our life is here now. That it's healthier for me.
The children are in New Orleans in school with tutors." He muttered
something else she didn't catch.

"What?"

" 'Unnatural,' I said. It's unnatural for a mother to leave her children, wouldn't you say?" He glared at her.

The horrific events of that evening cascaded across her vision, and she nearly burst into tears, except Chabot leaned across and grabbed her hands again.

"I'm sorry, Annie. This fever makes me stupid some days, forgive me?"

His usually jolly face looked so downcast that she struggled with the weight in her chest and nodded. She thought she might faint if she didn't get air soon.

"Dealie maintains her import business in New Orleans then?" She tried to sound indifferent, but her fingers ached from holding Mr. Audubon's sketchbook so tightly. For his part, Audubon pretended to make a study of the travelers, nodding companionably to those who passed.

Chabot tapped his lips with his finger and glanced beyond her toward the closed door. "You didn't know? She has become Jacques' partner here." He spread his hands. "The inn, all the furniture, and—" He nodded toward the two slaves setting the tables. "Another of their imports."

"Jacques wouldn't." She felt a rush of anger, then stopped herself. It had all changed in the time she'd been out of her senses. As if she had lost Jula and Jacques in one blow.

Chabot leaned forward. "I've upset you."

Smelling the almost poisonous combination of liquor and medicine on his breath, she opened her eyes and waved him off. "The heat—"

Chabot clenched his fists, his bloodshot eyes a bit wild now. "I told Jacques that you had no business going up there. Tomorrow early I will take you in the cart to study the herons, then have you back safe before the heat of the day. We can start at daybreak, if you'd like."

She replied that she would.

"Could I be included?" Audubon asked, his large eyes filled with interest. "I don't mean to presume, but I have a great interest in birds, you see."

Chabot glanced at her and when she gave a slight nod, he reluctantly assented. She had the feeling that he was hoping for a moment alone so they could discuss their spouses in greater detail, but she wasn't ready for that conversation yet. She was aware of growing more and more angry with Jacques, and of feeling a deeper satisfaction in that anger than she had felt in a long time. She had no intention of giving it up anytime soon, would not be talked out of it by anyone.

"Well, we're all gathered for dinner it seems." Dealie appeared in front of them, flushed red with the heat from the kitchen, her damp hair clinging to her face in limp straggles. Annie wondered if she was aware of how much she had deteriorated.

Dealie caught her staring and, an expression of defiance crossing her face, said, "You won't be eating, will you, Annie? You wouldn't have any appetite after sitting all day." Her tone was disguised with concern, but the blade of her meaning touched Annie.

She wanted to ask Dealie where her children were, but thought better of it. Instead she smiled sweetly. "I'll just keep company with your husband and Mr. Audubon while you supervise, Dealie," she drawled in imitation of Dealie's deep accent.

Jacques appeared behind her, putting his hands on Dealie's shoulders and whispering in her ear. She immediately swept to the front of the room and announced that dinner was to be served.

Chabot stood aside as Jacques lifted and carried her to a large chair at the head of what appeared to be the family table. When Audubon slipped in beside her on one side and Chabot on the other, Jacques stepped back and watched, his expression unreadable. He had changed shirts from earlier when she had poured the tonic on him, and for the first time since she'd known him, he was dressed in an extraordinary costume: ruffled white shirt, doeskin breeches, and a wide black leather belt with a large silver buckle depicting a woman's head, the expression on her face terrified or terrifying, with snakes writhing out of her head like hair. On his feet he wore a pair of fine black kid boots that rose almost to his knees. Had Dealie been dressing him or was this his doing? At his waist he wore a pistol and his knife, and she was certain that another knife was hidden in a boot. In the dramatic costume, his presence dominated the room, and all eyes were upon him as he swept around the table to sit at the opposite end, then raised a hand to signal for the meal to be served, the bowls of food carried in by a half dozen slaves. She had thought Dealie brought only the three, but now she had to wonder just how many there were. Did they fill the four small cabins now?

As soon as the food was distributed, wine and beer were poured and the eating began. Dealie slipped into the empty place at Jacques' right hand, and they acted more the married couple than anyone else at the table, confiding to each other, glancing in her direction, beckoning to the servers. Chabot ignored them, mainly drinking wine until his eyelids drooped and he pushed away from the table and staggered to his feet. Dealie signaled with her hand and two slaves appeared to help him away.

She looked resigned as she watched him leave, and when she caught Annie staring at her, Dealie gave a small shake of her head.

Audubon rested his fingers briefly on the back of Annie's hand and the warmth spread up her arm. "I will make sure he is well enough to take us in the morning." She pulled her hand away.

NEXT MORNING JUST AFTER SUNRISE, CHABOT FLICKED THE LINES ON THE horse's back and the cart lurched down the road away from the inn. At first the road followed the river and Jacques' land south, beside the fields his men were reclaiming by chopping down, uprooting, and burning out the trees, then draining it with ditches. The dainty parasol she was holding did little to dispel the dawn's heat, already lying across the land in a white haze, like smoke from a distant fire, even as they turned inland toward the swamp to the west.

Audubon, next to her, leaned across to point out the great blue heron in low flight to their left, long neck tucked into a crook.

"We'll see many more of those," Chabot said. He was livelier this morning, though his face bore the mark of ragged, gray exhaustion.

As the path cut close to some marsh, she pointed to the red-winged blackbirds bobbing in the bulrushes, tiny black feet clutching the ends of stalks, small black eyes glittering angrily at their intrusion.

"Wait." Audubon held up his hand for Chabot to stop the cart and pointed to a well-made cup of reedy grass attached to a bush with three pale blue eggs spotted and scrawled with dark brown and purple. The closest birds rose up and began to swirl around them, diving at the horse and Chabot's straw hat. He swatted at them with his free hand and raised the reins. The horse happily swung into a ground-eating trot.

The road quickly narrowed to a rutted path made by infrequent wagon wheels and the high weeds in the middle thunked and swished against the bottom and sides of the cart, but didn't seem to bother the little black horse. The orange dirt became softer, sandier and waterlogged in places.

They humped over a molehill and the cart wheel on her side caught the edge of a sand bog, tilting them with a quick jerk that dropped her straw hat over her eyes. As the horse struggled to pull them out, Chabot used his voice for quiet encouragement rather than grabbing the whip that stood in its holder beside him.

Sand bogs, which had appeared during the quake years, punctured the land, some close to the path. Dry during the hottest summer months, the sand bogs or boils quickly filled with water and appeared bottomless after rains. Jacques' men had had to pull enough cattle, horses, and pigs out of them that they decided to fence off the largest. Since the men were only beginning to clear and fence this area, several boils were still waiting, their malice disguised with the green lip that surrounded the yellow patch.

As soon as they were righted, Chabot stopped to give the horse a minute to catch her breath. The swamp to their left and the woody field to their right were filled with noisy birds flitting and feeding and arguing. A fat, gray possum, which had apparently been hunting in the marshy field, trundled across the path. The animal wouldn't be hurried as she waddled along, her belly swinging, small pointed pink snout twitching. The long hairless tail and small white paws with sharp claws made her look part giant rat, part raccoon. His face pinched in concentration, Audubon was taking notes and sketching quickly as the animal edged down into the underbrush and disappeared behind the knee of a huge old cypress.

When they finally reached the end of the path, Chabot turned slightly and pointed ahead to the dank swamp and marshland shaded with bald cypress, tupelo, swamp privet, water locust, pumpkin ash, water hickory, water elm, and black willow. The hum of mosquitoes made her hasten to lower the net from her hat brim over her face and quickly pull on the white cotton gloves Dealie had insisted she bring. The moldy heat coming off the trees, out of the air itself, clung to her mouth and the inside of her nose. Eventually she stopped being able to smell anything except the brackish water and the mildewed air with that sweet rankness of rot.

"Nigger wool swamp far as you can see," Chabot said. "Nothing but a canoe can get through it. Indians hunt it, but a white man does well to stay out." He abruptly rose and climbed down from the cart, leaving the reins wrapped around the whip holder. "Wait here."

Using a machete he began hacking a tunnel through the nearly impenetrable tangle of briars, grape vines, wisteria, dogbane, and poison ivy. Up to his knees in the brackish water, he grabbed at creeping vines hanging from the cypress and pulled them down, working methodically to clear the line of sight. A cottonmouth slid from a cypress knee behind him and released its long body into the water. The thickness of a man's wrist, with a fixed half smile on its face, it seemed to contemplate Chabot's leg, then eased back into the vegetation-choked water and swam out of sight.

She looked over at Audubon, who was capturing the snake's expression perfectly while his rifle leaned uselessly against his knee. Struggling to wrestle the pistol from her satchel, she uttered an impatient, "Damn it," which caused him to raise his surprised eyes just as the gun cleared and pointed at him.

"I surrender," he said, face solemn, a smile twitching the corners of his mouth.

Letting the gun drop to her lap, she brushed the mosquitoes collecting on the netting in front of her eyes. "The snake."

"Although the cottonmouth is an aggressive breed, it is probably not going to attack a man with a machete. Even snakes have common sense." He smiled and returned to his sketch, writing a note and date on the bottom of the page.

"I'd hate to rely on that."

As he studied the surrounding scene, he raised his brow and widened his large eyes as if to take in the entire panorama, but when he sketched, he squinted and bit his lip as if to focus on a single detail at a time. Or maybe he merely needed glasses. A bead of sweat dripped down his large nose, and without interrupting the line he was drawing, he swiped at it.

Chabot came splashing back, climbed to the path, and hoisted himself on the driver's seat again, grunting with the effort and swatting at the cloud of gnats that had found him. His face was very pale and covered with a damp, greasy sheen.

"Stay quiet now," he said in a low voice, "and look right through there."

She lifted the brass telescope from her satchel and put it to her eye. "A rookery!" She handed the telescope to Audubon, who took a deep breath as he brought into focus the swampy pool filled with white birds wading and nesting.

"Ahh," he breathed, "if I could but catch one." His mouth widened to a smile at the thought.

Chabot chuckled quietly. "If you were an Indian you could set a snare without disturbing a feather. Or—"

He looked over his shoulder at her. "You could just shoot it. They're standing still."

Audubon seemed to consider the idea, glanced at her, and shook his head, a small frown appearing. "Not today."

She thought about the eagle, his unwilling subject, and the cost of rendering such accuracy in the name of science.

"Get out your sketchbook," he ordered, abruptly setting aside his own.

She blushed as those serious eyes came to rest on her as if she were one of the specimens he was collecting. Thank goodness she had decided to bring a blank book today so he couldn't scrutinize her earlier poor efforts again. She pulled off the cotton gloves and picked up her pencil and commenced sketching a bird.

She had barely etched outlines of three tall wading birds when the drawing lesson was cut short by the simultaneous attacks of gnats, mosquitoes, and deerflies, which bit so hard they drew drops of blood on any bare skin. The gnats immediately clustered in the horse's ears and began making their bloody little nests, causing her to shake her head, shiver, and stamp her hoof, her irritation accompanied by the high jingling of the curb chain and the clicking of the bit against her teeth. The cart shivered with her motion. Annie slapped at a deerfly on the back of her wrist but it stuck, biting so hard it felt like a bee sting until she grabbed it roughly and flung it toward the swamp. The men were under more arduous attack, swatting at the air with their hats and hands. Audubon wore a tiny knot of blood on his cheek where a fly had bitten him, and Chabot was blinking hard to keep the gnats from clustering on his sweaty forehead. The horse began to back up and lunge forward, kicking to dislodge the flies attacking her belly and flanks.

"Time to go!" Chabot sang out, unwrapping the reins and giving the mare her head. She gladly surged forward into the harness, but abruptly stopped. She tried again, this time grunting when she hit the collar. Annie looked over the edge of the cart at the large wheel sunken to the hub in sand.

Although Chabot and Audubon climbed down to lighten the load, swinging their arms over their heads to fight off the insect attack, the cart still would not budge. She offered to come out, too, but the men shook their heads. Chabot stepped off the path and fanned himself with his straw hat while he examined the cart. Then he retrieved the machete and began to cut down small saplings along the edge of the swamp, with Audubon shoving them in front of the wheels until the path became a green carpet.

Chabot handed her the reins and staggered to the back of the cart. He was paler than ever, and his breath rattled unevenly in his chest as if he were coming down with lung congestion. He had no business being out in the heat, let alone pushing the cart.

Audubon was barely winded, she noticed. He removed his brown jacket and waistcoat, folded them neatly on the seat opposite her, and carefully rolled up his sleeves, as if he were about to relax at a picnic, except for a slight grimace at the annoyance. When he was in position to push the wheel beside her, Chabot braced his back against the cart and nodded. His shirt was dark with sweat, his face drawn and pale.

It was worry about Chabot that made her do the one thing she knew she shouldn't. She took the whip from its holder, raised it overhead, and brought it down on the mare's back, just as Chabot yelled, "No!"

The mare reared, tried to spin and lash out with her hooves, but the harness held, and she hit her again. This time the horse lunged forward, not letting the bite of the collar stop her. She dug her hind legs in and pushed so hard the cart groaned and leapt forward all at once. Feeling the weight-lessness behind, she lunged again, bolting for freedom so quickly she almost fell backward over the wheel.

Righting herself, Annie jerked the reins and managed to swing the horse around so she would run back the way they'd come, the cart jolting heavily in and out of the ruts and holes, her teeth clattering against each other, the bones in her hips and back feeling pulled apart. When the men jumped in the path to stop her, the horse took the bit and exploded into a mad gallop across the field. She was so furious that she bellowed every time she felt the traces against her flanks. Annie made the mistake of trying to pull back steadily, but her strength was no match for the horse's. If only she'd remembered to saw at her mouth instead. But the cart was tilting side to side, bucking over the uneven ground. She had to hang on for dear life or risk being thrown out.

"Whoa, stop!" she yelled, but her voice only seemed to excite the horse, who was lathered under the harness, with gouts of yellow foam flinging from her mouth into Annie's face. Finally she veered through a small open-ing at the edge of the field, clattered over a narrow drainage ditch, almost sinking the wheels, pulled out, and continued into a huge area that had been both cleared and drained, although for some reason not planted in the spring. The ground was thick with burnt dust from the burning off a few weeks before. Her hooves raised a veil of black powder that made them both cough, but she kept running. Then she just stopped, as if she'd hit a stone wall. One of the shafts cracked and broke in two, the jagged edge of the pole hanging dangerously close to her heaving side.

If the mare turned and moved now . . . She stood, though, head low, blowing.

Annie, out of breath, was relieved that not too much had happened ex-cept for the broken shaft, although an odd sense of motion remained. No, they were still in motion, the cart was trembling—a quake—she couldn't catch her breath! She quickly glanced about her, but everything seemed normal: The sun was shining brightly, the birds weren't flocking up and crying, the snakes weren't erupting from dens, the rabbits and foxes and deer were still hidden, and most important, she didn't feel unbalanced, sick at her stomach, her blood wasn't fizzing in her arms and legs. But the cart *was* moving, not forward, she realized, but down! They were sinking in a sand boil!

At that moment the mare began to struggle weakly, too exhausted to lunge out of the watery sand surrounding them. Annie lifted the whip again and struck her across the back. Nothing. She cracked the whip over the horse's head, shook it beside her face. The cart was sunk to the floorboards, and cloudy water was seeping in.

"Go! Move! Go on!" she yelled and waved her arms.

The sand was up to the mare's belly, and when she pulled her foreleg partially out, she found nothing solid to grab with her hoof and she let the leg drop in defeat. Looking over her shoulder, the mare's eye was filled with a terrible resignation. Annie had killed them both. Her head dropped slowly and with a groan she started to lie down in the harness, her weight tipping the cart forward. Annie held frantically to the side to keep from going over.

"Help me!" Annie screamed. "Help!" But the two men were nowhere in sight.

She jerked on the reins again and was rewarded when the mare's head rose a few inches. But the dispirited animal blew sandy water from her nostrils, closed her eyes, and let her head down again. This time Annie slackened the left and pulled the right rein as hard as she could, winding it around the driver's seat for leverage. As soon as the mare's head began to rise out of the boil, she wrapped the rein around the seat again to secure it.

At first the horse was inert, then she began to struggle, trying to pull against the rein and break it to release her head. The bit would have slid through her mouth except for the sidecheck. Thank God the leather on the headstall was new, so the stitching held. This time Annie tried talking to her as Chabot had.

"Good girl, now get up, come on, get up, you can do it, you're a strong girl, get up—"

The mare's ears flicked back and forth with interest, and for some reason the cart slowed its sinking, which gave Annie hope that perhaps there *was* a bottom.

She made extravagant promises of food and care and ease, and the mare seemed to listen, a light flickering in her eye.

"Come on, girl, you'll never be hurt again, I promise, come on—"

With the right shaft broken, the horse discovered that she could turn her body in the direction her head was twisted. Annie loosened the rein and clucked. Her boots were resting in the cloudy water up to her ankles, and the cart began to creak and groan as boards twisted and swelled, threatening to pop their nails and joints.

Somehow the horse half swam, half reared to the edge of the boil, so she was at a right angle to the cart. As soon as she struck solid ground she found purchase with her hooves and dragged her front end out. Exhausted, she laid her head on the ground, blowing loudly.

"Good girl," Annie soothed, despite the water that now soaked her skirt to the waist, making it pull at her back and legs. Damn her legs! She pounded her thighs with her fists, splashing watery sand into her face and mouth. She spat and ground sand in her teeth.

If she could only get out of the cart—

She looked around for her satchel, for the knife inside. She'd forgotten it. The satchel had fallen to the floor and was so waterlogged it took some effort to drag it up. She found the knife at the bottom, beneath the ruined books and sketches, and pulled it from the beaded sheath Chabot had given her the year Jula was born. The familiar wave of despair threatened to wash up her body, but she didn't have time for that now.

She quickly sliced her skirt down the middle and ripped it from her waist, freeing her legs, followed by the long petticoat, leaving only her drawers. Her legs looked too puny to be of help, shrunken, twisted, scarred, but they would have to do.

First she had to free the horse. She crawled over the driver's seat and perched there for a moment. She didn't dare hesitate. She unwrapped the rein from the driver's seat, releasing the mare's head, and wrapped the reins around her chest, just under her arms. Since her back had the only real strength in her body, she'd use herself as a pulley. Slipping into the boil was harder than she expected, and finally it was the cart lurching down another foot, starting to pull the mare backward, that propelled her to slip between the shafts and let herself down. The water was ice cold despite the hot sun. She had to hurry before her fingers were too cold to hang on to the cart or move. She had to work the shafts out of their holders and cut the traces and breeching holding the mare to the cart. When the last strap let go, the mare raised her head and looked back at her. This time the weight on the reins was Annie's, holding herself against the sucking sand. Going hand over hand, she began to inch her way forward along the reins. The problem was that she couldn't hope to get purchase with her legs. Even though the mare's sides were heaving with exhaustion, the horse would have to pull them both completely out of the frigid water. Would she have the strength?

Annie licked her lips and spat the sand out of her mouth. The sudden dark helplessness reminded her of those days during the quakes when she lay trapped in bed under the roof beam. This time she had to save herself.

They lay side by side for a few more minutes, sharing the same labored breathing. When Annie pressed her face against the mare's shoulder, the scent of sweat stung her nose, but the heat was reassuring. There was strong fighting blood in this mare—she'd survive. Annie knew it.

"We have to do this one last thing, girl." She pulled the mare's head around and whispered in her ear, "We're not going to die here, either one of us. You're my girl now." She patted her, rubbed her nose, working the reins around her neck. She had to be careful not to let her weight rip the mare's mouth apart when she started out.

Raising her shoulders, Annie urged her in a quiet voice, "Giddy-up, go on, pull, girl, pull us out."

As if she could feel the water closing over the driver's seat behind them, the mare propped her forelegs in front of her and lunged upward, grabbing solid ground with her front hooves, digging in, somehow pulling first one hind leg, then the other up, her haunches churning, reins tangling with her legs.

Annie hung on, not wanting to throw her off balance. With a final heave, the mare stood, giving herself a good shake from head to tail.

"Go on now, pull—" When she clucked at her, the mare looked back, her eye full of a softness and understanding Annie'd only seen once before, in the big dog she'd cared for that spring. "Come on, pull me out, girl." Again she used her quiet voice. "Please hurry," she whispered, loosening the outside rein.

The mare straightened her body, put her head down, and took a step forward, struggling to plant her hoof. When it was flat, she took a deep breath and fought her shaking muscles to bring the other leg forward. Step by step, she dragged Annie out of the sandy water as if she were a huge deadfall. Once they were well away, Annie called to her to stop. The mare looked back over her shoulder again, her body quivering with the expense of effort.

"Good girl." She reached up and stroked the mare's trembling hind leg. "Thank you." She unwrapped the reins from the mare's body, slowly untangling her hind legs. The mare stood quietly until she was free, not even lifting a hoof when a big green horsefly landed on her hock, because Annie was underfoot and they had saved each other's lives now. As soon as she felt the long lines free, the mare turned around and came to stand over Annie. Looking down, her eye was full of curiosity. She lowered her head and nuzzled Annie's loose, tangled hair, the hat long gone, then blew softly in her face. It was the sweetest breath she'd felt since Jula's—

Annie raised her hands slowly, so as not to spook her, and placed them on either side of her nose, black velvet grainy with yellow sand, and blew gently into the shadow of her nostril. The mare swiped Annie's forehead with her nose, nudged her shoulder, and began to crop the grass around her, staying there, shading and guarding her, until well into the afternoon, when at last the men found them.

II

IT WAS LATE AFTERNOON BY THE TIME THEY TRUDGED INTO THE STABLE yard, bitten and bloodied by flies, gnats, mosquitoes, and so sunburnt and parched they thought Chabot was starting to make sense in his delirium. The mare was limping, footsore and trembling as they slid off her back. Dealie burst out of the inn, calling for her slaves, who carried Chabot to bed, while Annie insisted on being taken to the stable to see after the little mare. With the help of a Negro stable boy, she took the mare to the water tank and a clean stall, where she told the boy—Boston was his name—to wash her well, pick out her feet, and make sure her legs were rubbed with liniment.

In the stall, she patted the mare's neck and whispered, "You're mine now. I'm going to ride you when you're better. You won't ever have to pull a cart again. We'll go all over, and I'll bring you apples and carrots and steal Dealie's sugar too." Annie rubbed the long forehead until the mare closed her eyes and blew a contented sigh through her nose.

Dealie directed a slave to help her carry Annie to the bathhouse next to the woodshed, another of Dealie's improvements. It had separate rooms for men and women, with high-sided copper tubs and stoves for continually heating water. As soon as Annie sank into the hot water, she closed her eyes and laid her head back. In the silence of the small room filled with the heady scent of cedar walls, the fire in the stove crackling and popping as it burned into a knot, she felt something let go inside her, as if she alone had been holding the pieces of a tree together, a tree that had already split apart and died. She gave her arms, then her back, and finally her legs to the water, feeling what a strain it had been to hold together that which must die, that which has already died and disappeared. No wonder her body ached at the end of every day. No wonder her calves cramped at the thought that came to her, and the pain shot up her thighs and clenched into a fist in her lower back, but she fought back this time. She was going to say it, she was going to—Baby Jula was gone. She was dead and there was nothing she or anyone could do or say about it. It wasn't Jacques' fault. Or hers. Or Dealie's.

Outside a bobwhite sang its own name over and over, a pure sweet whistle, and a large fly bumped lazily against the glass of the high window. She opened her eyes to the shafts of dusty light trapped in the late afternoon room. She didn't know if she would see Jula on the other side, as everyone insisted. She didn't know if Jula would be restored whole and sweet, her tiny fist pressed against her pink lips, those eyes so blue the whites were a milky sky to their bright orbs, those soft curls that smelled just like her and her only. Maybe she would see nothing more than the bloody cap she wore at the end, but she couldn't think of it again. She had to stop now. She had to. There was an answer but it was not to be hers today, or tomorrow. That much she did know. So she raised her head and reached for the soap and cloth.

The Negro woman had said to let her know when Annie was ready to wash, but she had no intention of letting a slave do for her what she was able to do for herself. Right then and there she decided to begin again to live as she believed, to believe again in her right to live. She sank down in the tub until her whole head was underwater. As she had with the mare that afternoon, she had an image of something not of this time. Now it was a woman, in the river, strangling on the water that whirled her so fast she kept being pulled deeper and deeper, unable to catch her breath until she was breathing water, drowning, the debris and mud at the bottom opening up, taking her in as if she were the most welcome guest in the muddy house at the end of the world. Annie jerked her head up gasping.

"YOU ALMOST KILLED CHABOT OUT THERE," DEALIE ANNOUNCED AS SOON AS Annie was deposited at the large oak-plank table in the kitchen.

"We got stuck in the sand," Annie said, eyes lowered. "Then the horse bolted."

Dealie slammed a glass of water with mint leaves down in front of Annie, who drank and put the glass down carefully.

"Maybe it's only a touch of the ague," Annie reasoned. "He'll be better soon."

Dealie hugged her arms around her waist and rubbed her red chapped elbows. She was even more exhausted-looking today, her wild hair uncombed, her fat face and neck glistening with greasy sweat that soaked the bodice of her blue dress. She pulled a chair out and sat across from Annie, laying both hands on the table. She turned them over and back as if they weren't quite familiar to her. When she looked up, there were tears in her eyes. "He's dying, Annie. You can see that."

Annie knew but to hear the words spoken aloud made her sick, as if the minty water in her stomach were boiling. "I'm sorry."

Reetie, the Negro woman who had helped her out of the bath, clanged a pan onto the stove behind them, and Dealie jerked around and frowned at her. The woman's back stiffened as if she could already feel the sting of the rebuke. Reetie was not the regular cook. Dealie gave a quick nod and turned back to Annie.

Her voice softer now, she said, "Don't ask anything of him, Annie. Even if he offers. An outing such as today's could kill him."

Reetie poured water into the huge pot waiting on the cookstove, and began to add pieces of cut-up chicken, the pale pimpled skin with the nakedness of human flesh.

Dealie leaned across the table until her face was only inches from Annie's and beckoned for her ear. "I'm pregnant again. I want him to live to see our baby, Annie." She sat back, a sob caught in her voice as she choked out, "But I'm afraid—"

Annie reached for her hand and pressed her cheek against it, unable to speak. Behind Dealie's back, the tall, angular Negro woman stood watching them, a knowing expression on her face.

AUDUBON LEFT A DAY LATER FOR A TOUR OF THE RIVER COUNTRY, WITH THE promise that he would return as soon as he could. He would write to her daily, he promised, which caused her to wonder how he imagined such intimacy between them, though at the same time she was flattered by his attentions.

Almost immediately, his letters began arriving via rivermen he befriended on his travels. She read them in her tree loft until she'd learned them by heart and could let the words play in her mind. She intended to burn them, but since she had never received letters before, the very paper on which the words were written felt precious and she held on to them vowing each day to be done. One letter included a drawing of each of them in a familiar pose. Annie quickly tucked it away in her notebook with his letters. He wrote of his travels and passed along news of his wife, Lucy, and the travails of his household, but he always encouraged Annie to spend at least "a good portion of thy day on drawing." He wrote often of their first meeting:

> It was this day dear Annie that I met thee at Jacques' Landing and not a day passes that I do not think of the dark hair blown free about your head like a wild child of the woods. Thou wilt delight in a picture I have sketched of thee, perched amongst the clouds in your tree house, like a beauteous bird—I take solace in thy presence on my pages along with my productions of the birds thou and I know so much better than others. I feel I must name thee if thy portrait is to join the others. When my pictures are met with approval and find a publisher, yours will be the most talked about as the happy days we shared are the only days I now remember and the tears blinding me are the vouchers of my hearts emotions. And no, do not tell your husband of our affection, as he will likely choose to end my misery most unkindly. Also I do not wish my wife to bear the pain of revelation until absolutely necessary. Bless thee my Dearest Friend for life.

Again, Annie was surprised at the intimacy of his tone, and shocked at his declaration. How in the world had he gotten the impression that she would ever leave Jacques? It was true that she was growing stronger of body and mind, but certainly not for Audubon.

In the following six weeks, she fulfilled her vow to draw daily, to restart her studies, and to regain enough strength in her legs that she might ride the little mare she had talked Chabot into giving her. As for Chabot, he spent much of the time confined to bed, too weak or fevered to rise. Annie spent the hot afternoons in the drowsy dusk of the netted and curtained room, ministering and reading to him. Although his conversation was usually broad, his taste in books ran toward travels, adventures, and humor. He enjoyed Washington Irving's *Salmagundi*, Mason Weems's *The Life and Memorable Actions of George Washington*, Bowditch's *The New American Practical Navigator*, and Walter Scott's novels. As a piece of ribald humor, one of the river raftsmen gave her a book entitled *Aristotle's Masterpiece* to read to Chabot. But as soon as she read the first page and glanced at the woodcuts of men and women in sexual congress, it was obvious that the book had as much to do with the Greek philosopher as the raftsman. Chabot managed a smile when he discovered the deception and Annie's red face. She did read him Mary Shelley's *Frankenstein*, but to his detriment it turned out, because his next bout of delirium was riddled with fears of his own monstrosity.

Dealie continued to grow with child, so large that it was almost as difficult for her to get around as for Annie. She huffed and puffed after walking only a few steps, and seemed more purple in the face than ever. In fact the color never left, nor the greasy sweat of illness. Despite her protests that she was healthy, several times Annie found her clutching her chest and grimacing in pain.

"I just need a good purging," she said one day. "Something I ate."

"Hawthorn tea is good for the heart, Dealie. It won't take any time at all to gather the leaves."

Reetie was told to accompany Annie. Although Annie was walking with one cane again and in little need of help, Reetie stuck to her through the underbrush and along the edges of Jacques' bayou and swamp. For the past several weeks Annie had been riding the mare astride, a pair of Jacques' trousers cut down and tied at her waist under her dress, though Dealie, unable to ride in her condition, had offered her own sidesaddle. Annie's arms and face were brown from her frequent outings, and she was growing stronger daily, able to saddle and bridle the mare on her own, supporting herself by leaning against the animal's shoulder as she worked. The patient little horse seemed none the worse for wear from their accident, perhaps because Annie personally looked after her. Her coat shone from the hours of brushing and rubbing she performed with the help of the stable boy, Boston.

That morning, Reetie followed on the house mule, used for errands and light work, an old jenny with gray whiskers and back so sunken Reetie's bare toes dragged twin trails in the orange dust of the path they were following. Annie's legs ached deep in the flesh next to the bone, but it felt good to stretch and sit upright without having to support herself. And it felt good to be on an errand. Jacques had told her how to find a hawthorn tree, where she would gather leaves for Dealie's heart tea.

DESPITE THE HEAT, THE MARE'S STEP HELD A LITTLE BOUNCE, AS IF SHE WERE tiptoeing, ready to run off at any provocation, though she wouldn't. But just as Annie leaned over to pat her, someone stepped out of the woods directly in their path. The mare planted her feet and shied, ducking right so hard Annie had to grab her mane and pray to stay on.

As soon as the mare stopped trying to turn toward home and settled, Annie looked at the person in the path. Audubon!

"Your hair—" she said with wonder at the waving locks that had grown to his shoulders, which he combed with the fingers of one hand as he studied her.

"Mrs. Ducharme." He bowed elaborately, sweeping his hat so low the brim brushed the ground.

His gesture made her blush. "What are you doing out here?"

"Looking for the ivory-billed woodpecker." He put his hat on and gazed up at the trees.

She explained about the need for a hawthorn tree. Following on foot, he told of his latest journey downriver, the specimens he'd drawn, the people he'd met. The intimacy that had grown in his letters made her awkward with him, and she struggled to keep her distance.

Finally she told Reetie to go on home since Audubon was there to care for her needs. Reetie studied the ground for a long moment, then untied the bundle that held their water and ham biscuits, handed it to Annie, and rode away staring back at them until she was out of sight. Audubon immediately helped her off the mare, pulling her against his chest where she felt the rough texture of his linen waistcoat against her cheek. He was shorter and less muscular than Jacques, and there was an almost feminine quietness about him. Jacques had that wild animal strength that took possession of everything he encountered and bent it to his desire, while Audubon awakened the part of a person that wanted to sit back and study and converse, almost without being touched at all by his physical presence. She had to admit that a part of her was drawn to him, but she rejected that desire out of instinct. Having been with a man like Jacques, she could never choose a weaker vessel.

He did not attempt to kiss her on the lips, merely smelled her hair and pressed his lips against her forehead, as if she were a child. Holding her at arm's length, he said, "How goes the work?" His eyes alive with interest now, face eager for what she could offer.

"I've been helping care for Chabot," she said, "and strengthening my legs." She was proud of her accomplishment and wanted him to notice.

"Yes." He brushed it off with an impatient wave of his hand. "But what of your work?"

She turned to the saddle and reached inside her new leather pouch, which resembled the one he carried. When her fingers encountered the notebook, she pulled it out. "See for yourself." They settled into a deer bed where the tall grasses had been flattened the night before, the mare in hobbles eating nearby.

"Butterflies?" He ran the tips of his long fingers down the page of painted ladies she'd drawn in a patch of wild daisies and mallow.

"What is this?" he said, turning to a page where she had drawn a large butterfly, paying special attention to the intense brown and black markings contrasted with a pale blue that caught the eye. "Ah," he said. "Excellent. *Hamadryas feronia farinulenta.* The vagrant, I see, has made his way here all the way from the jungles of South America." He turned a few more pages of butterflies, moths, and beetles. "But where are the birds?" His expression was both puzzled and hurt.

She took the notebook from him and closed it. "I wanted to study something on my own, something I could find in the fields with my horse. Besides, you draw them better than I ever could."

His eyes softened as he glanced at the mare and back at her. He picked up her hand and stroked her palm, following the ridges of callus formed by the cane before turning it over and inspecting the deep tan that ended at her wrists.

"You have a laborer's hands, my little hardworking lark."

Something about his silly words made her jerk her hand away. "And you have a wife, sir."

He laughed and grabbed at her hand. "And you a husband, milady, but tell me of the birds you've seen. You made a list, I'm certain."

She stared at him defiantly, but couldn't resist the small curls around his wide mouth or the bright merriment in his eyes, so she sighed deeply as if he were demanding too much and opened the notebook to the last few pages, where she kept notations of sightings and dates.

He read the list aloud: "Hermit thrush, marsh hawk, snipe, common crow, turkey hen and tom, black vulture, white-headed eagle, Carolina parrot. Yet you weren't tempted to draw them."

"I didn't want to kill them first. Besides, butterflies are easier." Perhaps that was why she'd never be a great artist or scientist, but she was grateful to him for not pointing this out. The disappointment in his voice was sufficient chastisement.

"There." He pointed to a butterfly settling a few feet from them, pulling a pencil from his pack while she opened her book to a clean page. "Capture it in a single line like this." In Audubon's hand, the pencil had a life of its own, and the shape flowed out of it as if of its own will. "Use your eye and let the pencil follow."

He put his hand around hers, not so much holding it as taking the resistance from it. With his other hand he raised her chin. "Don't look at the paper, look at the butterfly. Now sketch it. Don't think about what your hand is doing, let your eye consume the details of the form and it will translate."

It was resting on a hackberry leaf, brown, nearly black wings spread. A plain butterfly except for the straw yellow bands outlining the wings and the blue spots following them. He was right. When she finally looked down, the butterfly was there. She quickly made notes about the color so she could fill it in later.

"Mourning cloak, *Nymphalis antiopa*." He lifted his hand and she wrote.

"Thank you," she said when she'd finished.

"You should bring your colored pencils to the field for this work." He lay back in the grass, staring at the sky. On the far side of the field, beyond the tree line, Frank and McCord Foley were trenching to drain more of the swamp, and the Burtram brothers were clearing timber. Their distant laughter and occasional shouts punctuated the otherwise quiet afternoon.

"If that little viceroy will settle, you can practice on it. *Limenitis archippus*. Notice how the narrow band across each hind wing differs from the monarch." He yawned and rolled over on his side, facing her.

"Don't watch me." She quickly outlined the form of the butterfly, then looked down to make the grid of black veins and white dots.

"Take your time." He yawned again and closed his eyes.

The tension in her shoulders relaxed, and her hand gained a lightness that hadn't been there while he was scrutinizing her. A blue jay suddenly cawed overhead and flew to another tree. Then its babies began to mewl like kittens. The men across the clearing must have taken a break because they were quiet too. A group of small yellow butterflies fluttered across the clover a few feet away. *Sleepy orange*, she wrote, and quickly drew, making note of the black wing margins that made them resemble sulphurs. She would ask Audubon for the Latin name.

A very large reddish brown moth settled on Audubon's shoulder. On both back wings was a large round eyespot shaded with a light gray brown band beneath. Each front wing had a small spot as if an eye had tried to form and could not. There were faint traces of cinnamon scallops and bands on the front wings too. The size and delineation made it so beautiful she wanted to reach out and hold it. The polyphemus moth. Feathery antennae twitching faintly, it inched down his sleeve. She could not take her eyes from it, so large and beautiful, almost mystical, as if it bore the voice of prophecy.

For days she had been teaching herself to look for bands and spots and shapes of wings and precise coloration. She had forgotten the other part, how such a thing can fill your soul so completely that your hands have no will to record it, as if such an act would destroy rather than preserve it. Instead, she concentrated on the strange feeling it gave her to stare into those eyes. Something rising, but not quite at the surface, made her stomach light, and she shivered at the sudden coolness in the air.

She stood suddenly, collecting her things. Audubon opened his eyes and propped himself on his elbows. "I still have to find my hawthorn," she said with an anxious glance to the west.

"I can help." He picked up his walking stick and shouldered his pack, and they set off with her astride the mare and Audubon keeping pace beside them.

"I should explain myself," he began.

"No." It was the first thing that came to mind, but she meant it. "Look—"

A scarlet bird with black wings landed on a branch of an oak at the edge of the swamp.

"Male tanager," he said. "Listen to his song—*keep-back, keep-back, keep-back, keep-back, keep-back, keep-back.*"

"He's right," she said.

The male cocked his head and eyed them as they passed. Parting his swollen beak, he again uttered his song. *Keep-back, keep-back, keep-back.*

The trees were densely matted with a sprawling vine that obscured the swampy woods. At one point, Audubon pushed his way between the vines and disappeared for a moment. Upon his return, he announced that it was better going on the path.

"Supplejack," she said. "That's what we call that vine. Rattan vine. You can use it for furniture, but the fruit stains, so don't—"

But it was too late. His waistcoat wore a swash of purple. He looked down and brushed at it without result.

She couldn't help but laugh, which drew a thoughtful frown from him. He plucked a handful of the ripe fleshy bluish black fruit and flung it at her. Startled, the mare shied and Annie had to grab the mane to stay seated. The front of her shirt was smeared with purple, however.

"Now we are equals again," he announced, laughing, and took up his stick. As he turned away, she picked up the clump of berries from her lap and aimed it at the middle of his back, satisfied when the fruit stuck momentarily, then slid down, leaving a purple streak like the vertebrae of an exotic animal etched on his tan coat.

To his credit, Audubon laughed again. "They told me this was a wild country." He pointed his stick at a stunted tree. "And there is your hawthorn. Is it the fruit or the leaves for tea?"

The tree was only as tall as Audubon. "My mother used to say that her mother made jelly from the fruit, and had it every morning on toast to cure her heart troubles."

"Too early for fruit. We can take some leaves." He broke off a small limb, avoiding the needle-sharp thorns, and handed it to her.

"Jacques knows all about the hawthorn. He learned healing from the Indians he used to live with." At the reminder of her husband, Audubon grew silent.

After a time, she said, "How long can you stay?"

He fixed his dark eyes on her. "I have so little time. I came to see you, of course, but I must find commissions for painting." He glanced at his hands, the fingernails rimmed with black and brown paint. "My family depends on me." He looked at her again, his face solemn, distant, as if not wanting her to see the embarrassment this was causing him. "Would your husband pay for your portrait?"

She gazed off into the woods, silent for a time. His request was clearly a pained one on his part, and her own thoughts were equally contradictory.

Her heart leapt at the thought of the conversations to be had spending precious time sitting for him, yet she was shamed by the idea that he would use her to gain money from Jacques.

"You must ask him," she said quietly.

He flushed and opened his mouth to say something, but closed it again. They listened to the birds calling in the woods, a blue jay squalling like a human infant. She wondered if all of Audubon's kindnesses had been directed to the moment of gain, if he spent his spare time writing letters to women like her all along the river.

Finally she gathered her cane and notebook and rose. When he tried to help her, she shook her head, but quickly realized she needed him to help her into the saddle since her left leg was still weak. As soon as his hands were on her waist, and she felt the heat of his body against her back, she knew she'd have to ask Jacques for the painting. But it made her angry to feel something for Audubon, and when the mare danced under the settling of the weight on her back, Annie pulled her mouth too hard. She immediately repented, patting her neck and calling her pet names until the mare sighed and relaxed. She didn't offer to take Audubon with her on the horse and he didn't ask.

THEY ARRIVED HOME TO LEARN THAT ASHLAND, ONE OF THE BURTRAMS clearing trees across the field from them, had suffered a cut on the leg. His brothers Nicholas and Mitchell had brought him home to Clinch, who was especially good at sewing up wounds so they didn't turn septic. When Audubon and Annie went to his bedside, Jacques looked up, an expression on his face that Annie could not understand. It was only later that she realized he must have been looking at the purple stain she and Audubon shared.

THINGS WERE QUIET IN THE DAYS FOLLOWING THE ACCIDENT AS THEY WAITED for signs that Ashland would survive. Despite the heat that afternoon Audubon had decided to use the opportunity to have Annie sit under the bur oak for some preliminary sketches for the portrait he would paint when Jacques agreed.

A fly drifted lazily about her, landed on her hand, walked up her sleeve to the bend of her elbow, and stopped to rub its feet together. As soon as she waved it off, Audubon said, "Please hold still." He had been admonishing her to the point where she lost patience.

"Why not just shoot me and imagine the rest?"

Audubon said nothing, engrossed in his creation.

A mosquito buzzed near her ear, but she didn't dare do more than shake her head, resulting in his impatient sigh.

He put down his pencils, sighed, hooked his thumbs in his waistcoat pockets, and stared up at the house. "Your husband's own design, I take it."

When she didn't answer, he pointed to the front and said, "Classical Revival, but the entry is off. He would do well with a full-height entry porch and a triangular gable above supported by four columns. He needs columns, even with a two-tiered porch. Why is the roof extended out all the way across? Surely he doesn't intend that many columns. Is he working off a Palladian three-part plan?" He shook his head as if the house were disgraceful for its ugliness. "And those windows are never hung in adjacent pairs. Ever."

She looked up at the house, imagining porches all the way across the front, so she and Jacques could watch the river and the shore on the other side. She would be able to spend her entire day outside without the discomforts of her tree house. "He's building the house for me," she said.

Audubon looked at her out of the corner of his eye and shrugged. "To build a great house, a truly great house, is to make a gift to the world at large."

"Dear man, you will never be in a position to give such a gift." She laughed and took his arm, leaning on her cane as they made their way to the inn.

Jacques appeared from inside the inn, flinging himself into the open doorway. "Annie, where have you been?"

"What is it?"

He grimaced and shook his head. "Chabot."

The inn was dark and quiet except for a dim shawl of light from Chabot's room.

Before they went inside, Annie touched Jacques' arm, saying, "Is he?" But he pulled away and stepped inside. When she looked around, she saw that Audubon was gone.

Inside, Dealie sat in a chair at his head, leaning against the bed, her face in her hands. When Annie entered, she lifted her face. It was shocking to see the raw grief there, her swollen features blotchy red and tear-stained, her eyes bloodshot and dim, her lips trembling so hard she had to try twice to speak.

"He's dying, Annie. Chabot's—" Her shoulders shook with sobs she refused to let out, and the cost of the effort seemed to force itself down to her swollen stomach, which suddenly convulsed in a wave of pain visible through her soiled dress, causing her to gasp and bend. "No!" She slapped her stomach and Annie lurched forward to grab her hand.

"You'll hurt the baby!" she whispered loudly. Dealie resisted only a moment, then leaned against her and began crying quietly, interrupted by the rhythmic gasps that marked the start of her birthing.

Annie looked at Jacques, who had moved to the other side of the bed to sit beside Chabot. He raised his eyebrows and pointed his chin at Dealie, but Annie could only shake her head. How could they take her from him now?

Jacques' voice cracked as he spoke. "He's been growing weaker all day. His fever rose so high it seemed to be boiling his blood. I tried everything—" Jacques turned his empty hands out. "The Creeks would put him in the river to stop the heat, but she wouldn't have it." He tipped his head at Dealie, an infinite sadness in his eyes. "Now it is too late." He touched his friend's brow with a gentle hand. Chabot's eyelids fluttered, the fingers lifted on the hand lying limp next to his body, and his lips parted. It seemed that he might speak, but only a strange, whistling breath came out.

Annie leaned over and whispered, "Chabot, it's Annie. Can you hear me?" His breathing stopped for a moment as if he were considering, then his chest labored and he took another breath. He heard her.

"Chabot, I love you. Care for Jula, Chabot, don't let her be alone anymore." His fingers rose again, and his lips opened and shut as if he were struggling to speak again, but only the whistling air came out.

Jacques' eyes filled with tears. Dealie groaned aloud, and pushed Annie aside, climbing onto the bed with her husband. Her contractions were causing her to twitch and turn as she tried to resist them, banging against Chabot as she did so.

"Dealie—" Annie reached for her, but Dealie pushed her off. She looked at Jacques, who shook his head.

Then a miraculous thing happened. After a particularly loud, long, rattling breath, Chabot sat up in bed, knocking Dealie away, and staring at something in the doorway. "I'm coming," he said and reached out toward the dark emptiness. Then he fell back and stopped breathing.

"Chabot?" Jacques shook his shoulder, and the head lolled toward

Annie, the skin already beginning to sink from the bones, melting into the flesh so that he began to take on the likeness of every person who had ever died, the anonymous skull of our collective legacy, our common ancestor, until he was barely recognizable.

Jacques' shoulders shook with sobs. Dealie's eyes were swollen slits as she hugged Chabot's head, lifted his arm and tried to put it around her, but was hampered by the growing contractions of her belly. Then she began to wail and pound at her pregnancy with both fists, and it took Jacques and Annie to stop her, to drag her from the sickroom to her own bedroom, to ready her for the birth. The coincidence of the two events was remarkable, and Annie could not but wonder if there were more powerful forces at work. She could only hope that they would not have to bury three instead of one tomorrow.

When they entered Dealie's room, Reetie was sitting cross-legged on the floor next to her mistress's bed, a candle and some small bones in front of her, and a sparrow in her hand. Without glancing at them, she inserted the point of a thin knife in the bird's throat, catching the narrow rivulet of blood in a tiny copper bowl. Despite her grief and pain, Dealie grew furious when she saw what was happening and tried to kick at the woman and candle, but Jacques held her and dragged her to the other side of the bed.

"She's birthing," he said simply and Reetie sprang up. Instead of racing for sheets and water, however, she leaned over Dealie's body and dribbled blood across her stomach. For a moment it was as if the blood were boiling or acid, because it seemed to smolder and burn through the cloth.

"Get it off me! She's burning me alive!" Dealie cried, pulling frantically at the cloth, trying to rip it, until Jacques tore her dress open, revealing the red burn marks dotting her swollen belly.

"Get out!" Jacques yelled at the slave, who raised her bowl of blood as if to fling it on him, then lowered it, turned, and glided out.

Dealie was so far along it seemed that the baby burst forth without help as she screamed and cursed and pushed. In only a matter of minutes, Annie spied the hard bloody curve of the baby's skull. The shoulders were a bit trickier, but then, with one last big push, the sturdy body of a baby girl soon lay in a bloody puddle on the bed. After Annie held her upside down for a moment to clear the lungs as Chabot had taught her, she slapped the rosy bum and was rewarded by a gasp and bellow of outrage. She laid the baby on Dealie's chest and cut the umbilical cord with Jacques' knife, releasing mother and child to the world.

"Who does she look like?" Dealie asked, a sharpness in her voice.

"Chabot," Annie said without hesitation. "She looks just like her father, Chabot." She made her voice as sincere sounding as she could, and caught Dealie and Jacques exchanging a glance. *They think I don't know,* she thought, *but they're wrong. I just don't care where the seed was sown, as long as it happened. The baby could be mine, too.* Chabot was gone, Jula was gone, what difference did the particulars make? This was a good, new life. It felt right to welcome the baby into the world.

"What shall we name her?" Annie asked.

"Chabot wanted to name a girl after me," Dealie said, on the verge of weeping again, "but I don't want her to be cursed as I am."

"Maddie, then," Jacques said. "For Madeleine, my mother. We will make her resourceful." He glanced at Annie with that odd look again.

Though she was exhausted by Chabot's death and the birth of her daughter, Dealie managed to hold and suckle her. As soon as the baby fell asleep, Dealie asked that they send Reetie in to clean her up. Jacques and Annie looked at each other, wondering if it was safe, but when Dealie repeated her request, Jacques left the room with a shrug, as if to say he'd never understand women.

"Are you sure?" Annie asked. "She tried to harm you." She was rolling the umbilical cord in the soiled sheets.

"Leave that," Dealie said. "Reetie was ensuring my daughter's safe arrival, Annie. She knows more about such things than you or I, believe me. I've seen her magic. That's why I bought her, why I'll never give her up. I was out of my mind after—" A sob caught in her throat and her eyes filled. "My poor Chabot," she said, "never saw his beautiful daughter." She looked into Annie's eyes. "Do you think he sees us here? Do you think he knows?"

Annie nodded, not trusting herself to speak.

Dealie smiled and closed her eyes as Reetie appeared with steaming water, clean bedding, and a nightdress. Annie said good night, careful to avoid touching the Negro woman, or even letting her eyes, and perhaps her witchery, linger on her.

12

*T*HEY BURIED CHABOT BESIDE THE NEW HOUSE, UNDER THE OAKS AND CY-
PRESS, next to Jula, in what was fast becoming their cemetery. A few
months ago Dealie had ordered a granite stone with their names and birth
dates on it, a plain cross etched at the top. Though he was not particularly good with the chisel, Jacques himself cut in the rest of Chabot's
dates, the numbers slightly askew and varying in size. Dealie patted him on
the shoulder when he pointed out his failure, and the stone was placed at the
head of the freshly dug grave without further apology.

It was a sad time for all, as Chabot had been a great favorite with the men
as well. The normally noisy inn was subdued, no one offering evening musical
or dramatic entertainment. Jacques had draped black cloth over the entrance
to let travelers know that they were in mourning, and Annie fashioned a wreath
of willow branches woven with strips of black cloth and hung it on the door.

AFTER CHABOT'S DEATH, THE QUESTION OF ANNIE'S PORTRAIT WAS NEVER
broached. Audubon himself was scarcely present. Since Jacques left at dawn

and returned at sunset too tired to do more than shove food into his mouth before he fell asleep, hurrying to finish the summer's work, few words passed between them.

So Annie took pleasure in the little things that happened during her day, including the delightful progress of the baby Maddie, though it made her miss both Jula and Chabot. She also began to write the story of her life, beginning with the earthquake, because it seemed after Chabot's passing that we die so suddenly, without a final reckoning, slipping quickly from memory, that without children who continue us, we cease, become as common as dirt trampled beneath the feet of travelers. She could not stand the idea, so she wrote to give evidence of their lives for that brief moment.

WITH THE LOSS OF HER HUSBAND AND BIRTH OF HER DAUGHTER, DEALIE WAS NO longer able to run the kitchen and the servants, and gradually the work fell on Annie's shoulders, such as they were. Since she certainly couldn't manage cooking as Dealie had, she grew to entrust much of the kitchen to Oceana and Finis, a married Negro couple who had been with Dealie since her first husband. Their work in the kitchen possessed a silent harmony that produced excellent food and little disruption and made her wonder that there had ever been a crisis about meal preparation.

Annie began to spend her mornings sitting in a large cushioned chair in the kitchen, directing the servants to the cleaning of the rooms, overseeing the conveyance of foodstuffs for meals to come, and dispatching other tasks necessary to running the household and inn. Reetie spent all her time caring for Dealie and the baby and would not speak to Annie unless she grabbed her arm and forced her to a standstill. Oceana and Finis avoided any contact with her, and went so far as to refuse to touch the dishes she carried from Dealie's room until they had been immersed in boiling water and sprinkled with dirt, which meant yet another washing. Annie tried to reason with them that soap and hot water were enough to cleanse them, but they were stubborn on the issue.

Oceana was a tiny woman, under five feet tall, with short hair she straightened with heavy grease and flattened to her head under her mobcap. There was a thick scar running down the right side of her face that ruined her small, fine features, making her smile lopsided and dragging her eye just a bit so it appeared slightly larger than the other. After her first owner had made too many visits to Oceana's bed, his wife gave her a choice: make herself ugly or she would have her killed.

"And Finis?" Annie asked when she heard the story.

"He can't stand it." Oceana's voice cracked as if she'd confessed the most desperate sin of all.

"But he stayed with you."

Her eyes met Annie's for the first time, woman to woman, and Annie saw how they shared the terrible secrets of being alive.

"Oh, we got a dance going. I keep turning so he don't have to see it."

They all missed Chabot those mornings, and after a few weeks of Annie's presence in the kitchen, they began to talk about him, not mentioning him by name, as the two Negroes cautioned, and relaying only good or humorous stories when he came up in conversation. One morning, with her back to Annie, Oceana asked, "You going out to your studying today?" When they first arrived, Annie hadn't been aware that the slaves noticed everything they did, and knew more about them than they knew about the slaves. They reminded her of her childhood, silently watching and waiting her turn, memorizing gestures and moods, strengths and weaknesses of the ones in charge, the way a wife watches her husband for each turn of his personality.

"Would you like to come with me?" she asked.

Oceana turned, a rare smile lifting her crooked mouth. "With Miz Dealie down, I can't leave the cooking." She hesitated, then said, "Thank you."

Annie smiled and assured her the invitation stood. As Oceana turned, the light from the window struck her scar, making the pink flesh shine for a moment before it blinked off again.

She said, "You shouldn't take that Reetie with you. Take Boston, he can help with the horse. You don't want to be messing with Reetie. Let her stay with Miz Dealie and cook up her business."

"What business is that?" Annie put her hands flat on the table to steady herself as she stood.

"Never you mind. Just stay away from that one." She picked up an iron pot from the stove and set it back down hard.

SINCE LOSING HIS FRIEND, JACQUES SEEMED TO BE DRIVEN BY A NEW ENERGY TO finish the house. He had taken the men off almost all the other work and hired new laborers from the growing village. Annie decided to make a case for using Finis to help with some of the architectural and interior design, since neither Jacques nor she had an idea of what the house should look like, and Finis had what his wife Oceana called "a big eye for beauty." With this in mind, she made her way up the small hill to stand in front of the house and called for Jacques.

Ashland Burtram was mending quickly enough to sit on a bench and fashion the intricate designs of moldings for the porches that would stretch across the front on both the first and second story.

"Miz Annie." Ashland ducked his head as he spoke. He had been especially shy since his accident.

"Is Jacques about?" she asked.

He tilted his head to the interior of the house.

"Could you call him for me?" She had no intention of going inside. She would wait until Jacques was absolutely finished and ready for her, since it was his grand surprise.

Ashland turned his head and bellowed so loud all the pounding and sawing stopped and Mitchell came running out to the porch.

"What's wrong?" he asked, brushing at the sawdust covering his shirt and hair.

"Is Jacques in there?" Annie asked.

Mitchell looked startled, glanced over his shoulder, then back at the inn. "Can't say where he is, ma'am. I see him, I'll tell him you're lookin' for him."

She looked at the debris of wood and tools scattered on the ground, raising her eyes just as the two brothers exchanged a meaningful look. "Thanks," she said and turned to go.

She was almost to the stable when Jacques, breathless, caught up with her.

"You shouldn't be bothering the men while they're working," he said. "We have little enough time as it is before winter." His face was flushed and somehow struggling to stay closed, to wipe away some feeling or expression. Where had he been?

"I have a suggestion for the building."

His eyes lightened and his wide lips parted in a happy smile. "You do? *Qu'est-ce que c'est?*" It pleased him that she was finally taking an interest in his grand project.

She explained about talking with Oceana and discovering the talent of Finis.

"I could use some help," he conceded. "I have the shape of the house, as you can see, but the front is the problem. It's so plain. I am *dans la rivière*, in the river, as you say." He put his big hands on her shoulders, leaned down, and kissed her forehead. "Thank you, *ma chère*." It seemed that his sadness over the loss of Chabot was lifting slightly, and perhaps they would make love that night if he was not too overworked. Her spirits rose at the thought of his body pressed urgently into hers again.

There was a peculiar sweet odor on him that made her nose itch and her throat tighten as she looked up at his pleased face. It reminded her of the oranges and lemons Dealie had ordered from New Orleans a month earlier in hopes of making Chabot better.

"If you use him for your building, I'll need more help in the kitchen."

He clapped his hands and said, "*Bien sûr*, of course! Anything for my little queen."

He grabbed her waist and lifted her, spinning around giddily as he had when they were first together. When he put her down, she glanced over his clothing, every bit the wife as she inspected the trousers and loose-fitting cotton smock he had replaced his buckskins with. If anything Jacques was looking younger and stronger than the rest of them, a reverse aging having taken place. His rough face was smoother, more golden, and his dark eyes a richer brown. His smile had a boyish quality now, and his teeth seemed whiter—or was she imagining it all? Had she been so blinded by recent events that she had forgotten what her own husband looked like? She didn't honestly know.

"*Chérie*, why are you staring at me?" He grinned broadly as if he knew a secret and picked up her hand, running his fingers between hers in the secret way they had of letting each other know of their desire.

She could feel her face redden and quickly looked away. Why was she behaving like a silly girl?

"We will be happy in this house, Annie," he said, pulling her against his body, where she could feel his breath quicken and the hardening below. "I've changed." He said the words slowly, carefully, and something in them sent a shiver down her arms.

"You're cold, *ma petite*!" He wrapped her tighter in his embrace and bent his head into the place where her neck and shoulder met, pushed her blouse away and softly nibbled, which he knew would drive her mad. She felt the warm surge begin in her stomach, flowing down her legs, then rising upward to her breasts, and she wanted to give in, it would be so easy, not waiting for the darkness of their room.

But Jacques abruptly straightened, releasing her so quickly she almost fell, except for his hand steadying her arm.

From the trees at the edge of the clearing stepped Audubon reading a book, unmindful of them, it seemed.

Jacques growled. "Audubon *again*! The man has no home, lives like the fly off the crumbs of our meals. Paying nothing for what he takes, leaving a little drawing or painting—worthless, eh? Where are the coins? I do not agree to this bartering—do you?" He tightened his grip on her arm, actually lifting her an inch so she was almost on tiptoes as they watched Audubon turn a page, engrossed in his book.

Annie twisted out of his grasp, rubbing her arm and panting with the pinching pain. "What are you saying, Jacques?"

He smiled coldly, his eyes glittery with anger. "Are you trading something you don't own, *ma chère*. Is it true, what I have been told?"

"You're listening to gossip now? Don't be ridiculous!" She turned and waved at Audubon, who had just noticed them.

Jacques' words were low and furious, "It is true then, madam? I will divorce you, I will stop you!"

She whirled to face him, furious at his insistence when she had been nothing but faithful, while he—

"You're a fool, Jacques! Do you think I don't know that Dealie's child is most certainly yours? Poor Chabot, poor, poor Chabot, you might have killed him!"

Jacques' slap knocked her backward a step and she stumbled and fell to her hands and knees. Her cheek stung, but he had withheld most of the force. She spat as if he'd cut her lips, though he hadn't, and sniffed as if her nose was bleeding, though it was hot only from insult.

"Get up." He lifted her under the arms and set her back on her feet. "Don't insult me," he warned with a raised finger in her face.

"Don't insult *me*!" she shouted, swinging her fist at his face, not intending to hit him. Although he tried to turn aside, her blow caught the side of his nose, causing an immediate flow of blood. Jacques shook his head, stunned, put his finger to the blood, held it out, and glared at her, both of them speechless.

He turned and strode back to the house without another word.

"Damn you, Jacques!" He was not a man you wounded.

She was still shaking by the time Audubon reached her, looking up at last from his book. She wanted to send him away and let Jacques win his pride back. She would tell Audubon that he must leave first thing in the morning and not return without her permission. It made her feel better to have such a plan to resolve the differences between Jacques and her—a silly misunderstanding. She knew Audubon's character. He lived off the goodwill of others, yes, but he was an artist, a scientist, and they must forgive him. She would explain this to Jacques, a man who made his own way and surely expected others to do the same.

Also, it was her house and land as much as his now. They claimed it together. She'd already given a life to it. She could invite guests as he did. She saw no reason why she shouldn't. The thought made her stand straighter, pull her hair over her reddened cheek, and smile brightly. In the meantime, she sorely needed Audubon's help in identifying a species she'd found.

"Do your studies go well?" she asked as soon as the greeting was out of the way.

With a glance toward the house on the rise above them, he said, "I found the Louisiana warbler. Shot it and then discovered a new species! Shot the female, but couldn't quite get her mate. Oh well, painted what I could." His eyes were in constant motion, as always, searching the landscape for living creatures he could appreciate and perhaps kill.

Feeling faint, she said, "Then I'll leave you to them." She made her way to their room at the back of the inn and lay on the bed to cry quietly into a pillow. When she was done, she slept the afternoon away, awoke startled at the lateness, and hurried to the kitchen to check on preparations for the evening meal.

Oceana sat her at the kitchen table and promptly put a cup of cool greenbrier tea in front of her. After a few sips, she felt her disquiet slip away, and told Oceana that Jacques would like to use Finis on the house.

"Just as well," she sighed. "We'll have to get someone to help me here though." And as if she were reading Annie's mind, she added, "Not her. Not Reetie. You'll have to sell me downriver she comes into my kitchen."

"We'll find a way, don't worry. Maybe young Ashland can help, since he's still having trouble walking. I'll speak to Jacques."

"He can't walk, he's not going to be much help to me." She picked up the huge bowl of crawfish and dumped them into the roux. Stirring to cover all the tails, she added a small portion of water, stirred, and repeated the ritual several times.

"Is the venison pie done?" Annie asked.

"Waitin' on the corn sticks and gingerbread." Hands on hips, Oceana turned and smiled. "I have the cream whipped and set in the milk house to keep it from turning in this heat." She wiped her dripping face on her sleeve.

"And common bread?"

"Made last night. *Pain perdu* for breakfast."

"Good. Audubon especially likes that."

Oceana raised her eyebrows and gave a little shake of her head, but held her tongue.

"Likes what?" Jacques suddenly appeared in the doorway, left hand behind his back, his face red with heat, or so Annie thought until the sour wave of alcohol hit her. "What does Audubon like especially, besides my little wife?"

"You're drunk," she said. Pushing away from the table, she clambered to her feet to face him.

He grabbed her face and roughly tilted her chin with his thumb to get a better look at her. "And you have browned your face like a savage, madam."

When she didn't respond with more than a glare, he chuckled. "But you do more than study the insects, don't you? You don't even keep track of your notes these days. Lucky I saw you drop it." He held out the journal he had been hiding behind his back.

She reached for her notebook, but he snatched it back.

"This is childish, Jacques."

His face was so hard, her heart sank.

"Let us see how your 'work' progresses."

He opened the book, leafing quickly through the pages as if he already knew where he was going. They both knew. The letters from Audubon appeared flimsy in his large, soiled hands, and his fingers stumbled and tore the pages as he unfolded the top one.

" 'My dearest,' " he began to read, the ire on his face softening into sadness as he read the familiar words out loud. " 'I have vowed to name a new species in your honor, and will do so as soon as possible, in hopes that seeing it will remind me of you always.' "

He paused and gave her a searching look, his face unmasked, vulnerable as it had been in their earliest days together. Perhaps he wanted her to see what this letter had forfeited.

" 'I am your obedient servant and more,' " he concluded, letting his hand drop as he crumpled the thin paper into a small ball he threw at the fireplace. Annie's heart lurched to see the flames flare red and quickly turn the words to black ash.

"And this one is *très jolie*." Jacques' voice rose angrily as he nearly tore the next page in half in his eagerness to read it. " 'My love is on wings to you, my heart in safekeeping in her beak—' " He wadded the page up and spat on it before throwing it into the fireplace.

"You weep for letters? What about your marriage?" He shook the journal so close to her face it grazed her cheek.

"I'm weeping for you, you fool!" She grabbed at the book, but he snatched it away.

"And *this*, this—" He held up the drawing Audubon had sent. "Like husband and wife, *n'est-ce pas*? Perhaps he would like my house, too, to go with my wife!"

"Nobody wants your house, Jacques, it's ugly." She wanted to hurt him, and she did. His hands stopped midair.

"Then you don't have to live there, *ma chère*." His voice was sober and cold.

"I won't. Don't ask. Ever."

She tried to stand straighter as he looked her up and down.

"You have traded a puma for a house cat—a married one at that. He won't provide for you. The man is little better than a beggar. And thief."

He smiled in such a superior way that she guessed that many things must have happened while she was too absorbed to notice. Even now, he appeared younger, stronger, almost ageless. What was his secret?

"Jacques, what's happened to you?" She suddenly panicked at the thought of losing him, despite her anger. She'd meant to argue him out of his jealousy. She didn't care what he'd done with Dealie.

"Let's say I have had the *danse macabre*." He spread his arms as if to show off his new power. "And I have won!"

A gasp and the clatter of a pan dropped on the stove caused her to glance at Oceana, who held a smoking rag in her hand as she stared at Jacques with fear-filled eyes.

"Oceana, be careful," she said. The woman looked down at the rag and flung it into the fireplace as if it were a poisonous snake, staring as the flames immediately consumed it. Annie turned back to Jacques. "I've done nothing!" she cried out. "I've nothing to be ashamed of, Jacques! Do you hear me? Jacques? I've been faithful. I've loved you—which is more than you can say! Jacques!"

Oceana dipped her head next to her ear and whispered, "Can't you see? That man's cursed—stay away from him. He's been mixin' in that bidness with Reetie and Miz Dealie. He done a Asking Prayer for more than's his right. It gonna cost more than he has."

Jacques paid no attention to her. He read from the journal in a low voice that only he could hear and then tore the offending pages out and tossed them into the fire.

Annie, making her voice pleasant and sweet, said, "May I please have my journal back?" Jacques looked in her eyes for a moment, his own eyes as dark and deep and unknowable as those of one of Jones's terrible dogs. And just as empty. She recognized nothing in them. He turned suddenly and left the kitchen without another word.

Annie followed him into the dining room, which was crowded with travelers milling about, positioning themselves behind chairs at tables, waiting for the moment the food would arrive so they could seat themselves. Jacques was seated at a table with Skaggs, the two Foley cousins, Clinch, and Wyre arrayed around him like soldiers awaiting their general's orders.

Before Annie could go to him and renew her suit, a disheveled Dealie appeared before her, wearing a red and gold Empire waist evening dress so tight her bosoms were barely covered; the sleeves had split in so many places her flesh appeared to be exploding. On her head she wore a rose silk turban wound with pearls and topped with a bent ostrich feather, her hair spilling out in greasy knots all around. She looked like the victim of a robbery or worse. In her right hand she held a full glass of wine.

"Dealie, you shouldn't be out of bed!"

"I'm lonely," Dealie complained, looking around the crowded dining room. "I thought perhaps Jacques could entertain me."

An inspiration came to Annie then. Dealie seemed to have more sway over Jacques than she did at the moment.

"Can you imagine? He's decided Audubon and I are lovers," Annie said.

Dealie burst out laughing. "That's absurd!" She stopped as soon as she saw the seriousness on Annie's face, and scowled. "You aren't, are you?"

"Of course not. Why would you think something like that?"

Dealie refreshed herself from the glass, then smacked her lips and smiled with her mouth half open, her teeth tinged lavender, her tongue dark plum. "He's not much of a specimen compared to Jacques"—she paused, her thumb clicking against her teeth as she thought—"but there *is* something there. I've seen it."

"Could you talk to Jacques for me? Tell him he's wrong?"

Dealie sipped the wine, staring out the windows at the gathering rose apricot light of early evening until her eyes glazed. "Tonight may not be a good time."

"There he is." Annie pointed Dealie in Jacques' direction and gave her a push.

Dealie wove through the room, lurching into people, being placed upright again and pushing her way until she reached Jacques' side. She leaned over and said something into his ear, and he glanced in Annie's direction, holding her gaze for a moment, giving her hope.

Until then, no one in the dining room had paid them any particular attention. But then Audubon was brought in shoulder to shoulder with Little Dickie Sawtell, Quick, and the Burtram brothers, who surrounded him like jailers. He was looking very anxious, darting his eyes through the suddenly curious crowd in search of a friendly face. When he spotted Annie, he waved. It was the worst thing he could have done. Jacques had to be restrained by his men, and Nicholas Burtram pulled Audubon's arm down and forced him to be still, while Mitchell pulled the leather pouch off his shoulder, spilling its contents on the table before Jacques, who plucked the sketchbook out and raised it as he stood, a judge in his court.

"*Petit délinquant!* Thief!" he yelled, holding the sketchbook aloft for all to see. Audubon stood still, his face wooden, shoulders stiff, hands in fists at his side.

"Jacques!" Annie shouted, unmindful of the stares and murmuring of the crowd. She started pushing people aside with her cane as she made her way across the room.

The servers filed in with steaming tureens for each table, but stopped as soon as they saw Jacques and Audubon, face-to-face. The room fell silent.

The two adversaries stood glaring at each other. When Audubon reached for his sketchbook, Jacques planted a large hand on the man's chest and pushed him away. Audubon stumbled backward and caught himself against Mitchell Burtram, who shoved him forward again.

"Now, let's see what you have been stealing from me," Jacques said in a loud voice slurred with wine.

"Ah, here is a bird I own." He ripped a page from the sketchbook, wadded it, and dropped it on the floor.

"And this one also—and this—and this—" After destroying several pages, he looked at Audubon with fake astonishment on his face. "Why, Audubon, you have stolen everything!" He continued leafing and tearing out pages, until he obviously came upon the pictures he was looking for.

"*Bien sûr.* Of course. The rarest of birds." This time when he tore out the pages, he carefully folded them and placed them in his shirt. By then Annie was close enough to see that they were the sketches of her.

Rifling the rest of the sketchbook, he didn't bother to tear the pages out; he simply muttered in French to himself, and finally clapped the book shut. She didn't dare grab his arm, although she was close enough. Instead she tried to appeal to his public side. Surely he had forgotten the people around them, who were in danger of forgoing a delicious meal to witness the drama he was staging.

"Sir, you have provided enough entertainment," she said in a low voice, tilting her head to the surrounding tables. People cast worried glances at one another and stared wide-eyed at Jacques and Audubon.

He turned slowly, his maddened eyes hardly recognizing her, it seemed. "You are never to address me again."

She was ruined.

When Dealie put her hand on his shoulder, he shrugged her off and waved to his men. "Monsieur Audubon is leaving." The men grabbed him by the arms and proceeded toward the door, Jacques following with the pouch and sketchbook.

"Stop them, Dealie!" Annie cried, but she shook her head.

"Stop them! Someone—" She looked around at the travelers, who were already on their feet, making their way to the door to enjoy the spectacle that had apparently replaced their meal. Only Ashland Burtram remained seated, his eyes on her, his young face flushed with confusion and shame.

"I'll stop them," Dealie said. She gathered her skirts, shook herself, straightened her tilting turban and started for the door. Annie followed closely, with Ashland limping behind.

Annie took one last look at the Negro servers standing stiffly along the walls, staring at the flies settling on the surfaces of the tureens of chilling stew in their arms, unimpressed by the violence white men visited upon one another. One man, so lean he seemed to be made of sticks, licked his lips hungrily as he gazed into his tureen.

They dragged Audubon to Annie's tree, where they tied his hands behind him and put a rope around his neck. Jacques held the sketchbook high, shouting in Audubon's face, but to his credit, the smaller man stood still, staring straight ahead while the setting sun cast the scene in a bloody tableau, blessing it with all the anger that gathers at the end of the day to curse the night into darkness and regret.

Dealie was fully in her senses now as she marched through the crowd, shoving the reluctant bystanders aside with an oath, Ashland and Annie in her wake. When they reached the core of the group, Dealie reached out and slapped Jacques' face hard enough to leave the red imprint of her hand.

"Stop this right now!" she shouted.

He was so stunned he dropped his arm and took a step backward. His nose began to bleed again. Then he seemed to come to his senses, and he stepped up to face her.

She became a harridan, shouting obscenities at him, calling him a whore's son, a black bastard shit, and more, threatening him in both French and English. He took the battering like a man facing a wicked storm, stoical, yet gradually beaten to the point where he must turn his face away from the force or suffer disfigurement.

"Give me that thing!" she demanded. When he handed the sketchbook over, she walked down the path to the river and threw it in. Audubon gasped as it sank from sight.

"Untie him!" she shouted at the Foley cousins, who shied as if she had struck them with whips instead of words, then hastily complied.

"And you!" She turned on Audubon, pointing to the river. "Go to that boat, get on it, and do not come back. You hear me? Ever!"

He stared at her for a moment, nodded once, picked up the pouch Jacques had dropped after the sketchbook sank, and slowly made his way down to the dock and onto the boat, where his figure merged with the darkening shapes. Jacques pushed his way through his men, joined by Reetie, the slave girl, who wore Dealie's riding costume of bright green velvet, soiled shabby now that no one was taking care of it properly. In her hair, she wore a beaded butterfly clip that Chabot had given Jula when she was born. The two of them strode quickly across the field toward the swamp that lay beyond.

THEY WERE GONE FOR SEVEN DAYS. WHEN THEY RETURNED, JACQUES LOOKED ragged and ill, his arms and face striped with scratches from the deep brush.

He ordered the men to finish the house immediately. He drove everyone hard after that, brooking no disobedience from slaves or men, speaking to Dealie only when she needed to discuss the inn, refusing to speak to Annie at all. Nor did Dealie and Annie ever speak to each other again, for Dealie shunned both her and Jacques and drank herself into a nightly stupor.

Reetie returned with a new status. She smiled at Annie whenever she could, a proud, sly expression on her face. Annie knew who was sleeping in the house with Jacques now that the men were completing the interior rooms. It pained her to numbness again. A person cannot lose all more than once, perhaps twice, without giving the rest of her life away.

Despite these changes, it was Audubon who filled Annie's thoughts. Poor Audubon. His sketchbook, all those months of work, gone. Would he ever recover to paint again? She dared not inquire.

JACQUES WAS TRUE TO HIS WORD IN THE MONTHS AND YEARS THAT FOLLOWED. Not a word passed between them. There were many nights when she watched, from her platform in the oak, the red glow of Jacques' cigar on the upper porch.

Dealie and her Negroes were the first to leave, in wagons overloaded with all their worldly goods. Jacques discovered just how much Dealie had meant to the running of the inn. With much of the furniture, dishes, silverware, and cookware, and most of the servants gone, travelers found meager fare at meals and dirty rooms and bedding at night. There were several very loud arguments between Jacques and Reetie as to her assuming the work that had been abandoned, and arguments even between Jacques and his men.

Then, one by one, even Jacques' most faithful men left, to be replaced by a much harder-looking group who thought nothing of drinking day and night, fighting, and stealing. Annie kept her door bolted at night.

And so the years passed, their love fading to gray ruin.

THEN ONE FINE JUNE DAY THE RIVER RETURNED TO CLAIM HER. IT GREW FROM a hissing, gurgling flow to a low rumble, then a muted roar, huge and dreadful. It chewed up the banks and swallowed field upon field. It carried off cattle, pigs, horses, flatboats, canoes, buggies and wagons, parts of barns and corncribs and chicken houses, and trees that rose and plunged and rolled in the roiling water. It disassembled cabins log by log and spread them all across the countryside. A whole house surged on the tide with a riverboat embedded in its side, its windows filled with flickering light, as if the family inside had just settled down to Sunday dinner.

It wasn't clear whether the rising river caught Annie unawares or all too aware, but when it came, she was in her tree, with Jacques across the clearing on the upper porch, smoking a cigar.

Some said the flood was the result of an overabundance of rain. Some said it was a quake up north. And some, the hand of a destiny that would not be denied.

In the end, Annie stood there clutching the thickest limb as the river battered her tree, the vibration passing into her body as if tree and she were one. She gazed at Jacques on the porch, at the red glow of his cigar. And as the tree was brought low, she cried out for help. Jacques quickly stripped naked, tied a length of rope tied around his waist with a loop in his hand. But by the time he got there, it was too late. Annie was already waiting for him on the far shore, that they might enter Paradise together, husband and wife once more.

13

HEDIE

I DID A LOT OF THINKING THOSE DAYS IN BED. I WASN'T JUST SLEEPING, AS Monte Jean and Clement imagined. I was getting smarter. I started listening to Clement's phone calls and came to the correct conclusions about where the extra money was coming from.

"What do you mean? It was twelve cases. No, no I didn't . . . all right, yes, yes. I said I would, didn't I? Yes, alone."

The conversations frightened me, but I didn't say a word. I needed to learn more so I watched him waiting for phone calls in the hallway, sitting and worrying, smoking cigarette after cigarette, tapping ashes into the cuff of his pants and putting the stubs in his pocket like a hill farmer. In between he would get up and pace, running his hand across his scalp until it grew shiny with hair oil, which he didn't seem to notice. It left a sweet scent on my cheek when he came in to kiss me good night. And looking at the worried pouches under his eyes, I wanted to pull him down in bed and pet him to sleep.

He's a grown man, I heard my dead father's voice announce one evening. Let him do for you as I did for my wife and children.

I didn't argue. You don't do that with the ghosts. They're long past reason and debate. Yes, Daddy, I said. All right.

I began to slip into Clement's bed to wait for him. Oh, I knew he smelled of liquor and smoke and sometimes perfume, which made me want to bash his skull with Monte Jean's big iron skillet. But one night he came home with scraped knuckles, swollen cheekbone, and bruised ribs and I realized that out there, where my husband went to work, was a place he was just surviving. I started taking care of his clothes, sewing the torn shirts, telling Monte Jean to clean the spots from his trousers with gasoline, then hang them out to air. I polished his shoes. Why would you do such a thing, you ask? Because this man took me in when he didn't have to, and because I loved him and having his shoes shiny made him walk taller in a world that wanted to batter him to the ground. I had more than my father's voice in my head, I had his blood.

In late January, Clement and I went down to the Hot Springs in Arkansas, which the doctor told him would bring me back to myself. I wasn't not myself, I knew that, I just wasn't the same.

The long, hot, mineral soaks at Fordyce Bathhouse felt good though, and I started to relax enough to sleep almost the whole night through finally. My days became predictable, easy. I'd bathe in the morning, lunch with Clement, rest in the afternoon, supper alone, read and try to sleep. After a while, I was jumping out of my skin, so Clement took me out when he was free. Usually we walked down Central Avenue, looking in store windows, holding hands and planning how to refurbish the house. He had such plans those days.

"We'll have a whole household of kids," he promised one afternoon with a squeeze of my hand. "And I'll make enough money to stay home and help raise them. They won't be orphaned the way I was." He forgot to quit squeezing my hand until I pulled it away. What he didn't say was that he didn't want our kids to be left with an alcoholic uncle possessing dramatic aspirations and a memory gone south, as he had been. There was still a lost boy living inside Clement's skin, and I was the one who saw it peeking out from those sweet eyes crinkling at the corners with laughter, the small pegged teeth, the little mouth, the freckles on his nose like those of a boy in the sun. I think the best time he ever had was shopping to please me, as if that were all he ever wanted in life now.

One morning, he took me into a little millinery shop and bought me the silliest hat we could find—a complicated turban affair with feathers and gold braid and glass jewels. He peeled the dollars from a thick wad of bills and handed them grandly to the stern counter-woman, who was convinced we were mocking her creation and shop. Afterward, we tripped like children down the sidewalk, Clement keeping his arm around my waist and glancing proudly at the other men.

"You're such a tiny little thing these days," he whispered in my ear, bumping the turban sideways. "You need to eat more."

Straightening the hat, I looked carefully at the window of an eatery we were passing.

"Let's stop," I said.

"Here? You want to go in here?" he asked.

"Sign says they have home-cooked food. Might be a relief from the fancy hotel meals."

The walls were covered with battered mahogany panels and dark green figured paper that had been applied in some distant past. Paintings and framed photos of racehorses hung everywhere, along with jockeys' colorful shirts, tiny saddles, and bridles with rusty bits. Everything wore a layer of dusty grease, and even the smoky light seemed thick with it. The air smelled a bit funny, I noticed, not like food as much as cigarette and cigar smoke and a sweet grainy odor, but I couldn't see anyone smoking. Perhaps upstairs, I reasoned, as several loud thumps shook dust from the tin ceiling overhead. With my luck, I'd probably taken us to a speakeasy. I decided not to say anything, to see how far Clement would go to please me.

When the slovenly waiter brought two yellowed, stained menus, Clement grimaced and told the man to bring their best dishes. We tried to eat, but the overdone steak sat in a hardened pool of grease beside a gray clump of half-raw potatoes and limp lettuce. Men and women kept streaming past our table, set close enough to the window to be visible from the outside, yet the room never filled. When I asked Clement, he shrugged, but then leaned back, wiped his mouth with the yellowed, stained linen napkin, and smiled. His eyes darted to the back of the room, then settled on me until he leaned forward and tilted his head at a passing couple.

"We're probably the only folks here for the food, Hedie. There's a saloon upstairs."

I tried a cough to cover my laugh, and he squinted at me.

"What if there's a raid?" I whispered loudly.

He looked proud of himself. "Lucky for you I'm here. Safest thing for you would be to stay out of such places. I'm a man, I can read the lay of the land, but you—" He picked up my hand and kissed the back, taking a moment to straighten the yellow diamond. When he smiled, that little-boy joy spread to his eyes and made him glow. "You keep to the bathhouses and outdoor exercise. Do you want me to rent you a riding horse or a canoe?"

I waved the ideas away. "Can't I go out with you?" I put a hand on his arm and he covered it with his own and squeezed.

"Sometimes I need to conduct business, sweetheart, you understand." His eyes searched mine, to see if I was convinced.

"Don't cling to him," my daddy's voice warned. "He needs to be a man with other men. You wouldn't want the kind of man who couldn't leave your side."

"That's fine," I said. "Can I have some shopping money? I may want to return this hat and get—"

I realized that his attention was on the full-figured, red-haired woman in yellow who was sweeping through the room, casting a bold eye on every man. When she caught Clement's eye, he dipped his head and she lifted her chin. They knew each other.

Suddenly, the greasy food began to stir in my stomach and I rose abruptly, letting the napkin fall to the dirty black-and-white tiled floor. I wanted to throw a plate at her.

"Hedie, are you all right?" Clement took my elbow and I gave a quick shake of my head, dislodging the hat from its precarious perch. It thumped into the large bowl of stewed rhubarb with clotted cream that the waiter had set on our table as the final insult to our appetites. Both of us stared at the ridiculous hat until the waiter sauntered over and made to pull it out of the dish. We burst out laughing.

"Leave it," Clement said as he dropped some money on the table and handed me a sheaf of bills I put in my handbag.

"Was she a friend of yours?" I asked as he tucked my arm comfortably in his for the walk back to the hotel.

"Oh honey, it's just business. That's all it ever is—except for you." He dropped my arm and slipped a cigarette out of the monogrammed silver case we had bought last week, and stopped to light it with the matching silver lighter. They were so pretty, I thought about smoking the way women in the movies did. Smoking made him seem older, but more uneasy too because I kept seeing him pacing the hallway at home, waiting for the phone calls. If they didn't come, then what? Would we have to go into hiding? There were men in dark suits with heavy shoulders who walked down the sidewalks crowding visitors out of the way—was Clement afraid of them too? I had often wished I had money for myself, but since I married him, I prayed for money for Clement. He was one of those people who would be a fine father and husband, a good person, if given the chance. I just knew it. Maybe I could figure out a way to save him or at least help him, I decided in that instant as he opened the glass hotel door for me, kissed me on the cheek, leaving a dry smoky imprint, waved goodbye, and hurried down the street, trailing cigarette smoke in his wake.

I pretended to go upstairs, stopped on the first landing, watched just out of sight until I was sure he was gone, and then followed him.

He returned to the restaurant, walking directly to the stairs. I waited outside, afraid he'd catch me if I went inside, and ignored the curious glances of passersby, until the sun grew so hot it made me sick and I went back to the hotel to bed.

I slept through dinner, opening my eyes for a moment to see Clement in evening clothes, gathering his watch and money before slipping on the cat's-eye ring I'd given him and closing the door softly behind him.

After that day, I followed him often, finding clever ways of disguising my intentions. I don't think he ever knew, because after a month he grew bolder, openly walking with the red-haired woman down the main street one evening. They appeared as old friends or a long-married couple, the air both casual and intimate between them. It took my breath away to see them, but I still couldn't bring myself to the furious pitch. Was she an old friend? A business associate? What I had to do was figure out how to keep my husband, not drive him away.

"Clement," I said one day at lunch, "I *would* like to begin riding. Can you arrange a horse for my use?" He loved doing things for me. It made him feel useful, kept his attention on me. I made a show of eating a waffle smothered in strawberries, syrup, and butter while his face glowed with approval. His late nights were beginning to sharpen his features, make his skin pale, and smudge around his eyes. There was a slight odor to his skin, too, a bit oily, sweet and sour.

"A few lessons, too," I added. "I've only ridden bareback on my grandfather's farm horses. I'm as strong as an ox, you know."

Clement laughed and clapped his hands. "You'll need riding clothes." He pulled a fold of money from his waistcoat pocket and handed me four fifties—more money than I'd ever had in my life. "You'll have to make do with ready-made boots."

I took the money, working to keep a bright smile on my face. "Shall I come with you tonight? I'd love to learn how to play roulette."

"More exercise will help you sleep at night," he said. "Besides, those places aren't for young married women like you, Hedie. I'm working as hard as I can so you *don't* end up in those places. Just trust me, please?"

"You're the one who's worn out, Clement, I just want to help."

He twisted the cat's-eye ring on his finger and frowned. "If Keaton could do with a little less money for a few months, and cotton prices would just go up." He looked at me with his eyes wide and suddenly tear filled.

"Oh honey, I wish we could have waited. I want you to have everything you ever wanted, but I can't lose Jacques' Landing. It's all we have." He turned his head to the side, and said in a muffled voice, "Just don't give up on me."

I took his hand between mine and held it. After my mother made me leave to marry Clement when I was pregnant, I knew what it felt like to have people give up on you when you're trying your hardest to be brave. He was trying to take care of his family as my own father had done until it killed him. My mother never let up on him after the bank failed and they were broke. Those last months sitting in a straight chair on the front porch for all to see, as his wife went out to work clerking in a dress shop, a place she used to mock, my father dimmed and failed, like a lamp left to burn itself out in the dark. By the time the vessels in his brain burst, he had not spoken in a week. He had exhausted his explanations, and his excuses had grown too weak to mention, my mother said. I was not going to let that happen to Clement.

I learned to ride in a proper saddle. It turned out that riding bareback had given me a natural seat and balance. I began to enjoy my body again. The pleasure was compounded by the knowledge that Clement needed me to do these things so that he could have evidence of his success. He was making headway if I had riding lessons and mineral bath treatments and nice clothes. Maybe it helped him face the people he did business with too, the thought occurred to me one day when I noticed a man following me on horseback, stopping or cantering whenever I did. When I dismounted at the stable and got a good look at his face, I realized that I had seen him several times during the last week. I grew cautious, making sure there were other people around when I walked out or shopped and never mentioning the subject to Clement, who was half sick with nerves these days.

We had been in Hot Springs three months when we went to Oaklawn for the horse races one afternoon after a week of his being out all night and sleeping until noon. I was so happy and relieved to be with him that we were laughing and making silly jokes about the people in the crowd, the jockeys, and the betting. A good warm wind was blowing, and the horses were dancing on their toes as they walked to the start, coats dark with sweat, lather building between their hind legs. One black reared and flung his rider off, then galloped around the track alone, throwing his head from side to side as the little stirrups banged against his sides, and the reins flopped loose. The other horses grew more agitated, bucking and rearing while the men tried to calm them down. When the horse came lugging up the backstretch to find a wall of men in its way, it stopped and neighed at the other horses until one of the men got close enough to grab the reins. Then the horse followed docilely behind.

Clement shook his head, his hands trembling as he tore up his ticket. "I just lost five hundred dollars on that fool. He'll be feeding dogs by tomorrow." He had gotten a haircut with his shave before we left and was wearing a cream wool suit with a black pinstripe.

"Is that a new suit?" I asked.

He stared at the program, then lifted his head and smiled. "We'll take you shopping in the morning if you'd like," he said and covered my left hand with his. The diamond kept sliding from side to side, cutting into my fingers, I'd lost so much weight.

"You need to eat more," he reminded me. "I like my girls with flesh on their bones." His voice rose and a couple of men standing behind us laughed at his remark. When I glanced back, I saw that the man who had been following me was standing there. I pulled my hand loose, the ring slipping off and falling to the ground.

"That right, Ace?" He turned and winked at the strange man, who appraised me with a heavy raised eyebrow and nodded. I wanted to say that Ace should know, he'd been watching my behind for a week. For a moment, I thought about leaving the diamond there, its yellow brilliance shining among the ripped wager slips and cigarette ends. Then I bent down and picked it up and slipped it back on my finger. The diamond clunked against the bone as I slipped my hand in the pocket of my skirt. Was Clement paying Ace to watch over me or was I collateral in some kind of deal? The thought sent a shiver down me that I fought with a toss of my head.

"If you want to buy me a present," I said to pay him back, "I'd like that horse."

Clement looked at the program in his hand, then at me, his eyes sharp as if I'd surprised him for the first time since we were married. Then he gave a quick, sharp nod and turned his attention to the race, his jaw muscle tight. When his horse won the next race, he hugged and kissed me and slipped a hundred dollars in my pocketbook. "You're my girl," he whispered with a kiss to my ear, while I watched Ace watching us, his face giving away nothing.

EVENTUALLY, I GREW TIRED OF FOLLOWING CLEMENT, EXPOSING MYSELF TO bold stares and remarks outside the clubs he frequented. If I had a pistol, a Colt Peacemaker like my daddy carried as sheriff, I could go anywhere I pleased. Without protection though, I was at the mercy of men like Ace. So I suppered alone and rested or read, trying to distract myself from the obvious: Was Clement lucky at gambling? Was he a good thief? Was he the man to swindle widows out of their fortunes? Could he commit murder without falling apart? I shivered at the thought, but our lives depended on it. I stopped sleeping so well, watching the shadow by the lamppost across the street from the hotel as the red coal of a cigarette flared and extinguished like a clock I could set our future to. I vowed to get a gun and learn to shoot as soon as we went home. My future wasn't going to be run by any old SOB who felt like pushing me around.

JUST PAST THE BATHHOUSES ON CENTRAL AVENUE, THERE WAS A LONG ROW OF casinos that stayed open all night, and were wide open to gentlemen and others. No lady would be seen in them, Clement assured me when I tried to wheedle my way into his company one night. Emmie, the girl who bathed me at the large, luxurious Fordyce Bathhouse, said that there were gambling parlors all over town. Speakeasies, too. The Bridge Street Club, the Southern Club, and Kentucky Club were some of the big ones. Places like the Harlem Chicken Shack and Butler's BBQ had restaurants on the main floor, with gambling and drinking on the second floor. The White Front was a cigar store with a casino on the second floor. According to Emmie, there were also "places of assignation" on the third floor of some of these businesses. I'd stood outside them all, but now I had another distraction—the bleeding was coming back again, unstoppable, exhausting, and it made me stay away from Clement. I stopped the riding lessons, too.

The bathhouses were government regulated in those days, and although there was an assembly room at the Fordyce for men and women to gather and listen to music between bathing treatments, the government had forbidden any but the most sedate tunes to be played on the grand piano. No jazz, even though it was 1931. Too many ill people who might suffer from harsh sounds, Emmie said.

The baths were taken as a curative for wounds that wouldn't heal, arthritis, gout, cancers, any and all ailments. But during my stay I hardly saw any young women my age taking the curative baths, only matrons whose flesh wrinkled and sagged as they released the pains that had brought them there for restoration. Like me they breathed in shallow little sighs as if it might not be safe, and used the water to fill themselves, like sponges plumping, as the hot minerals scaled off the deposits of pain and grief.

And there was always the terrible politeness of the living that exhausted me. The young woman who cared for me, Emmie, with thin, white blond hair and white skin, was generally quiet. She spent her days inside the pools, bathing the maladies from us. Her small hands seemed to know how to move along your limbs, gently lifting and massaging your legs one at a time and helping your arms to circle without disturbing the water. Her skin seemed blue beneath the thin shine of water it wore, like skim milk at night, held in the moonlight. Her washed blue eyes should be elsewhere.

"Go outside," I told her one afternoon. "Get out of here. Don't you have any friends, a boy who comes to call?"

She pulled my shoulders back, letting me lay my head on her narrow chest; she was sixteen. "Mole on the neck, money by the peck," she whispered, and stroked my neck and cheeks. I closed my eyes and felt the luxury of going weightless for a few minutes before the water began to pull me under. We were never a family of swimmers, we were always too full of ourselves, my Methodist mother used to tell Daddy when he tried to teach me to swim. Stay away from water, she warned. My mother never took her clothes off, not even to bathe. She was like a novice in the nunnery, sponging herself in sections while she covered the rest, as if God had condemned our nakedness forever.

Maybe that's why I took Clement, who knew how to take my clothes off. Afterward, I wondered how Mother and Daddy made love, especially after he told her if she laid a hand on me he would leave her, so that I was never spanked after the age of five. That's the reason this happened to you,

Mother told me the day she sent me away to marry Clement, you were spoiled before you were ruined.

"I'll stop the bleeding," Emmie whispered. I felt her rest her fingers lightly on my stomach, probing without hurting, until they seemed to settle on a certain spot and heat it briefly. I opened my eyes as she raised her arms to the ceiling and whispered:

Upon Christ's grave
three roses bloom.
Stop, blood, stop!

Her arms fell lightly as spent petals. "I been a blood-stopper since I was twelve," she said. "It was give me by an old-time healer who was our neighbor. Now, you rest yourself. Don't worry no more." She began to hum a tune in that high thin mountain voice that so soothes. A ripple ran through the muscles of my abdomen and thighs, like a chill maybe, or an unclenching. I closed my eyes again and let my arms go heavy. There was something about Emmie that reminded me of Annie Lark, and it took some effort to let that last disturbing thought go.

THAT FATEFUL DAY, AS I WAITED FOR THE BUS TO TAKE ME TO JACQUES' Landing and Clement a year ago, I thought of my father, who had been gone for three years. The bank failure broke him, the family, and the town all in one stroke. He suffered the brain hemorrhage within six months of laboring to pay back the depositors and died with a dazed look on his long face. But what I remembered best was something I never actually saw— Daddy riding his white horse, a stallion by the time the story came to me, up the steps of the train platform in Coal Camp to meet his bride. As she descended from the train, he scooped her up and held her on the saddle in front of him while he spurred the horse clattering across the wooden planks and leaping off the end of the platform. He was wearing his Stetson and sheriff's badge, and no one dared stop him.

A white horse, my sisters and I breathed, our eyes filled with impossible hope, as we watched Daddy neatly slice his overdone roast into one-inch squares. Mother was a terrible cook, but Daddy never said a word about the meals. A man who would ride a white stallion and sweep a woman off her feet would never complain afterward. What about her luggage? I wondered as I sat there on the wooden bench outside the Skelly station, waiting amid the gas fumes and the curious glances of the men filling up their cars. Did my mother arrive with a single tan and cream striped cardboard suitcase, the way I had? Had that been her suitcase? I knew even then about the things we lost over time. Clement wouldn't ever meet me on horseback. That day, he had his coupe and a marriage license, and it was all I could do to get the smoky grit of the bus ride off my skin before I said I do.

"DO YOU WANT TO SEE SOMETHING?" EMMIE ASKED A FEW DAYS LATER AS WE waited to check into the pools. When I shrugged and pulled the belt tighter around my robe, she slipped out of line and headed down the hall. The bleeding had stopped, so I had to trust her. At the sign to the men's bath hall, she glanced once over her shoulder, and pushed open the staff door. The tiny room was empty except for a couple of pairs of shoes and two piles of clothing on a long red bench. She opened the door at the end of the room a couple of inches and peered out. Then she waved me over and cracked the door open a few more inches.

"Look up," she said.

On the ceiling was a huge domed glass mosaic predominantly in blues and greens that cast a beautiful muted light on the steaming pool below.

"Neptune's Daughter," Emmie whispered. "Eight thousand pieces of glass, brought from St. Louis. And look it there—" She lifted her chin toward a ceramic statue at the other end of the hall.

"De Soto receiving water from a Caddo Indian princess," she said. "It's all tile, too. De Soto came here and bathed when he was looking for his youth." She turned and smiled, her teeth as milky blue as her skin. They'd be gone by the time she was thirty, and she'd be an old woman by the time she was forty. Hill people, my mother used to say, wear out sooner than flat-landers.

Emmie, I wanted to say, you need to drink milk, and de Soto never came to Arkansas. Of course, it would turn out that I was wrong about that. Instead, I said, "They're beautiful," which seemed to satisfy her. Although Emmie was quiet, she sometimes whispered things about herself to me while we were bathing. Often I wasn't certain that I'd heard her correctly, that the words were what they seemed. Yesterday she told me that she and her two sisters and cousin had set a "dumb supper" to see the men they were going to marry, and the phantom men had appeared. All except hers.

"And I stirred the cornmeal and salt without a sound, like I was supposed to." Her voice cracked. "And the wind came blowing up, too, the whole time it was baking. Blew out the candles and the others recognized their men right away the minute they set down at their place."

She was getting agitated. "Maybe it doesn't mean anything," I said.

"No," she said, "it means I won't marry."

I watched her make swirling motions in the water with her fingertips.

"Least I didn't see a black figure with no features on its face—" She looked at me and bit her lower lip. Last week I had told her about my baby. "I'm sorry," she said.

"Maybe you can use your healing powers to find a husband."

She shook her head. "You don't understand," she said.

She was one of those Ozarks people with stones and bits of hair sewn in the hems of their clothes, their world so fraught with danger and mystery they could hardly take a step without some protection. I'd found little bits of weed and bark tucked in the pockets of my clothes, herbs in the toes of my shoes. We have so little that isn't too fragile to bear our living.

After we bathed, Emmie rubbed my stomach with sweet oil and tied a piece of red yarn around my waist.

"Don't take this off till tomorrow," she said.

IT WAS JUST AFTER MAY DAY WHEN A YOUNG WOMAN MY AGE CAME TO BATHE. She had short, straight black hair and very dark brown eyes, and her skin tone was all over dusky rose against her white suit. Of course, the baths were for whites only, the coloreds had their own facility elsewhere, so she must be from Italy or Spain, I concluded. She waded along the edge of the pool until she stood only a few feet away from where I was waiting for Emmie to come for our session.

"I'm Caitlin," she said, "from St. Louis." She spoke confidently, without the hesitation I felt being a stranger.

Then she pulled up the top of her bathing suit, which didn't cover as much as it might, and said, "You're Hedie Ducharme, aren't you?"

Looking around as if she were standing in the midst of a large party of friends, she smiled at the blue tiled walls, the other bathers sitting with their legs in the water or standing immersed to their necks, waiting with blank expressions on their faces. I followed her gaze, noticing the black mold etching the grout between the bottom tiles. Then, in the doorway of the women's dressing room, I saw the man called Ace who had been following me. He was leaning back smoking, despite the signs strictly forbidding it. Although a few employees looked up, no one made a move to confront him. Okay, I reasoned, all right.

"What business is it of yours?" I brushed a strand of wet hair off my forehead. She hadn't even gotten hers wet. Her eyes followed the yellow diamond on my finger, the other fingers clenched to keep it from falling into the pool.

"I met your husband at the casino the other night," she said. "He loaned me his jacket when I got cold."

I watched her wide red mouth, the little half-moon scar on her chin, and refused her words. She had small even teeth that seemed whiter than anything in the room, even her suit.

"This must have fallen out of his pocket—" She reached into the top of her suit and pulled out the cat's-eye ring I'd bought him as a wedding present. He didn't wear rings, he told me, but he'd put it on to please me when we dressed up. She held the ring in her outstretched palm, offering it back.

She was a pretty girl, just that blemish on her chin, and eyes a little too wide set, but she made up for it by keeping her bangs long and heavy and slightly dipped in the middle of her forehead. Her heart-shaped face was arresting, in fact, surrounded by the thick black hair. I tried to imagine the ring in his pocket. I glanced down at her wrist to see if she was wearing his gold Hamilton watch too.

"Doesn't it fit?" I asked, keeping my body perfectly still. Don't move, I thought, don't you do what you're going to do. Out of the corner of my eye, I caught a glimpse of Emmie stepping into the water, sliding toward us. Stay away, I warned her with a glance. Don't come over here.

Caitlin smiled and tried to slide the cat's-eye on her ring finger, but it was too small to go farther than to the second knuckle. She had a full figure, big hands, long fingers with long oval nails painted dark glossy red, and the ring didn't fit.

The warm spring water around me seemed to cling and pull at my waist as I turned and lifted one foot, then the next, carefully, up the stone steps. You must be extra careful when everything is an accident. Emmie opened her mouth, but I shook my head.

"What should I do with it?" the woman called after me, and her laugh echoed off the tile walls loudly enough to make everyone look at us. Just before I made it to the doorway, I heard something ping on the wall next to me and clatter across the floor. I didn't have to look to know it was the ring, a small cheap thing I had spent my last dollars on. Although my shoulders ached with wanting to reach for it, I left it there, to the clatter of Ace's laughter joining in. I didn't want to believe that Clement was sleeping with her, but I did believe that she was trying to provoke me into something— maybe leaving Clement so she would have a free field. I had no intention of doing that. My daddy taught me to fight for what I wanted.

"I need you to head home," Clement said a few hours later. "I'm almost done here. I'll be there by the weekend, Monday at the latest." He finished fastening his cuff link and reached a shaking hand into the top dresser drawer, pulled out an envelope and held it out to me, his hands ringless. *Where's your ring?* I wanted to ask. *Where's the goddamn ring, dear?*

"Listen, something happened today," I said. "This man and woman—"

"Here's a train ticket." He waved my words aside with the envelope. "Just tell the conductor you need to get off at Jacques' Landing and then you telephone Monte Jean to get Roe to come and pick you up soon as he's done with chores. Just telephone. Okay, darlin'?" I took the envelope and he held me tight until the tension eased from my shoulders, although I felt a slight tremor in his body as he released me.

He adjusted the black bow tie at his neck, and brushed at the long black sleeves of his new tuxedo with the habit of a cotton farmer who has to check for lint all fall long.

"This Caitlin, do you know her? And that man who's been following me—" I stopped and pulled his arm so he faced me.

"Honey, that's why I need you to go home, to be safe. Quit asking questions and start packing." His red hair darkened with oil, his light brown eyes sharp and shiny as a fox's, his thin lips curved up in a smile—he was a handsome man. I didn't know whether to stay or go.

"You don't even want to know what happened?" I sat down on the bed.

"Look, I've tried to tell you, this isn't a place for nice women. And now you're making it dangerous for me. I can't pay attention to you every minute and hold my business together at the same time."

"So you hired this Ace?"

He sleeked his hair back and sighed. "I would have told you that. No, he's one of the reasons you need to leave. Can I make it any clearer?"

"What are you doing here, Clement? Tell me, I can help." I stretched a hand out to him and he took it, playing with my fingers and twisting the yellow diamond ring around as if he were considering asking for it back, to gamble with, I imagined.

He bent down and kissed my forehead, leaving a wet place that stung. "I'm trying to make enough money to keep us going, Hedie. We're not a bunch of hillbillies or tramps, we don't pawn our jewelry to pay the bills. You have to trust me." He held both my hands up and looked deeply into my eyes.

"Can you do that for me, honey?"

I nodded, afraid to open my mouth lest I shout out, No! He picked up his money and key, looked at me for a long moment, and nodded.

"You look a lot better, Hedie. Now don't go moping around the house till I get back, you hear? Go shopping. You'll need to buy some things when you get back. There's a surprise for you." Then he added, "I just wish I could be there when you see it."

"Don't be gone too long," I said.

"Oh sweetheart," he began, but a shadow came over his face and he said, "In the back of the closet in our room, there's a loaded shotgun. Keep it by the front door during the day, and sleep with it in bed at night." He stopped and looked at his hands, turning them over as if he were inspecting them before dinner. "You can pull the trigger, can't you?" And without waiting for my reply, "Hold the stock tight against your shoulder, damn thing kicks like a bucket calf." He glanced at me again, and scrubbed his face with his hands. "Hell, this is a mess, isn't it? I should be teaching you, not telling you. Soon as I get back we'll practice with targets and I'll get you your own gun. Something to look forward to, isn't it? Annie Oakley."

I laugh. "Ma Barker maybe."

"Don't let anyone in the house, Hedie, and don't talk to strangers, and—"

I stood up and kissed his lips, tapping his teeth with the tip of my tongue. "Honey, Clement, everybody there is a stranger to me. Just relax, I took the bus halfway across the state to marry you, I bet I can stay safe until you get home. Now let me get some sleep." I patted his shoulders, picked a thread off, and waved him toward the door. Despite the trouble, I was looking forward to being on my own and figuring out how I was going to help Clement.

I woke up early the next morning to the empty room and hurried to dress and pack the suitcases I would take with me and the trunk he would send after me. If only Mother could see the good calfskin case, the shiny brass latches, the coy holders for my toiletries.

When I went back to the baths to say goodbye to Emmie, she pressed a pewter button into my hand. It was the Confederate States uniform button, a six-petaled flower in the center of a crisscrossed ribbon design.

"Put that on a charm string round your neck," she said. "And wear the red yarn round your waist until the snakes crawl."

I gave her twenty dollars, thought better of it, and added another twenty I'd taken off the dresser before I left that morning. She acted like it was a fortune.

"And don't forget the squawroot or smartweed tea if that problem comes back," she called after me. Out of the corner of my eye I saw the matron hustling over to chide her for being noisy. Some people enjoyed making you feel like you were just a wasp under a jar in the sun, slowly frying in the heat.

14

*I*T WAS CAT, THE BLACK HORSE CLEMENT GAVE ME AS A SURPRISE, WHO taught me the land as I waited for Clement to come home. The horse was still racy, so I had to take my time letting him down, walking for miles in the afternoon heat. At first he pulled so hard, my arms ached with holding against him to keep from toppling over his head. Then, he'd settle down, first to a jigging walk, finally a flat-footed plodding that ate up the miles, as if he were determined to walk his way back to Arkansas if he couldn't run. I talked to him the whole time, humming songs, repeating conversations I had in my head with the woman who had confronted me in Hot Springs—Caitlin with the cat's-eye ring. I'd grown to hate those colors of brown and yellow, which I'd loved before because they so went with his hair. I told her how much I would hurt her for trying to come between Clement and me. Sometimes I yelled out loud at Clement for missing a telephone call to me two days in a row, for sending me presents like the new bridle and the short whip with the engraved silver handle instead. I wanted him home, safe, but even as I thought of going back to Hot Springs on my own to get my husband, Daddy's voice kept counseling me to be patient.

CLEMENT DIDN'T COME HOME UNTIL THE MIDDLE OF JUNE, AND WHEN HE DID arrive, he was thin and sickly, and slept between meals for a week straight before he got up and began to tend the farm again.

That first morning he came down to breakfast instead of having it brought up to him, I made sure to serve him myself, to kiss him and hold his hand as he ate. He glanced up from the biscuits and gravy with grateful eyes and a wan smile. My poor man, I wanted to say, but held my tongue. In his travel case were three thick stacks of bills, and I could only imagine what they had cost him.

"Let's have Roe keep working the apple orchard, the cattle, the second cutting of hay, supervise tilling the corn and chopping weeds out of the cotton," he said as soon as he laid down his fork. He patted his mouth with his napkin, carefully refolded it, and placed it beside the plate.

"Monte Jean and I can share the housework, and she's teaching me to cook, Clement." I was proud of the biscuits he'd just enjoyed, and I could cook eggs four different ways, bake muffins, churn butter, and skim just enough cream so the milk wasn't too blue and watery. I wanted to be a good wife.

He stared into his coffee cup a moment before bringing it to his lips. "Cream's good. That brown cow must've freshened."

I nodded. "It's a sweet little heifer, just like her mama. You need anything else?"

One side of his mouth lifted in a devilish smile and he pulled me over to his lap. We kissed there for a minute before Monte Jean made a big show of noise coming into the kitchen, and I jumped off.

"I'll catch you later, little girl," he said. "Meantime, why don't we go out and take a driving lesson. Got something to show you yonder."

NOBODY HAD DRIVEN HIS COUPE SINCE HE'D BEEN GONE, AND WE HAD TO BRUSH the dust off the windshield with a rag before we drove it out of the barn. I was curious about the leather satchel he had dropped in the back. He drove slowly down the rutted track between the fields and pastures until we were out by the big sand boil in the farthest field, the house distant enough to look small.

"What're we doing?" I asked.

"First things first," he said, and I got nervous because he had such a serious expression on his face. "You never thanked me properly."

"What do you mean?" I asked.

"Why, look at yourself!"

I glanced down at my dungarees. "I'll change as soon as—"

"No, you're beautiful—healthy—and that horse is the reason. Don't you remember who gave him to you?" He laughed.

I punched his arm and he grabbed me and we kissed for a while, until it seemed that we'd have to get out and make love in the field and we stopped.

"My Lord, I missed you," he gasped as we straightened our clothing.

"I was just here waiting," I reminded him.

He touched my cheek with his fingertips. "I had this thing come up and the money was too good. Did you see what I brought home? Fifty thousand dollars, Hedie, imagine what that will do for the farm!" His excitement faded into thoughtfulness, however. He glanced in the rearview mirror. "Let's get out," he said.

The satchel held several revolvers, small and lethal looking. At the edge of the sand boil, Clement set up some rocks and a nearly empty whiskey bottle he found in the trunk of his car and began to show me how to aim and fire accurately. We practiced until my arm was shaking and my ears were ringing.

"That's enough, honey." He took the gun, careful of the hot barrel. "You did pretty good." His eyes reflected a new admiration which made me almost light-headed.

"I can go with you, Clement. I can help, can't I?" I put my arms around his neck and kissed his cheek, but he stepped back with a frown.

"What're you talking about?"

"You know . . ." I could hear my voice growing weak.

He folded his arms and looked at the ground, scuffed his shoe across the sandy waste at the boil rim. "Sweetheart, I couldn't stand anything happening to you. These are dangerous people I work for. Women can be hurt in ways a man . . . well a man is different, don't you see?" His voice was pleading with me to understand, and I had to step toward it. When I nodded reluctantly, he brightened. "I tell you what you can do, you can help me figure out a way to expand the farm here. We have the money now. What should we do with it?"

Since I'd started riding Cat, I had been dreaming of building a stable filled with horses, but I decided to wait a few days for us to talk more. I couldn't bear him laughing at me, so I just stepped to his side and walked back to the car with him, resting my head on his shoulder, certain that he would come to see how much help I could be.

"Get behind the wheel," he said with a wink.

"I don't know how to drive," I protested.

"No time like the present," he said, walking around to the passenger door and climbing in.

He showed me how to operate the clutch and shift into gear and steer without jerking the wheel so we stopped swerving from side to side. When we reached the farmyard, he directed me down the drive to the road toward town.

"I'm not dressed," I wailed.

"You're beautiful, even with a dirty face," he said, and I almost put us in the ditch trying to slap his arm.

In town we went to the car dealer and he bought a big black four-door Packard. When the salesman asked if we wanted to sell the coupe, he smiled and said no, it was his wife's car. It was almost better than getting a horse, I decided. Now I had four legs and four wheels—no one could stop me now.

But too soon the telephone began to ring at night again, ringing and ringing in the dark hallway. I'd wake to feel him climbing out of bed and hear him walking quickly down the hall, then the abrupt cessation of the ringing, replaced by the low murmur of his voice. Almost always, he would return to his room, dress, and leave, his Packard driving away slowly, without headlights, so I wouldn't be disturbed. But I was. I was watching the whole time, standing in the shadow of the balcony, hugging myself.

"Who is it?" I asked out loud. "He never asks, so it must be somebody local. Maybe that bunch at Reelfoot Lake I heard Monte Jean and Roe talking about. Maybe I can follow him some night now that I have a car." Those nights when the fog rose up from the river, I heard voices whispering their stories, stood at the window to catch a glimpse of the ghostly woman in blue limping along the edge of the road.

The next day I was out riding again while Clement worked in the barn with Roe, repairing the hay mower. I had on my bathing suit so when I was far enough from the house, I could take my shirt off and feel the sun sting my shoulders and back.

"He's a finicky man," Monte Jean remarked this morning as she watched me make a pot of coffee for him, then add the thick cream to the china pitcher and get out the good sugar bowl and fill it with cubes.

"You'll spoil him," she warned with a squint of her eyes, as if she could see nothing but bad down the road ahead of me. Monte Jean was tall, tall as a man, over six feet, and although her body was thick limbed, she moved with a quiet grace. Unlike me, she never bumped into furniture or let things slip from her hands. And she could hypnotize a chicken so it lay motionless on the chopping block before the raised hatchet. Her hands had that kind of power, thick yellowed nails she never trimmed.

I didn't want to explain how I was trying to keep my husband, so I smiled and shrugged and she thought I was young and foolish.

I watched her cleave thick slices of bacon from a slab, and throw them in the big iron skillet heating on the stove. Her wrists were twice the size of mine, and she wore a cheap man's watch strapped so tight the flesh pinched around it.

"Tell me about Reelfoot Lake," I began. "What goes on over there?"

She glanced at me quickly, then turned her attention back to the bacon, which she began stabbing and moving around in the boiling fat with a long-handled fork.

"I can't figure out—"

"You don't need to figure anything out." She flipped a piece and leaned back when it popped loudly, spattering hot grease. "Best stay out of that Reelfoot Lake business, honey." She stared hard at the frying pan without blinking. "Best not to get involved with it."

"What business?" I asked.

She lifted the fork in the air, opened her mouth to say something, then stopped.

"You make his toast yet? Eggs are done, soon as this bacon finishes."

Even after nights he was gone, Clement got up for breakfast, clean-shaven, face shiny red, hair slicked back, wearing a clean white shirt. Monte Jean was showing me how to run his shirts through the mangle iron so they came out stiff enough to stand on their own. No matter whether he was working the farm or driving to town, he started every morning in a clean white shirt and a pair of pressed brown cotton trousers. He was the kind of man who never got mussed, and I admired him for that.

When I met him in Resurrection, he was traveling on business, he said, stopping to see someone about a contract. He'd stayed a week in the Rains Hotel, taking every meal in the little dining room where I waited tables after school and on weekends to help my family. I could eat for free too, and that saved another mouth to feed, stretching our few dollars further. When

Daddy had his stroke, I was in college in Warrensburg, and was called home, never to go back. I left a trunk of books and clothes, and the silly little things that accumulate in a girl's life, but we could never afford to have it sent. Then Daddy died, and I took a job teaching in a country school in the hills south of town, and gave every penny to my mother, twenty-five dollars a month. My sisters were waiting to get married, so they worked in town where they could be seen and courted by the local boys. Clement was a surprise to them all—a man who courted, seduced, and had me promised in marriage in a week.

I was seventeen, and the oldest boy in the hill school was the same, having been held back for three years in a row. He had already trapped me in the cloakroom once, and waited every day after school to see if he could try again. I couldn't complain for fear of being fired. I'd lied about my age, you see.

"You're mine," the boy had declared as he held my shoulders against the raw pine wall. It wasn't until Clement said those words that I truly felt their power.

"Do your homework, Orvil," I told the boy as I pushed away from him.

It was love at second sight, as my granny would say, the kind of love you feel coming down on you like a train, and you daren't step out of the way, though you can feel it has your future happiness and unhappiness all on board. Women in our family know the men who will break their hearts and we marry them, she said. I didn't pay heed to anything she had to say.

When I had asked Monte Jean, she said, "You want to keep a dog at home, you bury some of its hair by the front gate or under the steps." She shook her head. "Doesn't work quite as well on men."

Cat and I walked along the river for a while, the horse slowing enough to dip his head and grab at clumps of dandelions by the road. Pretty soon he got more ambitious, shouldering his way into the brush, and the dust on the long sumac leaves shook down like flour when he nudged them, coating his face. He snorted loudly. Then we both froze at the next sound—a warning rattle that made me afraid to turn my head and look down.

"Jist stand still, he doesn't want trouble," a man's voice drawled.

"Are you going to kill him or wait till he dies of old age?" I tried to see where the voice had come from, but the brush was thick right there. I couldn't even see the snake.

"Here, brother, now you jus' come on out a there and leave folks alone," the voice coaxed. There was a slight rustle and then the air seemed clearer, empty, and I knew the snake was gone. Cat blew again and stamped his foot. I patted the sweaty neck and turned him back onto the road, forgetting to duck as we swept under a small cottonwood limb that raked against my face. The corner of my eye stung and watered where the tip of a leaf had caught it, and my cheek burned where it'd been scratched. I picked a couple of round leaves out of my hair and rubbed them together for the green scent.

"Sir?" I called, hoping the man would come out and be thanked.

"Yes ma'am." A Negro man in a pale yellow straw fedora stepped onto the road, a heavy, wet burlap bag hanging from his hand.

"That's not the snake, is it?" I nodded at the bag that twitched and shivered.

He didn't answer at first, just looked along the road ahead of us, then back behind us, then finally at me and smiled. "Catfish. Big mess a catfish." Then he smiled and a beautiful set of white teeth gleamed against purple-pink lips and his round, acorn-colored face.

My mother had taught us to be polite with Negroes, but never to be friendly, and my thoughts flashed to Clement as I said "Hedie Rails Ducharme" and held out a hand he had to step closer and reach up to take. He didn't even hesitate. His large hand wrapped around mine was so thick with calluses the skin felt brittle and hard as a june-bug shell. His fingers were well shaped and strong, the nails clean pink ovals. He wore a faded red and blue plaid flannel shirt washed so thin it followed the shape of his long muscled arms and shoulders. I was staring, and he cleared his throat and eased his hand out of mine.

"Jesse Gatto," he said, his eyebrows lifting with a question. His skin was smooth and shiny, like the surface of a deep-hearted flower petal or a black-bird wing that gleamed wet when the sun struck it. His small ears, beneath the fedora, folded tightly against his skull. He shifted the burlap bag on his shoulder and looked up the road again.

"Thanks for driving off the snake," I said.

"He didn't want trouble."

Cat blew hard through his nose and stretched his neck toward the man. Jesse let him nibble at the pockets of his overalls for a moment while he rubbed the nose and stroked the horse's ears.

"Thinks well of himself, doesn't he?" He laughed when the horse pulled a red and black handkerchief from his pocket.

"He's still learning to live in the world." I patted the sweaty neck and rubbed my palm full of wet hair on his mane.

"He the horse Mr. Clement bought in Hot Springs?"

"He's the one."

Jesse nodded, then flipped the horse's upper lip over, staring at the tattooed numbers there. "Uh-huh."

"What?" I picked up the reins and tightened my legs. The horse lifted his head and turned to look at me, then started to chew on the toe of my boot.

"No ma'am, he's a fine lookin' animal. Just fine." He paused and looked up the road a third time, lifted his hat and adjusted the brim, and gave the burlap bag a jiggle.

"Best get these fellas home." Then he looked at me, his eyes crinkling into a smile. "You like catfish?"

"I don't think he'll let me carry anything yet, still pretty skittish." I lifted my chin toward the horse's head.

Jesse tilted his head up the hill. "You never tasted anything as good as fried catfish and hush puppies my wife makes." He turned and started up the hill, calling over his shoulder, "Y'all coming?"

Cat started of his own accord, and I let him go.

The tiny house sat in back of a stand of stunted pines in the shade of a small grove of black walnut trees. As we approached, the screen door flapped open and a girl just a little younger than me stopped and leaned a hip against the railing of the porch, arms and legs crossed, scowling. She was so pretty and proud of it, you could see the kind of trouble she was. Her carefully waved hair pinned flat, her small hips and tiny waist sheathed in a soft yellow rayon dress that flared into a ruffle at the bottom and showed a hint of cleavage in the narrow, sleeveless vee of the top. It was a dress meant for an older woman, a woman who had been in the world, a woman who knew how to walk in high heels and sway her hips. The girl had painted on bright red lipstick and had darkened around her dark doe eyes, and as her father neared, she pouted for all her trouble.

"What's this?" Jesse dropped the sack and mounted the two steps in one stride. Taking her chin between his thumb and forefinger, he pulled down to stare at the lipstick. Her yellow-brown face darkened until it was the color of mahogany.

"I told her she wasn't going out with that fast boy," a woman's voice called from the dark interior of the house. "But there she is, all dressed up."

"What boy is that?" Jesse looked at the girl.

"Who's that?" The girl lifted her chin in my direction, her eyes cool, her voice flat.

Jesse stared at her a moment longer, then took his hat off and introduced us.

The girl, a daughter named India, mumbled hello and turned her attention back to her father. "He's not fast, Papa, he has a car and Mama says any boy his age with a car can't be up to good, but please, can't I go? All the girls are going and it's at the New Hope Bible Church and I never get to go anywhere at all living out here all alone. Please?"

Despite the yellow dress, India leaned against her father's chest and threw her arms around his neck, knocking his hat off and kissing his cheek. He laughed and lifted her away.

"Vishti?" he called toward the screen door.

"I knew it. You've let that child have her way again. First the dress, now the social dancing. You recall what comes next, don't you?"

Jesse looked sternly at his daughter. "No drinking. That boy has a bottle, you come home, hear? That boy drives fast, you come home. That boy, well, he better have you in this house before midnight."

"Thank you, Papa." She leaned over and kissed his cheek again, her eyes full of victory she was trying to keep from showing him.

"And get in the house now. No decent girl waits on the porch for a boy."

"He's afraid to bring his car down to the house on our path. I told him I'd come when he honked from the road, Papa, he'll think I'm not coming if I don't—" Her eyes teared up and she pouted again.

Jesse sighed heavily and leaned down for the sack, which had fallen open to reveal the thick muddy bodies of gasping fish.

"Next time that boy comes to the door proper, you hear?" He waved her off when she tried to kiss him again. She looked around him toward the road, unfazed by any of the exchange.

Then he remembered me. "Bring that ol' fella on back here, Miz Ducharme, he can keep my mules company for a spell. Do him good."

I made a decision then, I could feel it as making a decision, because I knew that Clement might not approve of my choice of friends, I knew that my mother would roll her eyes and say that I was taking up with low elements. I knew that even Monte Jean would tell me to stay home and mind my own business, but I was so darn lonely by then, it was all I could do not to run up the back steps of that house and burst into the kitchen and take my place at the table ahead of anyone. And I guess Vishti had to like me, she didn't have any choice, once I helped chop the heads off and gut the fish with Jesse, my hands dripping bloody red when I carried the fish into the house in a dishpan, the dogs in the barnyard fighting over the entrails. Soon as I washed up, I put my new cooking skills to work and made biscuits under the skeptical eye of Vishti, while she rolled the fish in cornmeal and made hush puppies to fry with it.

It was suppertime when I got home and turned Cat loose in his stall with grain and hay. Since I was late, I wasn't going to bother brushing him down. I was just checking the water level in his bucket when hands grabbed my face from behind—lavender and lily—

"Clement!" I laughed and turned my head to meet his lips. We kissed hungrily, and then my hands were undoing his belt and his were unbuttoning my blouse. We stepped out of our pants together, and he pressed me into the empty stall across the aisle and pulled my swimsuit top down, kissing, and I reached for him and it sprang free and he pulled my panties off and we did it there, standing up, my legs wrapped around his thighs. Oh, we wanted each other so much, it was like two starving people finding a cake.

"I've missed you," I whispered.

"I'm going to make it worth the wait," he panted and pushed himself deeper so it felt like he was buried inside me and I curled around him and rode out the bucking explosion that followed.

"You're even better now," he gasped. "So strong." His legs were quivering from holding us both up, but I didn't want to part yet.

"It's all the riding I do now," I said, stroking his hair smooth and taking his earlobe in my teeth.

"I've been waiting for you," he said.

"I'm right here," I whispered and we sank into the deep straw.

"Monte Jean's supper will be cold," he said.

"I like it cold." I kissed his chest, working my way down his hard round little belly . . .

CLEMENT HAD RETURNED IN EVERY SENSE OF THE WORD, AND WE WERE ONCE again planning our future family, although I wasn't getting pregnant as easily as I had the first time. We spent the evenings he was home talking through our farm improvements, planning to have the house and barns painted in August. I'd been reading the farm's bloodstock book and was tracking down original lines. Cat was a descendant of one of the farm's mares, and when I explained it to Clement, he grew as excited as I was. For a week we spent evenings on the porch, listening to big band music on the radio, my legs resting on his lap in the wide swing hung by chains from the ceiling, while we planned a return to the days of raising champion race-horses. And the telephone never rang.

That was when I began to tell him some of the Ducharme family history I'd discovered, but he was only interested in the parts about Jacques. "If we found the old pirate's hoard, we could buy the land on either side of us to the river. We'd never have to hear or see another person then." It was those words that made me understand why I was keeping my visit with the Gattos secret. Clement was living for the day when he would finally have the means to separate himself from the rest of the world. He'd be just as happy living as a hermit. I wasn't that way, however.

IT WAS EARLY OCTOBER, THE CROPS WERE DOWN, APPLES PICKED, CIDER SET, canning done. The new stable gleamed with whitewash, and I had already filled half the stalls with foundation stock. Clement was so pleased he bought me my own horse van with the Ducharme Farms name painted in gold and red on the green paint of the doors. It had a four-stall box with a ramp I could let down for loading horses. He let me order matching blankets and fine leather halters with brass nameplates, and all manner of buckets and equipment for the new enterprise.

He must have thought he'd already found Jacques' fortune. I came so close to saying something, but didn't want to disturb the good feelings between us, so I kept quiet, and he beamed with pride the day the big truck drove up the driveway, swung around, and unloaded two mares whose sire had come in second in the Kentucky Derby. And when they unloaded the Preakness horse, an aged bay stallion, Clement actually clapped his hands and hugged me as if I had made all his dreams come true instead of the opposite.

Every evening after supper, we'd walk down the brick aisle of the stable and give apples to our horses. Clement's face shone with excitement, his thin mouth constantly smiling, his small features like those of a boy at the circus. He carried his shoulders up, his chest pushed out, a smaller, more compact version of his powerful forebear. When the Preakness horse brushed a green smear on his white shirt, I held my breath, but he only laughed and handed the stallion an extra apple.

Nodding at the clean-swept aisle, the nearly dustless air, he said,

"You're just like me, Hedie. You like things neat. An operation like this could pay for itself, bring in people with real money—the kind of people Uncle Keaton knows."

"I could use more help." I brushed the stallion's sleek neck.

He frowned, and I thought I'd gone too far. I already had a man to clean stalls and feed.

"Training and handling. We have to break out the yearlings I bought next spring," I hurriedly explained. And it would really help if we built a training track, I wanted to add.

He bent down and picked up a piece of slobbered apple and held it out again. The old horse did his part, blowing on Clement's neck, then slicking his palm as the apple disappeared.

"Have anybody in mind?" he asked. The horse returned to licking his hand, moving to include his wrist, which seemed to charm Clement. He's doing it for the salt on your skin, I could've said.

I took a deep breath instead. "Colored man up the road. Jesse Gatto has some racetrack experience. We could use his wife Vishti's help too. Give Monte Jean time to clean more and Vishti's good with poultry."

He frowned. "You want me to hire *two* people?"

I looked past him to the stallion that was nuzzling the top of Clement's head. The horse sighed and rested his chin on Clement's shoulder, which sealed the deal.

"All right. Okay. I guess we can handle it," he said to the horse. "Have to give us some damn good babies, big fella."

That's how it all began, I guess. Jesse and Vishti agreed to work from six-thirty to one-thirty six days a week, and if there was extra work to do, their daughter India came along and they'd stay longer.

More horses arrived, and Jesse began to teach me how to train them in addition to the other chores. Although Monte Jean was used to running the household, she and Vishti came to an uneasy truce because of India. It took both women to keep her focused on a task long enough to complete it, and both women to discourage her lazy rebellions and desire to run out to complain to her daddy every time she was unhappy. More often than not, they'd find her trying on clothes or jewelry in one of the bedrooms instead of working, which seemed pretty typical for a girl her age, or rather, almost my age. But we were nothing alike, I assumed, nothing.

We had no idea, any of us, that someone else was watching her too.

The first time it happened, I came through the front door and stopped to check the closet under the stairs for gloves and scarves. I could hear Vishti and Monte Jean upstairs quarreling about the best way to clean windows, their voices loud enough to drown out other sounds. Although Vishti was usually quiet and somewhat reserved, Monte Jean had a big, booming way about her that drew Vishti into disagreements that often turned loud. Later the two women would laugh at themselves. I wasn't thinking much about it when I hurried into the kitchen. Clement and India looked like two people who had dropped the best dish on the floor, almost like they had just stepped back from it.

"We have us a right smart girl here," Clement said with one of his little smiles. India's face darkened and she turned and picked up a dishrag and began rubbing the clean counter in wide, lazy circles. Her scarf was off, I noticed, sitting next to the sink. I didn't think anything of it until I stepped around her to fill the coffeepot with water and saw the ruby earrings she was wearing. My hand on the faucet stopped for a moment. They looked familiar—then I shook my head and turned on the water. I glanced at her ears again. The stones were awfully big. Where in the world did India get something that nice? Vishti never wore jewelry, and they certainly couldn't afford to buy such things.

"You know, I think India's too smart to be doing housework," Clement said. I turned just in time to catch the wink he gave the girl. What was he up to now? I was more annoyed than jealous. He was going to ruin all the time we'd devoted lately to keeping India from becoming a problem.

"How about she helps me keep the farm books?" He caught my arm just as I was setting the coffeepot on the stove and steered me into his arms. He nuzzled my neck with his nose, sniffed, and abruptly stepped back, pinching his nostrils between his fingers. "Phew. Someone smells like a horse, dear."

India laughed behind her hand and gave up all pretense at cleaning the counter.

He was embarrassing me to entertain India. How could he? I gestured toward the cabinet in front of her. "Get the can of coffee out."

She stared at me for a moment, her face perfectly blank, as if I'd only mouthed the words instead of speaking out loud. Finally she shifted her hips and turned, moving as slowly as she could to get the coffee, which she set on the counter with a loud thump, as if to say, so there.

She's just a defiant girl, I reminded myself. She thinks of me as another interfering adult like her mother or Monte Jean, even though I'm only two years older than she is. My hand was shaking as I spooned the coffee into the top of the pot.

"So it's settled then." Clement clapped his hands. "She can start right now. I'm behind in the expense records, and I need to keep better track of the men's hours. I haven't even recorded the cotton harvest yet. That tax bill that came last week is somewhere. Have you seen it, Hedie?"

I wasn't happy, but I believed him when he said he needed help. He was running day and night. The man couldn't keep up.

He placed a hand on the small of the girl's back and began leading her through the doorway.

"Don't forget your scarf," I said, receiving India's glare over her shoulder for my trouble—which I confess, I found satisfying.

"Oh she won't be needing that," Clement said.

"Looks like that bay with the white socks is colicking," I said just to worry him. His head jerked around, and he none too gently gave India a push into the hallway.

"What's that mean?"

"Big stomachache, except it's worse than that in horses. They can't throw up, so unless it eases, they can die. We've been walking her for two hours. She keeps trying to lie down and roll, which can twist a gut, then she dies."

"I'm sorry, honey." He came back in and put his arms around me, and I believed him.

Part Two

OMAH DUCHARME AND LAURA BURKE SHUT DUCHARME

. . .

"My soul is a stranger"

15

IT WAS THE KIND OF AUGUST NIGHT WHEN THE HEAT AND RIVER SWIRLED time away, and sleep was impossible because it took all your effort just to keep breathing the thick, damp air. So it was natural when Omah, hearing the noise from the river, got out of bed to stand by the window in Jacques Ducharme's big house on the hill, where she'd moved after her parents had died. She could hear the voices of men and women laughing on a passing paddleboat, followed by the angry shouts of men fighting. The fog that had been drifting in all evening made the sound of laughter or words pitched between distant and muffled or as clear and distinct as if the person were standing in the same room. The fog was treacherous in that fashion, altering distances and shapes. Jacques had warned her not to leave the house when it was foggy at night. She could easily disappear, fall into the river, and nobody would ever find her. She shivered. But it wasn't the voices that had bothered her. A breeze pushed the fog off for a moment and she heard the sound again beneath her window. Startled, she looked down.

In the yellow light the face floating without a body appeared carved and grotesque. She cried out and sprang back.

Then it said her name in a loud, disembodied whisper, "Omah!" She recognized that voice.

One-Armed Jacques Ducharme was rich beyond anyone's notion. Even Omah's father and mother, who had worked loyally for him all their lives, had never calculated his real worth. Although Jacques eventually freed them, they stayed because he had saved them when the boat carrying them to St. Louis had struck a submerged deadfall and broken apart in a storm on the river. When the rest of the cargo of slaves had drowned, and only a few of the horses and cows had made it to land, her mother and father believed Jacques had been sent by the River Mother to save them alone. Jacques had hung on to the couple not only because he was superstitious but, above all, because he understood that they were forever beholden to him. He could find no more loyal servants. Faithful as dogs, Omah had reminded them every chance she got. But she had been a child then, confident in her own set of facts.

Again, "Omah!" She inched toward the window again and looked down. It was the lantern old Jacques was holding that made his bony old face appear so frightening.

"Come down here," he said. She stared at him for a moment, hearing her mother's warnings about men in her head. Jacques was old, so old no one knew how old he was, but she remembered how strong his body was, how he had the strength to lift that granite slab for her parents' graves with only one arm, how he pumped water effortlessly into two large buckets and carried them in his one hand to the house without losing a drop. She couldn't afford to underestimate Jacques, she warned herself as she pulled his dead wife's finely woven yellow cashmere shawl around her shoulders and went downstairs.

A MONTH AGO, WHEN HER MOTHER AND FATHER FELL ILL WITH LUNG congestion within hours of each other, Jacques sent food and medicine, but neither of them could eat or drink without coughing everything back up, and after a few days they were simply too weak to lift their heads, open their mouths, or do more than pant in shallow little gasps. For five whole days, in the middle of July, Omah kept a roaring fire in the cabin to warm and comfort them. As the rain made the air thick and damp, hard to breathe, the heat made her nauseous, and she hadn't been able to sleep or eat while she tried to care for them. When Jacques sent the local doctor, she waited outside until he was done, then threw clods of dirt at his retreating buggy and horse. She was too old to be acting that way, Marie the cook told her.

As soon as the sound of their rattling lungs stopped altogether, a terrible silence overtook the cabin, and woke Omah, who had been dozing upright in the chair next to their bed. She knew her own puny breath was not enough to do battle with that silence. That suddenly, she was as unimportant as a fleck of cotton fiber floating in a dusty shaft of light. Her Yoruba father, who had been destined to wear Obas's great beaded crown as king when his father died, had lost everything when he was captured and shipped to the New World, yet dreamed always of going home to his people. Her mother, one of many of his royal wives, was never to place the crown on his head and stand behind him, warning him not to look within himself, not to risk the blindness that could ensue. Omah, who had no memories of a better life where she was important to anyone except her family, was now nothing, would never be important again to anyone, she realized with sudden clarity. Saying goodbye to her mother and father, she was saying goodbye to herself.

Now she understood what it meant to be truly alone and free in the world. She would have eaten a bucket of river mud to bring them back. As soon as they were gone, she realized that for all her bragging about freedom, she had no idea where to go, what to do. She'd spent her whole life at Jacques' Landing. Where would a sixteen-year-old Negro girl go? What life was there for her out there? She had wailed her grief and fear to the dead bodies, taking up the three chipped porcelain cups decorated with hand-painted roses and smashing them against the hearth. She tore down one of the flimsy lace curtains her mother had been so proud of because they had come from the old man's house. The rotten lace she'd been so terribly ashamed of for the same reason shredded weakly in her hands—why wasn't it stronger? why didn't it resist her?—and she threw handfuls of the yellowed pieces on the floor and stomped them, then pulled down the rest and threw them in the fire.

Jacques came to their cabin, bringing Marie, who helped her prepare the bodies. He and one of his men dug the holes and buried them side by side in the little family cemetery up by the house in the rain that had not stopped falling for two weeks. When he started to erect the rough wooden crosses hewn from cedar and soaked red by the ceaseless rain, she stopped him and asked for a piece of the quarried granite he'd salvaged from a barge run aground seven years before. As a child she'd played among the slabs neatly stacked in the cabin next to theirs, lying full length on their cool grainy surfaces when she was hot. She wasn't even afraid of spiders or snakes there. Nothing seemed to like the granite slabs except her. She remembered how Jacques had hesitated, looking across the road at the brown river, full to its banks, gouts of yellow foam riding the surging waters like sickly blooms, catching on the trunks of flooded trees until the disappearing shore was lined with suds as if a giant had bathed in that basin of muddy water. Then he nodded curtly, his large hook nose white across the bridge, jaw knotted.

She drew the birds with charcoal first, then went to work trying to chisel out their forms. Her mother had told her that birds were the sign of a woman's power, and that she gave them to the man to wear. Obas's crown was figured with clusters of birds. Omah had only half listened to her mother's recollections and warnings, and now it seemed that all she could remember were the black figures floating between the trees, settling on the fence surrounding her mother's little kitchen garden, cocking their dark oily heads curiously at her while she worked. Were the birds a part of Aye, the visible, tangible world of the living, or Orun, the invisible, spiritual realm of her ancestors and of the gods and spirits? Her mother had said the two realms were inseparable, but what did that mean? Old Jacques sometimes cursed his God in French, and kissed the gold medal around his neck after a dangerous river trip, but he never seemed particularly concerned about spiritual matters otherwise. Never attended the Catholic church in the village. How was that belief different from the one her mother and father had? Who were her gods exactly?

It was much harder, nearly impossible she discovered, to neatly cut the outline of the birds and then the names and the year without the hammer slipping and pounding her fingertips, or the chisel gouging her palm, and she soon gave up, vowing that someday she would pay someone who could really cut the stone, rather than merely scratch it as she was doing.

Then one evening, while she was soaking her wounded hands in one of her mother's herbal balms at the table, Jacques came to the door, battered straw hat in hand.

"*Comment ça va?*" he asked. "How's it going?"

She shook her head and held up her gouged hands, the fingertips sliced and tender. He inspected her homemade dress, the only one she'd worn for the past three years. Since she'd sprouted up, it stopped just below her knees, and the bodice pulled so tightly across her bosom that she dared not stretch her arms too far for fear of ripping out the stitches her mother had so lovingly used. Her new dress lay in pieces where her mother had carefully stowed it the night she fell sick, on the shelf next to the door among the few pieces of crockery and two pans. It was a deep yellow, perfectly dyed by her mother, who had successfully resisted Omah's attempts to yank it out of the vat too early. Under his scrutiny, she tucked her elbows against her sides and pressed her knees together.

"Come," he said, "it's not safe here." She watched him take in the windows bare of the ragged lace curtains and the crude bed made of unplaned logs and straw pallet with the thin faded quilt, and suddenly she saw her life as he did.

"This is my house," she said, stretching her arms across the narrow plank table and gripping the edge in case he tried to take it away from her.

"*Naturellement*," he said. "Of course."

He stood there a moment longer, gazing out the door at the separate entrance to the bachelor's ell, which could be seen from there. The men who worked for him—St. Clair, Orin Knight, Frank Boudreau, and Leland Jones—were sitting on the grass, playing stick pig with their knives and drinking. They hadn't been working enough lately.

"It's not safe for a young girl out here, *ma chère*." He glanced at her, then shifted his gaze back to the men.

NOW HERE HE WAS NEEDING HER HELP THIS TIME. AS SOON AS OMAH FOUND him standing outside looking up at her second-story window, he turned, holding the lantern in front of them. A dense cloud of fog flowed over them and he took her hand, leading her toward the river, she thought, but she was disoriented and couldn't be certain. She walked on tiptoes since she was barefoot and couldn't see. They seemed to be walking through grass, then down a little hill where her foot got tangled in bindweed that grabbed like ribbons of snake, and she stumbled and cried out, and felt him pull her arm up, half lifting her out of the ditch, onto the dusty road. The cool dust like flour between her toes as they crossed to the other side, and then she recognized the riverbank by the heavy fishy mud stink and the sloshing of water. A willow whipped her arm and face and she pushed blindly against it.

As soon as the water lapped her toes, Jacques stopped and placed the lantern on the bank at their feet, where it made a small yellow halo of light. His face was a series of dark hollows as he turned to her and released her hand.

"I need a little favor," he said. His dark eyes streaked with yellow from the lantern resembled an animal's in their strangeness.

She shivered, and he reached out and pulled the shawl around her shoulders.

"Yes," she said. It was like being hypnotized, the way her mother had done to chickens before she cut their heads off, stroking the beaks until the eyes drooped.

"Just climb into this little *bateau*, eh, boat." He stepped aside and she could see an old flatboat tied behind him, surging in and out on the current.

"Why?"

"Can you do this for me?" He put his hand on her shoulder and it was as if his entire weight were pressing down on those fragile bones.

"All right."

He led her forward, helping her crawl onto the flatboat while he held it steady, lifting her gown so it didn't trail in the water, and in a moment she was kneeling in the middle of the boat.

"That's good," he kept saying, "that's right. *Doucement*. Gently. That's a good girl."

He lifted the lantern, turning his face into a mask once again, inspecting her while she sat on the rough-hewn planks, the splinters digging into her shins. Was he going to cast her loose out here? Return her to the river where he found her? She shivered and bit her lip to stop from crying out. Was he insane? She saw something scrambling just outside the circle of lantern light, followed by a muffled noise of something heavy entering the water. It wasn't safe out here.

"It might be better if you take off your *habit*," he said softly. "Your nightgown."

"What?" She shaded her eyes as if she could see and understand him better.

"Get out of the clothes now," he said. This time his voice was stern with warning.

She drew the shawl tighter around her shoulders and glared at him.

"*Tranquille*. I'm not gonna hurt you, *ma chère*. I just need a little help here." He lowered the lantern and knelt, pulling the boat close enough that he could touch her arm.

"*Très facile*," he assured her, helping her pull her nightgown over her head. The touch of his rough hand scraping her upper arms and back made her draw away and bend over to hide the rest of her body. He pulled the shawl out of her hands and gathered it with the gown in a ball he flung on the bank behind him.

"When I push you off, the current will take you, and pretty soon a boat comes and you yell, loud. You are lost, afraid. Call for help, that is important, call as if your life depends on it." He held up the end of the coiled rope attached to the boat. "I have the boat in hand, you see, waiting to hear your voice!" She knew that if she didn't do as he instructed, he would let the rope go and she *would* be cast loose on the big, ugly river in the dark, in the fog.

"Nothing is going to happen to you, *chère* Omah. This I promise. Just do this little thing and you will be back in bed long before the moon sets." He smiled to reassure her, but it was more a grimace in the eerie light.

As if on signal, the four hired men holding long poles stepped out of the fog and stood beside Jacques. She shrank down into a ball, trying to cover her nakedness from their dark shiny eyes. The tall thin one called Orin licked his lips and grinned. Leland Jones, the small, sturdy man, lifted his chin at her, as if they were passing in the road. Frank Boudreau watched up-river, head cocked, listening, and St. Clair seemed to look over and beyond her, as if he were as embarrassed as she by the situation. Jacques nodded and the men used the poles to push her boat out. Guiding the boat after the poles had cast her off, St. Clair stepped into the water, following the rope as it fed her out into the current. His face was only a foot from hers in the waist-deep water when he murmured "I'm sorry" and gave a last shove that finally separated her from sight of the shore and the men.

THE FIRST FEW NIGHTS SHE HAD STAYED IN JACQUES' BIG HOUSE, SHE'D BEEN suspicious and locked her door and shoved a chair under the knob, and left a rope by the window just in case, but neither Jacques nor the hired white men who lived in the bachelor's ell ever bothered her. Her mother had told her once that some people mated for life, like geese and swans, and Jacques was one of those. Despite his later wives, it was the first one he would always be married to. He had no interest in a young freed Negro girl, and had apparently warned the others not to go near her.

She had been in Jacques' house only a week after her parents had died when Marie woke her one morning with an armful of dresses. They smelled of cedar and bore deep wrinkles from being stored in a trunk for a long time, and the fit on Omah was loose and comfortable except for being short. When she looked in the carved walnut mirror in the hallway, the dresses stopped well above her ankles, and she felt the nakedness of her bare feet with their chipped toenails and calluses. She wanted to rip the dress off, but

Marie told her no, her old clothes were to be used for house rags now. These were Annie Lark's, Marie whispered solemnly, as if mentioning the dead required secrecy. At first Omah was tempted to leave, steal one of Marie's two dresses and go rather than wear a dead woman's clothes, but again she reconsidered. So she chose three to wear, all in soft colors and cut simply from cotton material. Sometimes when she put her hands in the pockets of a dress, she would find things—a blue jay feather, the seedpod of a lily from the beds beside the house, and once the small pencil drawing of a baby propped in a chair with its eyes closed. She did not remember ever picking up a single one of these objects. At first they frightened her, but before long she placed them on the mantel in her room. Under candlelight their edges seemed to gleam as if they had been touched with gilt paint, and at night she had dreams she was sure belonged to someone else, since she never recognized anyone or any place.

WAITING IN THE FOG, WITH ONLY THE SLAPPING OF WATER ON THE BOTTOM of the boat, other sounds muffled and distorted, she gritted her teeth to keep them from chattering. She made herself think of things she had seen during the day to keep from calling him by name and begging him to bring her back, because she knew he wouldn't. She was tethered like a goat, waiting for a panther.

She could feel the occasional tug of the rope keeping the boat from slipping around and around as a whirlpool caught at its edges. The men were watching her slip into the thick white fog, their eyes disinterested as birds'. Except for the one, St. Clair, whom she had noticed before, quieter, more thoughtful than the others, watching her not as they did, but with another kind of interest in his face.

Naked and cold, she huddled to shield herself, but the fog found her like thousands of tiny smoky hands, fingering her hair, the inside shell of her ear, the back of her neck, the tips of her nipples, the hollow above her buttocks, the sides of her calves, the bottom of her feet, leaving dampness like a malicious kiss. She was shivering so hard she didn't trust herself to shout, to call anything, didn't think she could do it when she heard the heavy pounding of the engine and the deep slosh of water. She waited a minute to make sure, then waited more because she knew now what the men were going to do. Her throat refused to open, she could not open her mouth, even as the sound grew so loud she realized the boat was going to run her down. Then the rope jerked, nearly spilling her into the river, and she shrieked.

"Help me! Help! Help me!"

While she was being jerked backward, she hung on to the sides, screaming. Then a dim light appeared in the fog to her right, followed by the heavy bulk of the boat rising high above her. A man called down, "What's wrong?"

She screamed again. "Over here, I'm over here!" And instinctively reared up so the men on deck could catch a glimpse of her, a beautiful, naked girl, alone on the river.

Still her raft eased back and to the left and the boat followed, men shouting instructions to her, arguing over her rescue and who would claim her, as they drew nearer and nearer to the giant snag Jacques and his men had floated into the river. When it struck, the boat heaved and groaned, stalled and listed amid shouting and cursing.

A few minutes later the fog thinned and rolled away to reveal Jacques and his men paddling close to the boat. Omah realized that she wasn't moving anymore and could see that the rope was safely tethered onshore. She could pull herself back if she wanted. Instead she watched as a hole blew in the hull and the boat began to groan louder and tilt heavily on its side like a wounded man sinking to one knee while the men fought on deck with knives and guns. Then the boat burst into flames with a great roar and men became ragged black figures against the orange-red glow, dancing in terrible frenzy.

Two horses swam by her, the whites of their eyes flashing in the darkness, their breathing stentorian, trumpeting fear as their hooves found bottom a few yards beyond and they used their last strength to clamber up to shore, where they stood shaking, then slowly descended as their legs collapsed beneath them. A crate of chickens floated within reach and she pulled them onto the boat, gasping with the weight of the dead soaked birds, took out the one remaining alive and shoved the crate back in, holding the nearly drowned bird next to the heat of her skin, where it didn't resist, but panted through the slit of its parted beak, eyes drowsy with something beyond fear. Something large and heavy bumped into the raft and began to swirl and lurch against her, threatening to shove her into the brush along the shore. She used her foot to push it off, and when it paused and caught in a small whirlpool, she saw that it was a young white man; his upturned face in the moonlight looked innocent as a child's except for the small dark hole in the middle of his forehead. Arms spread, he floated easily in his new sleep and disappeared.

"Hurry," she heard Jacques shout as the men struggled to lower several trunks to their waiting skiffs.

Suddenly her raft was tilting and she was sliding down into the water—something had hold of her foot. She let the chicken go and screamed just as she went in, taking a mouthful of water as she was pulled down and a large hand sought to hold her there. She fought, but the man had strong arms and she couldn't get to the surface for more than a gasp of air before he had pushed her down again. Finally she let herself be held under, and he relaxed for a moment, just long enough for her to wrap her legs around his head and push herself up. She shot into the night air gulping lungfuls of air while he thrashed below her, held down by her weight and the terrible squeezing of her thighs around his throat. He clawed her legs, but quickly grew too weak to struggle. She waited, holding the edge of the raft to keep from sinking, until she was certain that he was dead. Then she released the body. When she tried to pull herself back onto the raft, she was too exhausted and the flat platform kept tilting too far. By now the river felt warmer than the night air, so she clung to the rope, singing to herself the meaningless African songs her mother had crooned her to sleep with while she waited for Jacques to find her. She had killed her enemy, as the men and women in her mother's stories of old had done, and she felt blessed in the midst of exhaustion.

Once they were all onshore again, the men lugging the heavy trunks away to the back of the house, Jacques wrapped her in a blanket and led her to the kitchen, where he sat her down.

"Tell me," he said, as if he could already see what had happened to her. His face seemed to soften and fill as she related the story of her battle, and when he saw the deep gouges the man's nails had left on her thighs and stomach, he looked away, visibly moved, then poured two glasses of brandy. He saluted her with his glass and drank, new admiration in his eyes. She drank too, feeling the fine hot burn in her skin as she let the blanket slip off her shoulders. He was an old man, she told herself, a very old man.

"Here." He pulled the ivory-handled knife with the large blade, Annie's knife, from his belt and held it out to her, hilt first. Taking it she felt the ancient power in its heft, as if her dormant Yoruba blood awakened at the familiar weapon. She brushed her forefinger against the blade and felt its bite quick as a viper's sting. She laughed and sucked the blood. She wasn't afraid of anything now.

16

I T'S MY TURN," OMAH ANNOUNCED AS SOON AS THE MEN DISPERSED FROM the night's work. They had disposed of the body, quickly dividing the money, clothes, and weapons, and only the horse remained as evidence. In the morning, Boudreau would ferry it across the river and sell it to a family of half-wild men who had settled in Tennessee near the large shallow body of water called Reelfoot Lake, which had been created by the New Madrid earthquake. The men never asked questions and the Confederate military authorities avoided them altogether.

Jacques was trying to pull on the man's high oxblood leather boots, but he couldn't quite force his foot.

"*Merde!*" he cursed, tossing the boot aside.

Omah picked it up and slid her bare foot easily into the leather. "Small feet," she said, tugging the boot up her calf and lifting her leg to admire it.

Jacques brushed the matter aside with his hand. "Take them."

She smiled—not even a trade required! Old Jacques was thinking of something else.

"I'm ready. I can shoot at least as well as Boudreau, and I'm as good as you with a knife."

"Boudreau has trouble hitting the barn from five feet, *ma chère*, and as good as me?" Jacques shook his head and smiled grimly as he tapped a long finger on the dead man's packet of letters, which he had read as soon as they settled at the kitchen table.

"The war is changing things. We must work quickly now if we are to survive." He picked up his large knife and cut a chunk of cheese, then sliced into the fresh bread Marie had left on the table for their return.

"The war will be over soon," Omah scoffed. Taking the cheese he offered on the point of his knife, she nibbled the corner. She'd almost mocked him for being old and afraid, but in the candlelight, he appeared as strong as ever, as if he never aged. Was it true, what the slaves whispered, that Jacques had traded an arm to the devil for immortal life? Not much of a bargain for the devil. Omah smiled and shook her head.

"No, *chère* Omah, this war goes on. Already the Africans make plans for escape, as the Federals draw near. They want the river. Both sides try to control shipping. We could help them, but no one asks."

"Help which side?" she asked.

"This one, that one, both, for that matter." He laughed and picked up the gold ring with the onyx stone they'd plucked from the man's finger.

"Raiders, too, they fight the invaders to save the family, but some are like us—they work for themselves."

Omah paused, listening to the wind picking through the trees, rattling lilac bushes against the windows. Jacques had let the outside of the house grow shabby, wouldn't repair the broken windows and cracked roof shingles, hadn't repainted in years, so the paint peeled in long yellow-white curls. He wanted outsiders to think they were poor, without means. He and Omah had hidden furnishings and gold and jewelry and clothing in several of his secret rooms and in hideaways dug like fruit cellars into the ground of his property. The house was as bare as if the Yankees had already commandeered it, hanged them as traitors, and shipped off their worldly goods.

So far, every move Jacques made kept them ahead of the war. Still . . .

"It's my turn to plan one. You said so yourself after we took that boat from New Orleans. You said if I gave you my share of the wine, I could plan the next raid. That was a year ago!"

Jacques smiled. "You should learn a taste for wine, *ma chère*—the gods' fruit. *Et comme dit un vieux proverbe, 'Plus je bois, mieux je chante.'* The more I drink, the better I sing!"

Omah noticed that he could take on a heavy accent, change his age even, when he chose: one moment a robust man, the next an elderly peasant farmer. He was teaching her his tricks, too.

"Are you taking sides now?" Omah asked.

Jacques snorted. "Only the one that pays best. Now the Yankee captain wants to be paid a bond for each male, even the slaves—*merde!* They are thieves worse than us! You see, we need the new strategy. These letters say the Federals are trying to take the island in the river by New Madrid, the one controlled by rebel cannons, Number Ten."

Omah lifted her brow in question.

He held out the ring and dropped it in front of her, letting it bounce and spin to the worn cypress floor like trash, since he cared only for the precious jewels.

"River traffic will stop, we are without work, do you see?" He lifted a hand to stop her words. "No more like tonight—it will bring the soldiers. No, we must see what the armies need and get it for them, *n'est-ce pas?*"

Omah nodded sleepily. It had been a long night, and what she wanted now was to sleep the day away, dreaming of St. Clair perhaps, or of New Orleans, the way it was before the war, when Jacques had taken her downriver for that brief glimpse of Society while he gathered news of the upriver boats. Let Jacques devise his plans. She had already made one fortune and would make another by the end of the war. She was certain because everything Jacques touched turned golden, despite the fact that he was the most joyless man she'd ever met. He had helped her buy a house and land a few miles away, as well as partnerships in several businesses and rental properties in St. Louis, but he never turned his own money to use. As far as she knew, he simply hoarded everything they stole or salvaged, and acted like a poor man forced to merely endure his days on earth. The only time he seemed truly alive was when they were raiding a boat or robbing a coach or stopping a traveler. Then he was like a man her age, eighteen or twenty, filled with fierce, careless energy as they did battle, putting himself at risk as if he *knew* that he was untouchable—unable to be hurt or killed.

Jacques bent to pick up the ring. Omah yawned and rose.

He stared into the onyx as if divining a vision. Omah chuckled to think what the slaves would say about that; she dismissed their superstitions and wound her way through the empty house to the stairs. No one else shared the main house these days. He'd banished the men and slaves to cabins as soon as the war broke out two years before. He only suffered Omah's presence because she stayed out of his way, followed orders, and had become a vital part of "our craft," as he called it.

She placed her hand on the newel post in preparation for climbing the stairs. As she did, she turned to look out the front windows, then stifled a small cry and staggered backward, stumbling onto the bottom stair.

The woman in blue was peering in the window, staring directly at her. Omah clung to the rail as if the apparition could somehow fling her across the room or draw her through the window . . .

She tried to focus on the face's features, but it was as if the window glass were too heavy, the waves and whorls too frequent, and she could not bring the woman into sharp delineation. After a moment, the figure simply turned away and continued the length of the porch, thumping her cane so loudly, Omah wondered that Jacques did not rush out.

Wide awake, Omah hurried up the stairs, afraid to turn her back on the woman for more than the briefest moment.

Although it was not her first encounter with the woman in blue, something about the figure tonight seemed to portend danger. What was she looking for? Who was she? When Omah had first moved to the house, she'd asked Marie, then Jacques, only to be accused of an overactive imagination, the result of her race. But Omah knew the woman in blue was real, and that she was restless, maybe even angry about something. That night, Omah slept with the oil lamp burning beside her despite the unusual appearance of white moths battering themselves against the hot globe in March.

When she awoke late the next afternoon, the oil had run out, leaving an apron of dusty wings and white furred bodies, as if the lamp itself had fractured.

A COLD, STABBING RAIN FELL AS THEY STOOD BY THE RIVER WITH THE UNION soldiers a week later, waiting for the storm to pass. They could wait no longer. In fact, the storm would probably give the Rebel soldiers on Island Number Ten a false sense of safety tonight, Jacques reassured Omah.

"Come," he said, tired of the argument, "there is money to be made."

There were four skiffs in all, three so full of men and the iron poles they needed that the flatboats were in danger of swamping as soon as they cast off, and they had to row back toward shore to allow three men to jump out of each boat and swim to land before they dared set out.

Jacques, Omah, and four slaves were in the lead skiff, which rode like a leaf in and out of the deep swells. Behind her, Omah could hear the frightened cries of the men as the thunder clapped and lightning slashed the river with brief brightness.

"They'd better keep quiet or the guns will find us," Omah said as loud as she dared into Jacques' ear.

Jacques looked worriedly back at the other skiffs tilting wildly with their burdens in the stormy waters. They'd be lucky just to survive the crossing, let alone accomplish the task, but that wasn't his worry. He needed to get them to the island undetected, past both the sunken boat and the one gunboat, and help them land. He'd be paid then. Jacques had made certain the gold was on board the captain's skiff, just behind them where he could keep his eye on it in case of trouble.

The river was high, full of debris from the spring melt up north and the days of recent rain, which even now flung so hard against Omah's face, it felt like bits of icy gravel. The slaves, four strong men Jacques had bought for the Yankee canal dig, bent their heads and rounded their shoulders to the work. They wore no manacles and were clothed like Omah and Jacques, in the warmest wool pants, shirts, and coats they could find in the hidden room full of barrels and trunks of clothing they'd taken.

Omah pulled at the loose end of the wool scarf flapping wetly in the wind, wrapped it over her hat, and tucked it into her coat. She was dressed in trousers, boots, and a man's fur-lined greatcoat that smelled of wet cedar. When she'd pulled it from a trunk and offered it to Jacques, he'd started to yank it from her hands, then dropped it and shrugged.

"Snag." She grabbed his coat and pointed. He nodded and tapped the nearest rower with the long cane, and the men pulled the oars mightily to swing around the obstacle, looking back to make sure the other skiffs avoided it. They were just in time to witness the last skiff get caught on the edge of a whirlpool, spinning slowly while the oarsmen tried to pull them out; the skiff spun lower and faster until the men simply spilled out, the boat upended, and they all disappeared as the water sealed over.

The other skiffs were quiet after that, paying utmost attention to every wrinkle and swell in the dark water. Omah tried to remember the landmarks they used on this part of the river, but many were underwater, and the rain and wind combined to make it hard to see. She had no idea how Jacques could navigate.

When they finally saw the dark mass of the island barricades, they crouched or lay down so that their boat would look like nothing but more river debris to any observers. As soon as they felt the skiff grind against the shore, Jacques and Omah leapt out and secured the ropes to the logs jutting out to ward off invaders.

In a few minutes, the remaining skiffs landed also.

"The guns are just beyond us." Jacques pointed toward the shore curving away from sight.

"Let's go." The captain waved his men on.

Jacques put his hand on his knife.

The other man turned impatiently. "We lost the other men out there. I need you now. You'll get paid, and handsomely, but afterward. Now hurry before we're discovered." Again the captain waved his men on, and they took off at a trot, slipping and stumbling in the muddy brush.

"*Merde!*" Jacques spat, looked at Omah, then the place where the gold had been, which was empty now. "I am beset by thieves. Come!" He waved the slaves out of the skiff and led them after the soldiers, Omah falling in last. If they were caught—she stopped the thought with a shiver, wishing she'd brought the yellow dog who usually shadowed her on these nights. They were more exposed than ever tonight. Too much, for this was nothing like the easy scheme they'd used to dispatch the river travelers. Here there were soldiers, guarding, ready for them. She wasn't going to hang, she vowed. She'd die fighting.

They reached the cannons to find that the storm had driven the Rebel guards inside, but the captain's men had trouble hammering the spikes home.

"Here," Jacques said, driving a steel pin into a cannon's touchhole and pounding it flush with two strokes, rendering the weapon useless. He went from one cannon to the next, spiking each with the same efficiency. Omah almost laughed at her foolishness. What had she been afraid of? Even the sounds of his hammer blows were swept away by the raging storm. They hurried back to the waiting skiffs without resistance. But Jacques was furious.

When the captain again withheld payment until Jacques saw them safely back across the river, Omah saw him consider slicing the man's throat.

The other soldiers were too miserable, cold, wet, and fearful of the return trip to notice or care.

She laid her hand on his arm. "Later," she whispered, and somehow he heard her despite the storm.

The return was even more harrowing. They fought the current, moving a few feet upriver, only to be swept ten feet back. If the current swept them past the island, they'd be exposed to small arms fire, deadly enough even without the cannons. Finally Omah crawled to sit by the nearest African, placed her hands next to his, and began helping.

Jacques moved to the other side, using his one hand and hissing at his oarsmen, "What will the Johnnies do to you if they catch you?"

At this, the oarsmen dug deeper, and inch by inch the boats moved upriver through the swells with Jacques keeping the captain's skiff and their gold in view. At one point he leaned over to shout over the storm in Omah's ear, "If their boat swamps, take this rope and swim for the gold." She nodded though she had no intention of leaping into the boiling river for a sinking bag of gold. Again the whirlpools opened all around them, threatening to suck them over their edges unless the men fought harder, and the waves grew taller, until the little vessels were sinking out of sight one moment and rising to the tops of the shore trees the next. Several of the soldiers behind them were crying out prayers, and the captain had his hands full keeping them from leaping into the maelstrom. When they finally muscled their way to shore, the Africans, Omah, and Jacques collapsed, their throats raw and their chests heaving painfully. At last they sat up and found that though the captain's skiff was just landing, the others had apparently perished. At first the captain was going to withhold the money, but Jacques' knife convinced him to pay for the service, despite the loss of his men's lives.

"With the cannons on Island Number Ten spiked, the Yankee boats are able to pass through the recently dug canal, avoiding New Madrid, approach from the downriver side, and capture the Island, and New Madrid and our town will have to surrender, see?" Jacques explained to Omah later that night.

She shook her head, restacking the gold coins in rows of three and four.

"Who controls the Mississippi River and the flow of goods, wins the war. Now do you see?"

"The Federals will occupy us?" Omah asked, suddenly alert. "Is that good?"

Jacques laughed. "*Très bien!* They have more gold, *ma chère*, and their paper money is good. It will be a good time for the likes of us. They will win the war and we will do well too."

"What about your Africans?" she asked.

He shrugged. "They will be freed, and I will hire them back and they will do it because they are afraid of me, but they are more afraid of the Yankee soldiers. Such is war, *chère* Omah."

SEVERAL MONTHS LATER OMAH WAS AWAKENED BY THE JINGLING OF HARNESS and the raised voices of men in the yard.

"Jacques." She leapt from bed and squatted below the window.

The yard was filled with Confederate raiders wearing colorful embroidered shirts, which women made for the romantic figures who swooped into farmyards and towns, giving rebel yells and capturing anything of value while they shot Yankee sympathizers and soldiers. Omah saw little Billy Shut on his bay horse among the others and felt a rush of pity. Last year, his mother, Maddie Shut, had dragged him to the camp, demanding he be allowed to join and avenge his father's death. Billy was fifteen at the time. Anderson and Quantrill had agreed only when she produced fifty dollars in gold. At sixteen, Billy wore the sullen expression of a boy trying to be a killer, without much success. Omah was sure that she'd looked tougher than that at sixteen.

A tall, powerfully built man leaned over his gray horse's neck and said something in a low voice.

"You don't run me or mine," Jacques declared and swung his rifle off his arm directly in the man's face. The man straightened slow, hands in the air.

"Jist a neighborly call, Ducharme," the man declared loudly. "We'll be stayin' around here for a spell now. Things heatin' up on the river. Wouldn't want you and me tangling in each other's snares. Billy here"—he jerked his head toward the boy—"says you run this end of the river, so I'm askin' myself how the devil them bluecoats dug through that nigger wool swamp without you helpin' show where and how? Beauregard, McCown, Stewart had 'em all bottled up—then poof!"

Jacques was trying to back slowly toward the porch, but the men had been easing their horses around him.

"The young man is wrong, *monsieur*. I am an old man, a farmer. I know nothing of this Yankee war."

"The Rebels had 'em bottled up pretty tight there on the river till they swung around the whole town and came out below Island Number Ten—attacked from both directions. Now no Yankee, even Pope, is smart enough to dig a boat channel through a swamp, not without some local help, and slaves, I hear."

"*Monsieur*, consider my position, what Yankee would trust a slave-holder? No, you are mistaken."

Omah reached back for her pistol and rifle, kept at the ready beside her bed, watching while the raiders glanced uneasily at the slave quarters and one another. In fact, Jacques had been in charge of all the slave labor used on the channel.

"He's still an old pirate! He probably helped spike them guns, too!" Billy Shut yanked his pistol from his red-sashed waist, but the man next to him quickly bumped his horse into him and pulled the gun out of his hand.

Jacques laughed and shook his head. "Children's stories, eh?"

"He's rich as old King Croesus, I tell you!" Billy said, his horse stamping as if to reinforce his words.

Jacques bowed slightly. "It's true, as you can see." He swept the dilapidated straw hat from his head, indicating his ragged clothes and decaying house. Not so much as a single chicken, pig, cow, or horse occupied the weed-choked pens or fields. Jacques had them all well hidden in woods and sheds, even caves he knew about along the river.

The raiders studied the scene a moment, noting the one scrawny yellow dog slinking along the road to the house, mistaking that, too, as harmless. In fact, he would attack and kill on command, jaws locked to a throat until the end.

"Let's go," one of the men muttered. The leader shrugged and nodded. "I'll be watching, sir," he said with a finger to his hat brim.

Jacques bowed again. "You don't have any food you could spare?"

The men chuckled and turned their horses toward the road, except Billy Shut, who walked his horse to Jacques and said, "I know you did it. I know you sold us out, you old bastard. And I'm coming back for you."

Omah slipped the rifle barrel out the window, knocking the frame. Billy's head snapped up and his glare was so hate filled, Omah drew a quick breath despite her gun.

"Back for you, too, you black bitch!"

As soon as he had galloped away, Omah ran downstairs.

"How did he find out, Jacques?" she panted.

"*Ça ne fait rien.* We have work to do. It is time to earn money with our new information. Both sides must help us through this time of need, *ma chère.* How else will an old man eat?" He cupped a hand to his ear. "Is that chickens I hear?" One of his slaves emerged from the house holding a brace of chickens by their feet, their beaks tied shut.

Later as they sat at the kitchen table tearing the roast chicken apart, Jacques observed, "Children should not play at war. We will help young Mr. Shut with his mouth if he does not learn to keep quiet."

JACQUES WAITED, SOMETHING HE WAS GOOD AT, OMAH OBSERVED. IT WAS EARLY fall when they heard of the pending nuptials between the captain and Billy Shut's sister, Emma. Word from town was that the Yankees so infuriated the population with their fines and levies and seizures, none of the churches would marry them; the Methodist, Catholic, and Church of Jesus all locked their doors against the sacrilege. Jacques' face wore a sly smile when he heard that the judge was going to perform the ceremony.

That night he sent Omah north to Boonville, where the raiders were supposedly hiding with a family of sympathizers.

"Tell Billy Shut his sister's marrying a bluecoat officer in three days. He'll just have time if he rides like the wind."

At first she thought not to deliver the message, but to tell Jacques she couldn't find Billy Shut. Then she remembered the boy's threats to them and knew the old man was right. He always kept them safe.

As a Negro woman she could pass through the Yankee blockades and patrols with a little acting where a man would be taken prisoner or shot as a guerrilla. The only danger was that she would be taken prisoner and forced to work for the invading soldiers as a slave.

As soon as she delivered her message she took off at a dead gallop. Omah knew she'd better hurry if she was to witness what followed. Billy, meanwhile, was delayed as the other men tried to talk him out of returning home, tried to convince him that it was a trap. Eventually, he ignored the pleas, saddled his horse, and tore off at a gallop.

When the boy charged into town with his loaded Henry rifle, his sister and the captain were about to be married in the county courthouse, where the judge was performing the service with a saber at his back.

Standing beside Jacques on the second floor of the courthouse, looking down into the open rotunda, Omah watched the tableau unfold.

Young Emma Shut, who truly was in love from the expression on her face, was trying hard not to be a bride with tears ruining the front of her dress when she saw her younger brother Billy, rifle in hand, drive his staggering horse up the steps of the courthouse, fling out of the saddle, and prepare to pull the trigger amid the crowd of bluecoats.

The trembling horse, a bay driven near to death during the all-night ride, began to collapse in slow motion, knees buckling, salt-rimed sides heaving, bloody nostrils smashing against the green marble. A long groan that caught in the throat like a sob accompanied the last exhale, but the boy didn't dare look away from the officers, who were beginning to back toward the shelter of the marble columns while they drew pistols and sabers. A pool of rancid brown piss began to spread around the horse, and Emma lifted her long green muslin skirts and tiptoed through it to get to her brother. He was as wild eyed and worn through as the horse had been, his face drawn and haggard from eating too little and riding too hard for too long. She knew the horse, Rebel. He had been her brother's best friend before the war, and now Billy had killed him to stop her. She could tell from the wildly embroidered sky blue shirt that he had been accepted by the raiders, who were trying to protect people in the occupation up north. Union soldiers had started punishing families of resisters there, imprisoning women and children, seizing farms and houses, emptying entire counties on the western border of Missouri. Her cousins were starving in a St. Louis prison, and she must have remembered them because she was reaching for the rifle, meaning only to stop him before he was killed. She wasn't thinking of her soon-to-be husband, or the town's unforgiveness that awaited her for the rest of her life when she married the Union officer. She was thinking that her brother, her own sweet Billy, was too tired to do a good job with the rifle now.

They laid the brother and sister to rest in the cemetery on the edge of town, the one with the big earthquake spring hole that was still so active then, only fifty years after the big shakes. But it wasn't a watery grave they went to, the townspeople made certain of that, although they had to wait until the Union officer left for another assignment before they dug the boxes up and moved them to a more favored spot by the rest of their Shut kin.

It was a few nights after the funeral when Billy and Emma's mother, Maddie Shut, appeared on Jacques' porch, dripping wet from the steady rain that had been falling nonstop since the killing.

Striding past Omah, with no regard for the mud on her boots, the woman found Jacques in the front parlor, staring moodily into the smoking fire while he emptied a second bottle of wine. He didn't offer her a glass, though she knelt shivering to the fire and held her hands out to the warmth.

"Chimney needs cleaning," she remarked. "Birds, no doubt." The drips from her wool cloak hissed on the hearth, and steam began to rise from the sleeves of her dress. It seemed to Omah that if the woman stayed there long enough, she might well be cooked. Something about the matted gray-streaked hair and wildness in her eyes made Omah feel a stab of sympathy. She moved quietly to the kitchen and filled a tumbler with brandy and hot water from the kettle they kept on the cookstove.

When she held it out to her, Maddie rose and sat in the chair opposite Jacques and took the glass. Sipping it carefully, she struggled with her expression until it moved into calmness.

When Jacques didn't speak, she finally broke the silence.

"They're your kin, too," she said.

His eyes flicked to the woman sitting before him, then took in Omah standing in the shadows behind her.

He shrugged. "Maybe."

"My mother—"

Jacques held up his hand. "—was my friend Chabot's wife."

"—said that you were my—"

"Best not speak ill of the dead, *chère madame.*" Jacques drained his glass and refilled it.

"—which makes the children—"

"The dead cannot be restored," he said.

"At least avenged. At the very least, that—" She drank the brandy in one long draught and rolled the glass between her hands.

"I'm a poor farmer." Jacques shrugged. "They've taken everything. Look around you."

"Nonsense. My mother *told* me—"

Jacques held up a forefinger, then placed it against his lips.

"I won't forgive them, Jacques. Don't get in my way, that's all I ask. I don't know who or what you are to my family. I'd hoped you were blood to help me." She spoke without taking her eyes off the fire.

He waved her off with his hand. "Be glad the officer is gone. The war will end, and what is terrible now will be forgotten."

"Nonsense. Wait until their brother Alair comes home." She rose and left the room. The front door clicked quietly into place.

Sometime in the middle of the night, Omah heard Jacques in the bachelor's ell, rummaging in the trunks; later he was apparently crying, and there was the sound of a bottle tumbling on the stairs. Then silence. Had Jacques killed his grandchildren? As soon as Omah had the thought, she pushed it away. But finally knowing what Jacques was capable of, Omah decided that the slaves were right to be frightened. For the first time, Jacques frightened her, too.

17

*A*S OMAH WOULD LATER REMINISCE ABOUT THIS TIME IN THE LIVES OF
Jacques' Landing, Miz Maddie, as she was known in the county, had
married a thorough bastard named Clement Shut, who terrorized
slaves and whites alike after her mother, Dealie Chabot, died. Clement sired
a boy, Alair, who left as soon as he was old enough to slip downriver on a
barge and sail to England, then on to India. Although Alair would die before
he could return to avenge his brother's and sister's murders, he did leave a
widow, Laura Burke. While the two women sat by the fire drinking warm
whiskey that first night of her arrival, Laura invented a pleasing history that
included the claim that her son Keaton, asleep on a pallet at the hearth, was
Alair's natural son, despite the fact that the man had hardly laid eyes on the
boy. Laura would later relate the saga of her marriages to Omah with such
candor it almost destroyed them both.

On Maddie's side was the tale of her husband's mysterious accident,
which involved being kicked to death by one of the workhorses. Afterward,
the sympathy was all with the horse, who had suffered a severely pulled sti-
fle in one hind leg and was put to pasture for the rest of his days. There was

never a rounder, shinier horse on the place, Omah claimed. And it was said that Miz Maddie wasn't alone in ensuring that the animal had a daily ration of apples and carrots, cool shade in the hot summer, and a warm blanket in the cold, wet winter.

After Clement's death, Maddie bedded a man who showed up on her doorstep one morning looking for work. Since she preferred widowhood to marriage, she gave the two children born from this affair the Shut name and left it at that. Maddie, it seemed, was as unlucky in children as she was in men, and by the time she was forty-five, she was utterly alone, avenging her loss until Laura and Keaton arrived with Alair's ashes.

Two years after her arrival, Laura did something nobody expected of her. She began to visit old One-Armed Jacques Ducharme himself. As old as the hills by the reckoning of most, Jacques still ran the farm, albeit much diminished by the loss of his servants, slaves, and five hundred acres of land when the war was over. It was rumored that the only way he hung on to any of the farm was through the service he provided the Union in the form of women and liquor and an occasional bit of spying. After the war, he bribed all he had to and made sure those who wouldn't leave him alone disappeared.

So Laura and One-Armed Jacques became friends. She told her mother-in-law she was tending his illness, and she began to take her son with her to play in the barns and old slave quarters while she spent hours talking to Jacques on the long front porch spanning the house. Once she let him hook up the pony cart and take them on a ride around the farm, which still held five hundred acres of good bottomland along the river and two hundred more of swamp.

He was an old man with stringy white hair, failing muscles, and a stump for an arm, what could be the harm? She was a strong-minded woman with a young son to raise; it was already 1873, she wasn't growing any younger, and as far as she could tell, Jacques Ducharme was the only single man with any money in the entire region. Although her mother-in-law warned her that Jacques wasn't what he seemed, Laura continued to visit him several times a week. It wasn't until the order came in at LeFay's Dry Goods in town, that everyone knew the truth.

There was the wedding dress: French silk, hand-beaded with seed pearls, edged with Belgium lace, the bodice so low and waist so tiny that Laura had to stop eating for weeks to fit into it and nearly fainted when the day turned suddenly hot after a spell of cooling September rain. And then there were the apple trees, sticks wrapped in damp crocker sacks, bedded in sawdust, and crated all the way from upstate New York. Guaranteed to Grow, the label said. It had cost him fifty acres of apple trees and the boy sent east to boarding school and college within the year to wed her, and he hadn't said a word to anyone.

Maddie watched her daughter-in-law with new respect as the wedding plans proceeded. The only thing she asked was that her son's engagement ring be returned to the family. It was a band of gold with etched flowers and a square, two-carat, flawless yellow diamond set in the middle. When Laura gave back the ring, it had been changed, however. In place of the diamond was a dense blood-red ruby that absorbed the light, and only bits of the original etched flowers remained.

"The diamond fell out," Laura explained. "It's gone. And the flowers were so old fashioned, I asked that they be removed when Alair gave me the ring."

"I see," Maddie said, and pocketed the ring. She was afraid of losing her grandson Keaton now, and didn't argue.

IT WAS A FINE MAY DAY, CLOUDLESS AND WARM, THE LAST OF SPRING BEFORE the coming of the summer heat that felt like a drug in the body. Omah had just gotten back from St. Louis the night before and was out clearing weeds around her parents' headstone when the buggy pulled up.

Then Jacques himself hurried out the door and down the steps to help the woman to the ground. She landed lightly, holding her hat and tilting her head with a light tinkling laugh that made Omah stare harder. Was that flirtation? The woman slipped her arm in Jacques' and climbed the steps, picking her way carefully around the broken porch boards and exclaiming merrily when the screen door tipped dangerously on one hinge.

Omah dropped her scythe and hurried to the house. No wonder Jacques had seemed preoccupied when she arrived. Why, he'd barely acknowledged her before he had hurried off to finish a chore in his bedroom. She'd been too tired to be more than slightly hurt, but now she began to understand.

The old cock had found a hen at last. She found them in the parlor, the woman's red hair shining out of the dusty gloom, her hat slung carelessly on a chair, while she leaned against Jacques' arm looking at the paintings and books he was pointing out. He had begun to furnish the house again in her absence, although since the furniture had been stored so long, much of it looked too worn and dirty to please a woman—especially a woman like this one.

"Jacques?" Omah said.

When his head jerked around, she could see annoyance in his face. The old fool!

"Laura," he sighed, "this is Omah." Nothing more. That was it? As if she were his maid? Or hired girl? Laura half turned and nodded her head, taking little notice of the colored girl in the doorway.

Omah stormed upstairs, grabbed a small bag, stuffed it full, flounced downstairs and went directly to the stable to saddle her horse. She'd go stay in her own house if he was going to act that way.

Thus, Omah had to rely on gossip and servants' reports for the progress of the Jacques and Laura romance. She didn't dare go near Old Maddie Shut, Laura's mother-in-law, for fear the woman could ferret out the scent of her betrayal in the demise of her children Billy and Emma. No, Omah and Jacques had stayed clear of the Shuts since the war, and now here was one right in the middle of their lives. Had Jacques lost his mind?

THE FIRST NIGHT JACQUES APPEARED IN HER BED, LAURA WOULD LATER TELL Omah, she was awakened from a sound sleep by the sinking of the mattress beside her. She'd started locking her door as soon as she moved in, yet here he was. Seven times she obliged him as a wife should, waiting in the dark until he was done, then fighting sleep until she was certain he was snoring. She didn't want him to hear her slip out of bed to wash herself with Miz Maddie's decoction to keep from getting pregnant. But there was still that first time when he'd caught her unawares, and that proved to be her undoing, because by March she was certain.

As soon as her swollen belly began to show, the people of Jacques' Landing laughed. The old bull had found himself a prize cow. They had been growing resentful the past months as the barges unloaded her new furniture, dishes, and draperies, each special order loaded on a cart and hauled out to the house—this while their own houses had been emptied by the occupying army and the carpetbaggers who came afterward to pick the bones clean. So many had suffered losses of family and households and land that it was natural to begin to hate Jacques and his wife again. People even regretted forgiving him some fifty years before when his crippled wife disappeared in the river and the old reprobate had holed up in that mansion. The fact that the mansion was outside of town, on the river, where they didn't have to look at it all the time, had helped then, but now the envy was back with the special viciousness of a reopened wound.

There were matching ornately carved rosewood settees covered in burgundy brocade, Chippendale occasional chairs and tables with curved, cabriole mahogany legs so delicate they looked as if they could slip off their claw-and-ball feet, black walnut French Victorian chairs with balloon-shaped backs, tables with marble tops, a drop-front desk ornamented with carved roses, tendrils, and leaves. It didn't matter that the medallion-back sofa with the heavy black horsehair upholstery might seem odd beside the Chippendale table or the Louis XV side chair, Laura ordered what caught her eye or was expensive or the latest fashion. The overstuffed gold plush Turkish Victorian sofa and matching chair trimmed with tassels and fringe were high style in the East, she discovered, and immediately wanted them. Most of the American Empire pieces in the house were moved to the stable loft, where the cherry acanthus leaves filled with dust and the brass rosettes tarnished. The rough, plain cypress and oak furniture Jacques had made when he first built the house and had run out of money for a time, she banished to the servants' rooms, the nursery, and the kitchen—all except Jacques' "Sleepy Hollow chair," a particularly ugly clumsy affair he insisted on keeping in the library.

In mid-October a red-haired baby girl, named Little Maddie after her grandmother, was born, and Laura wasted no time convincing Jacques to bring Miz Maddie and a wet nurse to live with them. Hauling the rocker out of the hayloft, Jacques wiped the lion's-head design on the back and placed it beside his bed. Laura promptly moved it to the nursery. As soon as she arrived, Miz Maddie had it carried down to the family parlor, and Laura was forced to spend part of each afternoon rocking the baby before Jacques and Miz Maddie's approving eyes. Something about the lion's open mouth on the back of the rocker didn't sit well against her shoulders, and she always left those sessions with aching muscles, the pain sometimes so sharp it felt as if his teeth had been sinking into her.

WHEN LAURA DUCHARME REALIZED THAT HER HUSBAND JACQUES AND MIZ Maddie Shut intended to make her a prisoner to the baby, she developed a malaise whose only cure, at the suggestion of the doctor from Sisketon, was a journey to the restorative Hot Springs in the Quachita Mountains of Arkansas. The doctor, on commission from the Arlington Hotel, the newest and largest there, had begun to send all dubious cases to the Springs for the curative baths.

Leaving the baby to Jacques and Miz Maddie, Laura mounted the steps to the train with a lighter heart than she'd felt in years. She was at last free, with enough money and time to thoroughly enjoy herself. She looked forward to a new place with new entertainments. She was still a young woman, she told herself, anything was possible. Settling into her seat, she was about to close her eyes to avoid seeing her husband's weathered old face fill with disappointment at her leaving while the baby squalled in Miz Maddie's arms, when a tall colored woman opened the compartment door and took the seat opposite her. Obviously a mistake, since the Negro car was at the back of the train, but the conductor would straighten it all out. The woman was particularly well dressed in the most current fashion, so there was little to object to really. Besides, the company might be nice for a while.

Laura straightened her shoulders and glanced out the open window at the well-wishers on the platform. Jacques was moving toward the car, mouthing words she couldn't understand and gesturing. What was wrong with him? Miz Maddie wore a peculiar little smile as she rocked the baby in her arms. Oh, these people were maddening! Couldn't they just let her go for a visit?

But when Jacques reached the side of the train, it wasn't Laura he spoke to. It was the colored woman, who reached her hand out the window and accepted a small package in brown paper and twine from him. They knew each other. Jacques was shouting something in French, but the words kept being swallowed by the steam release and the grinding, whining of the wheels. They were moving at last! Jacques must have engaged a maid for his wife, Laura concluded.

On impulse, Laura kissed her gloved hand and waved at the little family through the window, then settled back against the green leather seat. Deep in her chest there was a little ache for her baby girl, but Laura really did need this time away, time she hadn't taken since all those years ago in Ireland, when she was pulled onto Michael Burke's horse and they had ridden away, thrilled by the cries of men she could hear chasing them, her father and uncles and younger brother. Seduced by a Catholic cousin, a highwayman no less, but she'd always had a weakness for pretty men. Oh why hadn't her family ridden harder, why had they given her up so easily, as if she were a woman swept overboard in a storm? Her eyes filled with the memory of how she'd been doomed to the abandoned cottage in Sligo where her shame and lover had taken her, left to give birth with no one but an ancient shepherd to hear her cries. When she escaped astride Michael Burke's horse in her dancing slippers and ball gown, she'd had no idea how hard her life was going to be, but she had been strong all those years. She'd saved her baby's life, and now he had the brightest of futures ahead of him. She had saved her own life, too, and now she was mistress of her own estate, planting an orchard and refurbishing a grand old house. As soon as Old Jacques passed on, she would be able to make more sweeping changes. She was a brilliant planner, she'd come to understand, and nothing was beyond her. So when she leaned back and sighed, she smiled with goodwill at the colored woman who had fixed her with a glare. What on earth could be the woman's problem?

As soon as the train pulled away, leaving the platform in a haze of coal smoke and dust, the woman began to unwrap the package. Because of the woman's unmitigated rudeness, Laura watched with open interest. First there was a folded sheet of paper that she recognized as Jacques' heavy stationery. The woman unfolded it, glanced at the contents, and passed it to Laura. Indeed, it was a note from her husband telling her of her traveling companion, who was not to be treated as a servant. Laura smiled and looked up just in time to see the woman tucking another letter and what looked to be a thick wad of money into her reticule. Of course, she was being given money to handle their expenses. Jacques thought of everything! Laura vowed to send him a telegram the minute they arrived to thank him. She also vowed to be a better wife and mother upon her return. Having a maid would make things so much easier. She'd explain it to the conductor and porter when they came by.

But when the conductor arrived for the tickets, he merely nodded at the colored woman, keeping his eyes carefully off her face. Why, Jacques *had* thought of everything! So they wouldn't have to go to the dining car, which was whites only, their lunch was brought to their compartment by a pair of young porters who seemed more worried about steering clear of the Negress than the white woman whose knees they bumped several times with the portable table.

When the scowling countenance threatened to ruin the pear salad and breast of quail *en croûte*, Laura put her fork down and stared at the woman until she looked up from her plate.

"If we're going to get along, you'll have to stop pouting, or I'll put you off the first chance I get and go on alone." She sounded harsher than she'd intended, but the creature was spoiling her lunch.

"Who do you think you're talking to?" The colored woman raised her magnificent head a notch, her eyes glittering dangerously.

"That is a question you should be asking yourself," Laura replied, picking up her knife in case the woman lunged across the table. Leave it to Jacques to hire this sort of person. He hadn't a notion about what made a good servant.

The woman's upper lip curled. "I know who you are, Mrs. Laura Burke Ducharme, late of Galway, half the British garrison at Sligo, and shall I continue?" She picked up her fork and took a tiny bite of pear, chewing carefully while she watched the scenery pass by the window.

She knew it all? Who was she? Some kind of detective? As soon as the baby Keaton was strong enough, she'd made her way from the cottage to the town of Sligo, almost immediately found military men who were happy to spend their money for her companionship, and eventually settled on a semidisgraced major being sent to India. But how did this scowling servant know all that?

"My name is Omah. Jacques has asked me to be your companion for this journey, a task I most reluctantly undertake, believe me. I am not your maid, servant, dresser, or colored girl." She gestured toward the entrée, which waited under a steamed glass dome between them. "Shall we continue to dine?"

THE TRIP WAS BY RAIL UNTIL THEY REACHED MALVERN, ARKANSAS, WHERE THEY had to board a stagecoach and travel the narrow, rocky, dusty road to Hot Springs. There were three men in the coach with Laura and Omah. Laura examined the men, who were dressed in the remnants of Confederate uniforms. She found them each wanting in some way, but did take in the fact that they wore pistols, and held rifles close at hand. When she tried to raise the leather curtain over her window, the man across the aisle put a hand over hers and shook his head. The fingers were long, the index bent permanently, yet the nails were clean and trimmed like a gentleman's. She looked at him more closely. Behind the unshaven face and gray skin, intense gray eyes the color of mica stared out of dark hollows. As the coach bounced over a particularly rock-strewn section of road, he grimaced with pain. His forehead was damp as if fevered, and he held his side as he shifted uncomfortably on the seat, his eyes never leaving hers. It should have been unnerving, but instead it made her curious. His gray-streaked brown hair hung limply to the shoulders of a dusty black coat that had once cost a good deal of money.

As a small groan escaped the man's lips, the fellow sitting beside him glanced over anxiously. That man was younger and healthier, although his arm was missing below the elbow, not as drastic an amputation as her new husband's, she noted, and his coarse gray wool shirt had been cut and sewn shut at that point. While his shirt was relatively clean, the legs of his heavy dark gray trousers with the black strip down the sides were dotted with dried mud and sticker weed. Pretending to yawn, she looked down and took in the expensive black boots smeared with mud on the man opposite.

When she looked up, the man across from her touched his hat, the corners of his mouth turning up. "Major Grayson Stark, ma'am," he said.

She controlled the smile on her own lips and gave a curt nod instead. "Laura Ducharme." She held out her hand and he gravely took the tips of her fingers and held them for a moment before bringing them to his lips.

"Forrest Pate." Grayson tipped his head at the man next to him, who nodded.

"And that gentleman on the other side of your colored woman is Chappell Jones." Omah stiffened but said nothing. The man next to her, holding the leather curtain open with one finger and peering outside, ignored them, his Spencer rifle between his legs, the barrel pointed at the roof while he held a Colt Navy on his lap, finger resting against the trigger. His trousers had a faint rind of mud to the knees, and his boots wore the same wash of reddish brown as the other men's.

"See anything?" Stark asked.

"Nope." Jones, younger than the other two, had a terrible red scar as wide as a bridle rein welting the side of his face. Saber wound. Laura had seen them often in India, where honor was fiercely contested amongst the British and the native people both. She'd grown to hate knives of all sorts. She much preferred guns and was happy that if the men carried knives, they were hidden in boots or under their arms. Jacques had tried to give her a knife in addition to the two pistols she carried for protection, but she had declined.

"What are we looking for?" Laura asked.

"Know it when you see it," Jones said.

Stark's gray eyes brightened and his glance slid to the man at the window. He licked his chapped lips, thought for a moment, as if deciding whether she were strong enough for the truth, then said, "No banks in Hot Springs, ma'am. Travelers carry too much cash. Coach like this is a rolling treasure chest." He lifted the barrel of the Spencer across his lap a couple of inches. Forrest Pate, the man with the missing forearm, cleared his throat, looked around, then swallowed. His rifle, an older army-issue Henry, was propped next to his knee.

Laura slipped her hand out of the reticule in her lap and laid the LeMat nine-shot revolver in her lap, pointed at the space between the man and the coach door.

Stark smiled for the first time and nodded. "That should do it." He fingered the shade open a couple of inches and squinted in the sudden sunlight, the smile remaining on his lips. Although it weighed four pounds, the LeMat had two barrels that could be fired separately, .40 caliber for the upper barrel, and .63 caliber for the lower loaded with buckshot, with the effect of a shotgun. She had brought the gun from India, where it had been carried by her British major. Not the only thing of his she took. She'd reinforced her bag to hold the weapon and learned to carry it as if she had nothing heavier than her lady's essentials inside.

"You might not want to wear that big yella stone till we get to Hot Springs, neither, ma'am." The man with the missing arm tipped his hat apologetically.

Laura frowned and nodded, slipping the ring off and hiding it in a secret pocket she had sewn into the skirt of her traveling dress. In India, she'd had to learn ways of protecting herself. Once she'd even shot a beggar who tried to climb into her carriage and yank off her diamond. She remembered the surprised look in his eyes as the gun appeared with an explosion that tore off his lower jaw. She could still feel the small hand tearing at the shoulder of her dress as he fell. He'd been a boy of fourteen, she was told later, a street thief with no family.

With two fingers, Laura quietly buttoned the hidden pocket shut over the diamond. There was a row of buttons on the outside of the skirt that disguised the ring's hiding place. It was irritating that in the one place she could wear the ring away from Miz Maddie and Jacques, she had to be so careful. She wasn't about to give the ring up, though, not after all she had gone through. Alair Shut had given it to her, an extraordinary yellow diamond ring so large she had doubted its authenticity until a jeweler examined it. A family heirloom, Alair told her, from his grandmother Dealie for his bride. So there was money in back of him, too, Laura observed. This was to be a wonderful marriage. It was true that she'd only been married to Alair for two weeks when he died, so it was difficult to feel a very deep and lasting sorrow, but she had always felt that the ring was hers alone. And she meant to keep it. She'd gone to a great deal of trouble to have that ruby she'd found in her husband's things mounted on the replica band to give back to Miz Maddie when she asked for it.

The stagecoach hit another rough patch of road, tilting and bouncing so hard that Major Stark clutched his side, turned white, and tipped forward in a faint. Laura caught his shoulders while the one-armed man struggled to ease the unconscious man back. In those few moments, Laura felt his full weight pressed against her breasts and smelled the sweet pungence of pine resin on his breath. Her face flushed as Omah helped push him back against the seat and she felt the sudden absence of his weight. Brushing at her lilac linen dress, she discovered the dark smear of sweat he had left on her bodice. As soon as the road smoothed again, she leaned over and loosened his collar and brushed the damp locks of hair off his face. The other two men watched her as if ready to spring against her should she hurt him. When his eyelids began to flutter, she pulled a small flask from her reticule, unscrewed the cap, held it under his nose, then put it to his lips.

"Brandy," she said. He coughed with the first sip, but took a deeper drink, paused and drank again without opening his eyes.

"Thank you," he whispered, then his breathing slowed and deepened, his fingers slack on the rifle. In a few minutes he began to snore lightly, his head sliding against the coach wall. His skin cooled and lost its clamminess. Laura could see that he had been a handsome man before the war, though his hair was prematurely gray, the deep hollows in his cheeks and around his eyes due to a wound that had apparently never healed. The major lifted the bent finger and muttered in his sleep as if he were making an argument.

Forrest Pate patted Stark's hand, crooning over him as if he were a child. When Stark's breathing deepened again, Pate looked at Laura and tipped his head. "Caught in that dang Lick Creek mess over in Tennessee. Siege of Knoxville, don't ya know. Never shoulda gone back to those Clinch Mountains. My people left there for good. Daddy tole me, Now don't none of us ever go back. Then we got driven to Zollicoffer, Greeneville. Almost caught 'em, they was out of food those days. Missed it though. Blue Springs, we took a beating there. Drove all the way back to Virginia about. Then

Lick Creek again. Seems like we was always going back and forth across that dang bridge. The siege wasn't much—just winter and everybody starving and such. Longstreet finally took off. We none of us fared too poorly then."

He shook his head and brushed at what was left of his arm with the care and tenderness of a new mother.

"This didn't happen till later. In December we snuck out and made our way back to Missouri. Major's men all blown to shreds, our company buried from Harlan County to Mossey Creek, we had nowhere and nothing, so we worked our way back to join up with some of the rebels at home. Mostly our families, I guess. We lost."

"Shut up, Forrest." The other young man spat on the floor and smeared it with his boot.

"You mind that window, Chappell."

The young man glared at them, then jerked his head back and fingered the shade open. As he did so, a revolver barrel poked in the gap and shot him through the outer cartilage of his ear.

"Oh you will!" he shouted and grabbed the revolver out of the assailant's hand, turned it on the man, and pulled the trigger. The leather curtain flopped and a man's torso bent through the opening, a large hole in the back of his neck as he bled from a gaping wound in his throat.

"Your side!" Chappell yelled at Laura, who had raised her revolver and sat prepared when the leather curtain suddenly bulged. She levered the barrel to the twenty gauge open and squeezed the trigger carefully. There was a surprised grunt, followed by an agonizing cry as Stark's shot also caught the man, who fell away, leaving the leather curtain flapping with light blinking in the two holes. Stark cautiously lifted the edge and peered outside, his gun at the ready next to his chin. Laura held her gun steady for the next intruder. She couldn't quite catch her breath though, with her pulse crashing against her chest. She was sure they wanted her diamond, just like before, and she was sure that she had killed again to protect it. More proof that it was hers!

The coach lurched forward, the driver whipping the horses into a gallop that threatened to spin them out of control on the rocky road. Major Stark let go of the curtain and smiled at Laura with a nod of his head.

"You'll do," he said.

Forrest leaned back with a broad grin that revealed a black eyetooth and shook his head. "Well, now I seen the elephant." His rifle was cradled against his body, held tight in the angle of his stump.

Omah, who'd sat stoically through the whole crisis, arms folded across her chest, glaring at the men across from her, now extricated a white cotton handkerchief from her reticule and held it out to Jones, whose wounded ear was bleeding down his collar and coat and threatening to scatter droplets on her dress also. He hesitated, then took it and pressed it against his ear. He looked at her and gave a faint nod of his head in thanks, then dipped his hat at Laura and went back to guarding his window. Laura caught a glimpse of the knife blade shining against Omah's dark skin before she slipped it back up the sleeve of her dress. It was worth noting, she thought.

A few minutes later, as the horses finally slowed from their wild gallop, Laura brushed the back of her neck, where her hair had started to come loose and now stuck to her wet skin. She hadn't realized how exhilarating the adventure was until she felt her skin begin to cool and chill. She took out her handkerchief and dabbed at her throat and forehead, while the major cast quick glances at her, following the motion of her hand. She smoothed her bodice and arched her back with a deep sigh before settling against the coach seat again with her eyes closed. Nothing she did surprised her beyond the first moment or two. She'd learned years ago that she would do anything to survive and protect what was hers.

18

LAURA DUCHARME WENT TO THE BATHS TWICE AND DECLARED THE sick people depressing, the air inside stifling, and the water dirty. She'd much rather be driven around town and into the hills at the side of Major Grayson Stark, his men cantering along behind the carriage on horses that had miraculously appeared the day after they arrived in Hot Springs. In fact, despite their first appearance, all the men had fresh clothing and money to spend after their arrival. Laura wondered at the sudden wealth, but kept her own counsel, deciding to explore its source at a later, more appropriate date. For the time being, she was enjoying the spectacle that made people turn their heads to watch the beautiful woman and her honor guard of war heroes.

Evenings the foursome began to attend the many entertainments that had sprung up since the war. Chief among them was a performance by bandmaster Patrick Gilmore of "When Johnny Comes Marching Home Again," which brought discreet tears to the eyes of Major Stark and his men. Next came a poet's recitation of "Thunder in the Barley" and "Death, His Fatal Dart," followed by a reprise of Mr. Gilmore's song. Laura and her companions were also part of the entertainment. The gossip that surrounded them added to the spectacle for others the moment they swept into a ball or party. Laura spent Jacques' money freely on fashionable gowns for parties and outings, boxes at the many concerts and theatrical presentations, and food she ordered brought to her room, where she and Omah would feast daily on real oysters, not the fried mock oysters of corn, eggs, butter, and flour Omah had endured just after the war.

Laura could not say exactly how Omah became her intimate, but the two women had grown close as soon as Omah had insisted that she stay in her own suite of rooms with adjoining doors to Laura's rather than in the maids' quarters as was customary. Laura wanted the other woman there for protection, too, so she invited her into her own bed after the first night. It soon suited them both to go out separately almost all night, arriving back at the hotel at dawn or later, and then to sleep away the day until the late afternoon heated up their rooms despite the heavy red velvet curtains and closed windows.

They had been living thus for several weeks when Omah awoke next to Laura one spring morning much earlier than they were usually wont to rise, the place where their bare legs touched radiating sufficient heat to push her out of sleep. She arose swiftly and dressed, quietly pulling the door shut behind her as she made her way downstairs to order cold oysters on beds of ice, cold champagne, and tea cakes with fresh butter and the imported French black cherry jelly the women savored.

The click of the door made Laura open her eyes, but she lay there without stirring, watching the dark shadows on the cream and cabbage rose walls, noticing how her arm looked with a light rose hue, almost the shade of the light red walnut that was Omah's. What a relief to finally have another woman to talk to, someone who understood so much. Although she had no children of her own, Omah knew what a mother and a woman must do to survive. Laura had already unburdened herself of part of the tale of Alair and the deception concerning her son Keaton. How understanding Omah was! Putting her arms around Laura, holding her while she wept for the man who was Keaton's father, the Irish highwayman.

Laura barely had time to pull on a dressing gown and slip back in bed when Omah knocked and the waiter appeared with their breakfast. As soon as he left, Omah slipped out of her dress and returned to bed wearing only a short white cotton shift.

"Shall we finish *Madame Bovary* today?" Omah settled the small silver platter of oysters on her lap, admiring the slivers of lemon. She chose a slice, pinched it so the juice dribbled across an oyster, then picked up the opened shell and held it over her mouth, head tilted, letting the oyster slide slowly into her mouth, then down her throat, leaving a brief taste of musky lemon. Feeling Laura's eyes on her, she looked over and smiled.

"They're very fresh," she said, holding out the platter.

"Champagne first." Laura smiled and brandished the wine bottle, dripping moisture from the ice bucket across her lap.

"To Emma Bovary," she toasted as soon as they had filled their glasses.

Omah wasn't much interested in the troubles of the French doctor's wife who lacked the courage to leave her family and strike out on her own, yet couldn't make peace with her household either. She much preferred Becky Sharp in *Vanity Fair*, who had lived a true life, full of adventure, or Mary Shelley's *Frankenstein*, which she'd insisted they read instead of Elizabeth Wetherell's *The Wide, Wide World* about some woman's life from childhood to marriage. Recently she'd discovered a writer named Jules Verne whose novels involved enough adventure to keep her more satisfied with their daily ritual, which she secretly considered somewhat silly and wasteful of Jacques' money. The real problem was, she herself had had more adventures and committed more crimes than any character in a mere novel.

Though she much preferred it when they lay in bed, shoulders touching, and read silently to themselves from the same book, she let Laura read the final pages of *Madame Bovary* out loud, and tolerated the sniffling and wiping of eyes that followed the ending.

"Poor Emma," Laura sighed.

"She's nothing but a boring little snob!" Omah exploded, thrusting the book from the bed and reaching for the nearly empty wine bottle.

Laura looked shocked for a moment, then the corners of her wide mouth rose and she squinted and snorted loudly, and burst out with laughter she could no longer hold.

"All that mooning around." Omah made a face imitating Emma.

"Tell me something—" Laura rolled over on her stomach and rested her head on Omah's thigh, her red hair spilling across the rich red-brown skin.

A wariness overtook Omah's expression, and she placed her hand carefully on Laura's head.

"Tell me what you did last night. Where you went, what it was like, who you saw, what you talked about. Tell me some interesting news or gossip.

Good Lord!" She lifted her chin and looked at the red and gold gown she'd worn last night thrown carelessly on the floor. "I'm sick to death of my life!"

"What about your major?" Omah slid her forefinger through one of Laura's red curls and wound it like thread around the tip, then let it go so it unstrung from its coil like a snake.

"He's so full of himself!" Laura pouted. "Strutting around in his uniform as if he hadn't lost the war. Every night somebody new comes over while we're dining and must have a toast to 'dear ol' Dixie and the cause,' " she drawled in a deep voice.

"Half the time I'm left to myself while he's off conspiring in that way men have of trying to look dangerous and important. When he finally comes back, he's full of compliments and telling me how much he admires me. Meanwhile, he's handing me off to some boring old couple from Birmingham or Atlanta, and I get to spend my evening listening to the wife talk about raising children with all the Negroes on the loose, while the husband plays roulette and cards and tries to put his hand on my leg."

She raised a long leg, pointing her toes to the ceiling, then lowered it and raised the other. "Last night I shocked everyone right in the middle of some story about the glories of the old South. They actually stopped talking!" Laura smiled at the memory.

"What on earth did you say?"

"That Victoria Woodhull should run for president of the United States, and that as soon as women got the vote, she would be elected!

"Mrs. Pettigrew of St. Louis and Atlanta turned white as a sheet, and her ugly daughter made the mistake of glaring at me. So I said that women would probably be happier practicing 'free love' as Victoria suggests, since marriage is so irksome. I even said that Victoria Woodhull and I were old school friends. These women are so dumb!"

She scissored her legs in the air. "That livened things up considerably. Sour old hens." She lowered her legs and turned to Omah. "You see what I'm forced to become. I'd probably welcome the Chicago fire most nights, just to have something new to do. So tell me, what's it like when you go out?" She began stroking Omah's leg from the knee to the ankle, pausing each time she reached the puckered round scar from the bullet wound in her calf. Omah wanted to snatch her hand away, but didn't want to draw attention to the scar.

"I usually go down to Malvern Avenue, the colored section, where we have our own places to eat and dance and gamble. Not as fancy as yours, but everyone dresses up, tries to look good," Omah said carefully.

"I was wondering—" Laura lifted her head off Omah's leg and rolled onto her side. "How you, I mean, where you found the money for clothes and jewels every bit as good as mine." She let the question hang in the air. "Jacques's paying you, isn't he?"

"I have my own money," Omah said. She made her voice light and smiled at the other woman. "Do you need to borrow some?"

Laura stared at her for a long moment, during which Omah didn't dare look away. If she only knew what Omah had done for her fortune.

When Laura finally looked away, raising her arm and studying its slim, unmuscled lines, she said, "So many people seem to gain and lose money in this country. It's remarkable. You can never tell who's rich and who's going to be rich. They'll impeach President Johnson, then acquit him. The war destroys Southern fortunes, then there's a financial panic in New York. You wouldn't dare count on any of that money. Those cattle barons out West, I'd like to meet one of those men. Last night that idiot Pettigrew said that they're going to have electric streetcars in New York this year. I'd still like to go to New York and live, but you know Jacques won't leave, and then there's the major." She sat up. "How am I supposed to make my way in a place such as this? That's why I'm asking you, Omah. I need your help. Old Jacques has a fortune, I can feel it. He gives me pearls and rubies and all manner of jewelry, but where does it come from?" She leaned back and stared at the crown molding along the ceiling.

"Some of the pieces are so old it makes me wonder if he were . . ." She looked at Omah, who was picking crumbs from the plate of tea cakes. "If he were a thief, a highwayman, or maybe a river pirate!" She smiled broadly and nodded. "That's it. Jacques the river pirate—a dashing figure indeed! An ancient, hobbled, one-armed pirate. My husband." She shook her head sadly.

Omah spread the black cherry preserves on a tea cake, took a bite and shrugged carelessly, hoping Laura wouldn't put things together too quickly. She was getting there, though, and Omah would have to alert Jacques. She held the bread out for Laura who took a big, unladylike bite.

"Better than home," Laura pronounced and pulled Omah's hand back to take the last bit from her fingers.

"Jacques doesn't have the culture or taste to purchase pearls of the quality he gave me. And the emerald brooch? It's so old it could have been worn by my Irish grandmother." She picked up a tea cake and slathered it with butter and preserves, carried it dripping red juice across the sheets to her mouth. Looking critically at Omah, she frowned and licked the red juice from her lips.

"And your pearls are every bit as good as mine, with that curious onyx and diamond clasp. I've only seen work like that done by one jeweler in London."

She paused. "You've lived there all your life, haven't you, but you have no idea where his money comes from." It wasn't a question. "Maybe you're a pirate too." Her voice was light.

Omah wanted to tell her to appreciate what she had. It was probably more than she deserved, but instead she climbed out of bed and began to pull the heavy drapes open.

"I was given the jewels years ago," she said. "Jacques' first wife came from a very wealthy family, and when she died childless, she instructed that her jewelry be given to the people who worked for her."

Omah felt proud of her instant lie. She smiled to herself as she picked up Laura's satin gown, one of the many she'd had made to replace the out-dated broad hoopskirts she had arrived in. The small attached bustle was accentuated by a large flounce and bow, a design Omah found bizarre and annoying, but a relief from the size of the crinolines required for the huge, old-fashioned skirts that constantly put a woman in danger of fire or entanglement with animals and wheels. Instead of ordering a new wardrobe herself, Omah had taken her dresses to a seamstress and had them remade. She was, after all, spending her own money, not some man's.

"They're bringing the bath up in a few minutes," she said. "We'd best be ready."

"A CORDIAL MAY DAY," THE VALET REMARKED TO LAURA AS HE HELPED HER INTO the buggy and handed her the reins. He was careful not to touch her fingers in front of the Confederate major, who sat stiffly proud on a big bay horse. The horse was shaking the bits in its mouth and pawing the ground while his two companions eyed the street and buildings around them.

"Perfect day for a picnic," he added as he tried to hand the basket to Omah, who simply stared straight ahead until he set it neatly on the floor between the two women and stepped back.

It was a spectacle to Omah's eyes. Laura's red mane picked up by the breeze and flashing brazenly in the sun, the three men on fat, sleek horses escorting them out of town at a slow, showy canter. They took the road south that led them past brimming creeks, meadows, marshes, and ditches alive with the pale pinks of vetch and verbena, wild rose and horsemint, the last of the redbud flowers falling in a startling pink rain of petals across the shoulders of the horses as they entered the coolness of the canopy of trees with new green leaves the color of watercress, then burst out on the other side.

Major Stark leaned dangerously off the side of his horse to pick a cluster of bluebells, then presented them to Laura, who smiled and held his eyes while she tucked them in the front of her dress. His eyes stayed on her fingers as they slipped deliciously into the shadow between her breasts, and Omah knew Laura was thinking of Emma Bovary. Some people seemed to believe that books gave them permission to do as they pleased. The major's horse crushed the yellow star blooms of wood sorrel with its hooves as it jigged against the leg and bit, sending up a sharp, not unpleasant scent that Omah could almost taste on her tongue like the quick scald of gunpowder. Dandelions, sorrel, and watercress made up her mother's spring salads. "A tonic," her mother had promised. "To ward against the spirits of the dead begging to come alive this time of year."

"Don't let anything happen to my wife," old Jacques had said the morning they left. Then he'd thrust a piece of his ancient gold hoard into Omah's hand to seal their bargain, as if she were a servant! It had outraged her, yet she had been doing as he asked for years because she found herself as beholden to him as her parents had been.

They found a comfortable copse for their picnic, two miles south of town, just before the road climbed up through pines and rocky outcroppings. Despite the seclusion and quiet interrupted only by the faint rustle of the trees and the birds that began to call once the group had settled down, Major Stark quickly posted the two men to the perimeter as guards. Omah carried the plates of roasted chicken, cold asparagus, and strawberries to them, receiving less than a nod. Meanwhile Laura opened champagne and filled glasses for the three of them. Omah could feel the eyes of the two men on her as she drank freely and at one point picked a strawberry off Laura's plate and put it in her glass of wine. She wasn't afraid of Forrest Pate or Chappell Jones; she'd handled men like them before.

As soon as their talk slowed and grew drowsy, Omah moved to the shade of a squat bur oak where she could do her own guarding under its knots of leaves and thick, corrugated bark.

Although her eyes were closed to slits, Omah could see the major's fingers ease down to Laura's shoulder. In her sleep she shivered like a horse dislodging a fly, but he left his hand where it was and deftly slid the sapphire and diamond earring from her earlobe without disturbing her. Slipping the jewel into the pocket of his bronze silk brocade vest, he looked up and around, but Omah had closed her eyes.

She touched the knife in the pocket of her dress, the blade so sharp it could shave a man's throat without his noticing. The gift from Jacques that first night.

She caught a slight motion out of the corner of her eye and turned to see the large head of a black snake rise up, the body as thick as a man's forearm, out of the center of the shorn tree trunk, just a foot above Major Stark's head. The snake paused, tongue testing the air before it rose out of the hole in the stump, collecting itself in thick loose coils on top. So still it could be taken as a continuation of the tree trunk, the snake appeared to crown the head of Grayson Stark as he leaned against the stump, his eyes closed while Laura rested her head on his shoulder, sleeping. A moment later the snake leaned down and oozed back into the dark hole.

Omah remembered before the war the dream Marie reported of a giant black snake wrapped around a white house. She gripped the knife in her pocket tighter. Pretending to pick a piece of leaf from her dress, she glanced sideways at Chappell Jones and was startled to find him watching her. She saw nothing in his dark eyes, not hatred, pity, or friendship. His was a watchful expression. If she threatened them in any fashion, he was prepared to deal with her. She shivered and wondered if her knife would be any use against the rifle the man cradled loosely in his arms.

STARK LOOKED AT THE SUN, WHICH HAD ADVANCED PAST THE MIDDLE OF THE sky. "Time to mount up. You, Forrest, put that horse back in the traces. Miz Ducharme, if your girl would put the basket right, we'll be ready to go."

Laura glanced at Omah and knelt by the collection of dishes. The major scowled but didn't look directly at Omah as he went to saddle his horse.

"Where's your earring?" Omah whispered as she knelt beside the other woman. Laura's hand leapt to her earlobes.

"It's gone! My earring's gone—" She knelt on the picnic cloth and began searching the ground, frantically picking up acorn shells and pebbles and twigs and tossing them aside. She lifted her hair and shook it, pulled out her bodice and peered down, stood and shook her skirt and brushed at it as if the jewel could cling like a leaf to the surface of watery silk.

"Major Stark!" she called. "Have you seen my sapphire earring?"

She turned to Omah. "Why aren't you looking?" Laura squinted her eyes. "Unless you already know where it is. Unless you took it."

"You know where it is." Omah started stacking the dirty plates in the basket.

Laura grabbed the plates from Omah and slammed them down so hard in the basket there was an ominous crack of china.

Omah held out a fistful of silverware that Laura took and jammed down beside the plates. She stopped and stared at the engraved silver handles for a moment. Then lifting her head she turned toward the major tightening the girth on his saddle. Her hand went to the remaining earring and fingered the bright blue jewel, the size of a dime.

"These were a wedding present from my husband," she said. "Jacques."

Omah didn't have to answer. She knew very well the source of the sapphires, even better than Laura, because she had been there the night they'd found the jewels sewn in the ragged coat of a man posing as a beggar on one of the last barges headed upstream before the Yankee blockade above New Madrid stopped shipping completely. It was his haircut and fine manicure that gave his identity away to Jacques. She had refused the sapphires, too big and gaudy. Not blue, she had told him, her mother had always told her to wear colors of the earth, not the sky. She had taken the matching ruby necklace and bracelet instead. There was a sapphire ring too, but Jacques hadn't offered it to Laura. Not yet. Now maybe he wouldn't.

"I'll tell Jacques someone in the hotel stole it," Laura said.

"Just put the glasses in their holders there." Omah pointed to the canvas pockets along the sides of the hamper.

Laura held up a wineglass with an inch of golden liquid in the bottom, saluted the other woman, and drank. "Jacques won't care. He can afford another pair."

"I wouldn't count on it." Omah picked up the champagne bottle, noted the wine in the bottom, and drank it down in a single swallow, the way they had those nights on the river when the cache of goods being shipped from New Orleans was for rich St. Louis families. She wondered briefly if Laura could survive on the river, the way she had.

"One thing." Omah snatched the white damask napkins from her. "Don't involve yourself in the major's business. I've asked around. He's a traitor, a renegade who used to be a raider, not a real soldier. Believe me, the only reason he's tolerated here is because half the people are afraid of him and his men, and the other half are sympathetic or don't care. He's danger-ous, Laura, don't make a mistake about that."

As if this were the most welcome news she could receive, Laura blushed and dropped her eyes. "I've known men like him before." She picked up the little crystal salt and pepper shakers shaped like acorns and placed them carefully in one of the glass holders.

"Just be careful." Omah grabbed the edge of the quilt and stood, shook and folded it. It was the wedding ring pattern, someone's heirloom. Now there was a pink stain on the white where a strawberry had been crushed, and gray chicken grease. She thought of her mother's quilts wrapped in tis-sue and tucked away in a trunk in her room while she slept under satin bro-cade they'd stolen from a paddleboat, which had pushed loose of the snare and continued upriver after a quick battle that began while they were un-loading baggage onto their flatboat. Her lover St. Clair had died that night, shot and drowned. Jacques had taken St. Clair's widow a final share and left it by her front door in the dark. Everything Omah owned reminded her of those river days. When would she ever live another life as thrilling as the old one was? She was ready for life to begin, but she wasn't going to marry some old man as Laura had done. She wasn't desperate, and she was eager to learn everything she could about the world. That's why she lay in bed with the other woman, exchanging caresses, kisses, until they were both breathless, hot, hungry for naked skin. That was something she wouldn't be reporting to old Jacques. But if Laura continued to allow these men into their lives, she was going to tell, oh yes, she was going to make sure the old man knew what his pretty young wife was capable of then.

AS SHE MADE HER WAY DOWN INTO THE NEGRO SECTION OF TOWN NOISY WITH evening revelries, Omah was certain that someone was following her. A white man. She could feel him in her wake, the crowded boardwalk separat-ing behind her, the space he walked through. She would be less worried if Jacques were here. He knew how to keep people off their trail, had taught her caution. She'd been reckless on the river in those early days, proficient and deadly. She remembered shocking St. Clair and that other one,

Boudreau, the night she had sliced a man's throat so quickly the blood sprayed them all. Was it because he was white, or because he had held a gun on St. Clair and she had come up behind him, slicking her knife under his chin as easily as slicing cake?

Now she was holding the knife tucked against the inside of her wrist and palm like a splint, keeping a tight grip on the ivory handle. Negro men stepped aside to let her pass, mincing in their boiled shirts, stovepipe hats, and store-bought clothes and tipping their hats at the woman in the yellow flounced dress making a wide swath with its old-fashioned crinolines. It was ten o'clock, early enough that the streets were still crowded, and the seriousness of the evening hadn't fallen like a veil across the hilarity ringing from the gambling parlors and eateries. Outside Fat Boy Baker's Cafe with gambling downstairs and women upstairs, she paused to look around and adjust the blade. There he was, Chappell Jones, the mean one, standing out like a fox in a dog run. Someone inside started pounding the keys of a piano so hard that the notes rang hard and flat, and then came a general stomping of feet. Several men on the sidewalk were eyeing the white man suspiciously, but since he carried his rifle in plain sight, no one tried to stop his progress as he drew so close she could smell the sour sweat and smoke on his clothes. They called to her instead, "pretty lady," "here come quality folk," and such things in high mocking singsong voices that abruptly stopped. She was just turning around when his hand darted out and took her arm, pinching the flesh. She swung her body close to his and rested the point of the knife against his stomach. He stiffened and relaxed his fingers.

"All right," he said, stepping away and holding up both hands. "I'm s'pose to take you to her, your mistress."

Omah kept the knife nudged against his skin. "I don't have a mistress."

He shrugged and tilted his head, eyes mocking her airs. "Miz Ducharme, I'm speaking of Miz Ducharme." Three colored dandies jostled his shoulder, and his head whipped around to watch them laughing down the boardwalk, a swagger in their hips, arms swinging loosely. The whole street seemed to be watching and laughing uproariously, and it made her ears ring.

"She's with Major Stark," Omah said.

"That's a fact," he drawled. Tucking the rifle under his arm so the barrel hung down, he nodded back the way he came. "They're waitin' yonder."

She had little doubt that she would find Laura with the major, but also that she would find some sort of trouble. Yet it wasn't in her nature to refuse trouble, so she flicked her eyes in the direction he'd pointed and slipped the knife into her secret waist sheath. He knew better than to think she was harmless now, and while that might be a problem later, for now he would be wary around her, and that suited her just fine.

Following Chappell Jones she became conspicuous, and the Negro men he shouldered aside glared or leered openly at her, a woman of color who must be a prostitute if she'd taken up with the likes of the dirty white man. At the end of the next block he cut behind the buildings and led her to a small house hidden behind a wall of overgrown lilacs that rose ten feet high and soaked the air with throat-thickening sweetness. The minute he turned toward the gate, Omah hung back, letting him move into the darkness by himself, while she kept her hand around the ivory hilt of the knife. A faint flicker of light shone from the two downstairs windows as he pushed through the gate and stopped, his rifle raised several inches so it was almost leveled at her.

"If she's not in there—" Omah said. Shifting her weight back on one foot, she drew the knife slowly, trying not to draw his attention.

"Nothin's gonna happen to you," Jones said. Then, clearing his throat, he lowered his voice. "Major just wants a word with ya."

His finger slipped onto the trigger and the nose of the gun came up until it was pointed directly at her gut.

"Where's Miz Ducharme?"

He waved the gun at her. "Git goin'."

She took a step back, and he steadied the rifle on her.

"You're nothin' but a nigger girl with a knife to me, so don't think I won't shoot." He bounced the rifle and jerked his head toward the house. "Go on. Git."

Once inside the house, she almost laughed out loud at the scene in the small, overcrowded parlor, where the dashing Major Grayson Stark bent carefully over the head of Forrest Pate, trimming hair in his shirtsleeves, like a public barber. If only Laura could see this!

Jones waved the rifle at the dark brown horsehair sofa facing a dirty red brocade wingback chair in front of the fireplace. Both pieces of furniture bore the evidence of muddy boots and greasy food spills, and she hesitated, then shrugged and brushed at the sofa and sat. So this was where the men had been staying. She wondered where the inhabitants of the house had gone. Surely no woman or servants had been in here recently, judging from the accumulation of bottles and dirty plates on the mantel and inlaid card table under the windows. A dismantled revolver lay beside a greasy rag on the occasional table beside the sofa. The table's surface was scarred with fresh yellow scratches. Looking around the room, she could tell that the men had had free run of the house for some time. The heavy tan velvet curtains had been yanked over the windows with dirty hands, and two portraits of a man and woman hanging from the picture rail along the top of the wall on either side of the fireplace were tilted, the man bearing a bullet hole in the middle of his forehead. The dust was so thick it hung in the light over the kerosene lamps with the blackened chimneys.

"There." Major Stark stepped back, brushing the front and sleeves of his shirt, as he turned to where Omah sat. The trimmed hair was left in a half-moon on the filthy cabbage rose carpet behind Pate's chair. Her mother would have made her clean every hair up and burn them to keep them out of the hands of other people, witches, who could gain your power and secrets with such a personal item. Again she wished that she had paid more attention to her mother before she died.

"Tell me about your master." He rubbed his hands on the sides of his gray trousers, which bore greasy streaks from previous hand wipings. Jones sat at the other end of the sofa, giving her a hard look. He was like a cottonmouth, just plain mean, stubborn mean. He wasn't going to get out of your way and he might come after you, the way a big ol' cottonmouth would, stalking you through the swamp if it took a mind to on a hot afternoon when the entertainment had run low.

"I'm a free woman," she said, keeping her voice steady, but not looking him in the eye. The material at the knees of his trousers was thinning, and a thread had broken where the cloth was starting to fray. He'd taken his collar and cuffs off, and there was a dirty rim around the neck of the shirt.

He laughed unexpectedly and rubbed his hands on the sides of his trousers again. His face was beginning to fill out and gather color from the days in the sun with Laura. He had cut his hair and now wore a mustache, but not the bushy side whiskers or beards men were adopting. His hawkish nose seemed less predatory now that his cheeks had filled out, but his blue-gray eyes were degrees of heated metal. The bushy mustache softened the thin, hard mouth that was smiling at her.

"Be that as it may—for the time being, at least. Tell me about Miz Ducharme's husband, this old man called Jacques."

His voice was cultivated, educated, and smooth as store-bought butterscotch, in the way of certain Southern men, but beneath it was a disdain and indifference that she feared more than men like Jones. Stark was more like a copperhead, pretty and so fascinated with himself that he couldn't be troubled with you, unless you trod on him by accident, then he'd crack around and sink his fangs in with no warning, hanging on to make sure he emptied all his venom in you, before he went back to admiring himself.

He took out a pipe with a long curved stem and tobacco, stuffing the small bowl and lighting it before he spoke again. "He's rich, of course. I know that." He blew a ring of smoke and watched it drift into the dust-clogged air before it shattered. His expression was empty of anything but goodwill and bemusement as he waited.

Then he nodded to the man at the end of the sofa, who lifted his rifle and pressed the barrel against the side of her face, hard enough to cut the inside of her cheek against her teeth.

"Tell me." He blew a couple of rings, puffing contentedly. "Tell me, does he love his wife? He's much older, isn't he?"

The gun barrel ground into her cheek. She grabbed it and twisted it off her face, but Jones brought it up again, this time pressing it painfully into the side of her breast.

"Jones's been known to shoot women." His eyes dancing, Stark smiled at Jones. "Bad habit, but we put up with it."

Behind her the other man laughed.

"I can find out on my own, but it will take time. One of the two things I'm in short supply of at the moment. So please—" He waved his pipe at her, the smile on his lips no longer matching the dead expression in his gray eyes.

She looked at his boots, the dusty surface spotted with grease from the latest meal. Jacques would know how to deal with these men.

"Mr. Jones." The major cleared his throat and raised his pipe.

"Wait," she said. "He's old. Old old old. Sits in dat chair on his porch all day. Drunk. Jist waitin' to die. Sooner he go, sooner I kin go." Her voice took on the grudging tone of the house slave.

Major Stark nodded, his eyes full of approval at her new submissiveness, and motioned for Jones to remove the rifle from her breast. "And the money?"

She gave the elaborate shrug of the freed Negro wanting no trouble with a white man. "I dunno where he keep it. He gots it but I never seen where he gots it. Gold, jewelry, truck like that." She worried that she was overdoing the dialect, that the men would catch on, but their eyes were gleaming brightly at the mention of the treasure they felt certain they'd soon possess. The little parlor was silent except for the guttering candle on the mantel that hissed and gulped, then died. Outside an owl *hoo-hooed* in the bushes by the gate, and Jones's body tensed. Stark continued to watch her with a slight frown now, as if he might detect a lie.

Out of the corner of her eye she watched Jones's gloating over the money turn to fear at the sound of the owl.

"He have anyone guarding the money? You know, men who keep a watch out for things?" The captain pointed his pipe at her and she flinched. When she got the chance she was going to slice that damn thing up and make him eat it.

Another elaborate shrug and shake of her head, her eyes on the floor as if she were truly afraid. "No sir, he only got the hired man and two old house niggers. Hired man he farms and don't come to the house none. House nigger couple is older'n the flood, so crippled they can't hardly walk up and down them stairs." She raised her face and looked at the major nodding his approval with the fixed smile of the snake just before it bit you.

"And Miz Maddie Shut's there takin' care of dat baby. Almost forgot 'bout her."

"Baby? What ba— Don't tell me that old man mounted her and—is that Miz Ducharme's baby?" The major jumped up and began pacing while the other two men watched the floor, their shoulders jiggling with suppressed laughter.

One more shrug. "It shore is Miz Laura's, but I couldn't rightly tell you who the father is. That old man or—"

"All right, never mind." The major's hand sliced the air impatiently. Then he stopped by the fireplace, and glared at her, his jaw muscle flexing. "You better be telling the truth, girl. I find out you're lying, I'll give you over to Chappell here, and he don't care for women or niggers."

She shivered and bowed her head. "I'm tellin' y'all the truth. Ask anyone if that ol' man don't sit and drink all day while the rest of us work like sharecropper mules. Ever'body in the county knows 'bout that gold."

"Then why doesn't someone steal it?" Jones asked, the rifle barrel pushing into the side of her neck.

She tried to look frightened and shook her head. "It's cursed. Ever'body knows it's cursed by his daid wife's hand and ain't nobody goin' to go up 'gainst a ghost. 'Specially an old swamp ghost like that woman. Old Jacques could leave that gold and treasure laying right out in plain sight, and not a soul would touch it." She lifted her chin. "Not even me."

The major's face lightened. "If I let you go, you wouldn't say a word to Miz Ducharme, would you?"

"No sir, my lips is sealed." She pressed her fist against her mouth and tried to look frightened.

He waved his pipe at her and she sprang off the sofa. "Let her go," Major Stark said as Jones started to stand.

SHE SENT THE MESSAGE BY TELEGRAPH, THEN THOUGHT BETTER OF IT AND also sent it with a man from the hotel on horseback. The message said, "Boat coming, light the way." She signed it St. Clair. By the time she got back to the hotel room, it was past midnight, but Laura was still out. She began to pack. Laura could stay if she chose, but Omah was needed.

19

LYING IN HER BED IN JACQUES' HOUSE AGAIN, OMAH FELT THE MEMories beneath the soreness of the long ride from Hot Springs. She had been dreaming of St. Clair, the week they spent alone in a cabin in the wooded Ozark hills just south of Resurrection, where his people were. It had been late fall when they had gone away, and she remembered the heavy woods ticking with rain that dripped slowly through the bare trees. The cabin was small and dark and smelled of mold and ash when they arrived, and they'd had to drive out a family of mice that had made a home in the shuck mattress before they spread their blankets. They'd laughed and quickly unloaded a week's worth of food, for they intended to spend all their days in bed. A honeymoon of sorts, after private vows to each other. They'd woken the first morning to rapping on the side of the cabin, and St. Clair had sprung out of bed, naked, gripping his big pistol. She'd been close on his heels gripping her knife. When he flung open the door, a large pileated woodpecker looked at him and continued up the wall onto the cedar shingle roof, pecking as it went.

"Shall we shoot him or just cut off his head and roast him?" St. Clair drawled and they hugged there in the gray damp morning, the sumac leaves bright as blood at their feet.

"Wait here, darlin'." He went around the corner to relieve himself and she went the other direction, where she found the staked outline of a kitchen garden, the wood fence fallen down, the streamers of rags to scare the animals so rotted they fell to pieces in her fingers. Beneath the fog, she spied a dull orange color in the heavy matted tangle of vines and weeds. She stepped carefully and knelt, pulling apart the vines to reveal the round shape. A pumpkin, the size of a child's head. She hacked at the dried stem anchoring it to the ground and lifted it out.

St. Clair was standing by the door with his finger to his lips, pointing. Only a few yards away in the ground fog was a big tom turkey in full display to several hens, which were moving slowly away with their heads down, murmuring while they searched for food among the fallen leaves.

St. Clair slowly lifted the pistol and squeezed the trigger. The tom rose in a sudden puff of feathers, then collapsed, his head gone. The females disappeared like smoke.

"Good shot," Omah said.

"Inspired by the idea of nothin' but hog and hominy for a week," he laughed. "We'll clean him up and give him a roasting along with that punkin there."

As he hung the bird up to bleed out while they climbed back in bed, she didn't dare tell him that she didn't know how to cook.

They were shivering with the damp morning fog that swirled along the ground and draped itself over the trees like silk. He put his cold feet on her shins and she tried to push him away, laughing, but he held on and touched his icy fingers to her nipples. He was the first man she'd ever known, and he was teaching her all the ways to pleasure herself. She ran her fingernails down his smooth chest, circling the curved knife scar under his nipple, and let her hand drift down to where he waited for her. He was teaching her to pleasure him also.

They slept like the dead until the afternoon, exhausted from hours of lovemaking. Then they rose and plucked and gutted the turkey and spitted it over the fire. Since it was obvious she hadn't an idea how to prepare the pumpkin, he laughed and stuck it among the coals to bake. The rest of the day was filled with wine drinking and the scent of roasting meat. Sometime in the middle of the night, they collapsed into bed, stuffed and happy, too tired for more lovemaking.

Then a thumping against the cabin wall woke her and she was as terrified as a child.

"It's a buck," St. Clair said, "rubbing his antlers along the wall, laying down scent. He wants us to know this is his territory. I'll tell him I already have a woman."

He pulled her to him, but she couldn't see anything and it was small comfort. It was so dark, the moon covered behind a thick layer of clouds, the trees making the dark denser. The fire in the fireplace had died, leaving only one small red coal in the ash. She felt as if she could put her hand through the inky liquid air and pull the light through the hole.

"Is this what it's like to die," she whispered. "You keep trying to see and you can't, it's just all sounds, is that the next thing you lose, then taste, and touch, and smell, and then you're—" Something rose up her throat, pulling her chest tight behind it, as if she were going to be turned inside out when it plunged out of her.

St. Clair shook her and pulled her hard against him, but that only frightened her more.

"No," she said, and wrapped her arms around herself, shivering, her breath caught in knotted gasps she couldn't stop. He eased out of bed and fumbled until he found a candle and lit it. The sudden sprawl of yellow light edging across the room made his face full of dark hollows, his eyes small and shiny as an animal's in the brush. When he opened his mouth, the words came out slow and full of echoes she couldn't understand.

"What? What did you say?" She sprang out of bed and reached for him, but the candle fell and flames roared up and he was standing in a fiery tunnel saying something, the hollow of his mouth moving, but she couldn't make out the words through the noise and light and she couldn't make herself put her arm into the fire to pull him out.

WHEN SHE WOKE UP, HER CHEST HURT FROM HEAVING WITH TEARS, AND HER throat was raw, but her face was dry. It was the way sorrow worked beneath the skin of her sleep.

What time was it? The sun was high enough that she could tell it was late morning, the air thick with the perfume of lilacs. It was a heady scent that drugged a person into thinking of the good.

"*Un bateau.*" She could hear Jacques talking with the men. There were always men who would do his bidding. Old Jacques was notorious for his mysterious ways of finding money. And the men, like St. Clair, were the most closemouthed and hard in the county. Leland Jones, one of the old river crew, was gone south to New Orleans, Jacques had told her when they arrived last night. Living like a king with all they'd taken from the riverboats and then the Yankees. But Orin Knight was still around. He'd bought land with his gold and owned all the way from the southern bend of the oxbow to the road to St. Louis. And he was planting cotton and had twenty men working for him.

"Can he be counted on?" she'd asked as they sipped brandy and ate cold fried chicken at the kitchen table long after Laura had gone to bed, exhausted by the time they arrived at midnight the previous evening.

"He'll do." The prospect of the coming battle brightened Jacques' faded brown eyes, and his hand was steady as he poured more brandy without spilling a drop on the old cypress table that took up a good six feet in the middle of the room. "How many will Major Stark bring?"

"The two who are always with him. Maybe a few others he's been recruiting, who want to win back what they lost in the war."

Sitting at the end of the table facing the door with her at his elbow, Jacques watched as she tore the meat off the thigh bone and sucked the grease from her fingers. The fire in the hearth flickered in his eyes, igniting them, giving his hard-lined face the patina of a bronzed mask. He picked up the brandy glass, carelessly jostling her arm, and drank, then set it down as if he'd made a decision.

"This major," he began, "my wife found him—agreeable?"

She nodded. They'd never lied to each other, and it never occurred to her that he might be hurt, but he looked as if he'd been struck across the face. His long jaw sagged, the lined hollows of his cheeks let go, and his mouth slackened. Although his eyes filled, he frowned and drummed his fingers on the thick cypress table.

"We'll stake her like a pig and wait for him," Jacques said and kicked at the fire, sending sparks shooting up and out across the hearth, where they burned away, leaving black specks on the granite.

He turned suddenly and walked swiftly back to the table. "Here." He handed her a diamond necklace with graduated stones leading to a large middle one that shone as clear and yellow as a spill of sunlight. "Take it," he urged.

"This was for her, wasn't it?" She fingered the yellow stones, icy cool to the touch. She wanted the necklace, it was beautiful, perhaps the most beautiful piece of jewelry she'd ever seen, but she understood the cost too.

"You don't take it, I'll throw it in the river."

She put on the diamonds, and sat with him in the quiet waiting.

WHEN OMAH CAME DOWNSTAIRS FROM HER LATE SLEEP, MARIA WAS IN THE kitchen putting away food from the noon meal, and Maddie Shut was at the table lightly rocking the baby in her arms. Laura was nowhere in sight. Omah greeted the women and smiled at the baby before hurrying outside. She found Jacques with Orin Knight watching two workmen unload bales of cotton, laying them along the side of the house and in the backyard. They had left a wide gap for the entrance to the little family cemetery.

Knight simply nodded at her. In their years on the river, they'd never exchanged so much as a word. He was silent and efficient, and she wasn't interested in him. He was a small, compact man with thin, almost white-yellow hair he wore long and parted in the middle, though it had long since ceased to be the style. With his sharp face under the sparse yellow-white beard and mustache, he resembled a fox wearing a disguise, and he was missing a part of his narrow nose, cut off in a fight—a bad night none of them ever spoke of again. The result of the disfigurement was that when he expended any effort, his breathing came in a high whistling. She could never pity him though. He was still alive.

The two men looked around at the river beyond the house and fields, and the graveyard behind a wrought iron fence. Behind them was the long wing of the bachelor's ell where Jacques had once kept the women he sold—a practice that eventually cost him his left arm—and where she believed the booty from his years on the river was safely stored. He was never going to give that up. Not even for Laura and his daughter. She didn't know her husband very well if she imagined that he would.

"What about Miz Maddie?" Omah glanced at the house. The other woman made her nervous, knew things, watched too carefully. Everyone said she was an Ozark witch, could put the spell on you, but so far she'd just been the baby's nurse.

Jacques shrugged. "Send them away." He scanned the road and river beyond again. "When she comes back from town."

Omah knew what that meant—Laura had gone immediately to Jacques' Landing to shop, unable to sit still for even a few hours. He wanted to wait to send the baby away so she could say goodbye, as any good mother would. He didn't understand how little Laura felt about the child, and that Keaton might as well have been her only offspring. She hadn't even mentioned the baby the entire time they were in Hot Springs, and she hadn't gone in to see her when they had arrived last night.

A buggy pulled up outside, and Omah watched Laura dismount and begin to fill her arms with the parcels in the seat beside her. When she went out to help, Laura whispered, "Guess what! He's coming. I can't wait to see Jacques' face when—"

Her hair was wild under the green bonnet she wore to match her green dress today, and the sun had brought out the freckles across her nose and cheeks. She'd powder them away as soon as she looked in the mirror. But there was something else in her face, some secret glee.

Omah looked carefully into the other woman's face. "What have you done?"

Laura blushed and hardened her eyes. "Nothing! I just want—oh, never mind!" She tried to hold Omah's stare, but looked toward the house. "Is that witch still in there with the baby?"

"*Your* baby."

Laura waved her fingers as if brushing off a fly and made a noise in her throat. "That old goat tricked me."

"The baby's—"

Laura grabbed the last package from the seat. "I already gave up one life to have Keaton. I'm not going to do it again." She climbed the porch steps and turned. "Not for anyone." She reached for the door handle, juggling the packages awkwardly in her arms, but managing to pull it open.

"Be careful," Omah said, but Laura was already beyond hearing.

A flock of crows flapping noisily settled on the roof of the house and in the oaks behind her, scolding with loud yaps. People who don't listen turn into crows, her mother had told her as a child. They spend their lives trying to tell people things but can never be understood. You split the tongue of a crow, it can talk like a human. Omah looked up at the oily black bodies on the peak of the roof, wondering if they could see what she couldn't— perhaps the riders on the road descending upon them in a matter of hours, or old Jacques' armed men hiding in the barn, along the riverbanks, and in the bachelor's ell. Where would she be tonight? On the river or lying in wait with Jacques? And what of Laura? Would she allow the romantic major to kill her husband?

The largest crow stepped to the edge of the roof, head tilted, beak parted as it gave three sharp barks, and then repeated them, body bouncing with effort. The sun sprayed around the shiny black head as if it were wearing a crown.

When Miz Maddie came out with the baby, Omah quickly loaded them into Laura's buggy, shoving the whimpering Maria beside them at the last moment.

"Wait." She dug at the back of her neck where the clasp of the necklace had been pinching her since she couldn't get it undone before she went to sleep in the small hours of dawn. This time the clasp came apart easily and the cool diamonds slid down her breasts like a reptile until she pulled them out of her dress.

"In case something happens . . ." She handed the necklace to Miz Maddie, whose eyebrows lifted at the sight of the yellow stones, so like the ring Laura had claimed was lost. Then she nodded and tucked them in her dress pocket.

"Go, go now!" Omah said and slapped the horse on its rump, startling it into a quick trot. For some reason, she felt her eyes fill with tears as she watched the courageous old woman and her granddaughter disappear down the road. She should have told her to get off the main road as quickly as possible, but maybe she'd know that. Miz Maddie had survived the war and Yankee occupation; she probably knew as much about tactics as Jacques.

When Jacques stepped out of the shadows, she noted the bright red scratch on his cheek and the mud up to his elbows. He put his hand on the back of her neck the way he used to do just before they launched a raid. His eyes had the mad shine they wore on raiding nights, and when he lifted his shoulders and straightened his back, he appeared to be a young man again. He nodded and lifted his eyes to the house. "She up there?"

IT WAS JUST BEFORE DARK WHEN THEY HEARD THE CLATTER OF THE HORSES ON the river rock road to the house. Jacques had let the fire die down, and the evening cool filled the room with the damp, sweet scent of honeysuckle and fresh grass. The peepers were starting to shrill in the trees and a passing paddleboat *hoo-hooed* from the river. Then the rhythmic clattering of hooves on rocks.

Jacques and Omah glanced quickly at each other and rose. He turned up the wick on the lamp, spreading yellow light like a shawl across the floor.

"Let them in," Jacques said.

Omah shook her head.

"It will be all right. Let them in."

"All of them?" She fingered the knife hidden at her waist.

"Just open the door." He patted her shoulder.

She opened the door before Major Stark's first knock.

"Is your missus home?" He had the same gaunt intensity she'd seen in the carriage when they'd first met, the burning eyes of the true believer, the exhaustion of a man fighting a war that would never end. Behind him Chappell Jones glared at her, rifle across his chest in case he had to fight his way in, and Forrest Pate grinned and dipped his head while he kept his hand on the pistol tucked in his belt.

"Let them in, *ma chère*," Jacques called from the parlor in the quavering voice of an old man. Major Stark looked at his men, a faint smile on his lips.

She stepped aside without a word, glancing quickly at the hitching rail outside where four other men waited on their horses—veterans, hardened fighters she could tell from the ragged clothes and indifferent stares. The setting sun fired their faces with orange-red, and the horses tossed their heads and pulled toward the rain barrel at the corner of the house.

"Y'all can water them horses over by the barn," she said in a slow drawl, the good Negro servant.

"Much obliged," they murmured and turned toward the barn.

Then the sunset collapsed and blue black filled the sky, drowning the remaining color. From the parlor she could hear the forced politeness of the men's voices.

"Every dog for his dinner," Chappell Jones was saying. "I don't want no more dealin's with politics, this side and that side. I'm riding on. Try my hand out West."

"Damn," Forrest Pate said. "I thought you were set on going back East? You are one three-hundred-and-sixty-degree-son-of-a-bitch."

Major Stark sat watching Jacques with his imperturbable gray eyes.

Out on the porch, Omah started when a sudden squeaky rush of wings swept by the porch, bats leaving for the night's hunting. She'd never been able to figure out where they slept. Her mother had promised to show her one day, but had died before so many promises had been fulfilled. Omah wondered if she'd see her tonight. Jacques was confident about his plans, but they could always go badly.

"Omah." Two dark figures slipped over the railing at the opposite end of the porch.

She glanced at the men watering their horses by the barn, and casually strolled across the porch, past the open windows of the parlor where the men inside were seated uncomfortably on the edge of the sofa.

"How many?" Orin Knight whispered. She glanced at the man behind him before answering. He looked familiar, but she couldn't quite place him.

"Three inside, four with the horses. There might be more on the road, but I see seven so far to our four."

Orin stood very still, cocking his head as if listening for the sound of a rattling bit or spur, a shifting of hooves, a creak of saddles or bodies. "We should have posted someone out there."

"Careless," the other man said and edged closer, so she could see his lean body and square-jawed face with the wide thin mouth and high cheekbones. His eyes were almost hidden beneath hooded lids.

"This is Frank Boudreau, remember him?" Orin Knight said.

"I could slip out and check the road."

"No, Jacques wants you in the house in case his wife—"

"These are dangerous men," Omah said. "Are you ready?"

Knight nodded. "And if *she* gets in the way?"

"I know," she said, watching Boudreau's eyebrows rise as he reassessed her.

"Stay awake," he whispered before he slipped under the railing, following Knight, and faded into the blackness blotting out the last of the light from the sky.

She stood there a moment because she thought she'd smelled the familiar pear scent. It couldn't be, but there it was again. "St. Clair?" she whispered into the darkness. Why does your skin smell like ripe pears, she'd asked him during those days at the cabin. He'd smiled and put his hand over her face, gripping the top of her head slightly with his fingers as if he could crush it if he wanted, and she'd smelled the smoke and sweaty sex of their bodies, and underneath the pulp of overripe pears.

"St. Clair?" she whispered again, and looked up at the stars winking like bits of slivered ice to give him time to appear.

"Omah?" Laura called softly from the porch above.

Had she seen the two men? Omah hurried lightly across the porch and down the steps so she could see her.

"What?"

"Should I wear the green flounced dress I had on this afternoon?" Laura leaned over the railing wearing only her corset and drawers, her full breasts on the verge of escaping.

Omah wanted to tell her that it wouldn't make any difference. They were all going to be dead shortly. "The green's fine."

"Can you come up and help me?" Laura asked in a plaintive tone that was particularly irritating.

"I'm coming," Omah sighed. Entering the house she heard Jacques explaining that "the family has already had their evening repast, but I'll see if my nigra girl can get something for you." It would be easy to take care of them as Miz Maddie would have, but the men demurred, they'd stopped for supper on the road and were just looking to camp for the night. Pay their respects to Mrs. Ducharme. Omah wished she were in there, watching the two men's wary maneuvers. Even with the open windows, heat seemed to pour out of the room from the huge fire that roared in the hearth now.

"Whiskey?" Jacques asked politely.

"If you'll join us," Major Stark said.

Omah went up the stairs to find Laura crouched at the top in her petticoats, trying to listen. She'd carried the lamp from her room and set it on the floor so the light pooled softly on her body.

"What are they saying? How does he look?" Her excitement put a red flush in her face, making the freckles stand out almost like insect bites.

"They're having whiskey and the major looks tired."

Laura grabbed her arm in both hands, surprising Omah with their strength.

"Has he asked for me?" There was a pleading in her eyes that gave Omah a small stab of regret. Maybe she really was in love with him.

"I'll help you get dressed." Omah tried to move past her, but Laura hung on to her arm, squeezing so hard that it felt like she could break the bone in two.

"Tell me."

"Yes, he came to pay his respects to 'the charming Mrs. Ducharme.' Now let go of my arm." She twisted loose and pushed the other woman away. "You're married." She rubbed her arm.

"I know." Laura's eyes filled. "It's just that I—" She stopped and raised her chin and hardened her face. "I have to get dressed." She picked up the lamp and turned toward her room.

Omah didn't know why, but she said, "Jacques will give you anything you want, especially now with the baby."

Laura waited until they were inside her room with the door closed and the lamp set on the elaborate mahogany dressing table. The room was already ablaze with lamplight. "Then he should let me go, give me half his fortune and let me go." She rouged her lips and touched her fingertip to a small ceramic pot of black that she patted along the edge of her eyelids. The makeup seemed to restore her confidence.

"Get my dress, will you?" She said it so matter-of-factly that Omah stepped back.

Laura pinched her cheeks and pinned a loose hair to the curls piled on her head and lifted her chin before she stood, her arms raised for the dress. As soon as it slid down and settled on her body, Omah began hooking the back.

"What about your child?" But as soon as she said it, she knew the answer.

"We've made our bargain. There's just an amendment to the contract now." Laura sat down and began powdering her face until the freckles gradually disappeared beneath a pale mask.

"You think I'm unnatural? You have no idea who I am." Her hand collapsed softly on the table and she stared deeply into the mirror. "Sometimes, I don't even know—"

It was fascinating to watch the beautiful face transform, the expression shifting between ruthlessness and innocence, the blue eyes glinting with guile one minute, becoming tear filled with hurt the next, as if there were still a young girl trapped inside the adult body.

Laura swept into the hallway, her voice full of music as she called out Major Stark's name.

"Why, Major Stark, shame on you for calling at this late hour!"

Omah waited until Laura was halfway down the stairs before she went to the second-story porch and peered toward the barn to see where the additional men were. The scent of pears—she peered into the dark, could just make out the four dismounted men, waiting with the horses, the tiny red glow of cigarettes as they smoked. Good, they were relaxing. But something felt wrong. She looked up the road to the east and west—nothing. Why was she so worried?

The scent of rotting pears, heavy and sweet, began to sicken her. The room danced before her eyes in the burning lamplight as if it were on fire. The floor gave a shimmer and the pictures on the walls rocked. She felt like she was climbing out of the river bottom as she made her way to the doorframe and clung to the solid wood. She stood there, willing herself not to suck in any more of the putrid stink of pears, the bile of grief choking her.

The floor stilled beneath her feet, and the fear faded, rinsing away. All that remained was the uneasy feeling that something wasn't right. She'd had that sense the few times their raids hadn't gone well too, although she and Jacques always survived as if they alone were unstoppable or damned by the murders they had committed. She couldn't imagine what force it would take to kill them. Or if death would be merciful.

She took a deep breath and willed herself to begin the work. First she must extinguish all the lamps. When that was accomplished, she felt her way to the top of the stairs, followed by the sweet scent of pears. "Be with me, love," she whispered. "Make my hand strong and true." She knotted the hem of her skirt up as if she were going in the river, slid the knife from her waist, and descended the stairs.

20

"NOW WHERE'S THAT NIGRA GIRL OF YOURS?" FORREST PATE'S LAZY, good-natured voice sent shivers along Omah's arms.

Omah paused on the stairs, keeping her feet to the outside of the tread, next to the rail where it didn't squeak. Something had happened in the parlor. She quickly glanced toward the gaping front door, squinting in the dark for anyone lurking there, then edged down the remaining steps, past the parlor door without pausing to listen, and in one fluid motion was out the front door onto the porch. She kept to the darkest shadows against the house and crept to the window, but she didn't chance looking in. Instead she waited in the silence for a few moments, making sure no one had followed or heard her, then went back along the porch, past the front door, and finally over the railing and dropped to the ground. At the back of the house there were two strange men, rifles ready, watching the surrounding yard. The cotton bales outlining the front yard stood pale and solid as hogs. She couldn't make it across to the little cemetery and trees on the far side. Where were the men Jacques had hired—Boudreau and Knight?

She was panting against the rising fear in her chest and had to struggle to keep herself quiet as she gripped her knife. She hadn't been this afraid since that first night on the river. Suddenly she remembered the way that dead man's face had looked, innocent as a sleeping child. She sank down, keeping her back against the planks of the house, which held the residue of the day's heat. The warm boards felt like strong fingers bracing her shoulders, telling her to stand up and move, she had to move. If she waited there, they would find her. She looked toward the barn, expecting to see the men with the horses, but they were gone, vanished. Nothing looked right. Everything was so still now, not even a breeze hushing in the trees. Which way should she go? Something was terribly wrong—Jacques had miscalculated. There were probably many more men than they'd thought possible, and they had a plan too, a military maneuver instead of the flounderings of some hapless men on a barge or a paddleboat full of gentry.

She pushed harder against the house, making herself as small as possible, and gripped the knife so hard, her fingers ached. The scent of pears had vanished, and only the early summer fragrance of lilacs and honeysuckle and new grass filled the air. Then the sudden sharp metallic sour of sweat. She stilled her breathing and got the knife ready, but the man passed a few yards from her without stopping.

From the house came a loud crash, followed by the sound of shattering glass, and Laura crying out. Old Jacques' roar abruptly stopped, and Stark was methodically cursing between the muffled thumps, "I . . . don't . . . give . . . a . . . good . . . god . . . damn." He was hitting or kicking Jacques. She tensed, ready to spring back on the porch and stop them. Strangely, Laura was silent. Had they knocked her out, killed her already? Whose side was she on?

The screen door slammed and heavy feet thudded across the porch. "You, Hazard, find her yet?"

The man who had just passed her said, "Not yet."

"Major says to burn this place when we're done. She ain't showed up by then, you'll have to stay and hunt her." It was Pate again.

"We'll find her," the man said.

"Chappell wants time with her, so bring her back in one piece. Then you can have her when he's finished."

"What's left of her."

"We're almost done here."

"He give up the gold then?"

"You just find that nigra girl and let the major worry 'bout the gold."

She heard Pate's boots clumping back inside, in no hurry now that they had control of the farm. They'd easily stop her. She had to hope that Jacques was strong enough. As the man named Hazard passed again, she held her breath but didn't dare look up for fear he would feel her eyes on him. What was it her mother told her about reaching the invisible realm— a chant to escape the living world in the face of your enemies? In the beginning when the slavers came, many of the people were able to hide, but eventually the old power began to break down—her mother never told her why—and by the time Omah was old enough to be told, it almost never worked. But she had to try. She mouthed the words, a prayer as much as an incantation, and waited, but nothing happened. The man stood ten yards away, slowly pivoting in a circle as he searched for any telltale motion. She was trapped. She'd have to simply run as hard as she could, and hope that she could make it to the river where she'd be safe.

She flexed her calves, preparing to rise, when she felt a cool touch on her arm. It was the small white woman, almost doll-like, dressed in the same pale blue gown as always, high-waisted in the old-fashioned style of fifty years earlier. A lavender shawl hung from her elbows and her face was as pale as a moonflower and smooth, as if the distinctive features were being polished down to nothing. In one hand she carried a cane. The woman put a finger to her lips, then beckoned Omah to follow. Slowly standing, she felt the coolness of the other body wash over her in a wave that stung her eyes. She blinked back tears and shook her head. Had the man seen them?

The figure beckoned again and began to limp away. Omah glanced quickly at Hazard, who was peering into the darkness in their direction, but apparently didn't see either woman, as if they were both invisible now.

The blue dress seemed to be reflecting the moonlight as Omah followed its ghostly glow toward the barn. And although the ground beneath her feet was smooth, the figure hobbled along. When they reached the barn, the woman slipped into the darkness without hesitating, but when Omah entered, she had vanished. A ghost. Omah quickly closed her eyes and said a defensive prayer. No matter what her mother had told her about being stained by spirits from the dead, this one had helped her. She opened her eyes and looked around.

She'd spent half her life playing in this barn, and although there was only the dim haze of moonlight through the dusty windows to thin the dark, she moved easily along the stalls until she found the door to the feed room with the false floor where they used to hide men and booty if they were being chased. Lifting aside several fifty-pound burlap bags of corn, she laid down her knife and brushed at the dirt until she felt the little wooden cup that would pull the trapdoor open. Her fingers had just touched it when a hand clamped her mouth—

She tried to grab the knife, but the man whispered, "Don't. It's me, Frank Boudreau—" and released her mouth.

"My God," she whispered, recognizing his voice, and slumped forward, her fingers finding the cool metal of the blade. "How many are there?"

"Just the seven we first saw. Knight sold us out. We never stood a chance."

"We have to work together," Omah said. She knew what to do. Jacques had taught her on the river how a few could baffle and defeat. Maybe Major Stark was overconfident now. He'd sent too many of his men away. They were down to five now, it seemed. She had to save Jacques and their money. She'd decide about Laura when the time came.

The smoldering cotton flamed at first, when Omah and Frank put the sulphurs to it, then produced a white rolling smoke that rose in thick columns, flattened and spread a choking fog across the cemetery, yard, and road. Behind the smoke, Omah had to drag and beat the five milk cows with a rake handle to crowd them into the smoke-filled front yard. Confused between the heavy scent of smoke and the blows of the woman, they bellowed and smashed into one another, creating the diversion Jacques had called for. Just as the breeze shifted and smoke began to boil toward them, a man came around the corner of the house fast, shouted and shot into the cattle. The bullet caught the red brindle in the throat and a spray of blood burst across Omah's face and chest. As the brindle went down, the other cows tried to climb over the sinking body, bellowing louder. Omah quickly wiped at her eyes with the dress sleeve to clear the red film and slashed at the cows, yelling and driving them toward the porch. The gun went off again, this time catching the brown and white in the side just as it was turning back toward the barn, blowing its ribs apart, the bullet burning a furrow through the upper flesh of Omah's arm. She felt it as hardly more than a hot jab, as she struggled to keep the cow from falling against her. Sinking to its knees, the cow grunted and mindlessly continued to scramble for purchase on the slick, bloody flesh beneath it. Omah was on her hands and knees, dizzy, uncertain which way to go, strangely light-headed among the hooves of the other cows churning the ground, groaning and pushing against the two fallen bodies, trying to climb over them in their panic.

If she didn't get up she'd be crushed, Omah told herself when a hoof glanced off the back of her head. Somehow she rose and hammered them with her fists because her arms felt too weak to hold the rake handle. Another rifle joined in shooting, plowing the thick air with bullets, striking the cattle with dull thuds. Omah ducked and clambered back behind the smoldering bales while the bullets flew around her. Amid the almost human sobbing of dying cattle, the horses began to rear and pull back until their reins broke and they scattered, whistling high through their red flared nostrils as they galloped down the lane to the road. The smoke had grown so thick, Omah could barely make out the two figures shooting at her. Then there was a muffled thump and one man disappeared.

"Hazard?" The other man waited, and when nothing followed, he shot into the smoke again, but the bullet only hit one of the cotton bales, causing it to rock back, leaving a momentary black hole before she scrambled over and pushed it back in line. She didn't even feel the scorched flesh on her hands. Her stinging eyes were filled with tears, and her lungs felt as if she had swallowed wads of hot cotton. She resisted the urge to rub her eyes, and for the first time became aware of the growing pain in her arm. When she looked, her hand was covered with blood that had soaked her sleeve. Then she heard another thump and the second man's rifle went quiet.

Through the smoke, she could barely make out the door to the house opening and a figure appearing. As soon as it reached the edge of the porch, the candles and lamps went out in the house.

"Omah?" Laura's voice sounded high and nervous, and she turned and said something over her shoulder.

"It's all right, Omah." Her voice was more confident now. "They only want the money. They'll let you—us—go when they get it. Major Stark has promised." She turned again and said something to the dark space behind her. "Jacques is fine. We're all safe, Omah. Just tell us where it is, where the gold is—"

Omah caught her breath, counting to ten slowly before she answered. She just hoped that Frank hadn't been hit.

"Let me see Jacques!" she shouted, then scuttled down into the darkness to the left so they couldn't track her voice with their guns.

There was another conference and the sound of boots on the porch, the screen door slamming. The breeze picked up again, swirling the smoke away toward the cemetery, and she realized suddenly that it was thinner; the fire was dying in the dense interiors of the bales. She'd have to hurry before they noticed.

"Jacques?" she called.

The screen door slammed again and two men appeared, a third propped between them, his head rolled forward.

"You've killed him!" she shouted.

"No, no, he's alive, I promise you, he's still alive, see—" Laura slid her hand into the front of his smock and held it there. "I can feel his heart, Omah. He just wouldn't listen, and they had to hit him. They promised not to hurt him again if you'll tell them where it is. Omah, please, I don't want anyone else hurt."

Omah felt the tall grasses near her give, and Frank was beside her. "I caught Knight sneaking around the far side a minute ago. Now there's three of us and four of them." He glanced at her bloody face.

"They get you?"

She raised her arm slightly, wincing at the surge of pain. He pulled the dirty blue scarf from his neck and tied it around her arm. Then he gave her a sharp look. "You up to this?"

When she nodded, he glanced at the porch and back at her. His grim face was smudged with soot, which had settled in the creases around his mouth and between his dark glowing eyes, giving him the appearance of an ancient mask used in sacred, bloody rituals. As he started to slide away, she put a hand on his shoulder.

"Is he really alive?"

"We have to think so," he said.

She took a deep breath, ignoring the burnt cotton thickness in her chest and throat, and stood. "All right," she called, "I'll show you. But you leave Jacques in the house."

There was a moment when Laura conferred with the men, after which Jacques was dragged back inside. Omah could feel herself swaying slightly as she stood waiting. Either she was light-headed or there was another quake, but it didn't matter anymore.

They left Jones to guard Jacques as Omah led the others down to the barn. In the lantern light, she noticed the cut on Laura's mouth and the swelling of her cheek, but saw that she wore a look of determination, her eyes bright and hard as she glanced at Omah and frowned. Laura was limping too, and the green dress was torn at the waist. Major Stark gave her his arm at the edge of the flagstone walk, and there was the slightest of hesitations before she tucked her hand in the crook and allowed him to lead her across the lane. Omah walked between the other two men, Chappell with his rifle pressed painfully against her bloody arm. The pain kept her alert against the waves of dizziness. There was a muffled cry from the house behind them, and she wanted to turn and look but didn't dare. Pate chuckled.

"Reckon the old man's awake," he said.

She could only hope that the other betrayer was dead now, and Boudreau was slipping through the darkness toward the barn. If not . . . They were several yards away when a strange blue-white glow like the dress of the woman Omah had seen earlier appeared in the loft window. She wasn't sure the others had seen it until Pate cursed under his breath and pulled her to a stop.

"What the hell—" On her right Chappell Jones lifted his rifle, aiming it at the barn.

She thought about pushing herself free and dashing for the brush, but that would still leave Jacques in their hands in case Frank had failed.

"There's a woman up there!" Pate said. "Did you see that? A woman in a blue dress looking right at us!"

Chappell pressed the rifle against her side. "Move."

"You seeing things again, Pate?" Stark's voice was full of amusement.

Pate shook his head and grumbled under his breath, but held his pistol ready at his waist.

"I hope your nigra girl isn't going to delay us any further tonight, Miz Ducharme," Stark said.

"She knows better," Laura said in her high flirtatious voice, which sounded so false Omah wanted to bloody the other side of her mouth.

"Nowhere to run," Pate said. "Nothing but nigger wool swamp surrounding these fields. The river—it's a knowed fact that nigger girls can't swim. Chappell already proved that, didn't you, boy? No, best give it up and get on down the line, that's what I always tell 'em. They usually wisht they'd listened to me, too."

Omah could feel his eyes on the side of her face, but she refused to look at him. The nudges of gun against her ribs every few steps were making her wild, and she had to concentrate on getting them all into the barn, over to the trapdoor in the floor. *Please, please, help me,* she prayed to anyone who might be listening. Out of the corner of her eye, she caught a flicker of movement, something moving parallel to them, but her relief was quickly shattered as one of the horses that had earlier fled crashed through the brush past them and swerved into the dark entrance of the barn.

"Must've run into the rest of the men on the road," Pate remarked. "They should be here in a few minutes." He stopped and peered into the barn where the winded horse could be heard blowing in the far darkness.

Omah felt a surge of panic at the news of other men, but fought it down.

"We'd best finish our work here now," Stark said.

Pate held up the lantern and stepped inside.

Omah stepped over the threshold. For a moment she was free of the gun and tempted again to run, but kept herself in check. If Frank had made it, they still had a chance—*St. Clair?* She tried to reach out to him as he had been reaching out to her, but the heavy scent of burned cotton was all she could smell. Maybe the lady in the blue dress, an apparition, but she'd helped Omah escape before—

As soon as the others were inside the barn, Omah looked around as if trying to remember where the booty was hidden.

"Hurry up, girl." Chappell shoved her with the rifle so hard she stumbled forward and almost fell, which gave her a chance to pull the knife from her waist pocket. Before straightening up, she hurriedly glanced at Laura, who had dropped the major's arm and now held her own small pistol half-hidden in the folds of her dress. Her furious eyes had seen the knife, and she gave an almost imperceptible nod. She wasn't a fool after all.

Omah straightened and with a sullen expression shuffled back to the grain room. It only took a few minutes to move the bags of grain and raise the door. While the others concentrated on the hole in the floor exposed by the lantern, Omah edged toward the entrance to the room.

"I don't see nothing," Pate said.

"Let me." The major stepped up and peered down. "You, Chappell, go on down there and take a look."

Without a word, Chappell dropped his rifle into the hole and eased down after it. Pate handed him the lantern, which left them suddenly standing in the dark.

Omah ducked and ran at Pate, stabbing him in the stomach as he turned. Ripping up with as much force as she could, she shoved him backward into the hole. His fingers squeezed the trigger on his pistol as he fell, but the shot went wild. The major was a shade slow in firing his gun, which gave Laura time to fire at his back. He fell on top of Pate, who was bleeding to death at the bottom of the hole, already too weak to push himself away. That just left Chappell, the most dangerous man. Already she could hear him scrambling out from under the others. Omah and Laura backed toward the threshold, listening to Pate's dying moans in the sudden silence. Then they heard someone talking and someone answering.

"The major's trying to convince Chappell to climb out first," Omah whispered to Laura. "Try to aim better this time."

Laura muttered something. Then suddenly, the lantern came flying out of the hole, smashing on the floor and spilling flaming oil that flared so brightly they were momentarily blinded. Instinctively, they slid back through the doorway as the two men rushed from the hole, firing. Laura emptied her pistol, but only managed to inflict a slight wound in the major's leg.

"Get out of here!" the major yelled and the two men leapt the line of flames, bursting out into the stall area where they were met with bullets from two rifles in the loft. This time Chappell was hit in the side of the face, the bullet shattering his lower teeth, smashing his jaw, and exiting his neck, but missing anything vital. He coughed blood and fired at the flash he'd seen above him.

Omah and Laura were crouched down in a stall across the aisle and one back from where the two men were positioned.

"Who's up there?" Laura whispered in a lull.

"It must be Jacques and Frank Boudreau," Omah said.

Omah could hear the disappointment in Laura's voice when she said, "Jacques? I thought—"

"Nothing kills Jacques, not until he decides to let it." She remembered her mother telling her that Jacques was one of the "old ones," whatever that meant.

Jacques called from the loft, "You toss them guns out, we'll let you ride away, no hard feelings."

A shot answered. "You wait us out, this barn'll burn down around you," Stark said casually.

"That's a fact," Frank said.

The flames seemed to be dying down on the dirt floor; however, the room was mostly filled with smoke.

"Is the gold really down there?" Laura asked, her body tensing, tongue flicking across her swollen lips. She glanced at the loft, then at the stall where the two men hid, ready to kill them.

Omah thought for a moment. "Tucked back behind the boards. They look like they're holding the dirt wall up, but they come loose if you just give them a good tug." Money, that's all Laura had ever wanted, and she wasn't about to let these men take it away from her. The major had only been a means to hurry along the process of getting it.

"We need your gun," Omah whispered as Laura edged around the stall partition.

She turned and smiled at her in a knowing, confident way, and started on her hands and knees toward the feed room.

"She's getting the gold!" Stark shouted and started after her. The slugs caught and spun him around before he dropped, which brought Chappell roaring out of the stall, a rifle and pistol in each hand, firing. He was cut down in an instant.

"They done?" Frank called from the loft.

Omah crawled to the two men, checking each, her knife point poised at their throats.

"It's over." She stood and wiped her blade absently with her skirt.

The two men clambered down the ladder and lit a lantern.

Jacques looked around, one eye nearly swollen shut, lips split and bloody, long gray hair stiff with blood from a wound over his right ear. Despite the beating, his dark eyes shone fiercely, as they had after their river raids, when the danger had made him a young man again. He kicked Major Stark in the head and spat.

"My wife?" When he spoke, there was a gap where two of his lower teeth had been broken off, and his mouth and jaw were so cut and swollen his words sounded garbled and mushy.

"In there, looking for gold." Omah tilted her head toward the grain room, which was now full of dark smoke.

Only someone who knew Jacques well would notice the grimace of pain and disappointment that passed in a quick shiver across his body, making his shoulders drop an inch, taking the life out of his expression so when he raised his hand to push the tangled blood-caked hair, his fingers trembled. He let out a deep sigh and started for the door.

"Don't—it's catching fire—" Frank grabbed Jacques' arm, but the old man shrugged him off with a surprising strength and slipped into the smoke. Almost instantly there was a thud as the trapdoor dropped into place, and Jacques reappeared, coughing and wiping at his eyes. Omah thought they must all hear Laura as she did—the banging of her fists on the door she couldn't lift, even standing on the dead man at the bottom of the hole there, in the dark. Omah shivered with sudden cold, overcome with sickness in her stomach. Her whole body felt weak as if it could no longer hold any more death.

Frank stared at the flickering orange beginning to appear in the dark smoky room, his eyes darting uncertainly between Jacques and Omah. "You sure about this?"

"Let her burn." Jacques turned and limped toward the open doorway.

Omah looked at Frank, who was watching the mounting flames, slowly shaking his head, his face suddenly red with reflected light. As much as Laura had done, surely she didn't deserve—Omah took a hesitant step toward the fire. Maybe she could still—

"Too late," Frank said and took her good arm. She tried to pull away, but she didn't have the strength anymore, and he hurried her toward the fresh clear night air, leaving the roaring fire to take the barn, the dead men, and the last idle dream of an old man.

21

HEDIE RAILS DUCHARME

IN EARLY OCTOBER IT BECAME CLEAR THAT CLEMENT'S BUSINESS WAS IN trouble. He slept little, spending the nights either watchful in the living room or on the second-floor balcony, the shotgun across his lap, a rifle leaning beside him. The telephone rang rarely, but when it did, he would hurry away, the leather satchel of guns in one hand, the rifle in the other.

"Keep the shotgun with you," he'd say at the door. "Don't let anyone in. Call Roe if anyone turns in the driveway. Hide if they try to come in the house. Go to the ell if you can't make the barn or the riverbank. Leave everything except the money in our dresser drawer." It was the same every time he left, as if he didn't trust me to remember.

"What's going on?" I'd ask, but he'd wave me off and duck out the door, turning at the moment before he stepped into his car to call softly, "I love you, Hedie, remember."

One night I cried, "You're driving me crazy! What am I supposed to do? I'm so alone I'm jumping at shadows."

He took me in his arms, but I could feel how his body wasn't even there.

The next day I made a decision. I rode Cat down to Jesse and Vishti's at suppertime and had fried squirrel, apple pie, and beer with them, released from my anxious vigil for the first time. It never occurred to me that I'd be bringing the danger to their household too.

"Let's play cards," Vishti said as we lingered over our plates.

"We'll deal a dummy hand." Although Jesse looked reluctant, we cleared the kitchen table and dragged him into the game and were soon playing a penny a point. In the lull after the hands were dealt, I began to notice the swelling under Vishti's eyes and the sagging lines around her mouth. Even when she lifted a hand to adjust a card, the motion dragged, as if she were resisting a greater gravity than the rest of us. I almost asked her right then. A few minutes later, I realized that Jesse looked just as tired, and that he couldn't even keep the bid straight. Finally, we all three laid our cards down and stared at one another.

"I guess we have the same problem," Vishti said at last. I'd never thought of her as flighty or nervous, but I realized that she'd developed the habit of grimacing with the right side of her mouth every minute or so. I wanted to reach out and touch her cheek to see if it would stop.

"It's India. She's running wild. Won't come home. Jesse thinks she's drinking. We've tried locking her up but she's strong and clever." Vishti grimaced again, and I understood the cause. "Ever since last summer, she's a different girl. I don't know." She shook her head and picked at the edges of the cards until her nail separated the cardboard of one, then she quickly gathered them all and shuffled the stack again and again, grimacing along with the snapping sound they made.

"She was supposed to be here for supper," Vishti murmured. Then she looked at me and grimaced again. "I'm sorry, Hedie, I didn't mean that we didn't enjoy having you. You have troubles of your own. I guess you don't need ours too."

I reached out and patted her arm. "I knew what you meant." I couldn't help but give a deep sigh. I *did* know exactly how Vishti and Jesse were feeling, except I knew that Clement was working, not running around, so maybe I had an easier time.

"You let me follow her some night, I'll find out who's got her scent," Jesse said grimly.

"You'll end up in jail."

"Oh my." Vishti looked out the window. "It's already dark."

I was hugging Vishti goodbye when the door flung open and India rushed in like a warm wind, all perfume and smoke and grainy liquor. She tossed her scarf and fur wrap on the straight chair by the door, stepped out of her high heels with open toes and rhinestone bows, and rubbed her hands on her hips. That was when she noticed me sitting at the table.

"Miz Ducharme," she said with a bigger smile than necessary. Was there something smug in her expression? I wondered. She hadn't treated me the same since last fall when she quit working for Clement. My eyes went instinctively to her ears. Those couldn't be diamond clips, could they?

"We've been missing you at the house, India." I smiled coolly, not certain why I'd reminded her that she had been my employee.

"Have you now?" She laughed and ran her fingers up the hair behind her ears, as if to make certain that I saw the earrings.

"Where did you get that jewelry?" Vishti asked. "I've told you how cheap it makes you look to dress like that." Vishti's hands were shaking and the twitch at her mouth was going nonstop. "And where'd you get money to buy shoes like that?"

The bold expression fell from the girl's face and she pouted to her father. "Y'all know how hard I worked for Mr. Clement last summer. He gave me some extra for doing such a good job the day I left. I saved every penny so I could buy some nice clothes. I'm tired of being the only girl without shoes and makeup when we go out to the picture show or a church social. I'm a good girl, Daddy, you know I am." She wiped at the tears in her eyes with her forefinger, being careful not to smear the dark liner around them.

Vishti looked at me and shook her head in despair. Jesse, on the other hand, wanted to believe his daughter so much that he went over and took her in his arms while her shoulders shook with what he believed was sobbing, but which I believed was quite the opposite.

Vishti didn't believe her act either. "Jesse, you tell her she can't go out with that boy again, whoever he is. And she's not to leave the house for a week, at least." For a hopeful minute, Vishti's grimace stilled while her eyes glowed in angry triumph.

India stiffened and pulled back from her father; for a moment it seemed as if she were going to explode at her mother. Instead, her face softened and she went to her mother, knelt on the floor beside her, and put her hands on her mother's arms.

"Oh Mama, I'm so sorry. I didn't mean to cause you to worry. You'll forgive me, won't you? Here—" She unclipped the earrings one at a time and put them on Vishti. "There, doesn't she look beautiful, Daddy?" She stood and looked at him, the picture of the good daughter. She rocked back on her heels, smiling while Vishti ran her fingers over the stones.

"You're right, Mama, they are too old for me." She threw her head back and laughed gaily, sounding much older than sixteen.

Vishti worked the earrings off and held them up to the light. "Why, these look real, India! Where in the world did you get these?" She held one out to Jesse for his examination, but it was clear that he didn't know a diamond from a piece of window glass.

"Oh Mama, I bought them at that secondhand store in Sisketon. You know the one, where we found that nice purse one time. They only cost a dollar. Who would sell diamonds for a dollar?" She smiled and glanced at Jesse and me to include us in the joke.

Vishti held the earring up to the light again, then took the pair of scissors from the pencil cup in the middle of the table and tried to scratch the surface of the large center stone. The blade slid off without leaving a mark. Vishti sat still for a moment, and I could hear India's long intake of breath while we waited.

"We'll take them back. They made a mistake." She looked right at India. "Didn't they?" If her mother had insisted that night was day at that moment, India would have agreed because Vishti's voice had a tone I'd never heard before, but which her daughter obviously had.

"Yes, ma'am," India said.

Vishti looked at Jesse and nodded. Then Jesse pushed back his wooden kitchen chair and stood. "I'll walk you home 'case that fool horse sees something he doesn't like."

We set out with Jesse beside Cat's head, a lantern in one hand, a lead line on the halter over the bridle in the other. The horse plodded along like a pony.

"Maybe we could work some of the horses in the evenings, now that the indoor ring is ready," I said as we neared our driveway. I would have paid him to stay with me the nights Clement was gone.

Jesse was silent until we turned on the stable lights, unsaddled Cat, and put him in his stall, where he settled to munching hay with a big sigh.

Jesse looked toward the house, which was dark since I'd left in the late afternoon. "Clement not around?"

I shook my head.

"When'd he leave?" Jesse ran a damp rag over the bit and bridle, removing dirt and sweat. The leather gleamed when he hung it up.

"Yesterday?" I said in a tiny voice.

Jesse snorted and slapped the rag on a hook to dry. "Shouldn't be here alone. What's he thinking? Anybody ever come around bothering you?"

I shook my head. It was odd how close he was to voicing my fears. "Who would do that? We're way out here in the country. I can shoot now too. I have a shotgun and a pistol I keep handy at night."

Jesse's expression said I was too dumb to get out of the way of a train. "He keeps some pretty rough company, Hedie."

"I know, but they never come around here."

"That you know of."

Jesse walked me to the house, waiting until we'd gone through every room, turning on lights and opening closets. I couldn't stand the thought of being alone though, so I offered to show him the farm's old stud books and Jacques' ledgers, where he apparently cataloged everything that passed through his hands.

"Star of New Orleans," Jesse read aloud, "run aground, all hands lost, baggage included: 500 bales cotton, 1 red bull, 3 spotted cows (kept) 2 draft horses 1 sorrel 1 black (brought good $), 100 bolts indigo cloth (10 for Negroes), various furniture, monies, jewelry, clothing and miscellaneous (divided equal shares)."

Another entry included a list of his slaves and their offspring, including "Omah Ducharme."

Travelers who suffered accidents, capsized coaches and buggies, men lost in sand boils—Jesse read aloud a long list of calamities the scope of which was so absurd that we laughed uncomfortably and glanced ruefully at each other.

"This old pirate's Clement's grandfather?" Jesse snapped the book shut.

"Great-grandfather, I think." I glanced around the room, seeing it through Jesse's eyes, a crowded museum of disconnected styles, periods, and tastes that defied any single vision. For the first time I wondered how much was stolen, and where the rest of the money was, the pirate's hoard.

"Look how late it's getting. Vishti's probably worried about you."

Jesse nodded, ran a hand through his closely cropped hair and looked toward the front door.

"You all right now?"

I nodded and thanked him.

He paused on the front porch, gazing at the dark outline of the barn for a moment. A coyote gave a little yip and coughed out a disgruntled howl, then went quiet. Jesse cleared his throat.

"Truth be told, I'm up half the night as it is. Vishti goes to bed early to read. I sit in the dark waiting for India or just thinking. Nothin' good comes from that. I might could stop back here around seven or eight, work the horses, maybe make a rider out of you yet."

Without waiting for an answer, he put his hat on and waved goodbye.

WHEN CLEMENT SHOWED UP A WEEK LATER, EXHAUSTED AND SICK WITH A gunshot wound in the fleshy part of his upper arm, I put him to bed and babied him for a few days until he was on his feet again, vowing to find some way to make more money so he could stop this dangerous game. He'd never hear of selling off any land, getting rid of the horses or one of the cars. In that way he was like old Jacques, he would do anything to hang on to this place, and now I'd become a part of the problem too. But I wasn't going to sit idly by.

"Come spring I'll take you back to Hot Springs for the racing season," Clement promised one night, his head in my lap while I stroked the ache from his temples. He clung to my thighs like a drowning man, and I leaned down and brushed his hair back and kissed the top of his head, admiring his small pointed ears again. One thing led to another after that and we made love with a desperation that turned us rough, unable to find satisfaction until we had broken through the very flesh sealing us from each other.

The next morning I slept in for the first time in months, and when I woke up Clement was gone. My first thought was to see if the Packard was still here, so I ran to the balcony and was surprised by a thick layer of early frost clinging to the floorboards and railing. His car was covered in its own silver sheen, but it was the front yard that held a surprise. In the frost-glazed grass he had walked out a giant heart shape that glistened like a bright green jewel against the white.

He was waiting for me at the kitchen table, with a cup of coffee in one hand, the paper in the other. At my place sat a little green velvet box. Inside was a ring set with a large square emerald, surrounded by diamonds. I gasped and tried it on, but it was so big I finally fit it to my thumb and held it up triumphantly for him to see, which made us laugh. We laughed even harder when I tried it on my big toe. Finally, I thanked him and said I'd take it to town to be refit for my finger.

"Don't," he said, all traces of a smile gone. "Just leave it be. Wrap it with string."

"It's too beautiful to be treated that way, Clement. Couldn't I just run it in to Boettcher's Jewelry Store and have him do it?"

Clement slapped his hand on the table, sending the coffee out of our cups. "Give it back if you can't wear it the way it is." There was an edge to his voice I'd never heard before, and I shook my head and put the ring back in the box, and the box in the pocket of my pants. He immediately repented, stroking my hand and saying how sorry he was, but I could tell that something was terribly wrong with him. Later, after he'd gone out to supervise the orchard work, I picked up the paper he'd been reading. It wasn't our weekly with local gossip and town matters. It was a St. Louis daily from a few days ago, with a story on the second page describing the lack of progress in finding the men responsible for the robbery of a courier carrying half a million dollars in jewelry. I dropped the paper, but immediately picked it up again and looked around the kitchen as if someone might see the story and connect it to us. Monte Jean! She was late today, but she'd be here soon—I grabbed the entire paper and a box of matches and ran out to the burn barrel where I stood watch until there was nothing but flakes of black ash in the bottom.

I went inside and hid that ring where no one would find it. For the first time I knew what being a Ducharme wife meant. At first it depressed me, filled me with fear, but by noon I had resolved to stand by him. I took the rifle and pistol he trained me to shoot and drove out to the sand boil with a box of bottles, which I lined up and shot so they fell into the boil and disappeared. When I was satisfied, I drove back and fixed us lunch, avoiding Monte Jean's pointed looks.

A WEEK LATER CLEMENT ANNOUNCED THAT HE JUST HAD A PHONE PUT IN AT Jesse and Vishti's house so I could call if there was a problem. "With horses, you never know," he said with a kiss on my cheek.

I was so touched I called Vishti as soon as he left the house to direct the fall plowing. Vishti and I spent hours on the phone the following weeks. Somehow it was easier than in person, sharing our stories of growing up, our secret pains and joys, though nothing about Clement or India. Still we never ran out of things to say, it seemed, that bodiless voice in the black receiver almost like talking to yourself. Clement would come in and smile at the picture of me with my feet on the kitchen table, the phone at my ear.

One day he said, "You know everyone else on the line is listening, don't you?" and laughed.

"We'll all be better friends then," I shot back.

Jesse came over four or five nights a week, usually on the nights Clement was gone or waiting by the telephone. The time flew. I guess, looking back, that I was happy. Not in the old way, when I was pregnant and full of green hope. This was a steadier, less raw thing, with hardly any hope involved.

I let the work take my mind off how my husband spent those nights and days, who had the power to call him away, and what to do with the money he kept hiding in fruit jars in the dug-out cellar, sheds, and barns. I didn't want to bother him with the obviousness of his stashes, I simply buried them in the stallion pasture where no one would know to search. The jars were waterproof and kept out the vermin, I told myself, and yes, occasionally I'd slip some bills into my purse and go shopping in Sisketon for horse blankets or saddle pads or a present for Vishti, who loved the tins of chocolates and gold-trimmed playing cards I found for her. She was a person it was easy to delight, and with India running the countryside, she needed it.

Jesse just stewed over his daughter's misbehavior. Finally, they sent her to an aunt in St. Louis, and that turned out to be the worst possible choice.

How I thought life had begun anew. What innocence, what pride—

ONE NIGHT IN LATE JANUARY JESSE AND I HAD LET THE FOUR BROOD MARES OUT to run loose in the indoor ring, since the ground was too hard outside for them to do more than walk gingerly through the frozen mud of their paddock.

"That Cisco mare's going to drop something special." Jesse pointed to a brown mare whose trot floated above the arena floor.

"Foal's as good as its ma. Could make the Olympics."

"You talkin' 'bout my racehorses?"

I whirled around to find Clement leaning drunkenly against the wall behind us. He looked like he'd been beaten up, with blood dotting the front of his white shirt, and his right coat sleeve half torn off. His left eye was swollen shut and there was dried blood on the corner of his mouth.

"You're hurt." I reached out and he took me into his arms.

"It's nothin', honey," he whispered into my ear. "Send Jesse home. I got a surprise for you."

His fingers were on my breast and I shivered.

"I'll be in the house." He staggered down the brick aisle, stopping to call over his shoulder at the door, "Don't be long now, honey."

Jesse was already collecting the mares and snapping lead ropes on their halters.

"He needs me," I said in an apologetic tone.

"'Course he does," Jesse said, but his eyes were flat, the skin on his face shiny tight.

"Tomorrow night?" I asked.

He handed me a lead rope.

I grabbed his arm and tried to swing him toward me.

"Listen—" I said.

But he pushed past with the three big-bodied mares.

At the house I found Clement passed out, snoring with his head in his arms at the kitchen table. I thought about leaving him there, but figured that wasn't fair to Monte Jean. How would I get him upstairs alone?

I looked out the kitchen window to the stable, where all the lights were still on. Jesse hadn't left.

As strong as Jesse was, it took both of us to drag Clement's deadweight up those stairs and haul him into bed. Undressing him was difficult too. He was bruised all along his right side like he'd been kicked. I felt sick for him, and was glad he was so drunk he couldn't feel it.

When he was down to his drawers, I got embarrassed and wanted one of us to turn away.

Jesse said, "That's all right," and I was grateful to leave them on.

At the front door, I stopped him. "I need your help—Clement's in over his head." I looked at the ceiling, imagining him up there, watching. I dropped my voice. "I'm so scared for him . . ."

"He's a grown man, Hedie." Jesse opened the door. "Nothin' I can say to change what he's bound to do." He patted my shoulder and left me to my worries.

"That's that," I said to the dark room, but it wasn't.

CLEMENT TRIED TO STAY HOME MORE AFTER HIS BEATING, BUT THE PHONE rang every night and whatever he was about, he left to do it, carrying his satchel of guns, with a new shotgun under a blanket on the backseat. Nights he stayed with me, he tossed in his sleep, crying out in nightmares that could only be stopped in my arms, as I soothed him with my voice. He never apologized for any of it, and I never expected him to. I took the gifts and measured them against the cost of my husband's life until one night after working the horses I proposed that Jesse and I begin searching for Jacques' treasure.

Jesse was brushing the thick winter coat of one of the brood mares to keep her skin healthy. Occasionally she'd cock a leg and give a little kick, one of the bad habits she kept from her racing days, although she was careful never to connect.

"So what do you think? Will you help me? I need someone strong enough to pry off some of the wallboards in the ell." I'd had a dream the night before in which Annie showed me where some of Jacques' treasure was hidden.

Jesse nodded, flat lipped, and dug the brush into the mare's rump too hard, receiving a soft kick that grazed his knee. "What's he gonna say when you present him with it? Think he's gonna quit criminalizing? Become an upstanding citizen? Go to church?"

"I don't go to church," I said. "He can buy more land and we can start our family, like we planned."

He crooned to the mare, who relaxed her leg. "Uh-huh. He'll want the youngsters to start racing in the spring, Hedie, and I bet you haven't even talked to him, have you?"

This was something we had debated since fall, that we worried about sending the two-year-olds out, wanted to give them another year's growth, although it meant losing a whole year's potential income.

"He sleeps all day, Jesse, you want me to wake him up? He'll never agree then."

I stuck my hand out and let the mare lick my palm, careful to keep it flat in case she decided to take out some grooming frustration with her teeth.

"You heard from your daughter lately?"

Jesse sighed and ran his fingers through the brush to release the dust.

"Aunt Lily got her a job in a library of some sort. Can't see it, but if it keeps her busy—"

"You all miss her, don't you?"

Jesse shrugged. "I don't miss the misery she was visiting on her mother and me."

I couldn't forget those words, which settled like a barb just under the skin. I worried that if I didn't find Jacques' money, I'd never have a child, never feel even the disappointment of being someone's mama. So after more discussion, we decided to start looking upstairs first, tapping the walls and floors, searching for hollow sounds, loose boards, any hiding place left by the builders. I intended to be thorough, regardless of how many before me had searched those same rooms.

We were up in our bedroom, pushing the bed back to the wall when Clement appeared in the doorway. "What's this?"

We were both so startled we jumped guiltily. "Nothing," I said. "We were just fixing the bed . . ."

"I see that," he said. His voice was so cold he was beyond anger.

Why wasn't Jesse saying anything?

"We were looking for something, Clement, that's all, you can see that. We came in from the barn, and thought we heard something up here, in the walls."

Clement shook his head, swung around and stamped down the stairs.

"I better go," Jesse said and quickly followed.

I found Clement in the library, drinking brandy and staring at the fire.

"All right, we were looking for Jacques' treasure hoard." I slumped onto the leather sofa. "I wanted to find it so you could stop, so you'd be here, safe, with me again." My voice sounded shaky, so I rushed on to explain the dream, but since he'd never read the journals, he had no idea who Annie Lark was, or what Jacques' treasure was.

"You mean your uncle Keaton never told you?" I asked in response to his revelation of Keaton's having read through the entire series.

Clement shook his head and slugged down the brandy, then poured himself another glass to the brim. Although his expression still showed a shadow of doubt, his suspicion appeared to be easing.

"You know I couldn't stand unfaithfulness," he finally said. "Not after all I've been through to protect the farm and you."

I went to him then, leaning over the back of his chair, holding his face to my breasts until the tension left his shoulders.

Part Three

LITTLE MADDIE
DUCHARME

. . .

"Our remedies oft in ourselves do lie."

22

"MY NAME IS LITTLE MADDIE DUCHARME," SHE KEPT REPEATING to pass the hours. Then she made up a song to go with her name: "I'll never marry, merry, mary, maree. Who would have me? Who could find me? My da has the key to my room." But he'd been gone three days now. She knew because she counted the scratches on her window. She made one for each day with her mother's yellow diamond ring. It was so big she had to wear it on her thumb. When Da locked her in here, he called her Laurie after her mother and cursed the color of her red hair, her blue eyes, her faithless heart.

"Da, please, I love you, please, I won't ever leave," she cried as the bolt slid home.

The water in the pitcher was gone, but it had rained that morning so she'd held her hands out the slit in the window and lapped the tiny puddles like a dog. The windows were nailed so they wouldn't open more than a few inches. He didn't ever want her to leave. Three nights ago, he called her Annie through the crack in the door, weeping as she'd never heard a man weep. She sat silently, hoping that he would open the door to find her whole and in his arms. He was her own da and no matter what he did, she must forgive him.

Maddie had searched the trunk in one of the unused rooms and put on a beautiful old pale blue silk gown with a high waist and stood at the window waiting for him to settle in the chair on the porch outside her room where he spent his days now, stopping her from something she had not yet contemplated doing. The shadows were morning-sharp across the planks, showing the sag and dark rot. She wished he wouldn't go out there. As soon as he stepped through the door, she heard the floor groan under his weight, and she began to pray that the house would not turn against him as the river and land had.

When he saw her, he stumbled and dropped to one knee, hand over his heart as if that frail body had finally broken. She had never seen a face full of such anguish, jaw slack, eyes stricken, as if he had seen the depths of hell.

She knocked on the glass, calling, "It's me, Da, it's Little Maddie, it's 1889, I'm just playing dress-up." But he stared so she thought he had had a brain seizure. His long gray hair hung in greasy clumps that morning, and the skin on his face sagged as if the life were fleeing. His sharp eyes seemed cloudy with that film old dogs and horses got as they went blind, and she wanted to go to him, clear the caul that was making him not see her as she was—his Little Maddie. She reached her hand out of the window slit hoping to show him who she was, but at the sight of the yellow diamond on her thumb, he gasped and backed away on his knees. She grew frightened that he would lean against the rotted wooden railing and tumble to his death, so she beckoned to him, which only seemed to frighten him more. "Come here," she said softly.

At that he wiped his hand on the front of the greasy old-fashioned smock he had taken to wearing of late, something from his early days, Omah said. He looked frightened out of his wits as he clambered to his feet, using the creaking railing for balance, and edged away to the door.

"Help me, Da, let me go," she pleaded, and his eyes widened with fear. He should stop drinking. She would tell Omah to hide the brandy and wine again. They'd had to do this three times since she could remember, whenever he went too far away. Omah knew. She would lock him in the bachelor's ell and ignore the ungodly howling until the poison washed out of his body. Maddie'd learned to stuff her ears with cotton and press her hands over them. Sometimes she slept in the barn with the horses just to get away from his noise. If only Omah were here.

Maddie waited all day with no food, calling until late that night, when he came to her door, muttering and weeping. He prayed to God, to someone named Annie, to Laura her mother, and to countless other names Maddie couldn't make out in his drunken garble. When she peered through the keyhole, he was lying on the hallway floor, staring at the ceiling, eyes fixed, only his lips moving mechanically. Again she wondered if he had had a stroke or if his heart were failing or if this time he were truly going mad. She thought that in the morning Frank Boudreau would come and let her out and see after Da. He had worked for Jacques since before she was born and understood the old man's ways. She thought all this while she watched her da, crusty white spittle at the corners of his cracked lips, tears staining his leathery face. Then he slowly sat up and pulled the smock over his head. The sparse silver hairs on his chest stood as if electrified, but the skin was still taut! He had the body of a young man—firm muscles instead of flaccid skin—she could not explain it. Only his face showed any aging. He stood and unbuttoned his trousers and stepped out of them. She should have turned her head, but she was too surprised by the strength in those long lean muscled thighs, the legs of a young man, and more. It didn't make sense, and she couldn't take her eyes off his figure.

Then he did a strange thing. He raised his arm, and yelled "*Espérez!*" which she took to mean "be patient," at the ceiling. She followed his eyes upwards and saw only the usual shadows from the lamps at either end of the hallway.

So she pounded on the door again. "Let me out, you bastard!" She had never sworn at her da before, and she didn't know why she did then. It just slipped out, but it was enough. He stared wild-eyed at the door, balled his fist, and hurled himself against the wood, yelling, "*petite délinquante*—you bitch, you thief!" She flung herself backward, certain the door was about to fall into the room, but it held, and the next thing she heard was the pounding of his bare feet on the stairs.

She had not heard from him or anyone since. Omah had gone to New Orleans on a boat. Grandma Maddie died a month before. Her brother Keaton lived in New York City, but she had never seen him.

We all want to belong to someone else, Miz Maddie, her grandma, told her. Little Maddie belonged to her old da and to this house and to her. She promised to watch over her granddaughter, then she died. How do you belong to the dead?

This morning, she determined to break out of her prison. Da wouldn't answer her, and she was so very very hungry. If he made her leave, if he disowned her, she would flee to her mother, wherever she was. Or her brother Keaton. Someone would have her. She was young and certain of this. If nothing else, she would go stand by the railroad tracks in the pasture and wave down the train.

She took the heavy porcelain water pitcher with the blue birds flying around its belled middle and threw it at the window. The pitcher crashed through, bounced on the rotten porch planks, and tumbled through the broken railing. It landed with a thud and crack on the bare dirt below. Grass wouldn't grow in their yard anymore. Everything Da put his hand to died now. It was Grandma Maddie who had kept the garden alive, the cows in milk, the pigs fat, the hens laying. Omah would raise the curse, she said, to free them. She'd better hurry. Maddie used a thick book of Annie's bird and butterfly drawings to push out the rest of the glass so she wouldn't get cut. The windows were wide and low, so it was simply a matter of stepping out onto the porch, which didn't resist her as it should.

"Don't let go," she whispered to the sagging planks. "Hold me."

She went to the railing, careful not to lean against the rotting slats that were crumbling dark orange where they met the floor. She looked for him across the yard, the dirt road, the wahoo and willows where dust was already clinging although it was only June, and the wide brown river where steamboats traveled day and night without one thought of her locked in this house. Where was her da? Was he afraid of the men on the river? Sometimes she thought he was. He always refused to answer their greetings, their calls for wood or aid, their curious questions.

Something as big as that river you can't do battle with, Omah said. Look at the horses—not one mare caught last spring. They should be breeding right now, she said, and looked to the river as if it had taken the stallion's heart too.

Stepping carefully around the weakest planks, with one hand on the wall of the house as if it could stop her from falling, she made her way to the end of the porch, looking out across the barnyard, fields, and orchard. Where were the chickens? Hadn't he let them out? The cows were milling in the pen by the barn, butting one another, lowing painfully as the heavy bags bumped between their legs. He hadn't milked either.

"Da?" she called out across the barnyard.

Back to the middle of the porch, where she forced open the window onto the stairwell far enough to squeeze inside. When she searched the house, she found no sign of him. There was an almost empty wine bottle on the kitchen table, and without hesitation, she picked it up and drank it to the dregs, the rich red wine sour on her hungry tongue.

"Da?" she called, "Da?"

She found a plate of cold biscuits in the oven and stuffed two in her skirt pockets and took a bite of one—Da's cooking. The biscuit was light and crumbly, flooding her mouth with buttery flavor. Omah couldn't cook. Da cooked most of the time unless he'd managed to convince a woman from town to come out and work for them, which happened about once a year. Each one would last a few months, then give up and quit, her pockets richer, but her mind turned against them.

The last of Grandma Maddie's blackberry preserves would be nice, but there was no time, so she pumped some water and gulped it down, then headed to the barns. Maybe he was out there, fallen, drunk, hurt, or worse.

She opened the henhouse, barely managing to step out of the way of the red, white, and black spattered chickens that came flapping and tumbling down the ramp. The sharp rank stench of their waste mingled with the hot feathery must of their bodies tried to push into her mouth, but she turned and hurried away. Later she'd fill their waterers and see if they'd laid any eggs. They might as well kill them and start over, Omah said before she left. The hens were either hiding the eggs or had stopped laying altogether. They were no good to them now.

But Da wasn't listening. Lately, he'd been paying attention to something they couldn't see or hear. Omah believed it was the spirit world. Ghosts.

"I saw her," Da insisted. "In the barn this morning while I was milking."

"You should quit drinking, my friend," Omah said. "Laura is gone."

Maddie's heart had leapt at the idea that she might have returned and that whatever had happened between her father and mother could be repaired. She was extra careful for the next week to keep herself neat and clean and to help Omah and Da. She polished the parlor and library furniture, and swept up the front porch without being told. They were wrong. Her mother never appeared.

The barn was the newest building. The old one had partially burnt years ago, and Da built onto it, but she could still see the char marks on the foot-square supports. It always smelled a little ashy in there too, like a fireplace when it rained.

"Da? Daddy?" she called into the dusty twilight, but heard only the soft mewl of a cat and the lowing of the cows just outside.

She let the three cows in and tied their heads loosely so they could eat, then quickly climbed the ladder to the loft and tossed hay into the trough from above. Some of it landed on their heads, but they shook it off and greedily grabbed at the flakes. You must always take care of your animals first, Da lectured her whenever she didn't do her chores. You owe them that, *ma chère*.

He must have gone to Jacques' Landing yesterday, she thought. He must have gotten drunk and stayed in the hotel, or maybe he met someone he knew and ended up staying there, or maybe he fell in the river drunk, or maybe he—she made herself stop. As soon as the animals were cared for, she would catch one of the horses and go to town herself. She was certain he was in town, and it angered her to think he had left her locked up, hungry and thirsty. Wait till Omah heard. If Grandma Maddie were here . . .

The cows knew her as the clumsy girl, so it took longer than it should have to coax the milk out. He must have milked yesterday though, which meant he was here. She leaned her cheek against the warm flanks and closed her eyes, letting the rhythmic sound of the milk squirting first against the metal sides, then into the liquid itself, lull her mind. If Da, then she was . . . The tail swishing flies caressed the side of her face like fingers, so real she almost imagined she felt the light scratch of nails on her skin.

When the cows were done, she carried the last pail of milk to the springhouse and prepared to pour it into the big metal urns sunk in the cool water. But there was yesterday's. He hadn't put it out for the people up the road or taken it to town. Where was he?

If they had a telephone as they did in town, she could call, but there was only the one, Omah said, so who would you call? A telegram, a messenger, or a letter were much more reliable. She'd call her da home.

She had to fight every nerve in her body that said hurry, find Da, don't dawdle, he needs you . . . hurry! She was the impatient one. This time she'd show him how much more patient she was than he was. She'd take care of all the livestock, then fetch him in his pitiful, drunken state. What if he'd fallen off the buggy into the bayou and drowned? What if he'd been killed by river pirates or robbers from Reelfoot Lake across the river in Tennessee? What if he took the ferry across to gamble or hunt? She shook her head to loosen the bad thoughts and filled a bucket of corn.

She spilled some corn on the ground so the stallion had to work to pick the yellow kernels from the dust with his black velvet lips. Then she slipped through the boards, hung the bucket on the post, and stood beside him. With a quick tap on the back of his knee, she said, "Down," and he lowered that leg to the ground. Despite the long skirt, she shimmied up on his back and grabbed his mane. As soon as he felt her weight, he grabbed a last bite of corn and turned close enough to the fence that she could handily lift the bucket as they passed, just as Da had taught her. He would be proud.

The stallion wanted to run, but she pressed her knuckles into his neck and cooed, and he stayed in his long, ground-eating walk. Maybe she should ride him to town. Imagine people's surprise when she showed up astride a black stallion. The stuff of fairy tales and romances. The Brontë sisters or Flaubert, the kind of books Omah gave her to read, but dismissed as mere silliness. Then why read them, Maddie asked, but Omah shrugged and offered Jules Verne and Mark Twain. She said that although Little Maddie couldn't leave Jacques' Landing, she could still know the larger world. There was a school in town, but she'd never been allowed to attend. Grandma and Omah taught her to read and write and do sums, and soon she would take over the farm accounts, Da said.

She pulled on the stallion's mane and said "Whoa," and he stopped and turned his head around to nip at the toe of her shoe, rolling his eye to demonstrate his dangerousness. As she often did, she surveyed the fields, the orchard, the swamp and woods that would be hers one day. Well, Keaton's too, but since they never heard a word from him, it was safe to call it all hers. He could fight her if he chose. She was Da's own girl and he was not a true heir.

She called, "Da? Come home, Da." The northbound train rattled by, hooting at her, the black smoke puffing the sky dirty. The ten cars were loaded with wood barrels, cattle, pigs, bolts of finished cloth, and furniture—what they had to offer the city this time of year. Da had promised that when she turned seventeen they would ride the red caboose all the way to St. Louis to shop and eat in a restaurant, and spend the night in a real hotel. Her birthday was only three months away, and she was already planning what to pack.

Little Maddie called for him again and again, raising her voice louder and higher each time, until there was a crack in her throat and she had to stop. If he were out there, she'd see or hear him, unless . . . she wouldn't let herself think of that.

She made herself glance over at her mama's apple orchard. She remembered when the trees bore their first apples, how she made the men pick one of each for her, and Grandma Maddie argued with Da that they should be harvested and given to the men and neighboring families if he was too stubborn to use them himself. Eventually several barrels ended up in the root cellar in the barn, but he was never willing to eat so much as a slice. Recently they'd all lost interest in the argument, and now almost all of the trees had bare limbs sticking out from the thick green foliage. At least two trees were dead, gray trunks surrounded by high weeds. The orchard needed culling and replanting, but Da didn't care. He hadn't cared for years. Omah had been running the farm for as long as Little Maddie could remember, and she'd told Jacques she was getting tired, she wanted to spend time with Frank Boudreau and their two children. Was she going to New Orleans to lift the curse or to replace it with one of her own, one that would free her?

"You're free to go, *ma chère*," he always reminded Omah, and she grunted and shook her head as if she knew what he didn't, which was possible, because he was so very very old, older than Grandma Maddie was when she died, older than anyone in Jacques' Landing. What he needed was one of Miz Maddie's nostrums to bring his spirits back, but Little Maddie hadn't been able to figure out which herbs and roots to use. Her grandmother had protected her secrets too carefully. Like an Ozark witch, which was what people in Jacques' Landing called her behind her back, even though they never hesitated to ask for help when they got sick. That was the way things were here, she used to say.

Da didn't bother with the horses anymore, and Omah had never cared for them, so it was left to Little Maddie and Boudreau, the hired man, to look after them. Even if they caught late in the season, their bags should be waxing up and their bellies should be swinging low and painfully full this time of year, but instead they'd just grown witchy and hog-fat like the stud who was acting like a gelding. They had ten mares, ranging in age from three to eighteen, and each one should drop a foal a year. But there were none so far. Da merely shrugged and muttered to himself when she brought it up throughout the spring. When she suggested the possibility of the problem being the stud, he looked scornful and snorted through his nose.

"Hasn't he stamped everything on the place with his image?" he asked.

"That's the most potent line in the country. Fastest, too." He shook his head and passed his hands over his face, pressing his knobbed, yellow knuckles so hard against his eyes she worried that he would damage them. "Problem is that damn girl—"

"My mother?" She asked stupidly.

His hands paused, and then he dropped them and peered out across the river, taking a sip of the brandy he had shipped from New Orleans despite claiming they were poor as field mice.

"You get Boudreau to do the breeding. The stud doesn't like girls."

She had stomped off with all the indignation she could muster. Why was it that men always resorted to her sex when they couldn't answer a question?

When she found Da, she was going to make him give her the horses. She could manage them better than anyone else on the farm. The thought swelled her confidence in finding him and getting him to put the animals to work doing what they were supposed to. Someone needed to take a firm hand here, she'd tell Da.

As she headed back to the barn, the morning sun was in her eyes, so she had to duck her head and peek sideways to watch where they were going. Her face was starting to sting with heat, and by the time she got back, the freckles would be standing out across her nose and cheeks. Grandma Maddie would be unhappy, but now there was no one to say a word and that gave Little Maddie a pang under her heart, a place only she knew about, where Mama and Grandma lived.

It was time to bring Da home, before the heat of the day made it too hard. She was certain where he was now.

She stopped only to put a bridle on, deciding that a lady could ride astride when it was bareback. She grabbed Da's old felt hat with the crumpled brim and stained crown and tucked her hair into it and pulled it down to shade her face. Immediately the sweat on the back of her neck cooled and dried. She pulled her long skirt down to cover her drawers, petticoat, and legs as best she could, but her bare ankles still showed that she hadn't bothered with stockings this morning. Her da was gone! How could stockings be anyone's business at all?

The stallion pranced for a while until she let him break into a canter which escalated to a full gallop, his head down, hooves scattering red dust in a great cloud that rose behind them.

When he finally slowed, they were at the tee where the main road led into town. They'd left the horseshoe of the river and all around them were the flat fields and bayou that drained the swamp backing up to their land. Scrub willow and cottonwood and wahoo grew along the road here, and so many wildflowers attended by blue and yellow and orange and red butterflies that she was thankful Omah wasn't here or she'd be making her collect specimens for identification. Such a terrific bore! Tell me about the world, Little Maddie begged her, tell me about the presidents and their mistresses, tell me about this French Statue of Liberty and the Brooklyn Bridge, tell me about New York City! She was going there as soon as she could.

Little Maddie didn't know that Omah had never been East, but she said that Maddie must have inherited this wanderlust from her mother, who came over the ocean to marry Jacques as a young widow. She sounded so brave and beautiful, Little Maddie wanted to be just like her when she grew up. She'd go back to her home in Ireland. They'd lavish presents and parties on her, their own dear granddaughter restored to the bosom of the family after all these years! Omah and Grandma told her as a young child about her beautiful mother, but cautioned that she must never speak of her to Da, who was too heartbroken to ever hear her name again. Little Maddie came from a long line of romantics, she saw, and she must strike out soon to find her fortune and love in the world now that she was almost a grown woman.

She pulled the front of her bodice and blouse down, hoping for the plump soft curve of breasts that the ladies' magazines showed, but instead there was only the dark emptiness of her small chest. Omah made Maddie's dresses too big on the sewing machine Da bought her, and nothing she could say or do changed the older woman's mind. She said the loose cloth was modest. Maddie had to cinch her huge skirts at the waist with one of Da's wide leather belts cut down, and when she asked about the tight dresses with small bustles tucked behind she saw in the magazines, Omah gave her a dark frown and said to mind her business.

Just outside Jacques' Landing on the old northern road there was a new building going up—a one-story red brick, the size of a cottage except the sign said Mississippi River Telephone Exchange. That's when she noticed the poles marching down the road into town, and saw that the tall old oak and cypress and elm trees that survived the quake and bombardment during the war had been scalped! A black wire strung from pole to pole had torn the heart out of the treetops. She was sick, then outraged—wait till Da saw this! Farther on, there were four run-down little houses, the unpainted porches tilting, steps rotting or missing, broken windows with oilcloth nailed across them to keep the weather out. Broken crockery lining the dirt path to the door told her that they were occupied by Negroes. The tulip tree to the side of the third house was hung with empty bottles to ward off spirits. Omah rarely took her this way into town; instead they usually turned and rode past the big houses of the local gentry. The owners of LeFay's store, the funeral parlor, the House of Hardware and Furniture, the farm implement store—all of them were clustered together in large houses with wraparound porches that took up half a block each, but were still dwarfed by the remaining plantation house with slave quarters and stables whose stone fence posts marking off a square block of land were a reminder of the past.

Their little town was hit hard the last time New York had a financial crisis, and everything needed a good coat of paint. Da never worried about money. For some reason they always had enough, although he didn't bother harvesting much these days. Why do you say we're poor then? she asked. How will I live when you're gone? He just smiled and told her not to worry—when the time came, he'd tell her his secret. The time has come, she would announce as soon as she found him. If you're going to disappear, then I have to know.

The stallion perked up as she approached the town square with the courthouse and blocks of stores and businesses that radiated in four directions from its big center. Two plump married women in tight corsets and bustles huffing down the street under their little parasols turned to glare at her in the early summer heat. She tipped Da's hat like a gentleman would and smiled at their red, overheated faces. The elongated bodices only emphasized their bellies, and the big bustles behind looked like sacks of grain tied on as counterweights to keep them from toppling over. On their heads perched little hats with stuffed pastel birds peeking out of bird's nests made of net and feathers; the hats matched their dresses, one yellow and white checked and one green and pink. Little curls framed the broad faces, making them look disheveled rather than coquettish as she imagined they hoped. The ladies waved scented handkerchiefs in front of their faces to dispel the red dust and stink of horse sweat. Little Maddie patted her own hair, which had come down on one side, making her look like a crazy girl. She held the reins in one hand and tried to tuck the hair back under the hat, but it was damp and heavy and wouldn't stay, so she finally lifted the hat and let it all spill down and tried to comb some of the tangles with her fingers.

Sensing her distraction, the stallion shied violently and almost unseated her when a man on a bicycle came pedaling furiously into the road ahead of them.

"Here now," she cooed to the horse, patting his neck and easing on his mouth until he settled into a flat-footed walk.

Qualls Saloon and Cafe took up half of the bottom of the River Hotel, a two-story red brick building where rivermen and stage customers alike stayed. It was also where Da was known and could drink on a tab as long as Omah brought the money round back once a month. But she wasn't here today, so it was up to Little Maddie.

She took a deep breath, squared the stallion so they were facing the double screen doors of the saloon, and yelled as loudly as she could: "Jacques Ducharme! Jacques Ducharme, you come out here!" Then she couldn't help but add in a plaintive little voice she recognized from somewhere deep inside her, "Da?"

23

Two miscreants pushed open the double screen doors with a shout and took a deep draught from their mugs while surveying her. She pulled Da's hat more firmly on her head and scowled back. They grinned like idiots, and she recognized them as the grown, ne'er-do-well sons of men who used to work for Jacques—St. Clair Jr. was one, the other was maybe Knight, she couldn't remember. They were dressed like cowboys from their year out West, when they went buffalo hunting and panning for gold, and ended up almost starving to death until a rancher took pity on them and taught them how to rope and mend fence and nurse cattle for twelve dollars a month. Omah said that they helped steal the herd on a cattle drive from Texas to Nebraska, and were drinking up the money. Soon as it ran out, they'd be up to no good again. She wouldn't let Little Maddie speak to them, though they'd tipped their big stained ten-gallon hats at her several times this spring. Looking at them on the porch, swaying drunk, she understood what Omah meant. Their jeans were so dirty you could sow oats on them and harvest a good crop before either of them realized it. Their high-heeled boots were so run-down and patched, they looked like they were about to split apart and leave bare naked toes in plain sight. The plaid had been almost washed out of their shirts, which were a dull stained gray with barely visible lines. They wore large filthy kerchiefs around their necks, something to wipe their mouths and blow their noses on as well as decoration. Their brown hair was so shaggy and uneven, they were probably cutting it with the big bowie knives strapped to their belts. One of them wore a pistol hung low on his side from a tooled leather holster, while the other had just stuck the gun unceremoniously in his belt. She glared at them, then hollered again.

"Jacques Ducharme!"

The two boys knocked their mugs together and drank again, then got pushed aside as another man came out to see who was making all the commotion. The stud took that moment to shy at his shadow, do a little jig, and then start to lift his front feet off the ground to rear.

She snatched at his mouth and kicked his belly hard with her heels. "Stop that!" He planted his front hooves, which was good. If he had really reared up, she'd probably have gone sliding off and landed in a dusty heap as free entertainment for the village idiots.

"My da in there?" She asked the new man, who had a trim gray beard and eyebrows and was more respectable looking in fairly clean black trousers and matching waistcoat. His bowler hat was coated lightly with red dust, so her guess was that he was a traveling man of some sort, new to town.

"Depends on who your da is," the man said, with a sideways wink at the two fools beside him. His voice was too smooth, and her da was inside her head warning her.

"Jacques Ducharme, you come out here this instant!" she yelled as loud as she could. The stallion began marching in place, knees lifting high as a circus horse.

"That's some horse there." The older man squinted and ran a hand over his wide, thin-lipped mouth, letting his fingers trail out his small beard as if he were overly fond of it. "What's a horse like that worth?"

"She don't know nothin'," Knight said. "Them Ducharmes is tight as a cat's ass with money and horses. Never sell nothin' to nobody."

"And you'd know about that cat's ass, I'm sure," she said.

St. Clair busted up laughing, slapping his friend so hard on the back that they both spilled their beers. His friend shrugged him off and glared at her.

"You won't be so smart mouthed next time I see you," he said.

"Are you threatening a lady, sir?" The bearded man's voice was suddenly deeply inflected with a drawl.

The screen doors pushed open, and Qualls, the saloonkeeper, leaned out.

"You can quit your squalling, he's not here. Hasn't been here. Don't want him here. Now go on, git—" He waved an arm as if he were shooing dogs and disappeared behind the dark screens again.

Almost immediately Frank Boudreau lazily pushed out through the doors, stretched, and looked around the nearly empty street before letting his gaze settle on her. When he realized she was riding the stallion bareback, he broke into a grin.

"You're lucky your pa ain't here, Little Maddie, he'd tan your hide for sure."

"He'd have something to say to you, too, Frank Boudreau, wasting your time drinking with the village idiots." He'd made her angry acting all cocky just because the other men were listening. He hardly ever took that tone with her at home.

"He's not in there hiding? Then where is he?"

Boudreau's grin slipped away, and he peered across the street as if the House of Hardware and Furniture held the secret. He looked like very perdition now that Omah was gone—greasy black hair hanging to his shoulders, dirty face and arms, stained holey red long johns with a pair of equally worn-out and filthy trousers over them.

"Thought he had you locked in your room?" he said.

"He didn't do chores today," she said. "When did you see him last?"

Frank straightened and ran a hand through his hair and wiped it on his trousers. "This morning like always." He gave a quick sideways glance toward the other men, who were now pretending casual disinterest. "Sent me to town to fetch a new hame for the work harness. Just stopped here to see a man about a dog." He frowned. "He said you were doing the chores for punishment."

The idiots couldn't suppress their grins, and the drummer inspected his fingernails. She finally understood. "I did them, but I came to tell him I'm sorry and ask if I can go buy a new hat I saw at Noble's last week. You think he'd mind if I went ahead and bought it anyway? I mean, as long as I'm here, and all." She made her voice plaintive.

His eyes narrowed and he gave an almost imperceptible nod. "You know how your da is. I'd be home whitewashing the henhouse or some such before I'd be spending his money, you want to please him. And I wouldn't be prancing around on his good stallion either, missy."

Ducking her head to hide the worry in her eyes, she nodded submissively, although it pained her in front of the idiots and that drummer. Frank was right. She shouldn't be here announcing the family business. Da would kill her, and Omah would personally take the willow switch to her legs. She was turning the horse away when the drummer spoke up.

"Nice young lady like that needs a man to see her home, don't you think?"

She swung the stud back around and urged him toward the boardwalk. The horse hesitated, so she kicked him and he lunged at the men, teeth bared, scattering them to the boards on either side with the clatter of his front hooves.

"Don't." Frank grabbed the reins under the bit and held the stallion's head while the men cursed and pushed themselves upright. "Go home," he said through clenched teeth, "and take this fool back to his pasture."

He released the reins, slapping the stallion's neck. The horse knew Boudreau, so he turned on his own, pulling his hooves off the boardwalk.

"That girl isn't right in the head," the drummer said, and the two village idiots found that greatly amusing and began braying loudly.

"I'll be there soon as I pick up that hame, Maddie. Tell Jacques I'll pick up those shotgun shells, too, after I meet Omah at the train station," Frank called as she started down the street. His last words sent a chill across her shoulders, and she pushed the stallion into a canter. She needed to get herself to the house, lock the doors, and get the guns at the ready. Something was happening. Was Omah really coming home? Anyone who knew them well would know that Frank made all their harness himself. She had missed that the first time he mentioned it. And they always loaded their own shells.

As soon as she was beyond the stores, she turned west and looped back to the road, then leaned forward, letting the stallion loose. The little houses and the telephone building flew by, and she could hear the distant shouts of the workmen as they became a dusty cloud. Her da said that when women in their family did ride, they generally rode like the very devil. It was not until they reached the tee that she pulled him to a trot, then slowed him to a walk and let him plod the rest of the way home to cool down. Her back felt as if a target had been painted on it, and her mouth was dust dry. She hadn't ever felt unsafe like this. It was so strange, the way her clothes suddenly clung to her body like they weren't enough to cover, and everyone could see right through them just because they were wet and sticky. The river too, by the time they reached it, seemed thick and dangerous, as if it could suddenly swell up and spill over the road, sweeping her away like an ant in its flood. There was a sudden shrill cry that shook her for a moment until she looked up to see two hawks drifting overhead, hunting. This was what Boudreau was really saying. They'd be hunting her. If Jacques was gone, then she was prey.

Not taking time to sponge the red dust and sweat stains from the stallion's chest and flanks, she turned him loose with hay in his box and raced for the house. Where were the dogs? She hadn't thought about that earlier. Just assumed they were with Jacques, since they went everywhere with him. Again, the hair on her neck prickled.

The house was empty. No Jacques, no strangers, although she thought that she heard a strange noise coming from the old bachelor's wing off the back of the house, a two-story ell that hadn't been used for as long as she could remember. Then she heard it again, whining or whimpering.

She pulled Da's pistol from the hidden drawer in the entryway reception table and went to the kitchen and pressed her ear against the door to the wing. Yes, there it was again, a dog whimpering. She hesitated a moment, checked the load in the pistol, and turned the knob. The door was swollen with the heat and disuse and it took her a few minutes of pulling and pounding along the edges to make it release. So much for surprise. The dog's whining had turned to yelping by the time she was in the long dusty twilight of the hallway; she tried to call it to her, but heard only scratching on wood coming from the end. Maybe Da was hurt—

Little Maddie hadn't been in that part of the house in years. Da forbade it when she was still a tiny child, and of course she had to disobey him a couple of times, but there wasn't much to see after all, so she forgot about going in there. Now she saw that the rooms were in disarray, old trunks flung open, clothing strewn about, furniture toppled and broken in the several bedrooms along the hall. When she had explored years ago, the rooms were mostly filled with outdated or broken furniture and trunks of old clothes and books and dark old paintings, but not this disorder. It looked as if someone had been looking for something. Were the men there already? She swung around in a circle, pointing the gun in front of her, ready to shoot any shadow that moved.

There was a rotten stink too, as if the dogs had done their business in the hallway when Da wasn't looking. She kept an eye out for the mess, but didn't see anything except the swirls and patterns of disturbed dust.

Why hadn't she brought a lantern?

Suddenly there was a loud noise and the floor trembled. Her heart thumped thickly until she realized it was only the passing train in the pasture, pulling enough weight to shake the house. It might even be Omah's train!

She was standing at the last door at the end of the hallway, and the scratching and whining were coming from the other side and she was finding it difficult to breathe against the stink, against the thought of Da, and the dog's fussing. She knelt down and leaned her cheek against the cypress door, a soft wood for a door, for a floor, for any more than standing knobby kneed in a swamp.

"Oh Da," she whimpered.

The dog heard and smelled her, and sniffed along the bottom of the door anxiously. She slowly slid her fingers under the edge and cooed to him. He licked the tips and scratched harder than ever at the door, began throwing himself against it, banging the door in its frame. She stood up, and put her hand on the knob. She truly truly would rather drown in the river right now than open that door.

"Not Da, please," she said as she turned the knob, "Not Da," and the door swung open with ease.

The little white dog rushed out and threw itself against her legs, leaping and scratching and whining, dark eyes wild. He caught her hand in his mouth, not biting, just holding and pulling her into the room, which was empty except for an old narrow bed covered with a dusty rose quilt, and a small crude table with the waxy remains of several candles crusting the top. There were pegs along the wall for clothing, and a tattered lady's silk nightgown hung from one. Nothing else. The window had been painted so only a milky white glow hovered on the wall. It would be pitch black in there at night. Why was the dog locked in there? What was that smell?

She stuck the gun in her belt, knelt down, and took the dog in her arms, whispering comfort and stroking his curly head. "Where's Jacques, Pete? Where'd he go? Where's your friend Vergil? Where are they? Go find them!"

Pete looked up at her, his small dark eyes filled with liquid wonder and what seemed at that moment to be an infinite sadness. Then he backed out of her arms and began sniffing the edges of the room and whining, as if he too was confused by the box he'd been locked up in. The old floor was made of wide cypress planks, roughly finished, not smooth and polished as the ones in the main house. She'd never asked Da what the ell was used for, why bachelors would need their own wing. How many were there back then? It was her impression that Jacques didn't have any brothers or sisters when the house was built, and that her mother was alone except for her son Keaton. Grandma Maddie's children were all dead too. Who were the bachelors? She ran a finger through the dust on the window frame, which was painted the same white as the rough cypress walls. The floor was swept, but not the sills. A quick glance at the table confirmed that it too had a thick dust layer. Why this wing of the house? Then she remembered that in the beginning her father had run an inn for river and stage travelers, and that it was swept away in a flood after he built this house. He must have added the extra rooms to rent. But only to men? When she found him, she was going to make him talk to her. No more pretending she was a child. She drew her shoulders up, straightened her back. If she was old enough to marry, then—

Pete began whining and scratching at the back wall, but as far as she could tell, there was no trick door there. She stomped on the floor, but it sounded solid.

"It's a wall," she told him. "Come on, let's go find Da and Vergil and get you something to eat." She swooped him up into her arms, and at first he tried to wriggle free, whimpering impatiently, but then he sighed and re-laxed as she pulled the door shut behind her and retraced her steps down the hallway. The kitchen seemed relentlessly bright after the shadowy ell, and when she slammed the door shut and let the little dog down, he gave only a few anxious whimpers before sighing again and trotting after her. For some reason, the dog gave her a sense of safety. He'd let her know if anyone got near. Sure enough, he ran down the front hallway barking furiously. She fol-lowed, gun at the ready, cautiously opening the front door in time to see the farm wagon coming up the road. Was Omah home? She stepped outside, the pistol tucked in her wide belt while the dog ran to greet them barking joyously and chasing his tail in tight circles, which never failed to make Da smile.

Her skirt was stained with a wide hoop of sweaty horse dirt down the front and back, but she wasn't thinking of that as the heavy wagon turned and the two big workhorses pricked their ears and lurched into a clumsy trot as they caught sight of the barn and pasture. Boudreau stood, hauling back on the reins, while beside him Omah clutched both her hat and the edge of the bench. Behind them in the bed of the wagon rode a large trunk so loaded that it didn't even shift with the rough road surface.

Pete began yelping and making quick dives at the massive legs of the team as Boudreau turned the wagon toward the house. By the time the team was settled in front of Little Maddie, Pete lost interest and trotted off to sniff and pee on the lilacs at the edge of the yard. Omah was different, elegant in new clothes that looked just like the ones in the ladies' magazines, with a brown and black checked traveling dress, trimmed in black with a row of buttons down the long checked bodice, covering a light tan dress. On her head she wore a large tan and black hat topped with the infernal nest holding the wings of a bird who seemed to be burying his head in shame.

Omah looked Little Maddie over, an expression of disapproval quickly passing across her face at the girl's disheveled hair and stained clothing. Then Boudreau was helping Omah down, and she was climbing the steps with her arms out. Maddie stepped into them, loving the feel of Omah's soft cotton gloves on her cheek wiping the tears. She smelled sweet, like the lilies and roses of the expensive perfume in Mama's old room.

Omah hugged her against her firm bosom, her strong arms steadying the girl, making her a child again. Then she released Maddie and held her at arm's length.

"Tell me," she said.

"I can't find him. He's gone." Little Maddie told her about the smell and discovering the little dog, but finding no sign of her father in the room.

"Just an old dog died in that room is all," Omah said, looking toward the ell.

Little Maddie backtracked and told her about the cows being milked, but the milk not being set out, and the chickens locked up.

"So you haven't seen or heard from him in how long?" Omah quickly scanned the barnyard over her shoulder.

"Two days." Little Maddie sniffed the tears up the back of her throat, swelling her nose.

"And where's Vergil?" she asked, half to herself, looking back at the ell.

"I don't know," Little Maddie whimpered. "I don't know what to do—"

Omah looked at her sharply. "Don't do anything. You let Frank and me deal with this. And you certainly don't go to town parading yourself like some half-witted girl. Now go upstairs and change and come right back down to help me put out some lunch and feed this dog before he goes after the chickens."

Omah swept past, pulling off her gloves as she opened the screen door, and entered the house as if she belonged there more than Little Maddie did. Maddie followed obediently while Frank turned the horses toward the barn, the wagon wheels in need of grease squeaking in protest and the harness jingling in a bright cacophony that overrode the hissing sound of the river's heavy bellying against the shore and the busy commerce of the birds.

DA IS GONE GONE GONE GONE GONE GONE. IT WAS OCTOBER ALREADY, AND THE song played over and over in Little Maddie's head as she directed the men chopping out the dead apple trees, trimming the living, and planting the new ones she had ordered last month. Summer flew by with all the work to be done and the quiet searching they did for Jacques so that no one would discover his absence. Telling people that he had taken to bed was bad enough. Suddenly Little Maddie found it difficult to have an evening's peace for all the local gentlemen callers, most not even gentlemen. The Knight, St. Clair Jr., and Jones boys were particularly difficult to get rid of until Omah shot at them one night as they were arriving. Maddie laughed herself to sleep over the expressions of terror on their faces as they ducked low on the horses' necks galloping wildly away from the house. They were lucky the horses had enough sense to swerve sharply onto the road and not continue straight until they plunged into the river. Those three had stayed away for a month now, and Little Maddie was mightily relieved. There was just too much work to do these days to spend evenings fighting off stupid children. The last haying was done, the oats and corn taken in, and now they were working on the orchard, the last of the canning from the kitchen garden, and mending fences and barns. But like every other farmer they'd been racing the weather to finish harvesting and preparing for next spring's planting.

They had a good fall day for working. The remaining apples, those called mummies, were hiding in the brown and yellow leaves, turned soft by the frost and ready for the cider press today. They had wooden crates set up for the ground falls and mummies, and in a while Frank Boudreau would fetch them and make a press. He'd leave ten jugs out to harden for another couple of weeks, then store them in the root cellar under the barn floor. At least that was what she had instructed. Da never used the root cellar, but he was gone and now Little Maddie was in charge even if Boudreau had some aversion to going underground. It's all right, Omah and I can take them down if necessary, she told him this morning to shame him. He had glanced at her with a quick shake of his head. They were going to see that although she was young, she was as iron willed as Da, and twice as strong.

A fourth of the trees were dead from insects, disease, neglect, rabbits, deer, and raccoons gnawing the bark off the trunks in the winter. In preparation for next season, they were pulling the last one out this morning. Over the past month she had inspected every tree and tied ribbon on the limbs that had to come off so the fruit could get light and air next summer. Although the sun had taken half the morning to burn the frost off the grass, the last of the summer heat would linger through the afternoon to die away suddenly at nightfall, giving them just enough time. She took a deep breath of apple-sweet air. She intended the orchard to be as her mother had planned it, in her memory.

"Make sure you clear around the base of the trees," she called out to Tom Spraggins and Nelson Foley, who, as the only Negroes there, worked together while the four white men paired off with one another. It was the usual dance of custom—nothing she could do about it for the moment, although it would make more sense for Foley, who was a huge strapping man, to help dig out the trees, and Caution Wyre, who was smallish and not very strong, to trim the grass. Instead she had to pay the men for ridiculous hours of inefficiency. Sometimes she understood why Jacques quit caring about the land. Almost every night since he'd left, she'd collapsed into dreamless sleep from exhaustion.

The sickle looked like a toy in Foley's huge hand, and he moved gracefully around the trunk of a good productive tree without wasting a motion. Just twenty, Foley was a good worker, who carried the name of the white family whose plantation house in town was all that was left of the old ways. She had seen him in the kitchen talking with Omah evenings when the work was done. There was a special soft tone they shared, and a kind of language that had nothing to do with Little Maddie or even Frank, who had to pretend not to be her husband and father of their children. Foley had yet to marry, and he came to Omah for advice, Little Maddie believed, because she had made her own way.

"Men worth having respect that in a woman," Omah said. "Don't be some silly girl like you read about in those magazines," she had chided in the past. "You have a responsibility here to this land and this house your father fought for so you would have a place in the world. Nothing is more important." She used to ignore Omah's words, but since Jacques left, Little Maddie was beginning to see what the older woman meant. Little Maddie had decided that he had merely left and would come back as soon as she proved herself, so she was working hard and taking practically any advice she could get, the sooner to bring her da home again.

Her mother's orchard was actually doing better than Little Maddie had supposed it was. The trees she had planted were good ones from solid stock, and Boudreau had quietly trimmed them in his spare time on and off over the years, used the apples too, she supposed. Little Maddie missed her da so much, but it was a relief to be doing the work he neglected, easier without his interference. Could she say that? she wondered.

Spraggins hit the tree with the big scythe blade again, notching it, then stopped and looked at the pale exposed flesh in wonder. Foley shook his head and glanced at her. Spraggins would be better used climbing the trees and trimming the individual branches she'd marked, though Clinch and Hazard appeared to believe that Negroes were incapable of using such highly specialized tools as saws.

"Nelson, you work the scythe. Tom, you come to the other end of the orchard with me." She took a saw and an ax from the pile of tools, and motioned for him to bring a picking ladder. Clinch and Hazard paused and watched her.

"You men stop standing around, hook the chain around that trunk and use the team to pull it the rest of the way out now. We have to finish clearing this end before noon and get the new holes dug. Boudreau's bringing the saplings from town as we speak."

Kamp, who was so quiet he seemed mute, laid down his shovel and went to fetch the team grazing a few yards away. Wyre looked worn out already, and she was tempted to suggest that he trade with Foley, but really she was sick of these men and their silliness. Clinch and Hazard were sturdier men, swamp bred and river raised, who already wore the perpetual brown skin and squint of a life spent fishing, turtling, and hunting to feed their families. They worked steadily because they had large families at home and winter was coming on. None of these men liked doing what a woman told them, particularly one who had recently turned seventeen. Boudreau set them straight every morning, and that lasted until late afternoon when their little rebellions started to get on her nerves, and her voice telling them what to do started to get on theirs. By nightfall, they were all thoroughly sick of each other, vowing not to renew acquaintance the following day, but there they were again at sunup, wading through the frost-tipped grass, leaving a dark trail like a finger drawn across a frosty window. They'd been working like this for more than a week now. Today they'd plant, and at the end of the day, they'd fire the huge pile of dead trees.

Spraggins stood holding the saw in his arms with all the awkwardness of a new father being handed his baby. He tilted his head and rolled his eyes toward the four white men working the chain and traces of the harnessed horses. "Those men won't like me doing this, Miz Maddie."

She didn't correct him when he called her by her grandmother's name. Maybe she'd stop being "Little" Maddie. "See the red ribbons up there? Those limbs have to come down. Work for a nice clean cut, all the way through. You trim and I'll collect the branches. Think you can do that?"

Her last remark had insulted him, and his long, narrow face closed up tight against her as he positioned the picking ladder that began wide at the bottom and grew narrow at the top so it fit into the canopy of the tree. He flipped the saw from one hand to the other and climbed up, his head and torso disappearing in the dying leaves. After a few minutes of sawing and showering leaves, a limb creaked, then there was a great deal of rustling, falling leaves, and shaking of the tree, until finally the dead branch dropped to the ground.

"Couple more up here," he called.

"Fine."

Dragging the heavy limb was more taxing than she imagined and she was beginning to wish they had a couple of carriage horses out there. They could probably be convinced to pull the deadwood. She was on the verge of going to fetch them when Foley came over and took the trunk of a big limb that Spraggins had just released, hefted it on his shoulder like a stick, and walked it to the pile at the edge of the orchard. In between carrying branches, he continued with the scythe and sickle, so that soon each tree was standing in its own clean apron.

Positioned under the last tree they trimmed, Little Maddie gazed up at the raw rounds of sawn limbs on the trunk and saw the bright blue fall sky staring back. She'd done what she could learn from the book in Da's library written by an Englishman who homesteaded in Vermont and who had sold her mother the apple stock. She closed her eyes, letting the air full of heavy ripe apples seep into her skin, dampen her hair with its sweet breath, and listened while the sounds of sawing, the whisk of the scythe cutting, and the murmuring of the men and jingling of the harness faded for just a moment. There was another sound, a tinny humming at her feet.

She looked down, realizing that she was standing unevenly, her right foot on a half-rotted apple. She lifted it carefully and stepped back and peered at the ground, suddenly aware of motion. Snakes? No, there were myriad forms of apple revealed now that the grass was short, from collapsed brown casings to almost perfect wholes still usable for cider. She turned one over with the toe of her boot, and bent to pick it up, but stopped. The half-hollowed-out apple had become a golden, glittering orb of wasps, writhing, no, turning and turning in the humming light. She stepped back and looked around. Wasps everywhere, feasting on the spilled apples as if it were their turn to take what they needed. Something in her suddenly felt longing and love, knowing that if Da were here, she'd run home and bring him back to show him such a wonder. Maybe even sketch it in a book, the way Annie Lark once had. Little Maddie missed her da so much, the way he'd throw his head back and laugh when she showed up with the oriole's nest like a long gray sock blown down after a storm, or the snake skins she'd collect and drape across the table beside his pewter mug of brandy, or his pride when she'd jumped on the stallion the day they were breaking him to saddle and had ridden around the pen twice before she fell off and broke her wrist. Those days were over now. She had no one but herself. Omah was talking about leaving for New Orleans again, and Boudreau wasn't kin. They weren't so much like the wasps; they had so little in common, any of them, and it was for so brief a time that it hardly mattered they even knew each other. The dark mystery of her heart would be hers alone to explore and hers alone to solve, which made all that lush brightness sad in a way that threatened to pull her down into melancholy. She shook herself out of her dark reverie and walked back to the men working on the dead tree.

The horses were leaning heavily into the harness, digging with their front hooves and trying to step forward with their hindquarters while Kamp urged them on, flapping the reins and calling ineffectually. Hazard was cursing loud and long, and she arrived just in time to catch him bringing a pry pole down hard across the huge bay haunches of the nearest animal. The horse faltered and threw its head up in pain, groaning loudly. The other horse stumbled and lurched to get out of the way, shocked because they were never hit. He cursed and started to raise the pole again.

"Here!" She sprang forward. "What do you think you're doing?" She snatched the pole and swung at his head, catching him with a glancing blow on the cheek before he could step away. He grunted and reached out for the weapon before she could hit him again, but she backed away, raising the pole.

"You're gonna pay for that, you brat," he snarled, and lunged, but she stepped back again.

"You, Wyre and Clinch, go around behind her."

The two men looked at Hazard and reluctantly took a step away from him. Kamp was hunkered down pretending to be busy with the trace chain.

"You men want to keep working here, you'll stay out of this," she said in as firm a voice as she could muster. In truth, she was scared to death, cursing herself for forgetting Da's pistol in her coat pocket that morning. Hazard had a big head and white blond hair and eyes so pale they looked like an eerie mistake. There was no fat on him either. He could break her in two like a twig. His children all walked around ducking when hands came up and kept their eyes from meeting another person's. Polite as church deacons too.

She glanced quickly at the road to the house, praying that Omah or Frank or somebody was coming, but except for the men working, the fields were quiet.

"You touch a hair on my head, my da will hunt you down like a snake and drown you in that river. You know he's killed more men than you can count, so killing one more will just be pleasure." She smiled as best she could and tightened her grip on the pole to keep her hands from shaking.

Hazard paused, doubt in his eyes for the first time. The other two men had stopped several yards behind him and were looking at their boots.

Wyre spoke up for the first time. "Old Jacques is a murderous sumbitch, Hazard. I don't want him on my trail. He's been known to flay a man alive and use what's left for his turtle traps. Takes a long time to die that way." Wyre shook his head and Clinch nodded in agreement.

"Just leave her be, Hazard," Clinch said. "You can't go around hitting women, and she's too big to be a girl anymore. Best you could do would be to marry her off to one of those lazy sons of yours."

Hazard thought about that as if it had the remotest possibility of actually happening, nodded, and broke into a sneering grin. "My boy could beat some good into her all right."

She couldn't help but shiver at the thought, and forced herself to stand straighter. "Get back to work," she growled. "Next man hits a horse loses a day's wages and a job." She paused for dramatic effect. "And they get to try to outrun my da."

She peered at the road from the house again, hoping to see Boudreau coming in the wagon, but still nothing. Turning, she saw Nelson Foley with the ax in his hand, half-hidden behind a tree. From his expression, she could tell that he was going to risk coming in to defend her. They stared at each other for a moment, his hazelnut brown face tense with worry, the dark eyes appraising her.

"You did good there," he said as she passed him. "But watch that Hazard once he finds out for sure that Jacques's gone."

She kept walking carefully so as not to stumble on the windfalls and give away her sense of imbalance. "He's upstairs in bed."

Foley shook his big head. "No ma'am, he's gone. The whole countryside's talking about it. There'll be more than them boys coming down on you like a hard rain soon. You best be prepared." They continued to walk down the lane between tree rows, wide enough for the team and wagon to pass along.

"You put on a good show back there"—he took a breath—"but you must needs get married as soon as you can. Any sort of man will do, long as he doesn't get rights to your land. Didn't old Jacques set up some paper with that lawyer in town? Didn't he tell you what to do case he passed on?"

She shook her head, unable to speak for the clog in her throat at the truth about her da. They all knew. And nobody but she and Omah were missing him. Just another old bastard, she bet they were saying, good riddance to that old river pirate. The thought made tears suddenly spring into her eyes, and she had to turn her head and brush them on her coat sleeve.

"I'm going to need help," she said, keeping her voice low.

He stopped and looked at the lanes of trees, then back at her and nodded.

24

FRANK CAME LOPING ACROSS THE FIELD ON A BAY HORSE. HE DISMOUNTED, looped the reins over the far wagon wheel, nodded at the men on lunch break, and walked over to where she was sitting with her back against a tree.

The mirthful expression on his face was enough.

"What is it?" she asked.

"You got visitors," he said with a shake of his head. "Omah says you're to get back there and see them." He couldn't stop himself from breaking into a wide grin. His hair was washed and neatly pulled back in the old style, and he was wearing clean clothing again now that she was back in charge. She was tempted to say something about that just to wipe the smart look off his face.

"Who is it?" She pulled herself up, stretching lazily. All that work was making her lean and strong, and her clothes were much too loose these days. With Omah's generous tailoring, she appeared to be wearing someone else's blouses and skirts. "It isn't more gentlemen callers, is it?"

Frank grinned harder and shook his head again. "You have to see for yourself on this one. Omah says you'll need to wash up and put on clean clothes too, so you'd best hurry before she reaches the end of her patience. I brought the horse for you. I'll finish with the planting."

"It won't take that long, will it?"

"Better hurry," he said, giving her a leg up on the horse, which of course allowed the men a glimpse of her bare legs to the knee.

She looked at them, nodding at the planting. "Not too close together, now, follow the pattern my mother set out and make sure the holes are deep enough, and you give each tree a good bucket of water, and don't tilt the tree in the hole, it has to be straight, and—"

Frank waved her off. "We'll be fine, Maddie. And we'll fire the dead trees when we're done, and yes, we'll dig a trench around the pile first, and keep water close by. Don't worry, I've been working this farm longer than a summer."

Passing the horse pastures, she was reminded of the next task facing her: culling the herd and putting it back into production. She'd been getting inquiries all summer about this year's two-year-olds and yearlings, and having to avoid them. They had no yearlings and only two horses old enough to be broken to saddle. Nothing looked racy either. If she didn't act soon, they'd be out of the business. They couldn't earn enough off saddle or harness horses. She let this problem occupy her all the way to the barn, through the unsaddling of the horse, and the walk to the house. Tied at the porch steps there was a fancy surrey lacquered black and painted with gold and red scrolls. The horses were a team of matching bright chestnuts with four white stockings to the knees, docked blond tails that had been cut, broken, and set so they perched high and immobile as decoration between the hindquarters.

Cap pulled low over his eyes, the driver was lounging lazily on the seat. It was the Knight boy, full of slouching arrogance, although he'd traded the cowboy clothes for fairly clean black trousers and a white boiled shirt with a stiff cardboard collar.

"Maddie, come inside," Omah called from the shadows of the house. As soon as she came through the door, Omah grabbed her arm and dragged her upstairs. There were murmurings of other women's voices from the formal parlor on the right.

"Who's here?" Little Maddie asked as soon as they were safely in her room. Omah pulled out her one good dress, which made the girl look like a child with its sailor collar and pinafore. Although she was of age, the skirt wasn't full length. Little Maddie reluctantly wiped the dirt off her arms, face, and neck as best she could with cold water from the pitcher and a washcloth. The drying cloth was streaked with dirt when she was done. She hurriedly got into her clothes while Omah tried to brush the knots from her hair, but finally just gave up and twisted it into a chignon at the back of her head, letting the straight strands that were supposed to be soft little curls hang down around her face. When Omah stepped back to survey the damage, she shook her head.

"That skirt is too short, and the pinafore—wait here—" She was gone only a minute before she returned with a dress over her arm. It was a lovely green, made of the lightest wool, with a long bodice and a wire cage bustle in the latest style!

"I was saving this for Christmas for you." She held it out, and Little Maddie snatched it from her arms.

"It's beautiful!" She hugged Omah and quickly began to undress again. No matter that it was wool and she'd be sweaty and itchy in the afternoon heat. It was her first real grown-up-lady dress! She pulled it on to discover that it actually fit. The length was perfect. Smoothing the bodice down, she realized that she did have a figure—slim hipped and small waisted—and with the bustle, she almost resembled those young women in the magazines!

Omah watched with misgiving on her face. When Maddie grabbed a hank of hair and groaned in despair, Omah stepped up and quickly fixed it again, this time braiding and pinning it so it rested on the girl's head like a crown. Not quite the current style, but it suited her. Her cheekbones looked higher now, and her blue eyes appeared deeper set and almost mysterious.

Omah inspected the image for a moment, then pulled something out of the pocket of her skirt, held her hand out, and dropped two large rectangular emeralds attached to gold ear wires into the girl's palm. She quickly slipped the wires into her earlobes, turning this way and that to let the light catch the icy green.

"These were my mother's," she said knowingly.

From her pocket Omah drew a large brooch, a huge oval emerald the length of her thumb, and diamonds and pearls wrought with gold. Little Maddie looked more closely and realized that the gold was in the shape of a mermaid, her hair sparkling as her pearl-encrusted body took ease on the green stone.

"I've never seen anything like this," she gasped. "How old is it? It must be very very old, and very very expensive—"

Omah said nothing as she pinned it to Little Maddie's bodice, but when they both turned to look in the mirror, Omah wore a tiny smile and patted the girl's shoulder. "You look just like your mother used to." Her eyes held a wistful memory.

"These aren't her jewels, though, are they?" Little Maddie said with sudden understanding. "They're yours."

"They're a gift, Maddie. It's not polite to question them. Now go meet your guests." She lifted a hand to her own thick curls, still black with only a few streaks of gray. Omah, like Jacques, was ageless, but Maddie knew she could not be as old as he was. She had children of her own—a boy and a girl had survived among the five children she'd borne—but she remained as lithe, straight backed, and strong as a girl. She never brought her children to the house though; in fact, Little Maddie had never met them, which seemed odd. She'd never seen Omah acting in wifely fashion with Frank either, and she had often spent nights and entire weeks there when Little Maddie was young and ill and again lately as Jacques had withdrawn from the world. Why the separation of the families? She was obviously a woman of means.

Little Maddie opened her mouth to question Omah, but she put a finger to her lips and shooed her out the door.

"I'll bring the tea and cookies," she said. "Remember, you're the mistress of this house now. Lift your chin and don't round your shoulders or cross your legs like a man."

Taking a deep breath before entering the parlor, Little Maddie lifted her chin a notch so she would be looking down on the seated ladies.

"Good afternoon, I'm Maddie Ducharme, welcome to my home." She greeted each one in turn, making them tilt their heads back and acknowledge her. Two of the ladies were the plump hens she had shocked the day she rode into town on the stallion, Dowsie Louise Binnion and Clara Boid. The third was Layne Knight's aunt Ethel May Zubar, the one clearly in charge. Without so much as a glance at her two companions, she initiated their business the minute Little Maddie settled onto the settee facing them.

"We represent the ladies of the First Methodist Church," Ethel May began, and Maddie smiled politely, which made the woman frown.

"Lovely weather for a carriage ride," Maddie said, which threw her further. Fanning herself with a lace handkerchief, Maddie glanced around the room as if she were noticing the opulent surroundings for the first time. When she had moved in, Maddie's mother redid this room in overstuffed, oversized furniture upholstered with red and gold plush, brocatelle, and velour and decorated with tassels and fringe reminiscent of Turkish style. Three of the walls she had painted bronze brown so the furniture stood out. The wall facing them was covered with wallpaper decorated with scenes from the Crusades, extending the Turkish theme, only the Christians were winning all the battles while the Saracens were lying trampled and defeated. Her mother had had a dramatic soul. With the heavy gold velvet drapes, the room was what Little Maddie imagined a bawdy house must be like. She was about to invite the ladies to peer more closely at the scenes in the wall covering when Omah strode in with a heavy silver tray of tea and cookies. The tea service was a Georgian silver one, gotten who knew where, but quite elegant and weighty. When she set the tray down hard, the Limoges cups rattled dangerously. Omah began to pour the tea, placing a delicate ginger cookie on each saucer, which Little Maddie then handed to the ladies.

Their first sips of tea caused such an array of sour faces, Maddie almost burst out laughing.

"What *is* this?" Dowsie Louise Binnion sputtered, the stuffed robin in her hat nodding violently close to falling off its perch.

"Why it's just your little ol' butterfly weed tea, Miz Binnion. Good for what ails ladies," Omah drawled.

Little Maddie looked at her in astonishment, realizing that Omah had entirely changed her demeanor and attire. She was now wearing her cotton slip as a shift with the oldest kitchen apron tied over it, and her hair was tucked behind a strip of white rag like she was a common washerwoman or cook. She'd even taken off her shoes! Any astute person could tell that her feet were better cared for than most lady's hands, the nails trimmed and shaped, the skin polished and smooth.

The white ladies hesitantly sipped again and smacked their puckered mouths against the flavor.

Her eyes merry, Omah drawled, "Good for nerves. Add a few lumps here, you feel like you sucking your mama's sugar tit." She went around and shoveled several lumps in each cup before the ladies could protest. They stared at their cups, uncertain what to do now.

"Stir it up good, that's right—" Omah poured her own cup of tea and added sugar, stirring so frantically the silver spoon rang against the cup to the verge of shattering. When her little performance was done, she lifted the cup and drank the tea straight down, finishing with a loud smacking of her lips. "Now that's a cup a tea, ain't it, Miz Maddie. We shore don't need us none of that newfangled Co-Cola here!"

Before the ladies could raise their cups again, Omah snatched them away, piling them haphazardly on the tray as if Limoges were the cheapest mail-order china. The ladies stared at the tray, Omah, and finally the saucers in their laps that still held the ginger cookies.

"Y'all eat them cookies now, 'fore I get back. They're real good, too. I feed 'em to my dawgs ever' day, parsley and ginger, gives them sweet breath and keeps the bowels nice and loose." Omah gave a big loose-lipped grin and marched away, sashaying her behind.

"Well, I never—" Dowsie Louise Binnion patted her lips with gloved fingers, a sweat bead leaving a track down her cheek as it made its way through the heavy powder.

"What do we do with these?" Clara Boid timidly held up a gingersnap by the very edge, as if more contact would prove lethal. Despite all the padding of flesh, she appeared to be a delicate eater, probably prone to fainting too, which Little Maddie immediately decided she didn't want in her house. The sooner these women left, the better.

"I'll take them," she offered.

The ladies passed the cookies, which she stacked neatly in her hand. Leaning back in the settee, she purposely swung her right leg up and rested the ankle on her left knee as Omah said not to, then began eating a cookie.

Ethel May Zubar raised her chin, keeping her eyes on the far wall, where a large, hand-tinted photograph of Little Maddie at five stared back. She had blue eyes and blond hair because the photographer forgot what she really looked like. Clearing her throat, the woman began again.

"I'll get right to the point," she said. "A young lady such as yourself cannot live out here alone. It's not proper." She swung her face toward Maddie, who had to stop herself from cowering under those blazing blue eyes. "It's not even Christian!" the woman hissed. The other two ladies looked uncomfortable, heads bobbing, but lacking the utter conviction of Ethel May.

"My father is right upstairs."

"He is not upstairs, Maddie Ducharme," she said. "You cannot hide behind that fiction any longer. The entire county knows that old river pirate has finally gone to his Judgment. Praise the Lord." The other two ladies repeated the sentence that was half benediction, half threat.

"Well, I'm not alone. Omah is here, and Frank Boudreau, and—"

"*That* woman is the worst of all! No respectable person would keep help like that, or that Boudreau man and his nigger wool swamp kin. Spawning children out there with anything that crawls out of the woods—" A small white glob of spit formed at the corner of her mouth, and her face stretched with such distaste and disdain that she began to resemble a rabid skunk.

"You are speaking of my aunt, madam, and I pray you stop this instant," Little Maddie said with the coolest tone she could muster. The aunt business was an inspiration from one of the ladies' romances she had read last winter, full of complications of hidden relatives and near incest.

"Your aunt! Such nonsense—who do you think you're talking to, sister?" Ethel May sputtered. "With your loud, cheap jewelry and crude manners—"

"You might as well get off your Methodist high horse, madam. We don't allow animals in the house." Maddie stood and went to the doorway. "You would do well to leave now. You've mistaken me for someone else. I am Jacques Ducharme's daughter, and if he's a pirate, so am I. You'd best escape with your jewels and horses while you can. And these cookies? They're the best ginger cookies you could ever taste."

She popped a whole wafer in her mouth and chewed loudly while the ladies quickly rose and almost tripped over themselves pushing past her out the doorway into the entry hall. Dowsie's bustle had been pushed to the side so it appeared that she had a large tumor on her hip, and Clara's bird hat had given up the ghost, slipping down so the robin appeared to be poised to eat her ear. Only Ethel May Zubar managed to keep herself together, but that was because she traveled like a ship at sea, with everything on board laced down tight as she pushed the prow of her bosom past and shoved open the screen door. She was still muttering about hillbilly witches, river vermin, and niggers.

"And these jewels are real!" Maddie called after them, furious that they would criticize her new treasures.

Outside Ethel May shouted roughly at Layne Knight to help them into the carriage, and Maddie tiptoed to the door to watch the spectacle of the tormented horses backing and lurching forward every time Layne tried to half lift, half shove a lady into the seat. The commotion brought Omah down the hall, and after laughing at them, she put a hand on the girl's shoulder and said, "You'd better go hold the horses or they'll never get out of here."

While the exhausted ladies were loaded, Maddie took the opportunity to stroke and calm the horses and loosen the check reins so they could stretch their necks and lower their heads. They blew loudly with relief as she scratched their chests where the flies had been biting so hard they'd drawn spots of blood. The fine chestnut coats were streaked with nervous sweat, and she was tempted to offer to buy the horses right there, except Ethel May would never sell them to her. Maybe she'd get Jacques' lawyer, Lee St. Clair, to buy them. She had the means now, and she loved the image of driving her horses past the Methodist Church on Sunday mornings. The nerve of that woman calling her da a common river pirate!

If only her da could hear them. Grandma Maddie, though dead, was more alive than anyone. She watched over her granddaughter. Little Maddie didn't see her, of course, not like the lady in blue who skimmed the grass on foggy nights, keeping Da restless as he hung out the lanterns. If her mother were there, she'd do more than poke fun at them as Omah had done. Her mother would high-hat them all the way back to town. She was such a grand lady. Little Maddie had seen the trunks full of expensive clothes, the jewelry in the room that was hers before she left. There was a great tragedy about her mother though—perhaps she ran off with a young lover, a pirate himself! Da was always old, and in novels, women did that, dying sadly alone or murdering themselves for the love of their children they missed too much. It made Little Maddie sad to think of that, so she joined in the better story. Her mother had died, swept away by the river, and her da had been in mourning ever since. Now he was gone, too, and she must construct his story before she herself was swept away by the greedy men around her.

That night after dinner, she asked Frank and Omah to join her in the parlor. It was time. She began by announcing that in the morning she intended to go to town to see Da's lawyer, and the county judge if necessary. She would tell them that Da was dead and that she was running the house and lands as her own now. She would notify the sheriff that any unwanted visitors would be shot on sight.

Omah watched her with a slight smile on her face, nodding. Frank stared at his glass of brandy, turning it in the light from the heavy chandelier hanging over the table, so the amber liquid broke into pieces between his hands. Then he raised the glass and drank as if it were a shot of whiskey, and settled the glass softly on the dark mahogany surface.

Little Maddie was still wearing the grown-up dress, and for the first time felt as if she were an adult. She poured a bit of brandy in a snifter and swirled it as Jacques used to do, smelled it, letting the smoky liquor rise and sting her nose, then took a tiny sip. At first it burned, then eased and warmed her throat and settled in her stomach with a smoky swirl.

"I will be stopping at the dressmaker also. Who do you advise?" she asked Omah.

Omah shrugged. "Alsie Taul does the best work in town, but she's talky. You could try Loy Greenlee." She glanced at Frank. "She's a young colored woman lives near us. Has a good stitch. You'd have to show her the styles and help her with the patterns though."

Frank refilled his glass, picked it up but set it down again without drinking, wiping his face with his big hand, the dirt so embedded in the creases it wouldn't come clean. He laid his hands flat on the table and looked directly at her. "Don't you think it's time to wire your brother?"

She let the question sit for a moment, picked up her glass and drained the brandy, imagining Jacques as she did, not allowing the smoky burn to rise up and choke her. She laid her hands flat on the table too, her mother's big yellow diamond glittering in the light.

"I have no intention of bothering Keaton. He is happy where he is and he shall remain so. His allowance will be continued as if nothing has changed, and I will not tolerate anyone interfering with this arrangement." She looked directly in Frank's eyes, as she imagined her mother or da might. "Is that clear?"

Omah was watching, her fingers tapping the tabletop lightly.

Frank shrugged and gave his head a slight shake as if he'd seen the world and it made him weary with its foolishness. "Well, I just hope you're prepared for what's coming then."

"And what's that?" She poured another brandy, this time adding more to the glass.

"We're always ready," Omah said, her voice hard. "Now let's talk about who we need to keep over the winter to help out here."

Little Maddie told them about hiring Nelson Foley, and wondered about Spraggins or Kamp. They decided on both men, and Frank said he'd talk to them. They were all reliable workers who could handle themselves in a fight and keep their mouths shut.

Then they discussed the horse operation and the prospect of replacing some of the mares and perhaps the stud, although Maddie argued against losing him. Finally she told Frank that she wanted to purchase the chestnut team Ethel May Zubar drove there.

"It won't do any good," Omah warned.

"Steal them if you have to."

"Now you sound like your daddy." Frank leaned back and laughed.

"We don't have money to waste on geldings," Omah said. "You need to be bringing the bloodstock back."

"There's a bloodstock sale in Hot Springs next month," Frank said. "We should take some of the mares, maybe the stud, and those two youngsters, and see what we come home with." For the first time he sounded excited, as if the idea of restoring the farm and its reputation were finally taking hold.

"No," Omah said. "No one is going to Hot Springs. Ever."

Frank and Maddie stared at her.

"Don't ask. Take them to Lexington or Memphis. Plenty of horses in Kentucky and Tennessee. No one from this family ever needs to go to Arkansas." She fixed the girl with a glare. "It's what Jacques wanted."

Maddie sipped the brandy, noticing how easy it was to become accustomed to the taste and the heady feeling.

"Good horses there, too, I guess." Frank poured himself another brandy, being quite liberal with her father's liquor. Her liquor now. She had to restrain herself from pulling the bottle out of his reach. She was surprised by how quickly ownership made a person selfish, and made a note to remember to watch her impulses.

"Good," she said. "Now that the orchard's done, we can cull the herd tomorrow and be ready to go as soon as we find an auction." She pushed away from the table, but Frank cleared his throat.

"One last thing—"

"All right." She settled back and crossed her hands in her lap, the picture of the mistress of the household.

"I didn't burn the trees like you wanted."

She waited.

"I thought, since we're clearing and logging the woods so fast, and that lumber is worth something these days, we'd best not be using it just for firewood. I thought that we could cut up the old apple trees instead and burn them for heat this winter. Your pa wanted to convert to coal but you still have so much wood around, I thought—" He shrugged.

She took a breath to think. What did a person do about someone disobeying an order? What would Jacques do?

"That's fine, Frank," Omah said. "He's saving you a lot of money, Maddie, you should thank him." Her voice was low and firm.

The girl thought for another moment, not wanting to give in too eagerly, then nodded slowly and said, "Fine. We need all the money we can find for the horses right now anyway. But Frank?" She paused and looked him right in the eye. "Don't ever do that again without speaking with me first."

He ducked his head. "Yes ma'am," he mumbled. Omah stiffened her back. When he looked up again, it was to catch her eye, and something passed between them that the girl didn't understand, awakening a sliver of jealousy in her for the first time. Who did Omah love more? Would she have to have someone of her very own now that Da was gone, someone who would love only her? There was an uncomfortable confusion in her chest as she looked at Omah, a light-skinned Negro woman, who had lived there her entire life, who acted as if she were the owner, the heiress, not—whatever she really was. And what was that? It had never been clear to Little Maddie because she'd never questioned it. Who was Omah? Why did Da let her tell him what to do? Why did he treat her as his equal? More than an equal, he acted as if they were—what?

"I'm tired." Little Maddie corked the brandy and stood, signaling an end to the discussion. She needed to think, now that her da was dead.

25

*L*ELAND ST. CLAIR'S LAW OFFICE WAS ABOUT AS INTERESTING AS A men's social club in a Henry James novel. On the walls hung pictures of St. Clair posed with a variety of cougars, bears, geese, deer, ducks, turtledoves, rabbits, any and everything that could be killed with a gun, bow, or knife. There he was, in every one of them, a man so small he could pass for a boy, with a little toothy smile on his face. His clothes were always so neat and clean in the pictures, she suspected that he hadn't killed the game at all, just had someone do it for him. Which was what she worried about—that he was one of those.

The door opened carefully, and she could see an eye peering anxiously in the crack. Then the door eased all the way open and the hunter himself came in, closing it softly behind him. Despite his gray hair, he was dressed in what could only be described as the current style for men engaging in sports, but rather than choosing one, he seemed to be representing several at once. Little Maddie smiled despite her efforts to remain stern. He had on a pair of brown wool knickers, yellow stirrup socks to the knee, such as a baseball player would wear, a bright yellow and brown striped wool sweater, as if he were about to set sail around the world, and the oddest shoes, low canvas uppers with rubber soles. She'd just seen a pair of them in the latest issue of a magazine, so she knew they were called "tennis shoes," but the rest of his outfit seemed to belie the activity.

He stood for a moment, frowning gravely at the papers in his hand, then sat in the Moroccan leather wingback chair next to her, facing the small, poorly drafted coal fireplace struggling to burn merrily that cold, damp morning, and emitting a certain quantity of smoke into the room in the process. Despite her vow, it had taken Maddie a month to come there. Perhaps because she was dreading the truth.

St. Clair placed the papers on the small table in front of them, which was laden with a tarnished silver bowl of brown-spotted apples and magazines that men might approve of: *Popular Science*, *Scribner's*, *Bicycling World*, and something new called *National Geographic*. The cover of the latter promised stories of African tribesmen, Antarctic exploration, and ancient Roman ruins. When he realized that she was about to pick it up, St. Clair leaned forward and eased it under the others, tidying the pile with a small sigh.

"I must apologize, this room is not usually where ladies—" He paused, admiring approval of her costume in his eyes. She was wearing the dress Omah gave her, without the emeralds, and was in town to pick up another, and order others. She had to bite her tongue from responding smartly that she had been hunting since she was old enough to shoulder a gun, and could outride almost any man in the county.

"Did you find my father's papers?" she asked instead.

He dipped his head toward the thin sheaf on the table. "What there is. I'm afraid he wasn't very forthcoming with details."

She reached for them, but he again anticipated her move and picked them up. He was beginning to annoy her.

"You understand that these are your father's private papers, and without proper evidence that he has, well, that he is deceased, then—" As he stumbled through these niceties his face swelled with redness, and she took a deep breath before she called him a donkey's behind and snatched the papers.

"Mr. St. Clair," she said. "My father is dead. You cannot expect me to wait until some fool someday fishes part of him out of that river. You knew him. Your family has known him since before the war. You know that he would never spend five months away from Jacques' Landing—he never spent five days away! My father never left that house or land once he put his feet on it."

"He came into town often enough." The little man stared at the smoldering coal fire, obviously considering her plight. Without ownership, she would be hampered from going forward. Unless, of course, she took a husband who could bully his way through, something she didn't intend to do.

"This town sits on *his* land, even if he did deed it over." She straightened her shoulders and held out her hand.

He shrugged and handed over the papers.

Jacques had made the simplest of wills, leaving his natural offspring all. There were two codicils that captured her attention, however. One stated that Keaton was to have his allowance as long as he maintained residence outside the state and did not contest the will. The second codicil affected her directly, and she was careful not to allow her expression to change as she read, but her breath seized in her chest and the acrid coal smoke seemed to rest on her tongue.

"Something needs to be done about this last item," she said, struggling to keep her voice firm.

St. Clair made an arch with his fingers and stared at the two stuffed pheasants taking flight from the paneled wall above the gray quartz mantelpiece. He had overly large brown luminous eyes, not unlike the old bay mare's they were sending to auction next week.

"I tried to talk him out of it, I did. Regrettably, he wouldn't listen. For some reason, it seems, uh, it appears, uh, that he wishes his line to end with, uh, you."

"That's ridiculous!" she snapped. "Why would you say such a thing!"

He raised his thin gray eyebrows and glanced at the fire, then the papers in her hands, and finally her face.

"Your mother . . ." He tapped his upper lip with his forefinger.

"My father *loved* my mother!" She stood, gripping the papers tightly in her hands.

"Yes, yes he did. In the beginning, it was hard to say a person had ever seen a man so much in love. And your half brother, Keaton, will benefit from that devotion for the rest of his life, in fact, but, then, as is often the case with May-December, uh, unions—"

She went to the fire, tempted to throw the papers in, but then she'd have to do something about St. Clair and God knew who else—just to have what was hers! But what was he saying about her mother? What did he mean?

"Please just speak directly, Mr. St. Clair. You are wearing terribly on my nerves with all this cat and mouse." She pressed her shoulders against the granite mantel, waiting for the blow, the heat of the fire warming the back of her skirt and legs.

"Your father seemed to believe that your mother, well, your mother might have been unfaithful to her vows." He couldn't look at her.

"Unfaithful," she repeated stupidly. Was that what happened? "She ran off with another man? Is that what you're saying? Yes, that's what you're saying, isn't it." She kept the tears from starting from her eyes by biting the inside of her cheek so hard she could taste the salty blood.

He shook his head. "I don't know. I don't know where your mother went. He never said. It was seven years ago when he came to me with the idea of making a will. He wanted to protect you, he said."

She considered the idea for a moment, taking a turn about the small room, past the pictures of St. Clair's triumphs. There was even a picture of a group of men on horseback, a ragtag version of an English hunting scene, with blue tick hounds milling to one side, and a row of dead possums strung from a stick raised on either end by two Negro men on foot. That was what she felt like right now, something on a stick, gutted by dogs.

"What else did he say? Did he seem to be in his right mind? Had he been drinking?" She stood behind him, as if to snatch the truth from his soul if she had to.

"I'm sorry," he began. "My father always said that Jacques was eccentric, but sane. I found him to be so. He had been drinking that afternoon, but he wasn't inebriated. He was French, one didn't expect him to abstain. He said he was going home to celebrate your birthday, your tenth, I believe."

She remembered that day. She had asked for a horse, not a pony, but a real, full-sized horse of her own to ride. She had also asked for her own gun, as she had been using Da's or Frank's since she was seven, and believed she was ready to hunt on her own. When she woke up that morning, anticipating what she believed would be the best day of her life, she discovered that instead of a horse she could ride astride, Da had purchased a lady's visiting cart with a little dapple gray gelding to pull it. The horse was so old, it wouldn't canter, and its trot was more an ambling walk than a true gait.

There was no gun in sight either. Instead, she was given a lady's archery set, with the target set up in the yard for her use. She flew into a fury, breaking the arrows over her knees, and throwing the bow in an oak tree before Da or Omah could stop her. Ignoring the horse with a red grosgrain ribbon tied in his sparse mane, she began attacking the cart with a broom. When Da tried to grab her, she turned on him with the broom, shouting that she hated him, that she was going to run away, like her mother had, because he was nothing but a hateful old man, he wasn't even her father.

The memory brought unwanted tears to her eyes, and she hiccuped trying to catch the sob rising in her throat. No wonder he came to see the lawyer. But who believes a ten-year-old child?

"Tell me the truth, Mr. St. Clair. The truth about my mother. I need to know." She settled in the chair beside him, leaned forward, and placed a gloved hand over his, as she imagined a grown lady would do to instill confidence.

He reddened to his ears.

"After the war she came here, you know, and helped Miz Maddie doctor people. When she married One-Armed Jacques, people got a kick out of how she brought him back to life. Being younger, of course, she wanted new things in the house, spent a good deal of his money with the merchants in town. It seemed to bring a lightness to his step again. The arrangements for your half brother were her idea, and Jacques did as she asked. He did everything he could to please her, and when you were born, he seemed to shed decades."

"Was she, was my mother a bad woman?" she whispered.

"Oh no," he hastened to say. "She was proud. She was beautiful and proud." His eyes said that she was like her mother. She pulled her hand free and leaned back with a smile.

"No one has seen her since she came back from Hot Springs after you were born. She was sickly, and your father and the doctor thought that the waters would do her good. That colored woman, Omah, traveled with her. I don't know what happened. No one does. She came to town one morning, then disappeared. Nobody ever saw her again. We just assumed that she ran away. We never mentioned her in his presence again. He wouldn't have it."

He put his free hand over hers. "I'm sorry."

"Your cousin worked for him, did he ever say anything?"

He spread his arms as if to indicate that the rest was unanswerable.

They sat there listening to the hiss of the coal fire, the fumes thickening in the room. Outside the heavily draped windows, the sky was low and leaden with an icy rain that had begun to fall just as she had stepped out of the buggy. The matching chestnuts were wearing good wool blankets to keep their backs warm, and without the tight check reins they'd stretched their necks toward the boardwalk, hoping for the sugar they were coming to believe every person must carry. She would not lose them. She would not lose anything.

"Mr. St. Clair," she began, leaning toward him and pulling off her gloves so he could see the huge yellow diamond she was wearing. Without effort, she slowed and deepened the drawl in her voice. "Is there not one little thing you could do to help me?" She put her hand on his arm and squeezed lightly.

His large eyes grew sympathetic. "I suppose I could file a petition to break the codicil. But—"

She took his hand in hers and brought it to her lips. "Would you do that for me, sir? Would you help a poor orphaned child like me?"

As soon as she uttered the words, she knew she'd overplayed it. He snatched his hand away and abruptly stood. The expression on his face said that she had a ways to go before she could use the persuasion of her sex on a man. She watched him pacing for a moment, then spoke.

"I am of marriageable age, sir. It is against nature to forbid that. A judge and jury would surely agree." She paused dramatically. "Of course, if you prefer, I will go to Sisketon or Cape Girardeau or St. Louis even to hire a lawyer. Rest assured, someone will want my money." She began to pull on the fine kid leather gloves that matched her new sheared beaver cape with the hood to keep the weather away.

He stopped in front of her so she had to lean her head against the back of the chair and peer up.

"There is no mention of marriage, my dear. It is offspring that is forbidden. Jacques wanted no continuation of your bloodline." His harsh words were matched by the harsher irony in his voice, and she had to stop herself from lashing out at him.

Instead, she pulled the cape around her shoulders and busied herself with the fastener. "And what sort of marriage would that be, sir? What sort of man would marry a woman who could never consummate her vows?"

She stood so quickly, her body was against his until he stumbled backward and had to push against the fireplace to regain his composure. There was a mirror etched with hunting paraphernalia by the door, and she stood in front of it adjusting her hair and cape, and watching his expression. When he sighed deeply, she turned and smiled.

"I'll file this week," he said. "The judge should be sitting after the new year. We'll have the hearing then. In the meantime, please see if you can find any evidence that Jacques is deceased. They will want that in a court of law. Hard to break a will if the person is still alive. You see what I mean."

"I do. Just make sure you remember who's in charge *now*." She opened the door without waiting for him and swept out of the offices with a smile and nod for his clerks.

Outside, the rain was freezing as soon as it touched the ground, and despite their blankets, her horses were shivering against the cold, heads low and dispirited, ice sheathing their necks and faces and harness. When she untied the rein, it crackled and pieces of loosened ice fell like splinters of glass. The iron step into the buggy was so slippery it took her three attempts to keep her boot from sliding off as soon as she placed her weight on it. Despite the top of the buggy, the leather seat was covered with a layer of ice that cracked when she sat down and pulled the heavy damp bearskin robe over her lap and picked up the ice-stiffened reins. The street was empty as she turned the reluctant horses in the direction of the rain and the dressmaker. Beside them the river seemed almost stilled by the icy rain pocking its surface, and the sound of ice hitting the trees and roads was a tinny noise clattering against the thoughts that occupied her now.

She was still too stunned by the lawyer's revelations to pay attention to where the horses were going, and they had turned into the road to their old stable at Ethel May Zubar's before she realized it. There was nowhere to turn around without gouging the grass, and she was cursing by the time they reached the stable yard behind the big house. Instinct had brought them to the nearest shelter, and it took some few minutes of cajoling and backing to convince them to even turn their heads around. She was just on the point of climbing down and leading them when a man came running from the house, tan mackintosh flapping behind him like a sail while he held the broad brim of a tan cowboy hat on his head. For one wild moment, she thought it must be Da come to rescue her from the rain and cold. But then she remembered where she was and thought of Layne Knight, Ethel May's nephew, and his cowhand apprenticeship out West before he came home to become a drunk, and she wondered if she was about to be subjected to some kind of rough play. Reaching into the brocade bag at her side, she pulled out Jacques' large revolver and laid it in her lap. The horses stubbornly refused to move from the closed stable door. Apparently no amount of kindness could overcome the instinct for survival. Horses would freeze to death rather than move from a place they perceived as shelter, tails turned toward the wind in an ice storm.

"Ma'am?" It wasn't Layne Knight. The man was over six feet and easily peered into the buggy as he raised his hat slightly off his forehead. He had a long, drooping dark brown mustache with threads of silver in it, and the creased, permanently browned face of a man working the land. The dark brown eyes were crinkled with amusement, something she was not in the mood for at the moment.

"Please step aside, sir, I have to get down and move my horses," she said as stiffly as possible, embarrassed by the gun she was trying to shuffle under the robe.

He put a large sun-browned hand on her arm, and she had to stop herself from flinching. "Now you just stay put. I'll get these ornery mules turned around and headed the direction they come from."

"They won't take to a stranger's hand—don't—" Her words were ridiculous and only made him smile happily as he coughed, then worked his way carefully to their heads, moving along their bodies with reassuring pats and quiet words. By the time he took the reins under the snaffle bits, they dropped their heads and leaned against him, as if he were going to save them from the ice biting into the thin skin around their eyes and noses. He rubbed their foreheads, coughing and murmuring as he began slowly walking them away from the stable. They didn't even shy at the coat flapping around him. His sleeves were too short, and when he reached to pull the ice from the horses' ears, the knob of bone on his wrist stuck out, suddenly making him seem vulnerable. His hands were crisscrossed with old scars and lines too, probably from barbed wire and rope. Even from her seat, the thick calluses padding his fingers and palm were visible. No wonder she could still feel the hand grasping her arm.

Coming back to her, he gave the near horse a reassuring pat on his rump, frowned at the docked, broken tail, and scowled at her.

"Think I should ride with you, ma'am. This storm's fixing to give us a good lickin' 'fore it's done. If you'll just wait while I—" He glanced toward the stable and coughed into his fist.

"I'm certain I'll be fine, sir," she said, preparing to thank him in the next breath. But he was already pulling the stable door open and sliding inside as her words were swept away with a snow-filled wind that was starting to gust hard enough to make the flimsy cloth of the buggy top appear to be on the verge of ripping. She pulled the hood of the cape around her face and pondered her next move. If she left, she'd seem ungrateful, but if she stayed, she'd be obligated to a strange man. Why wasn't she afraid? she asked herself. She looked toward the large Zubar house, scanned the heavily draped windows for some sign of life, but not even Layne Knight's face appeared. She put the gun back in her lap, in plain sight this time. It was true that she could use help with the horses who were even now starting to back, trying to turn toward the stable again. She spoke in a low voice, but her words didn't even reach them above the wind that was starting to howl as it flung ice and snow as hard as small rocks at the landscape. The horses flinched and ducked, and began to dance in place, and she had to resist jerking their mouths to get their attention.

She was moving the robe aside to dismount and go to their heads when the stable door opened wide enough for the stranger and a big spotted horse in a Western-style saddle to step out into the storm. The stranger lightly sprang into the saddle and urged the horse forward. Walking was more difficult on the road to the street, which was also building a thick coating of ice, and the horses stepped as if they were on marbles or bird eggs as they rolled forward, following the big spotted horse.

At the street, the man waited for her to come alongside, then leaned down and asked which direction they were headed. Deciding to forgo the dressmaker, she pointed west and shouted the place to turn. He leaned down farther and said that the ice would all be snow soon, the temperature was dropping, so they'd best be at it. She nodded and they set off, his shoulders humped against his coughing. It was reassuring to see him, wide hat tied down with a knitted wool scarf covering his ears, the mackintosh replaced by a red and black plaid blanket-wool coat, hands in leather gloves lined with wool, riding beside the buggy giving confidence to her horses, and giving her something she wasn't used to, a feeling that took some of the edge off what Jacques had done. Her da was a strange man with old-fashioned ideas. It wasn't the first time he'd been wrong. She wished she'd been able to say goodbye, that was all, that was all, that was all, the wheels lurching over the ice-coated ruts seemed to say. When her eyes filled with tears she let them, and she soon felt the frozen moisture stiff on her cheeks.

Half the town would be watching the strange little caravan from behind their curtains and store windows, but beyond the anxiety of making it through the increasingly treacherous storm, she had Omah and Frank to worry about when they reached home. Frank had become obsessed with the notion that some man would trick her out of Jacques' land, and despite her assurances, he had become worse than her da, promising to lock her in the bachelor's ell if she dared to think about a courtship or marriage without his approval. You don't have to worry anymore, she'd tell him tonight, Jacques fixed that problem for all time.

The iron shoes on the horses eventually made their step so difficult that she signaled the stranger and halted. They fought the ice-sheathed harness and released the horses from the buggy, leaving it beside the road. Throwing the heavy bear robe over one horse, she mounted astride, and gave the other to the man to lead. At first her horse refused to move, the snow so thick they could hardly see the road, let alone the trees on either side. She squeezed her thighs and calves as best she could through the heavy robe and clucked, and he took a tentative step, then another. When the stranger moved out in front, her horse slipped in behind to catch the only shelter from the wind. She clutched the hood across her face and held on despite the fact that the thin kid leather gloves she was so proud of were now soaked and frozen, numbing her fingers. Her other hand holding the reins she buried under the edge of the fur cape, but when she went to change hands for relief, she couldn't release the fingers cramped around the edge of the hood. Her horse stopped but she was so worried about her hand that she didn't notice for a minute and when she looked up, she was surrounded by swirling whiteness and the howling wind. The other horses had disappeared!

She kicked the horse, but he wouldn't move, as confused as she was. "Help!" She yelled, startling the horse into shying hard to the left, but she stayed on and yelled again and again, frantically searching. Then she remembered the gun she'd returned to her bag and somehow pulled it out and cocked it. Steadying the horse between her hand and legs, she raised the pistol in the air and shot. She worried that the storm muffled the sound so much it would be a miracle if he heard it, but suddenly a shadowy figure appeared in front of them, coughing more deeply.

He looked amused at the gun, but quickly went to work on her hand as soon as she shouted the problem to him. Taking off his own glove, he fit it over her dead white hand and lifted her cape and stuck the hand under her arm, brushing his fingers across the front of her bodice. There was no time for reprimands as he tucked the cape back around her body and tried to shove it under the back of her thigh. Giving up on that, he pulled the bearskin around her legs and lap, wrapping her like a mummy. His big horse was snorting and eyeing the bearskin nervously, but didn't move a hoof. Her chestnut pair were too beaten by the storm to worry about such things.

The stranger leaned down and shouted hoarsely in her ear, "How much further?"

"At the tee we turn north, not far then. Keep the river on your right," she yelled back, the wind ripping the hood off her head and taking the last words with it. He pulled the hood back, unwound the knit scarf holding his hat on, and quickly tied it around the lower part of her face, anchoring the hood. It smelled of wood smoke and horses and something else, him, she believed.

He took his hat and tucked it into his coat, leaving his own head bare. His ears were already red. He'd lose them if she kept the scarf. She started to untie it, but he stopped her hands.

"You'll freeze!" she shouted.

"I'm used to it. Let's go." He took one of her reins and wrapped it around his bare hand with the other horse's lead and tucked the hand into the front of his coat, then urged the spotted horse forward into a slow trot. The other horses had no choice but to follow.

They almost missed the tee, but the spotted horse swerved at the last moment, and she almost spilled as her horse scrambled to follow. For comfort she started to recite Whittier's "The Barefoot Boy," but couldn't remember anything past the second verse. Omah was right, a person never knew when they'd need to know something. Her frozen fingers were starting to ache as they warmed, and her eyes were almost frozen shut. She could only see a sliver out of each, but then the wind shifted and there was the line of huge old cypress and bur oak and she shouted to the man in front.

The horses turned naturally and hurried toward the barn, the wind at their backs. The man reached down and unlatched the door and they ducked and rode inside, the three horses jostling each other briefly in the crowded aisle. The man sat slumped in his saddle, not moving except for the spasms of coughing, as she slid off and unwound the scarf. The barn was warm and heavy with the sweet scent of apples, horses, and cattle. The battering storm was working on something in the loft, lifting and clattering it down again, but otherwise there was only the warm muzzling silence of big animals resting, a horse blowing lightly through its nose, cattle chewing contentedly. No one was even disturbed by their presence.

She lifted the robe and wool blanket from her horse's back, followed by the rest of the harness, leaving the bridle hanging down the spotted horse's side, then quickly put her horse in a full blanket and rubbed his face and neck down. Turning him loose in his box stall, she went to the other chestnut. When she tugged on the rein, the stranger roused and slowly pulled his hand from his coat. She had to unwrap the reins, noticing the heat in the man's skin despite the cold. After rubbing the second horse down and blanketing him, she forked fresh hay into three stalls, made sure their buckets of water were full and not frozen, and returned to the stranger's horse. The storm howled, but the banging against the roof and rattling windows seemed muffled in the barn's warm twilight. Above them in the rafters, there was a soft chirp from a bird.

"Sir?" She shook his sleeve, uncertain what to do. He appeared to be asleep. "Sir? You need to dismount and let me settle your horse now."

"Got to go back for them," he mumbled, lifting a hand, then letting it settle back on the shaking thigh. With horror she watched the shivering roll down his body in waves. His trousers were soaked! He was freezing!

"Come on." This time she pulled his sleeve hard enough to tip him. "Step down. We have to get you warm. Come on." She took his horse's reins out of his hand and led the animal down the aisle to the box she'd prepared. At the sight of the deep straw and fresh hay, the horse bolted through the door, knocking the man's leg hard enough to produce a grunt. When the horse started to go down for a roll though, she snatched its head.

The stranger seemed to come to himself, looking around with a bewildered expression.

"Get off the horse so I can unsaddle him," she ordered, and he slowly swung his leg over and slid down, stumbling when his feet touched the ground. If he lay down, she'd never get him up, so she led him to the stall divider and leaned him there while she quickly took care of his horse. The animal was grateful for the attention but shied so violently at the heavy canvas and wool blanket she tried to put on him that it was clear he was a Western cow pony who had never known the niceties of stabled life. His thick winter coat was standing up and drying quickly after the rubdown, and his eye was still bright as he dipped his head to grab a mouthful of hay. Obviously he was used to the elements.

The man was another problem, however, leaning against the wall with his eyes closed. His face was pale and damp with sweat as if he were fevered, and when she placed her palm on his cheek, it was burning up.

Could she make it to the house without this stranger collapsing? Should she go to the house and see if there was someone to help? What if they all went home to their own families today? When she left this morning, Nelson Foley had harnessed the horses and planned to spend the day repairing fence. He was going to move into the bachelor's ell after the holidays, and Kamp and Spraggins arrived early every morning and left at dark so there would be men around to help, but not during a freak storm like this. Frank and Omah had been taking turns staying with her, but last night she had sent both of them home. She was probably alone.

Taking a deep breath, she put her shoulder under his arm and half draped him across her back. "We have to make it to the house now. I need your help. Can you walk?" she shouted, startling the spotted horse, who lifted his head and stopped chewing as he watched them stagger toward the stall gate.

It took longer than she liked to make it to the outside door. At that rate they'd die in the cold, but there was nothing else to do. Leaning against the wall to catch her breath, she took down a length of rope.

"I'm just going to tie us together," she said. "We can't get separated out there." She wound the rope around their waists and tied it loosely. If he went down, he'd take her with him, but it was better than losing him altogether.

"Sir? Are you listening to me, sir?" She slapped his face, bringing his eyes into brief focus. "We have to make it to the house. You have to walk on your own now. I can't carry you. We'll die out there if you don't walk. You understand?"

He coughed and gave a dazed smile. "Tough girl," he said.

"I'm a grown woman!" she sputtered. "Come on now." She yanked his arm over her shoulder and pushed against the door the wind was holding shut. It took both of them shoving to finally open it, and then the wind whipped it out of their hands and slammed it hard against the barn with a loud crack that startled the animals inside. It took as much effort to close it again, and a little drift of snow had filled the doorway by the time she managed to latch it shut.

The wind was blowing harder than ever, gusting and slamming against them, but the outline of the house appeared long enough for her to get her bearings. In her long skirt and thin kid boots, it was difficult to stay upright on slippery footing with the wind buffeting the cloth, not to mention the weight of the cowboy draped against her, but they stumbled forward, heads down like horses. She'd left her soaked gloves in the barn, and her hands quickly began to freeze again. There was nothing for it now though, so she began to recite the Whittier poem again, each word a step. "Bare—foot—boy—"

They were halfway there when he staggered and coughed so hard it sounded as if he were strangling, threatening to pull both of them down. She yelled and punched his side and back through the thick coat, but it did no good, so she reached up and boxed his ear with her freezing hand, which brought him to his senses. He straightened and staggered forward again, dragging her with him.

By the time they made it to the porch steps, they were both so exhausted that they collapsed and crawled on all fours. At the door she tried to untie the rope, but her fingers were so stiff she couldn't undo the frozen knot, so she had to work the rope down her body and climb out of it. It seemed to take forever getting the door open, shoving him inside, then shutting it and dropping to the floor, closing her eyes in the shelter of her house at last. But it was cold inside. The fires had gone out in her absence and she must quickly rouse herself again.

Her wet skirt was so heavy that she took it off and hung it over the back of a kitchen chair, then stepped out of her soaked boots and stockings before putting fresh wood in the cookstove and starting the fire so she could put the kettle on for hot tea. Then she went around the other rooms, lighting fireplaces and stoves, hurrying because the floors were so icy on her bare feet. When she at last returned to the entryway, the stranger was sitting up, coat unbuttoned, staring with a dazed expression at the broad winding stairway.

"L. O. Swan," he said.

26

HAT'S FINE," SHE SAID. "CAN YOU GET UP? I HAVE A FIRE GOING IN THE kitchen."

When he didn't answer and kept his eyes closed, she realized he was in a stupor. His face, reddened from the cold, glistened with sweat, and his breathing sounded hoarse. He couldn't stay in the entry hallway, and he probably shouldn't be on the kitchen floor if he was sick.

"Oh damn it, where is everyone?" She stamped her foot and looked up the stairs to the second-floor landing, and saw something. What was that? It looked like an odd shadow hanging in midair just beyond the railing. Her stomach lurched, then she heard the clicking of her little dog's nails on the wood floor, and he appeared at the top of the stairs.

"Pete! What are you doing up there? Come here, boy," she called softly. He whined and looked over his shoulder, then back at her, but didn't move. He should be barking at the strange man in the house, she thought, what was wrong with him? The shadow seemed to move along the railing and stop over the small white dog. She squinted and stared harder. It must be the odd light from the French doors to the porch. When she looked away and back, it was gone.

"Come here, Pete," she called again, and he bounded down the stairs as if he had just realized that she was home. The moment he saw the man on the floor, he backed up and commenced growling and barking.

The noise roused the man enough that she managed to get him to his feet and turned toward the upstairs where she could put him to bed. If Nelson Foley were moved in, she could put the stranger in the bachelor's ell, but not now.

Once she had him safely on the bed in Grandma Maddie's old room, it was no small feat getting him out of his soaked pants and shirt, but she was used to undressing her da on nights he had drained the brandy bottle, so she managed the task at last. His body was younger than she expected from the weathered face and hands, the pale thighs taut with muscle where her da's were thin. Pulling off his socks, she took a moment to study the delicate bones of the long toes, which looked so fragile in the storm-shadowed room, the nail on the little toe torn to a sliver. His foot was so cold she rubbed it between her hands to warm it as she used to do for Da. The stranger muttered and pulled his foot away, flinging an arm across the covers as if he were too hot. Quickly pulling a blanket over his feet, she lit the lamp on the dresser across the room and hurried down to the kitchen for tea.

If only she'd paid more attention to her grandma's concoctions when she nursed the sick or gave nostrums to the heartbroken. Da had always doctored everything with brandy and comfrey tea, but he respected Grandma Maddie's skills and grew solemnly quiet when she was working in the kitchen with her herbs and teas. What would she do for a fever?

"Feverfew tea, flowering dogwood for malaria, fever and blood, that's what the old Indians used," she told her. It was coming back! Maddie could hear Grandma's voice, as if the old woman were standing behind her!

"Viburnum bark," her grandma whispered, but when she whirled about, the kitchen was empty, except for an odd, canted shadow on the opposite wall that must be from the way the snow was piling up on the windowsills . . .

They'd left her jars and tins of herbs and teas and salves where she had always kept them, in the pantry and on the cupboard shelves next to the sink. The cheesecloth strips for holding the tea leaves were still there too. It was as if her hands were hovering over her granddaughter's, guiding them as she pinched the crumbled bark into the square of cloth, then tied it up deftly. Filling the teapot with water from the steaming kettle on the stove, Maddie let it steep until the color was right before she carried it upstairs to the patient.

She fell asleep in the chair next to his bed after rousing him to drink some tea and making certain the fire was going to stay lit despite the cold and wind pressing down the chimney. Pete came upstairs and paced the hallway while she dozed, his nails clicking louder and louder until he was past the room, then growing distant, then louder, then distant, back and forth like a living clock. Somewhere in her sleep, she imagined his claws leaving tiny commas in the soft cypress floor that decades from now a woman her age would discover, kneeling down on her hands and knees and running her fingers over the pattern, and she'd see them waiting out a snowstorm one afternoon while everything in the world dug in and slept, even finally the dead.

Maddie woke at dusk to the dog's whining to go out, despite the wind that continued to pound the house, shaking the shutters and windows in their very frames. When she looked over, the man's eyes were open, watching her. She returned the gaze without shyness, as if they had known each other for a very long time.

"L. O. Swan," he croaked weakly. "My name—"

She raised her hand to stop him. "Maddie Ducharme. Are you feeling better?"

Pete's whine grew into a yelp at the door, and she rose and hurried out. "I'll be right back—"

SHE WORRIED ABOUT THE ANIMALS DURING THE NEXT TWENTY-FOUR HOURS while the storm raged on, but there was nothing to do. The chickens and ducks were safely housed, although they would need water and food soon; the cattle and horses had shelter and would wait out the weather as they always did. The barn cats were safely burrowed in the hay, and except for the necessity of going outside twice, the dog was content to curl up in front of the fire she kept going in Mr. Swan's bedroom. She made periodic trips to the kitchen for soup and more tea, and to stoke the fire, but she spent the majority of the time in his room, hauling firewood upstairs from the kitchen so they could stay cozy. He slept and awakened as his fever rose and fell, and he coughed in terrible fits. She gave him some sassafras tea for the cough, but it didn't seem to help. Although she waited to hear her grandmother's voice again, it had disappeared. She prayed though, prayed to her, prayed to her mother, and prayed to Da, thanking them for bringing a man just when she needed one, prayed that they kept this L. O. Swan safe for her, because sometime during the long vigil, she fell in love.

"WHAT WOULD YOU HAVE ME DO, L.O.?"

It was May, and the winter and cold spring that lasted so long had finally broken, so they were able to get out and work the farm at last.

"You could leave." He was mending the halter the stallion had broken trying to get at one of the new mares in the spring pasture that morning, and she was cleaning and sorting the tack room Foley and Kamp had built by adding walls and a door to a stall. She lifted a canvas horse rug and a mouse went flying out of the wool lining and scampered out the open door.

"This is my home, L.O." She lifted the heavy rug caked with mud and gave it a shake. Several tiny red bodies dropped to the floor and lay there squirming silently. Mice. Damn it. She lifted her foot but couldn't do it. Instead she stooped down and lifted them one by one into her palm where they squirmed like infested rosebuds—

"But we can't be together here, Maddie." L.O. punched the awl through the double-stitched leather strap and caught the thread on the other side. He was using good waxed linen thread they had ordered from the saddlery in St. Louis, and evidence of his repairs gleamed in most of the equipment hanging on the bridle and saddle racks now. He'd even patched the torn blankets and fly sheets. In fact, he had designed the tack room, planning it as soon as he was able to get out of bed for a few hours at a time, and demanded something to put his hands to. Besides her, that was.

"We can too. We just won't tell anyone. We can get married in another county—go to New Orleans, that's far enough." She looked at the tiny hairless red creatures in her hand. Would the mother disown them because they had a human's scent? There was no question of killing them now, that was the kind of thing you had to do right away before you thought about it.

"Put them outside in the weeds beside the barn. She'll find them." L.O. glanced up, smiling at her dilemma.

"Or something else will. Where are those darn cats? I thought they were around here." She looked out into the main barn where the sunlight lay in big yellow dust-filled squares from the windows and outside door.

"The longer you wait," he reminded her. They already had hutches of rabbits filling one of the box stalls from the nest she had found in the lilac bushes last winter after the freak storm. The mother never returned, and she had made Frank bring the babies inside to be nursed. She didn't know what came over her, but she couldn't stand the idea of anything dying then.

She didn't know she was so tenderhearted. Everything surprised her these days. She smiled and hid the mice in a tall mass of four-o'clocks, covered with pink flowers that would stay closed until late afternoon. L.O. was responsible for this. God knew these mice would probably grow up and gnaw the trunks of her young apple trees next winter, and she'd be cursing this day.

As she paused in the doorway to the tack room to watch him, it was as if she could feel the dust motes like gold a person could breathe in to coat their lungs, to make them last forever, outliving the world as they knew it. Suddenly the day seemed so fragile, and tears sprang to her eyes. She would never have this again. She knew it. She could feel Grandma Maddie's lips against her ear, a wisp of hair on her cheek. Remember this moment, a voice said, and her heart became greedy for the man whose thin shoulders were bent over his work. The head of long hair, as long as Da's and tied back the same, gone silver with his illness, the big competent hands so agile despite their ruin. He was wearing Da's linsey-woolsey smock, wide suspenders holding up the high trousers. On his feet a pair of Da's moccasins from the old times, made from deer hide. He was even wearing Da's stiff old leather apron, scarred and stained from decades of leatherworking.

Would she dress another man in Jacques Ducharme's clothes if he were still alive? She should ask that of St. Clair and the judge. Proof, they said. Proof was this man living under her roof—proof was her naked body in his naked arms at night. She shivered at the thought of their bare bellies against each other, and her stomach pulled and dropped and the familiar distraction came over her. A mare in heat, he'd laughed this morning when she mounted and rode him a second time. "You've inspired us all!" She had laughed. "The mares and stallion haven't ever bred like this. I have to suppose it's you, L.O. Some magic you sprinkle into the very air and water." He had kissed her nipples, slowly and deliciously, until she arched her back and lost herself.

How had L.O. and she come to this? The steady companionship of a person other than those she had spent her life with was such a heady experience. Everything he said and did was new and different. She listened for hours as he told of his life, of his home. And what he loved, she learned to love from the way his lips shaped the words, the way his eyes changed color with memory.

"Left home at fifteen to work on a neighbor's cattle ranch near the Wind River Reservation in Wyoming," he told her when pressed about his family. "Pa and I stopped seeing eye to eye. Lucky the neighbor, Ellis Weaver, was a decent man with a family. I worked hard, but he was fair. Made foreman by the time I was twenty-five. Drove herds over to the railhead in Ogallala, Nebraska, fought cattle thieves, blue tongue, black leg, rattlesnakes, wolves, blizzards, drought, and every other kind of trouble.

"Ended up in Montana, working on a spread owned by an Englishman who had some kind of 'row' at home and came here. Like me, I guess, except he had money. He liked to hunt some, so I spent five years roaming with him, shooting animals for their heads and hides. Not to my liking to waste meat that way, so I moved on to a big operation near Bozeman. Got busted up on a horse, spent the winter laid up in the bunkhouse. Come spring the owner died. Company bought the place let me go. Back to the Englishman. He'd grown tired of hunting and was raising cattle and horses and goats. He figured to market those goats all over the place. Me, I couldn't see it. Goats were a lot of trouble—getting out, chasing the livestock around. Nubian goats, they were. So when he sent me by train all the way to Kentucky to oversee the purchase and shipping of a billy goat, I planned to ride back through Missouri, then hop the train again in Omaha, head on home to my family ranch in Wyoming." His eyes shone, and she liked to think it was surprise at having so much luck in meeting her.

"Took sick on the trail and laid up at the Knight kid's place, waiting for it to pass, but then you show up. A blessing and worse—"

"You have your own place?" Little Maddie asked.

"It's my folks' place. Pa died. Ma passed on. My two brothers and sister want nothing to do with it. They left, like I did, soon as they could."

For a girl who had never even been permitted the luxury of attending school with other children, entering the houses in town or attending church with other families, the luxury of listening to this man's tales was intoxicating. At first she contrived simply to brush her fingers across his cheek as she lifted him to sip from a cup of broth or spooned his soup to his mouth, those lips she longed to kiss! Then when he had accepted her touch, she grew bolder, letting her hand linger on his chest or arm, until one day he closed his hand over hers, naturally it seemed, and her heart leapt!

"Tell me the worst day and the best day you ever had, and I'll do the same." She felt inspired now. It was so difficult to get L.O. to talk about himself that she wanted to keep him going.

"Don't you have chores to do, Maddie?" he teased.

"The worst day?"

He took a deep breath. "I'd say the best day was also the worst—the day I left home. Pa had been gone for a week with Ma in the wagon. He'd given her only time enough to pack the one satchel with clothes, then half lifted her onto the seat. She hadn't even time to say goodbye to Jake, the little one, who was running after them, crying. He was the last, eight years old. And Molly, a year younger than me, but already in charge of the cooking and outside chores. Ma was having a bout of her 'sadness' again, and could barely climb out of bed of a morning. At night I'd hear Pa's angry whisper, 'Can't you do any better than that?' " L.O. glanced at Maddie, who wasn't even blushing.

"I asked Molly where they were going, but she kept her mouth clamped shut and shook her head. I think now that she knew and was afraid I'd take out after them if she told. She didn't want Ma to leave, but she didn't want me to get a beatin' either. And likely her for telling me. My brother Nelson, who was twelve then, was standing there with his hands in his pockets, lips quivering, trying hard as he could not to cry, as if Pa was still there getting ready to knock him in the head for being a baby. Pa was just one miserable old bastard. Funny, we were alone on the place for a week, yet none of us ever talked about where Pa took Ma, how we felt about things. We just took up living as if Pa were still there, watching our ever' move like a hawk, ready to pounce on any little mistake. Nelson's hands shook so bad when he bridled a horse, I had to look away and bite my lip to keep from reminding him that the old man wasn't even around. Jake, even at eight, cried himself to sleep every night, and wouldn't eat. I finally went into my folks' room, took the coverlet off the back of the chair where Ma kept it when the bed was being used, and gave it to him. He sniffed it, curled up like a puppy, and fell asleep. When Pa got back, he never noticed Jake had it. I imagine the kid took it with him when he left soon as he could.

"When Pa got back, first thing he did was stomp around complaining about how shabby we'd let the place get, and made us work well into dark cleaning and patching. Most of it was things he could've been doing right along, but we didn't dare complain. Nelson had to climb the hayloft and pull down the cobwebs over the stalls below. I had to muck out the run-in for the horses, piled with ten years of manure. Molly had to clear the straw out of the henhouse, whitewash the inside, and restuff the laying boxes. Poor little Jake was in charge of soaping and oiling all the saddles, bridles, and boots.

"He fell asleep over his plate three times before Pa excused him to go to bed. The rest of us weren't much better, but I reckon he'd planned it that way because when he told us that Ma wasn't coming back, we were too tired to argue. He'd taken her to a place for crazy people in Cheyenne. That's how he said it. She wasn't crazy, I wanted to argue. She's just sad . . . and who could blame her for feeling that way. Look at us. I didn't say a word, of course, none of us did because he was waiting for it. Knife in one hand, fork in the other, gripped the way you would for stabbing something, muscle in his jaw working, and something bright and wrong in his eyes. He was waiting so he could whale on someone, and I wasn't going to give him the satisfaction, you see. By the age of sixteen, I'd learned that much. I never saw her again. Thought about trying to find her over the years, but I never did. No letters or messages came for us either. She was as good as dead, and for all I know, that's what he'd actually done, murdered her and put her in the ground, the way he'd do an old cow who'd gone dry. That was the worst day, the one where he came home without her.

"The best part came in the morning, when I swung onto the horse I'd raised and broke myself. The old man looked up at me and said, 'That'll be fifteen dollars you're owing me for the horse.' He grinned meanly, thought he had me, but I knew the old bastard through and through. So I pulled the money from my pocket and threw it at his feet, spun the horse and galloped out of there. Left with the clothes on my back, a bridle I'd made, no saddle, blankets, or coat. I did have the old rifle my grandpa had given me when I was a boy Jake's age, some powder, and a hunting knife. I hadn't even taken a handful of oats for my horse. The fifteen dollars only covered the horse, nothing else. I suppose if he hadn't been so surprised, Pa would've made me pay for the clothes I wore, or stripped me naked and told me I owed him for my bones and hide too. Couple of times I wrote Molly, then she married and moved on to Nebraska. Lost track of Nelson and Jake."

"That doesn't sound so wonderful to me," Maddie murmured.

"Believe me, it was."

He must have loped down the road from their place, cursing the old man for all he was worth, until he came to the main road where he stopped to look behind him to the east. No dust but his own. Nobody was coming after him. Then he looked west and north and south—all one big empty space.

"Couple of hawks riding overhead, wind pushing the grass in waves, sun shining. It's all so still I can hear my own heart beat, and it comes to me that I'm the freest man alive. I don't ever have to live that way again, some mean old bastard taking it out on me," he said.

Maddie stayed quiet for a while. Although her da was strange, he had loved her, and she was lucky. Sometimes being related was an accident, she realized, and people didn't necessarily have to care about each other just because they shared the color of your eyes or the shape of your face. L.O. seemed more fragile to her now, and what stirred in her breast was something she'd felt only for small animals in the past, the urge to protect them from pain and suffering. She wondered if this were that part of being a woman that prepared you for motherhood—first you discovered the vulnerable places in a man, then you tried to protect him—perfectly absurd, she knew.

As his condition improved, she had read to him, selecting stories that had lovers in them, finally holding his hand while she read the afternoons into dusk, and one day he raised her hand to his lips as naturally as if he were already her lover. She knelt on the floor beside the bed and raised her face to his . . .

After that, she had locked the door when she came to his room, and quickly dispensed with her clothing, climbing into his bed, but continuing to read so the sound of her voice would provide the reassurance that Omah and Frank needed.

" 'The Mississippi River will always have its own way . . .' "

All the while L.O. made love to her and she was pressed to keep the gasping pleasure from obscuring her ruse, her volume rising with her passions: " '. . . no engineering . . . skill . . . can persuade . . . it to do . . . other . . . wise!' "

She remembered almost nothing of those books, and how her lips formed the words while her body twisted with hot pleasure, she would never know. She only hoped that Mr. Twain, Mr. Hawthorne, and Mr. Melville, especially Mr. Melville's Ahab, forgave her for such inattention. She would read them again one day when she was so old she had forgotten the comic torture of holding those heavy tomes while L.O. did battle with her virginity.

THE SIGHT OF THOSE HANDS NOW WORKING THE THREAD SO DELICATELY INTO small stitches in the leather, oh, this was what it meant to be alive! She finally understood the novels she'd read for years, the stories in magazines. Omah hardly looked at her these days, and Frank hadn't uttered a word in weeks. They thought their disapproval could take this away, but she would never let go of this man. Never. She crossed her fingers in promise, wondering at the sudden chill that came into the air and seemed to turn the light opaque. A cloud crossing the sky, she told herself, nothing more, nothing more, and heard the echoes of that old poem. Nothing more.

"If you conceive," L.O. said this morning, "you'll lose all this—" He swept his arms out to include the house and barns and pastures and orchard and woods. "But then we can go away, out West to my little ranch, raise cattle, horses, and kids. You'll see, Maddie, you'll fall in love with it." His eyes always grew a little darker and distant when he spoke of his West, and she worried that one day she'd wake up alone, so she slept with a hand or foot always touching his body. He'd have to cut off a part of himself, leave it in the bed under her fingers, to make his escape. He loved her. She thought he did. Last night she had asked him. "As much as Antony and Cleopatra? As much as Tristan and Isolde? Troilus and Cressida? Would you die for me, like Shakespeare's Romeo and Juliet?"

He laughed, said, "*Leaves of Grass*. My love is like the uncut hair of graves—" This morning she had hastened an order to her St. Louis book dealer for Walt Whitman's poems. She was not a great reader of poetry, knew only those slight verses deemed appropriate for young girls. Mr. Whitman was not approved of for ladies, but Omah wouldn't know, and at seventeen now, she was too old to listen to anyone but herself.

"I had not known you to be so well read," she had said this morning over coffee.

He looked puzzled, then laughed. He always laughed at her. "Only book I had to read one winter up in a line cabin my first job cowboying. I ended up memorizing most of it to keep myself from going crazy. Read the labels of cans, the newspapers tacked up to cover the holes in the walls. Sang every song I knew until I was making up new words. Could hardly wait to forget some of the poems and lines so I'd have to reread the dang thing again." That was when he had gotten that distance in his eyes, looking over her shoulder out the window toward the pastures and orchard. "You have no idea what that high mountain loneliness does to you."

She could tell it wasn't all that bad, or he wouldn't be staring off like he'd lop an arm off and leave it on the kitchen table if only he could get away now, go home. Her heart felt sorry for him, it did, as much as for those rabbits and baby mice, but she just couldn't let him go. He was hers now.

"What say we go fishing over to Reelfoot Lake today," he said. "We can take lunch, ride down to the ferry."

When she shook her head, a cloud of disappointment descended on his face. "I have to see my lawyer this afternoon," she lied and turned to examine the bosal on a breaking bridle. One of L.O.'s inventions, it was a rawhide-covered oval that went over the horse's nose for control instead of a bit. He was already working the four fillies they had bought last winter to supplement the herd. They'd go racing this summer, then come home to breed unless they proved valuable on the track.

"Fine," L.O. said. "See him, then we can cross the river right there." He laid down the halter and looked at her.

"I don't think there'll be time. I have to see if that new Montgomery Ward catalog is in. Stop at the dressmaker too."

"Maddie!" He stood up and reached for her arm, pulling her against him. He smelled like oily old leather and tobacco, which he used when there was some, but most of all, he smelled like Da. She twisted away and gave a short laugh, hearing the uncertainty in its note.

"You scared me for a minute there," she said breathlessly.

"Dear girl," he said, but instead of stepping closer, he ran a shaky hand through his hair and turned to look out the window. As if he were arguing something, he folded his arms, shook his head, and nudged a wooden brush box on the floor with the toe of his moccasin. "Am I to be your hired hand then? A kept lover, one of those useless men in those novels of yours? Someone you hide in the attic every time the town ladies come calling?"

He turned to look at her, his long face solemn, mouth grim. "I can't do that, Maddie."

She was going to lose him. Her lungs clenched tight, and she could hardly breathe. "I'm too young."

He shook his head. "Don't start lying to me now. What is it you would have me do here?" He spread his arms. "I can't order the men to work. Hell, I can't even look your colored help in the eye."

It took her a moment to understand who he was talking about. "Do you mean Omah? She's not—"

He raised a hand to brush her words away and sighed deeply. "I don't mean Omah. Hell, she's more mama to you than anything. You see what I mean, Maddie. I'm a man and you aren't giving me—" He groped for the word. "Respect, I guess that's what I mean. I don't feel like anything here, except someone who does your bidding and beds you at night. I don't know what that makes me exactly." He looked her straight in the eye. "But it's not good, is it?"

"My da," she said. "I can't leave him."

He watched her for a long moment, then dropped his eyes. "I know, darlin'." He opened his arms and she stepped into them, tasting the bitterness of victory for the first of many times.

"Just stay till fall," she murmured into his ear, nuzzling the stubble of his cheek, and reaching for his trousers. "You can cut the timber and drain the swamp separating the two eastern fields. Wait till you see the size of those trees—cypress, oak, sweet gum, sycamore, elm, and more—you can build us a pole road to the railroad, make it easier to move the horses and cotton. We can start charging for the use. Haul what's left to that little sawmill town below Jacques' Landing, that's all I ask."

He moaned as her fingers found his swollen sex. "You're witchin' me, Maddie Ducharme."

She laughed and licked his cheek like a cat. "Of course I am, L.O. And you walked right into my gingerbread cottage, didn't you?"

He pulled her down to the plank floor, and they made hurried love, skirt to her neck, drawers still tied at the knee keeping her legs from spreading too far when he entered her, but they managed.

"Marry me," he said as they lay in each other's arms. In the young black walnut tree outside the window, the baby blue jays set up squalling, sounding just like human babies.

"In the fall," she murmured. "When the apples are done ripening." She'd think of something by then. She had the whole summer to make him love her. She'd just have to be careful not to get pregnant. Omah would know what to do.

"YOU'RE GOING TO RUIN HIM," OMAH SAID WHEN SHE WENT BACK TO THE HOUSE to change her clothing for town. "He's not a boy or a pet." She was sitting on the front porch, fanning herself with a letter she had received that morning, but Little Maddie was too irritated to ask her about it.

"He can do what he pleases," she said.

Omah gave one of her looks that somehow reminded Maddie of her da, and she was suddenly glad he wasn't there.

"My my my," she said, lapsing into that little singsong Maddie hated. "Missy give dat por man his freedom. Such a gud mistress, she goin' to let dat man drain her ol' swamp and cut dem trees all on his own self. Wat next? She goin' gib ol' Omah the right to wash her drawers for her?" She stuck out her lower lip and left her mouth slack while she widened her eyes until they bulged.

"Just stop it," Maddie said crossly, rolling her own lower lip out and flopping into the chair next to hers.

"Listen, little girl." Omah tapped the envelope against her lap, staring out at the purple blooms of the lilacs at the edge of the yard, which filled the air with a narcotic sweetness.

"Whatever it is, I'm not giving him up. You can't make me!" She stamped both feet on the floor, sending the chickens flapping down the steps.

"I have to leave soon. Take my daughter and son north so they can go to school." She glanced at her. "I mean to have this Mr. L. O. Swan business settled before I go."

Her words stunned Maddie. "Is Frank going too?" she asked in a dreamy voice. She should be saying I'm sorry, please don't go, or something, but instead she felt a secret joy rising in her heart. Yes! They'd be alone to do as they pleased!

"No. Frank is staying here." She looked at her. "With you, Maddie. He's staying to watch after you."

"But I'm of age," she pouted.

"You are not to marry that man, and you are to stop sleeping with him as of right now!"

Something rose inside Maddie, making her look at Omah with her eyes and face set hard, unmoving as she said, "All I need from you is how to keep myself from conceiving a child until I manage to convince those old fools in town to break Jacques' will."

Amazingly, Omah's lips curled into a smile—not a sweet, but a knowing smile. "You're more like your mother than you'll ever know."

"Tell me then—" Her heart leapt at the mention of her mother. "Tell me about her, something you've never told me before. I'm old enough now. I won't be shocked."

She didn't know whether it was revenge or an urge to finally reveal the truth behind her childhood misconceptions, but Omah told her how her mother married Da, how she went to Hot Springs to recover her health after the baby was born and put with a wet nurse, a young colored mother whose own baby died at birth, how Jacques paid the woman in gold coins that so raised the suspicion of the townspeople that she was beaten and jailed and hanged herself out of grief before Jacques could get to town to save her. She was buried here. On the farm.

"Where's her grave then?" Maddie asked, shaken to the bone by the awful details.

Omah waved her hand vaguely toward the family graveyard on the north edge of the yard. "Jacques never got a chance to put up a stone."

"He had years!" she protested, hot tears stinging her nose.

"It's not as easy as it seems sometimes," she said.

A detail of the story bothered her though. "Where did the money come from? The gold coins, where did he get those? I thought he was broke. He always said we had no money."

Omah stared out across the tops of the lilacs to the river on the other side of the road. "Oh, he had money all right. He wasn't going to spend it if he didn't have to though." She glanced at Maddie, the lines in her face deeper, making her finally look her age, whatever that was. "He wanted to make sure you didn't have to struggle as he had. That you wouldn't have to do things you'd ever be ashamed of."

Now she really felt guilty. "Like now?" she asked in a tiny voice.

Omah nodded once, slowly. "You're headstrong as a portage pony though. He should've seen it. Or maybe he did." She tapped the top of Maddie's head with the envelope she had been turning over and over in her hands.

"Where's my money then?" It was the obvious question.

She grimaced and looked toward the bachelor's ell, then back toward the barn. "I'm not sure. He never told anyone where he hid . . . where he put it. And when he disappeared, I can only guess that he was looking for it, that he forgot himself where he'd hidden it." When she chuckled, there was a bitter apron on it.

"Where did he get gold coins?"

"He was a good saver, like I said." She smiled, her eyes sly.

"No. Where did he get the gold, and my jewelry, my mother's—where did it come from?" She'd taken the yellow diamond off while they worked around the farm, but it was the ring she'd be married with.

Omah stared at her, a small smile pulling the corners of her mouth up.

"You're not going to tell me, are you? I know people call him a pirate, a river thief, is that part of it?" Her voice rose and L.O., still working in the barn, stepped outside to gaze at the house.

"Never mind that pirate talk. You need to pay attention to what I tell you, missy. That is a grown man there, and he doesn't belong to you or to this place. You'll ruin him you keep him here."

Her words stiffened Maddie's shoulders, but she couldn't ignore the wet seeping into her drawers from their lovemaking. "Who are you? What do my family and my concerns have to do with you?" It's a question she'd been dying to ask.

"Why, I'm my mama's child, same as you." Omah glanced down at the letter. "I grew up here. Lived in this house. And—" She took a deep breath, laying the letter in her lap and holding out her scarred hands. "Jacques and I were on the river together." Her voice dropped to a whisper. "But don't you never, ever, tell a soul about that." She seemed transformed, her voice roughened, her eyes turned crafty.

"Pirates? River pirates? Really?" she whispered.

Then it was gone, as suddenly as it appeared. Omah shrugged and tilted her head with a whimsical smile. "Treasure Island, Maddie?" she laughed. "No, I'm afraid we were just simple, hardworking folks. Your da sold wood to the riverboats, and ran an inn for travelers. But that was before the war, much before you or your mother's appearance."

Maddie shook her head. "What about all the furniture? The gold coins you told me about? What about the horses? There wouldn't be a stick of wood left on the place and he still wouldn't have been able to buy all this."

She smiled at the envelope and picked it up again. "Oh, you'd be surprised at how grateful folks can be when you relieve their journeys, Maddie."

"And what does that mean? People *gave* him furniture and horses?"

"What it means is that he was a man in love, and a man in love will do things. Anything, for the woman he loves. It isn't often pretty but that's the way of it sometimes. That man put together a life from his own fearlessness."

Little Maddie threw her long braid over her shoulder. "Who did he love? It wasn't my mother. They met after the war. Who was his first love, tell me. Did you know her? What was her name?" She leaned toward that woman who held so much knowledge inside her, taking her hand, feeling how soft the palms were, much softer than hers. Omah did little work anymore, but not because she was old, she was as timeless as Da was. Frank looked much older, his hair gone gray, the skin on his neck loose, deep grooves around his eyes and mouth while her face was smooth, unblemished. Maybe Frank was right when he said she made a pact with the river god one night, whatever that meant.

Omah brushed the back of the girl's hand with her long slender fingers, then tapped the knuckles. "Annie Lark, I believe is her name. Somewhere in the library or attic there are some pictures she drew, and a journal or two. I saw them when I was a girl, but they disappeared after that. Your grandmother told me about her. Annie knew your grandmother Maddie's mother. This was a very long time ago, you understand. When your father was a young man—she died tragically."

Little Maddie was thrilled by the notion of a tragic romance and vowed to search the house from top to bottom as soon as she had the time. "Was he very very much in love with her?"

Omah nodded. "I don't think he ever got over her." She glanced at the girl and squeezed her hand. "Until he married your mother. He was the happiest I'd ever seen him that day." She smiled. "That's why I hope you'll wait for the right man, Maddie, not just the man who's convenient."

She didn't understand! "Did you wait?"

Something crossed her face and she dropped Maddie's hand and turned the envelope in her lap so it was held vertically. "I haven't had the fortune of love, Maddie, not much of it anyway."

Little Maddie wanted so badly to ask about Frank, but something in Omah's voice and the way her shoulders sagged made her stop. You can't push on a person so hard that they have to give up every single secret, she was discovering. Some things were better locked away in the heart where they could remain the hard, bitter kernel they had become in such darkness. Glancing toward the barn where L.O. was still standing in the sunlight, his face upturned, as if he meant to blind himself, she wondered if he would become that splinter in her heart, the luck of love that turned bad. Not if she could help it, she vowed. She'd keep him close and teach him how much another person could mean in his life. He'd never want to leave her! But even as she said it, she felt the shadow behind her, against the screen door, something watching and waiting.

27

WHEN THE STRANGE LITTLE MAN WITH THE YELLOW-BROWN SKIN trudged up the muddy road at noon carrying a carpetbag, Little Maddie thought he was just another drummer, come to sell them something. They'd had heavy rains for a week, so the road was impassable by buggy, and the man's tan trousers were stained red to the knee, his boots carrying heavy gouts of mud. Despite the added weight, he walked with a spring in his step, lifting each foot with the ease of one of her chestnut carriage horses. When he reached the grass, he picked up one of the many sticks blown down by the almost constant wind that had accompanied the storms, and began to pry mud from his boot soles, giving her the opportunity to call Omah and Frank from the kitchen, where they'd been planning the rest of the summer work.

They met at the door. "Valdean French," he announced. He lifted the tan bowler soiled with splashes of red mud, displaying a head of orangish brown hair given a distinct ball shape by the weight of the hat. To Maddie's surprise, Omah opened the screen door, forcing the girl aside.

"Omah Ducharme." She used the family name without hesitation. "I wrote your mother."

He hesitated only a moment before smiling enthusiastically. "Started soon as I could. It took me a while, river flooding all the way to New Orleans." He looked out across the front yard toward the brown water, which had swallowed its banks and was lapping the road. It had finally stopped raining yesterday, so they were hopeful it wouldn't cross the road now.

"I have a message from Mama for you." He spoke in a light thin voice that was highly pleasant to hear, with almost no trace of the deep accent. When he set the carpetbag down, it clunked loudly.

"Your tools in there?" Omah asked. Maddie looked over her shoulder at Frank, who wore the same puzzled expression she did.

"Yes ma'am. Won't do to lose those." When he knelt to open the bag and search the contents, she noticed the worn seams of his old-fashioned blue frock coat, the frayed edges of his collar and shirt cuffs. Presently he stood with a thick packet of paper bearing a yellow wax seal and handed it to Omah.

"She sent nothing else?" Omah glanced into the bag at their feet.

Valdean French shot his cuffs from under the coat sleeves, straightened his slightly soiled white cravat, and stood almost on tiptoes, as if he were perpetually trying to make a good impression.

"Did she send anything else?" Omah said again.

He smiled and shook his head, lifting the bowler again. "Said to give you that letter. Remind you that the indigobush can take care of the whole household."

Omah grimaced impatiently, looked him up and down, and turned abruptly on her heel. "Might as well come along, then," she said over her shoulder. Frank and Maddie stepped aside as the little man picked up his carpetbag, lifted his bowler hat once again, and sidled between them through the door and down the hallway to the kitchen.

"Now who do you suppose that is?" Maddie asked.

"She doesn't tell me much these days, not that she ever did, mind you. Omah is a close one. By the way, indigobush is a good way to poison a critter giving you trouble." He looked out at the river and yawned. "I might could go turtling, this flood lets down a little. Those big ones'll be hungry. Think L.O. would like to come along?"

They both gazed toward the training ring he'd built, where he was sacking out a rank gelding he bought as a saddle horse. The horse was lying on its side, four legs roped together while L.O. rubbed him all over with a burlap bag. A horse had to learn to tolerate some things on this earth in exchange for a full belly and a little work, L.O. said. They had come to this agreement of late because the farm was too large for Maddie to manage alone despite her initial plans. Now he was in charge of the horses, a job Frank was happy to relinquish, as his back couldn't take the work anymore. Maddie was in charge of the orchard, fields, canning and kitchen gardens. Frank cared for the cattle, pigs, and poultry. They all pitched in during haying, corn, and cotton harvest. The three hired men, Tom Spraggins, Nelson Foley, and Artie Kamp, did the heavy work and assisted Maddie. Omah had charge of the house with the help of two young colored girls who happened to be the daughters of their dressmaker. There was never any question of Omah's own children coming to work for the Ducharmes. Sometimes Maddie wondered if they even existed, they were so little in evidence. When she mentioned this, Omah told her that they were hard at work with their studies. They had little time for play. Frank and Maddie never discussed his family. It was an unwritten rule, and this was one of the rare occasions when he mentioned Omah directly.

"We cutting hay this week?" Maddie asked.

"Soon as it dries," he said. "You know what happens we cut it and it rains. We need a few good sunny days now. Don't go runnin' ahead of your horses." He grinned and looked sideways at her.

"I sound like Jacques, I guess," she laughed.

"No question who your pa was."

"He loved this place, didn't he?" It's something she wondered about these days, because she loved it so much she'd do anything to keep it.

"Sometimes more than others. Toward the end, well, old people get some crazy notions. Can't judge a life by the end."

She glanced quickly at his face, the pensive expression, the sagging flesh that nonetheless didn't obscure the handsome features.

"There's so much I don't know about my father," she said.

"I think L.O. has that son-of-a-buck licking his hand, will you look at that!" Frank pointed toward the pen where L.O. was rubbing the muzzle of the now-standing horse and the animal was letting its head hang affectionately on his arm. "How's he do that?"

"Sugar, sometimes salt, or carrot and apple pieces. They all come when he calls now. Practically stampede him."

"That ol' stud is acting like he's a colt again too. What'd he do to him? That's no sugar."

"Got a teasing mare and that two-year-old colt so the old man has some competition. He just forgot what his job was, L.O. says. He's so studdy now I can hardly get near him, but we need him like that for the time being. Soon as the mares catch, L.O. will put him to work."

"That stud's not the only one doing his job, is he?" Frank said this softly, without a smile.

"We'll have a good crop of babies next year. Maybe we'll finally make some money again. Horses have to start paying for themselves soon. Omah and I went over the books yesterday, and we're a little tighter than I like. We need everything to come right this year." She paused and gave a sigh. "I just wish I knew where my da kept that gold of his."

Frank's face grew still as if he were listening to a barge voice from the river.

"Frank? Do you know where Jacques' gold is?" Her heart was pounding as she said the words, as if there were some terrible meaning tied up in them.

He turned and tilted his head, examining her, then said, "For a minute there, you sounded just like your mama. Almost like she'd come back from the grave . . ." He brushed at an imaginary fly on his cheek, trying to be casual, but his hand was shaking.

"Were you there when she died?"

He looked shocked, almost spoke, then shook his head quickly.

"How long did you work for Jacques, Frank? Did you help him on the river?" She took a wild stab at the truth, and was shaken herself when she heard his next words.

"I was nothing but a kid. Things we shouldn't of done. It was hard times, hard hard times. A person did things to feed his own, things—"

"Frank!" Omah's voice made them both jump. "Can you help Mr. French, please? He needs to get started today. Maddie, you come along, too. You have to decide where yours will go."

She pushed the door open, giving Frank a frown, as she led the way down the stairs with the little man in tow.

"What's going on?" Maddie asked, hurrying to catch up.

"Mr. French is a stonecutter. He's here to engrave my parents' headstones, and I thought you'd want Jacques' done too. And your mother's. I'm having mine done, and you might as well do yours too." When she didn't mention Frank or her children, Little Maddie turned and glanced at him, but he was staring at the grass that needed cutting, as if Ducharme business were none of his.

"The stones are in that shed." She pointed to a small tumbledown building raised up on stone blocks Maddie had always been afraid to enter because of the cane rattlers that lived beneath. It was an entire den of snakes, as far as she could figure. Blue racers, black rat snakes, and maybe even copperheads would winter together, and she just knew they were dug in pretty good under that shed. She wouldn't be surprised by a big old cottonmouth either. Even the dogs steered clear of the tall weeds surrounding the stone steps and foundation.

"I wouldn't go in there without a stick or gun," Frank said. Omah cast another dark frown at him.

"Where's Nelson and Kamp? They can carry the stones out to where you'll be working. You just tell them what you want." She looked over the little man's head at Frank and scowled again.

"May I see the grave sites?" French asked.

Omah led the way to the large family cemetery on the edge of the yard. Although the wrought iron fence was overgrown with wildflowers and grass and thick with years of leaves from the bur oak and willows, she managed to unlatch and push open the four-foot-high gate. Inside wasn't much better. They had to tramp around to find the rotting wooden crosses, and even then it was unclear who was buried there. Omah knew though. She pointed at two sunken places along the far edge of the fence as belonging to her parents. Then she named several others Little Maddie didn't recognize, except that they must have worked for Jacques at some time.

They were at the edge of a little pool surrounded by the pale sand that marked a sand boil when Little Maddie asked, "Where's my mother's grave?"

The exchange between Frank and Omah was so quick the girl almost missed it, then Omah looked around and pointed to an obscure spot in a tangle of wild grape at the foot of the bur oak. "Why'd he put her way over there?" Little Maddie stepped through the grass, careful to watch for snakes, and looked for signs of a grave, but the ground wasn't sunken or even raised, and there was no marker.

She wanted to protest, but Omah wouldn't look at her and Frank was studying the sand boil like it was going to send up a treasure ship next.

"So where's Da's first wife?" It was a lucky hit, and Omah pointed to a place far from her mother's, where the grass was flattened as if deer had been sleeping there. Frank's head whipped up and he stared at the spot with his jaw flexing. Again there was no sinking or headstone or cross. They might be standing on the dead, so little care had been taken of them. Maddie stepped backward, stumbling into Mr. French and almost falling over the carpetbag, which was so heavy it didn't budge. How did this little man carry something that heavy with such ease?

"Where will you be, Omah?" Little Maddie asked. "With Frank and your children?"

It was Maddie's turn for the dark frown. She knew from experience that Omah was not a person to fool with, but neither was she now, so she smiled back.

"Get Foley out here to clean up this mess," Omah said to Frank and Maddie. Turning to French, she said, "Will you be working out here?"

He lifted the bowler again, giving them another glimpse of the round orange mat of hair. "I need flat, hard surfaces. These are sharp tools I use. One mistake can ruin the whole stone. Someplace behind your house would do." He pointed to the arbor draped in muscadine vines that filled the shade inside with a heavy, grapy sweetness. A flagstone path leading from the house to the structure sprawled out to provide a floor. Little Maddie used to play there as a child with the barn cats and dogs as her companions. Sometimes she'd corral a chicken or duck and trap it in her baby carriage beside the china-faced doll. She never liked that doll much. Her face was too hard and cold. The feathers were much softer and warmer and she took to leaving the doll out of the carriage when she played; eventually it was left outside in the weather for so long the cloth body mildewed, then rotted, and only her doorknob-hard head and tiny hands and feet were left, like the skeletal remains of an ancient tribe of miniature people. Maddie liked those pieces better than the doll, and kept them tucked away in her cedar keepsake box. When she had a child, she'd give them to her and let her puzzle out their meaning. When she had a child—the thought hadn't really been in her head until that moment, and she patted her flat stomach lightly. Da, she vowed secretly, you can't stop me, I'm mistress of all the world now.

AND SO THE SUMMER DAYS WERE NOTCHED WITH THE SOUND OF THE CHISELS chipping careful designs on Omah's headstones. Once when Maddie asked him about the intricate bird and water scenes, Valdean French said that they were tribal, African, and that Omah knew what they meant, although he could only guess. Valdean, as they called him, had to work slowly because his small hands cramped, swelled, and stiffened if he worked too long in one sitting. It was a leisurely job, then, marking the dead, and he spent many of his free hours resting in the shade of the grape vines as they grew green knobs that began to blush and darken. Often she saw him reading a book he'd taken from their library or writing, whispering words as he composed. When she mentioned this to Omah, she told Maddie that he was a poet, that his work was published in several northern literary journals, where he was celebrated as a fine lyricist.

"How did you find him?" she asked.

"His grandmother was once a slave from Jamaica, and your father helped free her and her brothers. She's always kept track of the Ducharmes. I met her on a trip to New Orleans years ago after your mother left. The woman was quite powerful. She passed it on to her daughter. Valdean is a different sort." Omah wasn't looking at Maddie as she said her little speech, and the girl could only imagine what she'd left out.

"Da freed a slave? I thought he owned—"

Omah slapped the table with her hand and clucked impatiently, something she'd always done when the girl said something she didn't like or wouldn't answer. Frankly, Maddie was getting tired of all the mystery.

"So how old is Valdean?" she asked. What she wanted to ask was when Omah was leaving, if she was coming back, what Maddie should do with Frank, with L.O., where her mother really was—there was an endless list of questions, but she found herself unable to speak with Omah anymore. She was already gone, Maddie realized. She'd already left her. Like Da before her. All the old ones were gone. Omah opened her letter and began to read instead of answering.

SUDDENLY IT WAS AUGUST, AS IF TIME WERE A WISP OF OAT STRAW TOSSED ASIDE after the heavy heads were taken. Valdean had finished Omah's family stones, and this morning he was putting the final touches on Jacques'. Annie Lark's, Miz Maddie's mother's, and Maddie's were all done, except for the dates. But Maddie didn't mention this to L.O., who had turned his yearning face west again. The ditch he started to dredge was only half finished, and the timber cutting had stopped until they finished draining the swamp between the fields. But Little Maddie was learning that you don't nag a man to work, not if you want him to stay with you. You must tease and promise—

Lately L.O. had taken to sitting with Valdean midmorning while he worked in the shade of the arbor, the two of them deep in conversation that stopped whenever the girl approached. She imagined they were sharing their travels, the South and the West, but when she approached silently this morning it was politics.

"The Dakotas, Montana, Idaho, and Wyoming. All admitted for statehood. The West is closing. Those poor sons-a-bitches don't have a chance," L.O. drawled.

"My father's mother was a slave in Mississippi for an Indian chief." Valdean tapped the chisel with a small hammer, cutting the L perfectly on her mother's stone. "I guess I'm part Indian myself, but I don't feel very good about it."

"Looks like you have some white blood too—that orange hair and light skin, you reckon?"

Valdean laid the chisel down and picked up a charcoal pencil and marked off the next letter along a straight line he'd drawn bisecting the pale blue-gray stone. "My mother's not the kind of person who's very forthcoming with details. She was Jamaican, but whether she was a slave at some point, I couldn't say. She's said things to suggest that her mother had been a slave as a young girl, but then it seems she was free to come and go as she pleased. I suspect that I'm the result of such freedom." He laughed lightly.

"At least you got an education," L.O. said.

"She insisted on it. We lived in my grandmother's cottage after she passed on. It was filled with books, and I think my mother would have burned or sold them to make room for her herbs and concoctions, if I hadn't shown an early interest in study." Valdean painstakingly finished tapping out the letter A, then ran his forefinger along the grooves. L.O. was silent whenever Valdean put chisel to stone.

Little Maddie was standing in the shadow of the vines, the heady scent of ripe grapes drawing bees and wasps and birds. They'd harvest them soon for juice and jelly, and perhaps some homemade wine. In an unexpected act of generosity, Omah had offered to make it as her mother used to for Jacques. Perhaps her impending departure had made her realize all she'd miss in leaving Jacques' Landing. Lately she'd been going through the trunks in the bachelor's ell, and the furniture and boxes in the attic. Was she looking for Jacques' gold too? Maddie wanted to stop her—

"I never had any trouble with Indian folk," L.O. sighed. "Shared some food, we bump into each other, fresh-killed deer or antelope. Let 'em have a dry cow if their kids looked hungry. Hell, they always looked hungry." He stared at his hands, idle in his lap, then gazed past Valdean and the row of blank waiting stones, out toward the cemetery. If he would turn his head but a few degrees, he would see her, his wife. She was. She had declared it so. She was his mistress, he her master. They were wed truer than anyone knew. Little Maddie had married! The thought made her want to spin around. She had taken to wearing the yellow diamond on her ring finger, and only Omah glanced at it and frowned.

"It's some world we live in." L.O. shook his head as he spoke, dropping his eyes to his empty hands again, turning them over.

"That it is," Valdean said. "Yes sir, that it is."

"You ever think about going out West?" L.O. asked and her heart bumped. A wasp wavered drunkenly toward her face, and when she waved it away, L.O. caught the motion and turned.

"Maddie," he said. "Didn't hear you."

"Good morning," she said in her gayest tone and glided around the heavy vines.

Peering over Valdean's shoulder made his hammer pause midstroke, and he didn't begin again until she eased back and settled on the granite bench beside her husband.

"Were you just speaking of the red Indians?" She kept the brightest note in her voice, although she wanted to pull the knife from her little boot and march L.O. to the ell to lock him away.

Valdean set down the hammer and swiveled to pour a glass of cold sweet tea from the small silver pitcher sweating beside him. They had ice now, shipped downriver and stored in sawdust in one of the stalls of the barn. Da would have loved that. When he'd had a long drink, Valdean set the glass down carefully beside his tools; he stretched until each shoulder and his neck cracked loudly, then shook his fingers and hands until they flopped like bits of cloth. "There." He settled back in the kitchen chair he used.

"I read something in the St. Louis newspaper yesterday—" She waited expectantly, but neither man seemed inclined to listen to what a young and foolish girl would say, even a girl a man twice her age was poking. Yes, she used this language now. Poking. Ugly. But if he left her—

Valdean rested his gaze on her and smiled encouragingly. He was raised right. "When you're done with that paper, I'd appreciate a chance to read it," he said. L.O. stayed so silent, he might as well be her little dog Pete asleep next to Valdean's chair. They had become fast friends, and perhaps the dog would run off with the stonecutter when he left.

"It's about a new religion the Indians are joining. They dance and starve until they fall into a trance. They believe they can bring the dead back alive again if they all dance together, all across the country. The Ghost Dance. That's what they're calling it. They wear special light blue shirts that keep bullets and knives from hurting them." She was proud of her story, and looked from Valdean to L.O. for approval.

"Wonder if it works," L.O. said.

"Be fine if it did." Valdean began to build a cigarette using the loose tobacco and papers he bought in town now that his premade ones were gone. He lit the end with a kitchen match, crossed his legs, and leaned back, inhaling deeply and letting the smoke out in a thin stream that rose and disappeared in the heavy grape vines overhead. He smoked slowly, with the same kind of meticulous pleasure he took in his cutting tools. The finished headstones sat around them in a semicircle, like finicky visitors, stiff necked, uncomfortable.

"Well," L.O. sighed and glanced toward the house and beyond to the barn. "Guess I should get to it." He sounded so worn down that her heart went out to him.

"Let's go fishing," she said. "Celebrate the end of your job." Standing, she waved toward the house. "I'll run and pack us a picnic. We can go to Reelfoot Lake." She gave them her best smile, knowing that L.O. was always after her to go across the river to that damn place so he could experience the fishing he heard so much about. Being men, they took their time, but came around.

"I'll see if Frank wants to come." L.O. sprang up and hurried to the house while Valdean carefully packed his tools into the carpetbag. He was wearing his only other pair of pants, a gold brocade waistcoat, white shirt without the collar and cuffs, and his bowler hat.

"You might want to see if Frank has clothing that will fit," she said.

He waved his hand and said, "I don't fish. I'll just sit and watch with the ladies or sketch. Finish the last dates tomorrow."

At the word *dates* he glanced toward the house, then busied himself straightening the tools at the bottom of the bag. He liked to have them lined up side by side before he closed the top. They couldn't be overlapping, despite the fact that once he picked up the bag, you could hear them being jostled around. The problem with dates was that she hadn't been able to get anyone to give her any. Not for her mother, and Jacques' stone listed only his name and the year of his birth as "B—?" Her mother's would have nothing if she didn't come up with a date. It would be as if she must still be alive somewhere, or as if she were just a figment, a hallucination, a spirit or haunt, since she was neither born nor died. Where were the letters, the odd things they saved, as she did—a green glass earring, some uniform buttons from the war that she found when she was playing out in the field by the big sand boil, the china hands and feet of her doll, the little engraved silver lady's knife Da gave her when she argued for a big bowie knife like he wore? There were any number of things she saved, where were theirs? Everywhere she looked there was evidence that Jacques Ducharme lived here: the house and lands, the town that bore his name. Omah who took his name. And Little Maddie who was born with it. Why would he try to stop her from passing it on? The thought had plagued her since last winter. The lawyer and judge kept putting her off, but she wouldn't stop. She would win. She knew she would.

Omah and Frank decided to join them at the last minute, making a merry group that went riding down to the ferry at Jacques' Landing, where they loaded the horses and buggy, and began the journey across the river, being hauled by pulley ropes. It was early afternoon by the time they made it to the Tennessee side and traveled the few miles down the dusty road to the lake. Appearing during the New Madrid earthquakes, Reelfoot was a shallow lake stretching over some distance, ghosts of giant old trees left standing in the water, roots rotted. A person could maneuver a shallow-bottom boat around them if they were careful. Some places the cattails were so thick a person could get stuck in them forever if they had to swim out. The cottonmouths looked pretty much like the water snakes in Reelfoot, so snakes were to be avoided. They stopped at an old slab-sided shack beside a rough plank dock. While Frank dismounted and went inside to work out the renting of a fishing boat, Omah and Valdean drove the buggy down the shoreline some three hundred yards to the clump of elms where they'd have a picnic. Maddie was riding astride, wearing a pair of Jacques' old trousers under her skirt. The men didn't know it yet, but she planned on going fishing too.

She reached over and grabbed L.O.'s hand. "I have a surprise for you," she said impulsively. God knew why she said that, but she'd think of something by tonight.

He lifted his eyes and smiled at her. Although he didn't mean to, she could see the sadness lines around his mouth and eyes. He was missing home.

"You're going fishing?" he said. "Female in a boat, bad luck." He shook his head and spat to the side like one of the old men who sat out front of the hotel summer days.

Frank stepped off the plank walk and spoke to L.O. as if she weren't there. "If you'll ride over, tie the horses in those trees by Omah, and come back here, I'll load the poles and bait." He began to untie the short poles and bucket from his saddle, while L.O. started off toward the buggy.

Urging her horse into a trot, she passed L.O. and had her horse hobbled and unsaddled by the time he was pulling the saddle from Frank's horse. She grabbed her straw hat from the back of the buggy, and raced back to the dock. Frank looked surprised when she stepped into the boat, rocking it dangerously, and promptly settled on a bench at the end, clapping the straw hat on her head.

Frank arranged the short poles and bait bucket in the middle of the boat and straightened, shading his eyes with his hand.

"You don't need to be doing this," he said in a quiet voice. With a glance toward the figure of L.O. walking leisurely in their direction, he added, "Let him be."

She tried smiling, but he just stared until she got up and climbed out of the boat, taking the last step so awkwardly, she almost fell in and he had to grab her arm. She flung him off and stomped down the dock planks, making as much noise as possible, passing L.O. without a word.

Omah nodded her head knowingly and Maddie had to bite her tongue as she flung down on the quilt and pulled the straw hat over her eyes so she didn't have to watch the boat drifting away. She didn't mean to fall asleep—she wanted to tell someone how she was being wrongly treated by L.O.—but the harmonic murmur of Omah's and Valdean's voices soothed her hurt feelings and eventually lulled her.

She dreamed first of her da, young and strong, laughing at something in the sunlight by the river. The next image was an old old man, so old his skin looked toasted, crisp and brown, huddled in a cupboard beneath a stove or fireplace. The room looked familiar and she was trying to place it when a voice came over the dream saying he was dead, but still she stood there waiting to make sure he was dead.

She worried herself sick that she'd killed him—and woke up, numbers rolling in her head—dates—the dates on the headstones. She had to find her da. She thought she knew where he was.

As soon as the men returned from fishing, she hurried them to pack the buggy and head back without supper.

"What's wrong?" L.O. kept asking.

But it was dark by the time they rode up to the house, and people kept watching her to make sure everything was all right. She would have to wait until morning to do this alone.

She thought she wouldn't be able to shut her eyes, but the opposite was true. She fell into a deep, dreamless sleep as soon as L.O. pulled her into his arms.

Rising before anyone, she tiptoed out of the house into the first rose-yellow light, her little dog pattering behind, still blinking away his sleep.

Valdean had finished sometime in the night, she discovered, filling in Jacques' death date, the day after he locked her in her room. He was truly dead, then. She turned to her mother's marker, whose death date had also been carved—the year after her daughter's birth, the month of May. She was gone, too. Only Omah could have given Valdean those dates, she realized, Omah who had been here the whole time.

In the dream at Reelfoot Lake she thought she had recognized the room, but she hesitated . . . what if he was there? Suddenly she was walking quickly back into the house, through the kitchen, pulling the door to the ell open. Pete stopped in the doorway, whimpering, would not follow, but she kept going, down the dusty hallway to the door at the end, which she had to yank on with all her might until it let go, sending her sprawling. She stood and looked. The room hadn't changed. The dusty rose quilt on the bed, the guttered stubs of old candles on the table, the tattered nightgown hanging on a peg. The only change was that the rotting smell was gone now, as it would be after this much time.

She tiptoed in, trying to sense anything or anybody; not knowing what to expect. She discovered another change—the sill of the boarded-up window was black with the bodies of flies, the large, slow ones you find covering dead things. As she neared the back wall, the brittle bodies crunched underfoot.

Leaning her cheeks and palms against the faded cypress planks of the wall next to the window, she whispered, "Da—" and felt the faintest puff of air on the side of her cheek. Startled, she pulled back and carefully examined where the wall met the window frame. There was the slightest line, as if the window wasn't sitting quite right. She followed the line with the tips of her fingers trying to sense the tiniest difference in temperature. She could feel it, yes, as if the window could be easily removed. It took her awhile to figure out that she could simply pull on the windowsill and the frame would begin to inch toward her, away from the wall. It was ingenious. Eventually, the entire window frame swung into the room like the top half of a stall door in the barn, revealing a dark passageway on the other side. If the design was truly an imitation of a horse stall, there should be a latch for the lower half, which she could see now that she knew what she was looking for. The craftsmanship was so good that a person wouldn't be able to discern the door's outline unless they knew it was there. She found the latch on the other side of the lower door that swung open on hinges heavy enough to hold a foot-thick partition designed to sound solid when knocked.

Peering into the darkness, she discerned steps going down into some kind of tunnel or underground room. She looked back at the candle stubs on the table. With all of them burning she might just make it down and back. She found the sulphurs in a closed tin on a shelf just inside the door, but looked in vain for more candles. If she stopped and went back for candles or a lamp, she ran the risk of encountering another early riser. No, she'd make do with what she had.

The first candle took her to the top of the stairs before it went out, and she hastily lit two this time. She held the candle in front of her and stepped down, surprised at how solid and soundless the steps were. She heard a slight rustle in the darkness ahead of her, stopped, and called, "Da?" Were there snakes down there? Rats, big river rats, the most terrifying ones of all—she shivered at the thought, but continued down nonetheless, feeling the air grow cooler as the stairs went underground. The floor was covered in ancient staw mats that muffled sound, and by holding the candle high, she was able to make out several fixtures holding candles set into the bricked walls of the tunnel. She stopped and stretched on her tiptoes to dislodge two long tapers. With their light, she could finally see the tunnel room in detail.

The room was so crammed with furniture ruined by gnawed wood and chewed-up upholstery, paintings blooming mold and mildew, and antique trunks held together by rusty hinges and damp, warped wood, that only a narrow path enabled her to pass through.

Da was down here. She stepped carefully, pausing to look under heaps of rotting drapes and bedding, chairs that mice had chewed into and riddled with elaborate nests, and trunks with lids thrown open, spilling their booty of photo plates, books, and velvet curtains. Where was her da? Where was the fortune he hoarded?

She wandered through the series of rooms, some of which were actually ancient caves carved out of the limestone by the river and springs. She had always heard that the subsurface of Missouri hid a maze of caves. Here was the evidence. She had to wonder how many more he had filled with his loot, much of which was rapidly being destroyed or was already too far gone to be of any use. The waste, she thought sharply, this was too much waste for one person.

She was coming to some kind of end of the tunnel, she discovered. The dirt beneath her feet was wet, and she thought she could hear the whisperings of the river ahead. When she finally turned the last corner and emerged into the final large room, the opening was barricaded by rock and timbers that apparently failed to keep out everything. She could hear the river louder now, as if the room sat almost at water level. She held up the candles.

There he was, propped in a rocking chair, a blackened figure so mummified as to be without identity, except for the bowie knife clasped in his hand and resting in his lap, the simple peasant smock, the flowered scarf tied around his neck, and the knee-high deerhide lace-up boots—all of which she recognized from the trunk in his room. He was dressed as the French fur trapper he once was. She moved close enough to examine the body for wounds, but the skin seemed intact, albeit weathered, burnt almost, as if it were a thousand years old. Then she noticed that there were clumps of hair on his shoulders and the floor. He had apparently cut his hair, but there was something wrong—the hair was black now, not the silver of late. She picked up a clump and felt the odd stickiness. The strands were coated with some kind of heavy grease . . .

When she moved closer, she kicked an empty brandy bottle. Looking down, she saw that he was surrounded by empty brandy bottles. He had come here to die.

The candles fluttered, threatening to go out, and she cupped the flames with her hand until they steadied again. When she looked up, the woman in blue was standing in front of the barricaded wall, the breeze leaking around the stone and timber heap pushing her dress alive. Maddie couldn't discern any features, but felt the other's gaze upon her. Although the figure didn't speak, Maddie heard the words in her mind. Jacques was home now, with her. The treasure was in another cave, just below this one, the entrance beneath Jacques' chair. Maddie was to wait, however, until there was great need, so great that Jacques' Landing was in danger and she was unable to work harder to save it. Maddie felt shame suddenly because she knew that the gold and jewels were all stolen, that lives had been lost so Jacques could pass on his fortune to her.

"Did he suffer?" Maddie asked.

The woman in blue began to fade.

"Da? Annie?" Maddie called and the air stirred around her, caressing her cheeks. She thought she heard the sigh and snuffle of Jacques' old dog, but could see nothing. She didn't feel like crying now, which was strange, she thought, but maybe it was because she had already mourned her father . . . and her mother. Now she was saying goodbye, seeing them off, as if they were boarding the train for St. Louis, and she wouldn't see them for a while. She pictured the white linen tablecloths, the heavy silver coffee service, and the deep leather cushions of the chairs as the world passed by their windows.

She wasn't even going to go down there and see the treasure. She didn't dare. But she told herself to remember to write a letter about how to find it and give it to St. Clair for her children. She was confident that she would never need Jacques' money. She was quite capable of making her own fortune.

She raised the candles and looked around the room that was her Da's forever now. "Goodbye, Da, sleep well," she whispered, and a cool breath stroked her face. It was only the breeze from the river, she told herself.

28

"EVERYTHING I HAVE IS FROM MY OWN HARD WORK," LITTLE MADDIE SAID.

"No one can fault you there," St. Clair said. Although it was 1902, nothing had changed there, except Leland's gray hair was now white and shaggy, and he had stains from past meals marching down the front of his lavender brocade waistcoat. His black formal shoes and white spats had sloughed through the red mud and been ruined. There was no clear indication as to why he was wearing formal shoes during the day in his office, particularly with the heavy brown tweed box coat, creased black dress trousers, and of course the oddly ornate waistcoat. His hair was unwashed and overlong too, hanging almost to his shoulders in the old style.

His face and body had registered every one of the past thirteen years since she first sat in this office discussing her father's will. Once they had finally agreed that he was dead, and she wasn't about to pull him out of that hole and parade his bones around to satisfy their morbid curiosity, it should have been a matter of declaring the codicil unenforceable, but the court had been holding her hostage for years. Now she made an annual pilgrimage each May first into Jacques' Landing, threatened to go to St. Louis to hire a competent lawyer, discussed the price of cotton and timber, shopped at the growing number of stores in town, and went home.

When he came from behind his desk to stoke the coal fire, adding more noxious fumes to the overly warm room, he hobbled stiffly and the poker shook in his hand. It was as if he'd weakened in the few minutes since she arrived. There was dust on all the sporting pictures too, and they seemed as dimmed by the past thirteen years as Leland himself.

And when Leland settled on the settee a little too snugly pressed against her, his ancient hunting dog, a German shorthair, shifted uncomfortably beside the fire, bones clunking on the slate hearthstone. It sighed, lifted its head, and looked blindly in their direction, the eyes filmed and dull. Leland had to lift the dog's leg to help it pee outside. She'd been watching him do it for three years.

"I might could argue at the state supreme court," Leland said slyly, thinking of the money he'd make. His body might be wearing out, but his mind was still sharp.

"We can't even get a local ruling," she argued, tempted to mention that the wiry hairs sprouting from his nose and eyebrows could use a trim, which she'd be willing to pay for since he seemed convinced he was too poor for a barber.

"How's L.O. holding up?" He made an arch with the tips of his fingers and peered at her with one of his intense gazes.

"L.O.? Wishing he was out West. He's buying horses like I'm made of money, selling the timber off as fast as he can chop and haul it to the sawmill. I think some days he's clearing his way to Wyoming. The Ozarks are going to be a little problem, I tell him."

"Those railroad people hook up with your line yet?" Leland asked. He knew very well that the Cotton-Belt Line, built just four years ago, joined hers and that trains were moving day and night, keeping her awake and L.O. jumpy.

"Can't you do something about that charcoal-making business that man's started right on top of us? I would never have sold him an inch of land if I'd known he'd take up such a filthy business." She fanned herself with the latest issue of *McClure's*, welcoming the cool rush of air that almost succeeded in pushing the coal stink away.

Leland sighed heavily. This had become his trademark, that and sitting too close and sliding his hand to her knee and upward. They did silent battle during the little interview sessions. She didn't say anything because she didn't think he even realized he was doing it. But since he knew the case and Jacques, unlike the other three lawyers in town, she continued to retain him. Anyway, it was just like dealing with a slightly ill-mannered but persistent puppy: The hand climbed onto her, she pushed it off, it climbed on, she pushed it off . . .

"You ready to sell me that big gray horse yet?" he asked.

"That horse is crazy. He'll kill you," she said, like always. The gray had been dead for five years, as he *well* knew. More games before they got down to it.

"You tell me when you get ready to sell him," Leland said, raising a shaky finger to the corner of his eye to rub a bit of crust away.

Good God, she hoped she never grew old.

"Don't you have a good carriage horse?" she asked.

His great-grandson delivered him every morning and picked him up every evening, driving as recklessly as his father had those many years ago. She had no idea how that idiot boy convinced the Dobson girl to let him sire her child. From cowboying to drinking, he and Layne Knight started a sawmill downriver and a whole town on raised timbers grew up around it. Now they were the most respectable citizens around. She was not fooled though; she still saw the stupid bullying glint in their eyes.

"Yes, yes I do. A fine black horse you sold me. Thank you. My grandson says we should get another to match it. I said I'd look into it." He pulled absently at one of his long earlobes. A person had plenty of time to think in a conversation with Leland St. Clair.

"I'll see what L.O. says." She always used this dodge when she couldn't come out and tell the truth—she'd rather cut off an arm than give that little ruffian another one of her horses. If that black hadn't been the most iron-jawed, ill-tempered, cow-hocked, pigeon-toed horse on the place, she would never have sold him to Leland. Some people never had the knack with horses—his was a whole family without an ounce of horse sense. Dogs, dogs they cast spells over, trained them with a look and a pointing finger. The old German shorthair was the most famous hunting dog in the county. He lifted his grizzled muzzle, stared in her direction as if he could read the appreciation in her mind, then flopped his head back on the hearth.

"I came to see you about something else today, Leland," she said, and the lawyer that lay beneath the aging surface came alive.

"Yes." His voice strengthened as if he were an old dog himself, chasing a bicycle the first nice day of spring.

"I need a will. I want to make sure that when the codicil is broken, any children I might have will inherit."

His rheumy eyes brightened. "Wise decision. Children come first."

They went over the details with him taking notes in a large nearly indecipherable scrawl that covered many more pages than necessary. By the end of their session, he seemed suddenly confident that he could file the petition and the court finally would hear it. It was as if with another generation involved, and the potential of future business, he finally believed in her case.

Leland sat back and scratched his chin, staring into the smoldering coal fire. "Let's see, Bonner Willson's sitting in court June. He's a stickler for the law." He glanced at her with amusement in his eyes. "But he has one vice."

"What's that?" she asked.

"Horses. Man loves his horses." He squinted at the wall over the fireplace. "We used to hunt raccoons on mules of his could jump a six-strand barbed wire fence. He's master of a hunt north of here, keeps a pack of fifty hounds. Racing, too. Man would give his right arm for a decent racing horse at a good price, you happen to know any."

"How decent does this horse have to be?"

"How much is your property worth?"

She nodded. So it came down to trading the best horse in her stable for the land she owned anyway. She didn't know how L.O. was going to take this news.

"You'll let me know where and when to send the judge this bargain, right?"

"I'll inquire and get back to you. Man's a fool for a horse."

They discussed the forecast for cotton and he told her that a man in St. Louis had put in an order for twenty thousand sticks of lumber at his son's mill.

"You hear anything from your people in New Orleans?" he asked, meaning Omah and her children. "They're fine," she said like always. He told her there were mutterings about dredging the swamps, diverting the water into bayous, and cutting the rest of the timber, which would include the old-growth cypress, oak, sweet gum, black gum, sycamore, elm, and hackberry. He listed them off on his fingers as if each tree were a personal acquaintance. "I hunted those swamps all my life," he said.

"How soon you think they'll start?"

"Won't be long now. People want it all these days."

"I just want what's mine."

He nodded his head slowly as if he'd fallen asleep, and they sat there in the stuffy office listening to the slow tapping of his secretary on her typewriting machine. Outside, through the heavy drapes, they could hear a motorcar pass, its loud engine sweeping past all that was the old world, leaving it as remote and finalized as dust in its wake.

Standing up, she was struck with regret or sadness, she couldn't say which, the sensation that she was departing his office for the last time. Immediately she felt bad for making fun of Leland St. Clair over the years, especially now when he was simply an old man and couldn't help his eccentricities. He'd served her faithfully, so she did the best she could by him—she gave him a sudden hug and pressed herself against his body hard enough that he could feel her full breasts.

He smiled and promised to send the papers out for her to sign, then waved her off absentmindedly, as if she'd come to sell him something. The secretary in the outer room nodded politely as she left. She was her old dressmaker's daughter who'd been hired by Leland's family to type as well as to care for him. She was wearing ready-made clothes these days, the first thing she did with her paycheck each week, although they were expensive. Maddie complimented her on the white blouse with the man's brown tie at the collar and the large loose brown tweed skirt, but thought nothing as nicely fitted as the clothes her mother could make.

At the end of the street, the boxcar serving as train depot was surrounded by crates of chickens and eggs to go out on the morning train for Sisketon and St. Louis. The town should have been set up on timbers, but the same mad optimism that put them back on the Mississippi after the big quakes ninety years ago led them to build the post office, livery stable, Masonic lodge, flour and grist mill, barrel and stave mill, hardware, dry goods, recreation hall, and bank only two feet above ground level, with the elevated plank sidewalk running along in front. The courthouse was set back sufficiently and made of native granite and limestone, so tall and massive a structure that water had little effect on it.

Last fall fire had destroyed a block of the business strip, and men were busy rebuilding there this morning. It was the second time that block had been rebuilt: once after the Union army burned the Methodist Church in 1864, and now when the beer tavern, pool hall, bakery, and barbershop went up. That block was cursed, anyone in town would tell you. Nothin' and nobody would thrive there. It was on account of Miz Maddie's children, they'd assure you, although they were making it all up. Miz Maddie's two children gunned down in the courthouse itself by Union soldiers, all sorts of human misery her family had been blamed for. But the more optimistic had hold of the economic reins this morning and were gaily rebuilding a neat line of storefronts, topped by second-story offices or rooms to let.

Although the continuing tremors made people prefer the ground floor, the continual flooding down here made a second story essential. She was lucky that Da built his house on a hill and lifted it up too. So far, they'd never been flooded out, although twice in her life the river had come lapping at the bottom step, depositing cottonmouths and dead fish as it departed.

Her next visit was to the doctor's office, using a side entrance up a flight of stairs above the dry goods store shielded from prying eyes. The meeting was brief and to the point. Afterward, she repaired to LeFay's department store, making the first mistake of the day.

Ethel May Zubar, who had never forgiven her for the chestnut team she took from her, was arguing with Hillis LeFay and Dowsie Louise Binnion about the Negroes again. This remained a topic of conversation on every white person's lips here, whether they were Methodist, Catholic, Baptist, or Holy Roller.

"They're having that convention right here in town," Ethel May said, stamping her big foot hard enough on the plank floor to rattle the array of pots and pans, dishes, and hardware sitting on shelves behind her.

"It's a revival meeting," Hillis said without looking up from the tissuey pages of Mr. Ward's Wish Book he was flipping.

"They need to have it in their own town," Dowsie said in a timid voice that seemed squeezed out of her heavy body. Both women were as usual in the height of fashion, bustled, corseted, bound and hobbled like fat sleek horses whose owner was afraid they'd run off.

"What town would that be?" Maddie couldn't resist their stupidity. It was like flypaper.

"I don't believe you're part of this discussion," Ethel May sniffed.

Maddie smiled, remembering the expressions on their faces when Omah made them taste her medicinal tea and cookies that day years ago.

"Well," Dowsie sighed in a put-upon way. "I'll just have to keep my grandchildren in the house this weekend."

"They're not Gypsies," Maddie said. "They won't steal your children. Which church is having the revival?"

"First African Methodist," Hillis said. He glanced up at her with a twinkle in his eye. "You thinkin' of gettin' saved?"

"That'll be the day!" Ethel May snorted through her nose like an old hog, and Maddie smiled brightly at her.

"You must have some advice for me," she said. "Let's see, what could it concern? My farm? My husband? My men? Or just little ol' me?"

Hillis gave her a warning frown, but she was on her high horse now and couldn't see the ground very well.

"Husband?" Ethel May gathered her considerable size and looked Maddie straight in the eye. "My dear girl, you and that man have been living in sin for thirteen years and you know it. As for the rest, your family has always loved the colored too much. Heaven only knows how many light-skinned brothers and sisters you have. And your precious Omah? Everybody knows she was your father's concubine, Frank Boudreau notwithstanding. He just traded her off to Boudreau like she was a cow or mule in exchange for some work."

Her jaw dropped, but nothing came out—she was too furious for words. The doctor said not to let herself experience extremes of emotion, to rest, take up a ladylike pastime such as reading or knitting. He didn't have any idea what she dealt with in this town.

"Don't forget that colored man she killed." Dowsie made her contribution, blushing wildly, her eyes fixed on the men's sleeping garments page of the catalog.

"What!" Maddie had to stop herself from knocking the turnip-shaped head off Dowsie's shoulders.

"Valdean French." Ethel May drew the name out with relish. "We heard all about it, although even I was surprised by how far you'd go, Maddie Ducharme."

"I haven't even the slightest idea what you're referring to, Ethel May. You wouldn't know cow dung from pecan. That man's alive and well in New Orleans!"

Hillis waved at her, trying to stop them, but she ignored him. He turned the flimsy catalog pages so quickly he tore one almost in half and ironed it out with the side of his hand.

Ethel May straightened her shoulders, put a hand on the counter to claim its solidity, and glared. "The citizens of this town are mighty sick and tired of being bullied by you and your family!"

Maddie said, "Do you even know who Valdean French is?"

For the first time she was stymied and glanced quickly at Dowsie, then pursed her mouth and glared again. "A colored man your father hired from New Orleans to paint your house. As if our local men aren't good enough!" Her eyes grew crafty. "You and Frank Boudreau conspired to murder him because he was having an affair with your Omah."

Maddie had to laugh out loud at the lurid, conventional imagination at work. As soon as she did, of course, Ethel May scowled and looked uncertainly at Dowsie and Hillis.

"You really should be writing for *Police News*, or one of those yellow rags that publish rumor instead of fact, Ethel May." She laughed again, enjoying how Ethel May's face was scrunching up like an old sow eating turnip greens. "Valdean French is a well-known poet and stone carver. And—" She paused dramatically, figuring it couldn't hurt since he lived so far away. "He much prefers men to women, which means that Frank or L.O would have to be the object of his affections. A matter which I'll be sure to mention to them as soon as I get home. They'll probably want to come discuss it with you and your family."

She'd made up part of it, but the woman didn't need to know that. "And if he'd preferred women, Ethel May?" Hillis was really waving his hand now, and the door jingled open, but Maddie plunged ahead.

"I would have been his lover in a heartbeat. He has the purest soul I've ever met, but you wouldn't know about that, would you?"

Ethel May clenched her teeth, her eyes becoming so small they were almost buried in the plump creases of her face. "You're nothing but a nigger-lover, Maddie Ducharme. And that puts you one rung lower than the bottom."

Maddie flapped a hand, forcing herself to laugh. "Oh, you're just jealous—"

The woman appeared close to combustion, and since Maddie had been curious lately about the subject of self-immolation, she was hoping she'd actually burst into flames, but Ethel May disappointed her by turning on her heel and marching out of the store without another word, Dowsie in her wake.

"Burning more bridges, I see." L.O. grinned wickedly and tipped his hat as if they were merely acquaintances, something he'd been doing in public for years now.

"L.O." Hillis nodded his head in greeting. "What can I do you for?"

Frowning, L.O. looked around. "Thought you had a pair of nippers I could use on horse teeth, or did I see that in a catalog?"

Hillis stared straight ahead, running the store's stock in his head. He knew every single item in the store: drugs, hardware, clothing, meat, groceries, feed, and seed. In spring he'd order the baby chickens, ducks, turkeys, and geese most farmers needed to raise for food. His family had been in business here since the beginning, and Hillis, though a young man in his twenties, appeared to wear the collective wisdom of the family in his thin face, bemused eyes behind the wire-rimmed spectacles, and brown hair already streaked with gray. It was not that there were lines in his face, but even so you could see his ancestors just below the thin surface of skin.

While L.O. and Hillis went off into the dark bowels of the store in search of nippers, Maddie wondered if living in one place for generations made all of them appear to each other as Hillis did to her. Ethel May saw the outrage of Jacques Ducharme every time she saw his daughter, so it wasn't her at all, not entirely or mostly, it was the collective wrongs of another person's life she wore like a suffocating robe over her own. Only it wasn't just Da she was responsible for, it was his first wife Annie, Omah and Frank and their children, her grandmother Miz Maddie and mother Laura, and now Valdean French. Maddie barely had room for her own crimes and L.O. No wonder Ethel May and the others were so outraged, it was a burden having to carry herself and her encyclopedic history. Human memory—what a compendium of lies, half truths, myths, bound by the flimsy string of a person's life. No wonder there was something of guilty relief when a person died, got themselves off the page, gave everyone around them the chance to close at least one book. Maybe they were better off not knowing one another very well, but then they had to make up what they weren't witness to—and that was even more arduous.

She wished Ethel May could see the way L.O. put his hand on the quivering flank of a frightened horse, calmed it with his touch, how that same hand had eased the grief up and out of her shoulders, lifted it like a yoke from her neck, and replaced it with loving. Or the way Frank Boudreau tended their cemetery now, trimming around the beautifully carved birds on the headstones for Omah's parents, Jacques, Annie Lark, Miz Maddie, and Laura. Although some of them had only a crudely cut initial and date, Valdean reminded them that there was beauty and recompense in honoring the departed, that they must order life so, or descend to the howling animals who waited outside the gates every time they crossed into the world. They must not join them, though the temptation was mighty, Valdean said in a poem L.O. showed her. How puny their defenses against the devouring world.

She was so philosophical this morning, it made her tired and nervous, and she didn't want anything to interfere with the good news she intended to give L.O. When he and Hillis sauntered back down the aisle, the large nippers in one hand, a bright sawtoothed rasp in the other, she slipped an arm through her husband's. He blushed, surprised at her sudden show of public affection. Were they married? As much as Omah and Frank, more she would say than her mother and father. If Da were alive, she would have him, the progenitor of this tale, perform the ceremony.

"Are you ready?" L.O. turned to her, package tucked under his arm.

She smiled up into his lean face, the trailing silver mustaches, the quick brown eyes that saw past her into a distance she could only imagine. "Don't bury me here," he had said last night after their lovemaking. She hadn't answered him. All this planning, she'd thought—my God, how quickly we're swept off our feet, poured down the road, to ride the floods! And all we can do is say a quick prayer, not go mad, and hang on until the end.

Part Four

HEDIE RAILS
DUCHARME

. . .

"Angels are bright still, though the brightest fell."

EPILOGUE

*T*HE REST OF LITTLE MADDIE'S STORY I KNOW FROM CLEMENT'S UNCLE Keaton, who heard the facts repeated often enough that it seemed as if he too had been there to witness it.

On December 24, 1902, Clement Ducharme Swan was born. Little Maddie and L.O. were extremely proud of their little boy, but kept him a secret until the following summer when the horse Little Maddie bartered for his future won a stakes race in Kentucky, and Judge Bonner Willson ruled Jacques' codicil null and void. The horse went on to win many more stakes races, and to become the foundation sire of a famous line of horses. All black, with a white teardrop on the forehead and one or two white socks.

Two years later in February, L.O. was killed in a hunting accident by one of the Knight boys, and in early April Little Maddie succumbed in the diphtheria epidemic.

It was later described as a miracle, the odd ice storm that came down the river, suddenly encasing the landscape in a glittering sheen. The eyelashes on the horses drawing the casket from the Methodist Church home to the family cemetery became frozen so quickly that the animals stumbled nearly blind the last half mile, and had to be led up the entrance to the yard. When the men went to lift the casket, it was so thick with ice they had to hammer at the rope handles to free them. The cortège crunched noisily across the front yard, struck by the way Jacques' house seemed emblazoned with light from the sudden appearance of the sun, and the ice that continued to fall rattled like tiny slivers of glass against the sides of the casket.

There were reports of a woman in an old-fashioned blue dress with a yellow cashmere shawl at the edge of the yard. A couple of people watching from the shelter of the bur oaks saw her, and some swore it was old One-Armed Jacques Ducharme himself peering from the corner of the second-story porch. What everyone did agree on was that it was a miracle that the tulips and daffodils, lilies and four-o'clocks that had mysteriously sprung into bloom together the week before, as if to comfort Little Maddie as she lay dying, weren't beaten or broken by the weight of the ice. Instead it appeared to enclose and hold them tenderly in a brilliant embrace that none could break to lay a single stem on the coffin as it sat beside its new dark home.

Little Maddie would have it that way, Frank murmured, and Tom Spraggins, Artie Kamp, and Leon Wyre, what remained of the men who worked for her, stood waiting before beginning the slow process of shoveling the wet red dirt onto the plain cypress box. In the end, a delirious Little Maddie had asked the dead L.O. to build her box of their best cypress because it could withstand the dampness and flooding, and Frank had seen it done, although he'd had to pry several floorboards from the upstairs hallway to accomplish the feat in such weather. The golden orange wood bore a patina that appeared as if it had been painstakingly etched with tiny commas, and even Ethel May Zubar, on the arm of her nephew Layne St. Clair, remarked on its beauty. It was the first time some of the townsfolk had ever stepped foot on Old Jacques' land, and for others it had been years, so everyone was taking in as much as they could without seeming inconsiderate to the dead. Who knew how long it would be before they were allowed another visit.

At the last minute, a tall Negro woman appeared, stepping through the crowd with such confidence they automatically moved aside. The finest carriage the livery stable owned stood waiting on the front lawn, the matching pure-white horses splashed to the knees with red mud, having been driven right to the steps of the house so the woman could dismount without soiling her pale green watered silk shoes. In her arms she bore sprays of fresh-cut wild indigo, yellow spicebush, and redbud blossoms, which she laid across the coffin. Then whispering a few words, she rapped the lid with her knuckles and turned back to the house.

Drawing a mink-lined cape of the smartest style around her as she mounted the steps, she entered the house without hesitation, moving toward the cries of the child, which the mourners now realized had been so steady since they'd arrived that they had forgotten them, much as they would the irritating buzzing of a fly at a window glass. Only Frank Boudreau knew who the woman was for certain. Leland St. Clair gazed after her with a smile on his face as if he knew her, too, but no one could be certain what Leland knew at that point.

Omah stayed long enough to make certain the baby Clement would be cared for, despite commenting to Frank that the baby's name was another unfortunate mistake—it wasn't a family name, as Little Maddie had thought to use to honor her grandmother, rather it was the name of a ne'er-do-well the woman had once married and promptly discarded. Before Omah left the house a day later, she paid a visit to her parents in the little cemetery, stood over Jacques' headstone trying to conjure his fortune, sprinkled a handful of Union and Confederate uniform pewter buttons she'd found over the years across Little Maddie's grave, and bid the family a brief parting, certain in her bones that she would be returning before long. She had, after all, written her story in the family book.

After Omah left, Leland St. Clair, the lawyer, contacted Keaton, Little Maddie's half brother, to come home and take over the farm and raise the child. If indeed Little Maddie had ever written the letter about Jacques' treasure, it was never transferred to her son or his guardian. What Clement later became was often laid on the doorstep of Keaton's indulgences, but perhaps it was more the result of two motherless boys facing a comfortless world.

ALTHOUGH I VOWED THAT IN THE NEW YEAR OF 1932, I WOULD FIND JACQUES' fortune and save us, things were different this time when Clement left at night, and he was not comforted by my assurances that we were closing in on the treasure, which of course even I didn't quite believe. It all sounded so childish, yet I couldn't stand the way Clement looked after his nights. He wore a permanently haunted expression, his eyes constantly watching the doors and windows, his body jumping at sudden noises. I had to make sure to announce myself entering a room, and put my arms around him carefully so he didn't overreact and knock me away.

It made me so angry to have him this way that one night I locked the doors so he had to sleep in his big, fancy car. I fought with him when he wanted to leave too, watched his face grow desperate and mocked him. I hid his evening clothes, cut the soles of his patent leather dress pumps, scraped his razor on the rough underside of the porcelain sink to dull the sharpness so he'd cut himself shaving. I put horse pee in his hair pomade. Nothing stopped him. It only made things worse. He stayed away for days now. Then he was gone for two and a half weeks and I did the stupidest thing possible— I called the sheriff out to the farm.

He acted nonchalant, his narrow, hungry face sullen as he eyed the rich furniture and the big yellow diamond ring I wore as a talisman now.

"In his bidness, got to expect he be gone irregular like—don't ya think?" he drawled.

"Farming?"

The sheriff cackled and brushed the rose silk brocade of the sofa with the side of his hand as if collecting crumbs.

"Never heard it called *that* before. Say, lady"—he leaned toward me, his brown teeth bared—"you tell Clement I ain't needin' much of a cut, but I ain't doin' without one neither." He winked and I felt sick at my stomach. If I'd had the pistol on me, I'd of shot the greasy son of a bitch right then.

"Tell him yourself." I stood and headed for the door. Clement kept a gun in the entryway table, but the sheriff sighed heavily, stood with one last look around as if marking what was going to be his, and followed me to the door.

"Shouldn't think a lady like you'd want to be in the same house as a man bedding that girl, but a person can't never tell, I say. One man's poison is another man's meat."

"Don't you ever bring that filthy mind back here." I held the door open, ready to lock him out.

"Don't you be callin' me neither, then. I come out here again, I'm takin' someone to jail for sure." He looked over my head, giving the house one last inspection, like a man buying livestock at auction. "And we'll take this place while we're at it, too."

I slammed the big door on his snickering face and ran upstairs to search my husband's closet and dresser.

There were plenty of matchbooks and napkins and hotel receipts from

Sisketon, Cape Girardeau, even Hot Springs, St. Louis, and Memphis. Why he was everywhere! I tore his suits off hangers and dumped the drawers from his huge cherry armoire.

In my head there was a singsong toothpaste radio jingle, "Brusha, brusha, brusha," playing as I carried his things out to the snow-covered driveway, poured kerosene over them, and threw a lit kitchen match on the pile. He wasn't going anywhere anymore. We'd find Jacques' hoard to-gether . . . we'd have our houseful of children . . . I put the promises to the rhythm of the toothpaste song and sang them over and over as I tore back through the house. I'd been to the bachelor's ell fifteen times already, but I went again, trying to hear the hollow sound in the walls that would tell me where it was. Nothing. Nothing. Nothing. I sank into bed that night weep-ing and praying for help.

Even Jesse couldn't soothe the fear mounting inside me that something was terribly wrong. Jesse had his own worries now. India had run away from her aunt's house and was reported being seen in the saloons and clubs and after-hours joints of East St. Louis. Vishti was almost ill with the thought of what was happening to her only child.

And then the oddest thing happened. Every year for Saint Valentine's Day, the Jacques' Landing Volunteer Fire Department held a benefit sweet-heart pancake supper which featured, among other things, a kissing booth, a roulette wheel for prizes donated by local merchants, and an amateur tal-ent contest. Vishti, Jesse, and I hadn't planned on going. We never attended those kinds of gatherings, and I had just settled on reading a Wilkie Collins novel in the library when I heard footsteps on the porch and the door burst open. I leapt up, looking for the pistol, when Clement strolled in, face flushed red and sweaty, wearing a white dinner jacket and formal trousers with a satin stripe down the side. His bow tie was askew, but I wasn't going to tell him. Although he was dressed impeccably, his skin wore a sick, sweaty sheen, and his eyes were so bloodshot they must have been plucked from the last drunk he passed on the way home.

He went immediately to the cabinet with the brandy and poured him-self a large snifter, which he drank quickly, his hands shaking so hard he had to use both of them to steady the glass. Pouring another, he glanced at me and winked.

"How're ya doing?" he said—as if I were a coat-check girl.

"Where have you—"

He held up a hand and shook his head as he poured another drink. "I'm here to take you to the sweetheart supper, Hedie. You're still my sweetheart, aren't you?" The smile that used to make me love and forgive him, made me suspicious now. I could tell that there wasn't any use in arguing though, so I set the book aside and stood.

"I have to change," I said.

"Hurry—don't want to miss the fun—" he called after me.

Since I wasn't feeling very loving at that moment, I put on the tweed suit I sometimes wore shopping to Sisketon and Cape Girardeau, and once to the Methodist Church to look up the records on Little Maddie's family. I didn't bother with makeup except for some pale lipstick. In the mirror, I looked like someone's sister instead of a young wife. I nodded to myself. If he wanted a sweetheart, he would have to come home more often.

By the time we got there, they were almost done serving pancakes and were out of bacon and sausage, but Clement didn't care for food anyway. He gave me the three silver dollar–size cakes and watched as I dribbled them with hot butter and syrup.

"Women your age have to watch what they eat," he remarked. He took out a cigarette and stuck it in the corner of his mouth while he searched for his lighter.

"I'm only nineteen," I protested.

"And look at yourself," he said. "Then look at the other girls here." He took the cigarette out and examined the end as if it were already lit.

It was true that I had grown a little shabby lately. What did he expect? The tweed suit was a mistake, I saw that now. I had forgotten what being a sweetheart, especially his, meant. I was just reaching for his hand when he lit his cigarette and waved it over my plate.

"Go ahead and finish. I was playing." He wasn't paying attention to me anymore, I could tell. He kept looking around the room as if he was going to see someone much more important or interesting. Following his gaze, which bounced like a mosquito from person to person, I noticed Jesse and Vishti sitting with the Negroes at the far end of the room. Surprisingly, India sat on the bench next to them, plate balanced on her knees, the way theirs was, and looking for all the world like a librarian in training rather than the wild girl who hung out in nightclubs.

"Wonder what they're doing here," I said, preparing to stand up and go sit with them.

"The girl's in the talent show, I believe," Clement said around a mouthful of smoke.

"How do you know?"

"Ran into her the other night, place called Red's in East St. Louis. She sang there and knocked them off their chairs. That girl has a very fine voice—"

"Think I'll go say hello to Vishti and Jesse. Where will you be?" I wasn't mad exactly, I just didn't like him knowing India outside her family this way.

He smiled and peeled a ten-dollar bill off the thick packet he drew from his pocket. "Games of chance, Hedie, they have no chance at all when I'm around. Now go play some games. I'll meet you at the talent show. Save a seat."

The little family sat in grim silence, and when I said hello, they each looked at me with a fake smile that didn't quite reach their eyes. This was not a happy reunion. It was about like mine. I stood waiting for them to invite me to sit down, until it became obvious that they weren't going to do it. I sat down anyway, drawing curious looks from the people around us, as well as from the white faces surrounding us.

"I hear you're going to be in the talent show," I said to India.

She nodded with so little expression on her face I had to wonder if she was sick.

"She shows up an hour ago demanding that we bring her here, and now she says she's going to sing in front of all these crackers in this costume." Jesse practically spat the words out and waved a fork over the tight black satin cocktail dress with the sweetheart neckline that by contrast made me look like an English nanny on holiday. She was wearing a different pair of high heels this time—black satin with open toes and ankle straps lined with rhinestones. In her ears were the diamond earrings.

Vishti patted her lips with the square of torn newspaper the firemen provided the Negroes with to use as napkins. "At least she's home safe," she murmured to her husband. "Let her be."

I took that as good advice for myself too, got up and pushed through the crowded room looking for Clement. I found him at the kissing booth, a fan of dollar bills in his fist as he leaned across the counter to touch his lips to a young woman who had to still be in high school.

I wanted to make him lick the concrete floor of the firehouse, but instead I walked over and linked his arm in mine. "Let's play roulette, winner gets to name the game in bed tonight," I whispered into his ear. It used to work.

"Anything?" He winked at the girl and she arched her brow and gave us both a knowing look as she moved across the booth to another customer, a boy more her age.

He shoved the dollar bills back in his pocket, tucked my arm in his, and strolled toward the back room with the roulette wheel. People whispered to one another as we passed, and it dawned on me that we were infamous in Jacques' Landing—the bootlegger thief and his child-bride. I raised my chin and walked as if I were wearing a movie star ball gown instead of my librarian tweeds. I wished someone like Omah was around to give me advice. Even Little Maddie seemed smarter about men than me.

When we got to the backroom, it was so crowded that we had to try to push our way through to the table. The problem was that no one was willing to give up their place, until the man next to us tapped the shoulder of the man in front of us and whispered, "Clement Ducharme's behind you," and as word passed, the space in front of us miraculously cleared. Not one of those men looked directly at us. I noticed that I was the only married woman in the group. There were three other women, all older than me, in shabby dresses they must have worn to the highway roadhouses. They had dark red nails and bright red lipstick, bottle-blond hair and cheap jewelry that was already leaving green lines around their necks and wrists. They were the kind of women who kept their cigarettes stuck between their lips as they leaned over the roulette wheel, yelling and pounding one another on the shoulders and back.

"What do you want?" Clement tilted his head to indicate the list of items attached to the red and black numbers on the wheel.

"One hundred pounds of oats from the feed mill," I said. He smiled and gave me a quick peck on the cheek.

"That's my girl. Nothing frivolous about you. Steady as they come." He put twenty dollars on the fifteen red.

Something in the way he spoke made me feel as if he was comparing me to other women. I flashed on that Caitlin woman from last spring, but knew in my heart that he wasn't involved with her now.

The other men placed small bets, avoiding Clement's number, and the wheel was spun. It came up fifteen red. We stepped back and found the man with the prize slips. When he looked up and recognized Clement, he stuttered, "Oh, oh, oh, here it isss," but he had trouble letting go of the paper and actually tore it in half, clearing his throat and repeating the same phrase like a needle stuck on a record.

"Too hot in there," Clement said and led me to the chairs set up in front of a makeshift stage in the large fire truck bay. "You wait here while I get us some RC."

Although I was the only person there, it felt good to rest in the metal folding chair. My stomach had been acting up for days, and tonight was no exception. I closed my eyes and let my body go slack for a few minutes. I must have nodded off, because when my head jerked up and I opened my eyes, the chairs were nearly all taken. I left my coat across both our chairs and hurried down the aisle.

I found him, standing in the dark shadows of a locked doorway, his arms around a woman, talking very earnestly. I knew it was Clement from the white dinner jacket that glowed in the darkness. I could not make out who the woman was, but it didn't make any difference.

Although I wanted to run out of there, I didn't feel strong enough. I was a little dizzy and my stomach kept rolling, so I made my way back to the talent show. India was waiting to go on first, before people were completely settled in their chairs. The announcer was standing to the side of the room, refusing to come forward to give her name, so after waiting a few minutes, she simply marched out and began her song without musical accompaniment. It was a low-down, slow, bluesy ballad, and her smoky voice handled it well. In fact there was something heartbreaking about a girl her age able to sing as if she'd had all the experience of love and betrayal the song described. A hush fell over the room as her haunting voice overtook us. At the end, there was silence, followed by a smattering of applause, because we were all so stunned and the announcer hustled her off stage as quickly as he could so the twin baton twirlers could follow.

I stood to leave also, wanting to speak to her some encouragement, but Jesse and Vishti were already leading her out the door. Clement came and took my elbow and we left by a different door. He took me home, dropped me at the door, and promised to be back in a few hours. "Just going to town to see a man," he said. I think I'd guessed by then, but I just never said it out loud to myself, so it wasn't really true.

By March neither Clement nor India had returned and we were all terrified. I was alone in the stable late one night after a wet March snow when I heard a car rumbling over the bridge, swinging onto our road, stalling, then the grinding of the starter until the engine caught. Someone gave it too much gas and the engine roared and sputtered and the car spun its tires before it began to inch forward without the headlights on. I grabbed the rifle from the tack room and stood in the shadowy doorway.

Finally the black hulk lumbered up the slushy drive hesitantly, like a dying bull.

At the top of the drive, the car kept inching forward until I recognized it and started to go to it, but there was something wrong—and suddenly I saw that there were dark holes stitched across the doors, and the windows had been shattered.

"Oh my God, Clement! Oh my God—" I ran to the driver's door first. I had no idea yet—and yanked it open. Clement was sitting bolt upright, his eyes closed, hands on the steering wheel. In the moonlight and snow his face was violet and the whole front of his starched white shirt was a shiny purple that was flowing down his pants, spreading across the seat, and dripping onto the floor. The side of his face was shadowed with bruises.

I reached in, turned off the engine, and pulled the hand brake. There was the metallic smell of blood and something like meat starting to rot that I had to hold my breath against as I worked my arm behind him to lift him out—his back was dry, the bullet still in him. He seemed smaller than when he'd left the house a few weeks earlier, and heavier. I didn't think I could lift him.

"She no part of it—leave her—just helping the kid out—" he muttered. Staring at me without recognition, he said, "She all right? I said don't hurt her—just a kid—her mama wants her home—she all right?"

"Who?" I looked at the empty passenger seat. Did he mean me?

"Backseat. She all right? Just a kid. . . . she all right?"

I looked over the seat and immediately stepped away from the car, folded my arms around myself, and shivered so hard I felt one of my molars crack, heard it, and the stab of pain brought my hand out reaching for the door.

She looked so young lying there, her bluish-brown lips parted in surprise and probably pain, judging from the cuts, swollen eyes, and smashed nose. Her clothes were in ribbons, her right arm looked charred to the bone, and from the odd angle her left was probably broken. Then I saw the small dark hole in her left breast. India Gatto was dead.

"Who did this! Did *you* do this? Clement! Wake up, goddamn you!" I shook and punched him awake, but he only mumbled deliriously.

"They're coming—" His eyes wandered over the car and the darkness surrounding the house. "Hide us—they're coming!"

"Who's coming? Who did this, Clement? What have you done?" I yelled to keep him from dropping off again. The bleeding was slowing, but still steady, and a ribbon of blood was stringing out of the car onto the snow at my feet. "Goddamn you!" I slapped his face.

"Caught me at the river—" he panted. "Told her, stay in car—"

"Why is India here?" I dropped my voice. "Clement, why is India in your car?"

He seemed to brighten at the mention of her name. His eyes widened and stared as if reliving the scene as he spoke. "All she had to do—stay in car—" he sobbed. "Bringing her home—" His fingers wandered through the blood on his chest, and he held them up and stared in wonder. "Shot me. Can't feel anything." He showed me his dark shiny fingertips.

I stepped back, looking up and down the road. I couldn't take him to the hospital in Sisketon—he'd never make it.

"I'm dying," he said matter-of-factly. "Hide me. If they find me, they'll take the farm. Hide me." He looked at me with recognition on his face for the first time. "Hedie, honey—"

"I'll be right back." I took off running to the house, yelling back over my shoulder as I ran. "Don't die, Clement—"

When I phoned the Gattos, it was Vishti, the light sleeper, who answered, and I had to fight with her to get Jesse.

"It's India and Clement—it's bad," I said and heard a muffled sound like the breath being punched out of him, then he hung up.

When they arrived a few minutes later, Vishti jumped out of the truck and ran to Clement's car before we could stop her. The horror struck her in the face like a board, and it wasn't until we carried India's body to their truck that Vishti would leave. We watched her drive away so slowly it was as if she were using braille to make her way through the dark slushy snow to home. It was the horror of the journey alone that must have undone her, I realized later, the struggle to move her daughter's ruined body out of the truck, up the steps, into the house. How she must have howled and cursed.

"Hide car, save yourself—" Clement whispered, wonder in his voice when we looked inside again. "Sand boil."

"No, I won't—Clement, you listen, damn you, sit up, tell me how to help you!"

I glanced at Jesse and he shook his head. Clement was dying and we couldn't take him for help now. It was too late. They'd find us—and the sheriff already made it clear we were on our own. There was only one place where they'd never find him.

I shook my head. "I won't do it. He won't die. Clement, don't you die now!" I took his head in my hands and shook it and kissed his cold lips and tasted the metallic brush of blood and threw up in the snow by the car. Jesse grabbed my shoulder and spun me around.

"Get in the car," he ordered.

"I'll drive," I said. I couldn't let anything happen to him.

Navigating around to the farthest hay field wasn't easy in the dark without headlights in the heavy wet snow, Clement sliding on the blood-slicked seat between us. My shoes soaked in his blood, I had to concentrate on keeping my foot from slipping off the gas pedal, too. Jesse and I kept looking over our shoulders toward the house and road to make sure there was no sign of headlights. Nobody came down this road at night unless they had business with us.

I was numb, I wasn't really reacting to anything but keeping the tires out of the sand boils and the shallow ruts that wound beside the fields. It began to snow again, big thick flakes that splatted on the windshield and stuck to everything.

When I finally swung the car into the hay field and turned off the headlights, Jesse said, "Car won't make it," in a voice so quiet, I glanced at him.

I stepped on the gas as we started to wallow and catch in some sand, and the hood rose and we bulled straight across the field to the big boil, the one we'd lost the manure spreader in last summer. It seemed solid in the snowy moonlight, but that was the dangerous part of sand boils. The slightest vibration, from a car or machine, instantly turned the surface liquid again.

Jesse's face was so still, so void of anything, I worried that he wasn't going to be able to help me. Then he shook Clement's arm, and grabbed him by the back of the neck like a misbehaving schoolboy and shook his head, until Clement groaned.

"Who's coming?" Jesse asked. "Clement, wake up! Who hurt my girl?"

Clement's head rolled back and forth, then he opened his eyes. "They're coming."

I looked behind us and thought I saw a bobbing light.

"Jesse, he's still alive. What should we do?"

Clement's breath was fluttery now, light as a butterfly struggling in a web—

"Lights," he said and I squinted and thought I saw them, yes, casting two thin streams of light on the road. If they saw us—

"She was the beauty of my life," Jesse whispered. "Just a girl—"

Clement's breath feathered on, the blood pumping ever more slowly.

He moved in and out of consciousness, words on his lips unintelligible. But he didn't stop breathing.

I stumbled to all fours when I climbed out of the car because my shoes were so slippery with his blood and the snow. Would they see the blood in the driveway? Did I remember to scuff it with my foot or had the snow already covered it? My heart was beating so fast my arms ached as I stared at the sand boil, then looked at Jesse on the other side of the car before I ducked back inside. Clement had slid down so he was lying half on the seat in his own pooling blood. I peered closely at his chest, the feathery breath still rising and falling. Damn him. I wanted to damn him to hell for dying— it was outrageous—and now we were all going to die.

My feet were cold. I glanced down. I was still wearing my house slippers. I'd forgotten to take them off when I went to the stable, and now they were dark and shiny instead of pink with ostrich feathers. Clement loved shoes, loved young feet . . . I leaned in the car again, had he stopped yet? No, his lips fluttered with the whistly exhale—

"They're turning into your driveway," Jesse said. "I'm going back there."

I glanced over my shoulder. We were out of time.

"Let me go, honey," Clement whispered. "Take the farm if you don't— do it—all for you—love—"

I leaned over and kissed his forehead and smoothed back his hair. "Good night, sweet man, good dreams," I whispered. Then I straightened, unable to move.

"I'll do it," Jesse finally said. "Get out of the way." He held the tire iron from the trunk, and his voice was so low and tight, I didn't know what he meant to do.

The Packard only needed the weight of the tire iron jammed on the gas pedal, while Jesse pushed and I released the brake, to get rolling forward. It stopped as soon as the front tires hit the sand and it took both of us pushing to force it the rest of the way in. The car sat there on top for a moment like it wasn't going to go, then the surface seemed to split and the car began to sink, first to the top of the hubcaps, then with a sucking whisper, to the bottom of the doors. The engine continued to rumble until the sand rose almost to the windows missing their shattered glass, then it gurgled thickly and stopped. I flung myself forward, but Jesse grabbed me just as my toes found the soft edge of the boil. Maybe we could save him—we'd been in too much of a hurry. Then the sand sucked over the window frames and the car lurched and squatted as the wet sand began to fill the interior with its weight. Was he—

The car paused for a moment when the sand reached the top of the seats, and I panicked that it might not sink. Then there was a long screeching sigh, and it continued down, inch by agonizing inch, until the surface was flat again.

It was so quiet then, all I could hear was my own hiccuping sobs. Clement was dead. I'd loved him, no matter what happened at the end. He was still in my heart, and now I had no one. Our baby gone. My husband gone. I'd killed him. I killed Clement. The words pounded my chest and I couldn't catch my breath, couldn't—Jesse's arm around me, I leaned back, and let him hold me up for a few minutes until my chest opened again. I could breathe, and wished I couldn't.

I imagined Clement's mouth and eyes full of sand before his mind and body recognized what was happening and it was too late to push his hands up through the heavy surface and save himself. He wasn't conscious. He was dying. I know that. He told me to hide him. Told me to save his precious farm. Jacques' land. I kicked at the snow and stumbled. This goddamned land.

It began to snow more heavily, as we walked back, then changed to icy rain when it warmed up midmorning. It covered us quickly, diluting the blood on our clothes. By the time we staggered up to the stable, the men had turned around and driven away. I have no idea to this day who they were—revenuers, federal agents, local police, or gangsters. I stripped the rank clothes off and stepped into the scalding bath, which turned pink from the blood, so I had to let the water out and start over again. I felt certain that the men would be back, that they'd kill me this time, and I wasn't sure I cared. I had nothing and no one now. Clement—how could he do this to me? I loved him, I kept sobbing until the water turned icy and my skin blued with cold. I didn't stop shivering for a week. I just drank and stared out the front windows waiting for someone to come and take me away for killing my husband. No one came. Ever. I have no idea why.

We were lucky, I guess. We never saw the men who killed them. That always bothers Jesse. Not me.

Jesse and Vishti hid India in a shallow hole at their farm and waited for four months until they felt safe enough to bring her here and bury her in the Ducharme family cemetery.

Vishti never spoke another word after that night. Her last words were to curse the Ducharmes and smash Jesse in the face with a porcelain box I'd given her. We waited six months before we contacted the lawyer for her family trust in New Orleans. He arrived the next day and made all the arrangements. It turned out she was Omah's daughter—a Ducharme after all.

I think back to the morning when the little family arrived at the farm to work for us—they had driven their battered truck, the bumper held up with baling wire, one headlight hanging from its socket, the passenger door so dented it wouldn't open. Yet Jesse got out with all the ease of a man stepping from a new Cadillac, shoulders thrown back, brown fedora cocked on his head, hands stuck casually in his brown pants pockets, jingling change—for all the world like a man alighting from a train in a new town. He began to whistle a sweet, complex melody and nodded in my direction as I stepped onto the porch. Clement was still sleeping, I remember, and I put my finger to my lips and Jesse nodded again and turned back to the truck.

India slid under the steering wheel and jumped out, landing light as a cat, but immediately crossed her arms and looked around scowling. She wore a faded blue checkered scarf on her head in the manner of colored women who worked out of the house, and I could almost feel her long tapered fingers with the bright red polish itching to snatch that rag from her hair. Although she wore a shapeless, faded dress that hung to her calves, her mother's most likely, the hard young curves of her body peeked out more tantalizingly than if had she worn a fitted dress. She turned to say something over her shoulder, and her mother eased under the steering wheel and stepped carefully to the ground beside her daughter and husband.

Vishti was small and willowy, and if at times she lacked a certain vitality, she was the one we all centered on, with her rich deep whiskey voice, surprising from that slight body, and a face that seemed to mirror every emotion a person had. A red felt hat slouched on her head belying the old housedress she wore. Her daughter said something, and with a quick glance in her direction, Vishti straightened her back, lifted her chin, and walked toward the house as if she lived here. As Omah's daughter, she had the right, I suppose, though I didn't realize that at the time.

We also didn't realize that the rumble of the arriving truck had awakened Clement, who stood at the upstairs windows watching as India gathered the extra dress material at the waist and pulled it tight, revealing the flared hips and high, firm breasts. Jesse swatted his daughter's bottom with a laugh and she scampered out of the way like a long-legged colt, suddenly a child again—

IT IS YEARS LATER NOW, 1950, AND THE TELEPHONE HAS BEEN RINGING FOR some time when I pick it up, already knowing what it is. Clement is long gone. Now it's Vishti's turn. I have spent the night waiting as I used to so many years ago, reading the family books, waiting.

"Is she—" I say.

"She's found her peace." Jesse's voice is quiet, firm. He's found his peace, too.

"That's it then," I say stupidly, for I know this is the end.

"Yes."

"Will she come here?" I ask.

"In the morning."

"Yes," I say. "I'll call someone—"

"No," he says. "I'll be there first thing."

So soon? I want to say when we hang up. Couldn't we wait a day or two?

"Vishti?" I say her name out loud in case she has joined the others, but am met with silence. Have they all gathered in a far room to meet her—is old One-Armed Jacques Ducharme there to welcome another river wife?

I put the Jack Daniel's bottle to my lips and fill my mouth with the hot smoky liquid, swallow, and take another mouthful. This one I hold until my tongue burns and my gums ache, then let it slide down my throat.

I pick up the pen and begin to write what I promised Vishti and Jesse I'd never tell a soul.

I take another slug from the bottle. I'm going to tell my story from the day I married Clement Swan Ducharme. Fill in the missing pieces. How Omah arrived for burial and Keaton, having only a vague recollection of her as Jacques' servant, had the hole dug beyond the fence for the family cemetery. No amount of discussion could convince Keaton that he was wrong, not even pointing out the headstones of her parents and their son, which Keaton to his dying day believed were markers for some distant relatives of Jacques, who must therefore be white. Clement's only reaction when I told him was to laugh.

Omah's grave remains today, a jigsaw piece cut out of the cotton, with a stone on which the most beautiful birds and trees are carved. It leans toward the fence, as if to reunite with the stones of her parents and daughter on the other side.

We're all silence in the end, you see, our flailing done, our hearts hung on the last of the gray light as it settles on the land, another storm on the horizon, until we stop urging each other toward the wild limits of ourselves.

Entering another person's family is probably the bravest thing a person can do, I figure. There's just no way of knowing the infinite devices we have to stitch ourselves together across time. How we come to hold hands with every dead person, every ghost, every wrong, every beloved, and every lost soul. They become us after a while, the scent of pears in the hallway, the faded blue gown crossing the yard nightly to the family cemetery, the whispered pleas, the tinkle of laughter and hot breath on your arm, the cool touch of moist lips on your cheek, the heavy press of a body sitting on the edge of the bed while you sleep—and the way the dog pauses in the living room, eyeing the doorway, hackles rising. This is what it means to live with the old ones, to inhabit the farm at Jacques' Landing alone, as I do now.

At night it's just me calling Jacques' name into the darkness, because it's the dead hand of Jacques passing misery down like heirloom china. And he replies in the low moan of the river, in the cries of things caught and killed, in the blunt stare of the moon's broad face. That's why I spend the day wearing myself down to the bone, because the nights are too hard. Only the horses with their bright flickering coats and big kind eyes can save me so I can fall asleep as quickly as a torch extinguished in the river—

Tomorrow I'm going to the old bachelor's ell to break through the walls and floors, maybe find Jacques' treasure, save our land for the last Ducharme, my son, born Swan Ducharme six months after Clement died. He's at the university, majoring in agriculture and girls. Jesse and I have worked hard to make him a proper man, but we must wait and see how the blood runs. So tonight I return to the story I am now writing in the family book, the story that really begins in 1930, the day I, Hedie Rails, married Clement Swan Ducharme. I was seventeen, and he was a grown man almost twice my age, but I had come to believe in love's evil angel . . .

ACKNOWLEDGMENTS

My thanks to my longtime editor and friend Jane von Mehren and my friend and agent, Emma Sweeney, for believing that I could tell this story. Thanks to my family, fellow travelers on the river—Jackie Agee; Cindy Boettcher; Brenda Bobbitt; Cindy, Ross, Mike Jr., and Travis Agee; Talbott and Blythe Guy. Thanks to Lon Otto for remaining my writing companion for over thirty years. Thanks to many friends who have cheered me along the way: Bill Reichardt, Jim Cihlar, Heid Erdrich, Leslie Miller, Tom Redshaw, Greg Hewitt, Tony Hainault, Sharon Chmielarz, Andrea Beauchamp, Barbara DiBernard, Joy Ritchie, Ted Kooser, Hilda Raz, Pat Fleming, Mike Dalton, and Sharon Warner. And thanks to the people in 202 Andrews, who make every day easier and better: LeAnn Messing, Elaine Dvorak, Sue Hart, Janet Carlson, Kelly Carlisle, and Linda Rossiter. Thanks to Molly and Terry Foster for seeing me through the last year. Thanks to my many graduate students, who make writing seem more a pleasure than work. Thanks to Kati Cramer, Cindy Olson, Daryl Farmer, Dave Madden, Julie Kraft, Allie Avant, Caitlin Teare, Arra Ross, and Corey Schroeder, who've given their personal time to help during the writing of this book. Finally, I'd like to thank Linda Pratt for her support and friendship, and for bringing me to the University of Nebraska, where I have at last found a home for my work. Thanks to the Hall family for providing me with the Adele Hall Chair and financial support to continue my writing, and to the University of Nebraska–Lincoln.

THE
RIVER
WIFE

JONIS AGEE

A Reader's Guide

A CONVERSATION WITH
JONIS AGEE

A Jacques' Landing Roundtable

Random House Reader's Circle moderated a discussion group where Jacques Ducharme, Hedi Rails Ducharme, Annie Lark Ducharme, Laura Burke Shut Ducharme, Omah Ducharme, and Maddie Shut had the chance to speak with author Jonis Agee about her strategies for writing about—and her *interference* in—their lives. We are pleased to present a transcript of that discussion here.

Random House Reader's Circle: Thank you all for being here today; we know you've all been looking forward to this. Jacques' Landing residents, is there any one in particular who would like to begin?

Jacques Ducharme: Why a pirate? And why, *cher*, this particular pirate? What you want to go and give away all my secrets for? Why could you not have let the river take me, so I could join my dear little Annie?

Jonis Agee: Your wives were recording your secrets, Jacques. You should know that there is nothing that stays hidden, especially wrongdoing. You tried to hide the evidence in your tunnel room, but eventually even that was discovered. I thought that you should die with the thing you valued most—your heap of stolen goods, the fortune you made. Besides, the river wouldn't have you, not after you put so many souls in it. Nothing could kill you, Jacques, you had made yourself a force beyond nature. Only you could decide to die—that's why you had to spontaneously combust or self-immolate. If you keep helping people in the afterlife, maybe your ghost will finally be permitted to leave the house and join Annie's.

Hedi Rails Ducharme: I shudder to ask this, since it brings back such a painful memory, but can you say something about sand boils?

JA: They're one of the most intriguing by-products of the great quake—seemingly bottomless pits where the ground actually liquefied. They periodically fill with water, too, and nothing grows on top of them. Farmers have to be careful not to drive their machinery over them, because the boil never gives back what it takes. If you fly over the Bootheel region of Missouri, you can look down and see the yellow areas on the land which are sand boils. When the next big quake hits, those boils will probably spit back what's in them.

Annie Lark Ducharme: What was Jacques doing in the woods that made him so strange? He never grew old after that.

JA: Jacques found something or someone with the power to grant him his desire for a vast fortune, and all he had to do was use everything he had in himself to bring it to fruition. He didn't quite trade his soul in a pact with the devil, but he found that without a heart, he could be utterly ruthless. By shrugging off the burdens of morality, he could stay young, without grief or care, ageless.

Laura Burke Shut Ducharme: I don't have a question for y'all, except to say that I was not a gold digger! I did love Jacques, no matter what they say! Didn't I?

JA: No, Laura, it's pretty clear to everyone that you wanted his fortune and the security it offered. Lots of people marry for those reasons. Your problem arose when you miscalculated what and who Jacques was, but then, you weren't alone there. I'm sorry that you had to die in that awful hole, but you are much more like Jacques than you realize, and you share a similar fate.

Omah Ducharme: What is it about Jacques that cast a spell over so many women, ole twisted stick of a man with on'y one arm?

JA: I'm surprised that you'd ask this question, Omah. Surely you saw his quixotic personality over the years, his vast powers, his ruthlessness. Why did you fall in with his schemes? You may not have been his mistress or wife, but you did fulfill his plans for you, didn't you? You became like Jacques, shared that power. It was exhilarating, wasn't it? Remember the first night on the river, how strong you felt after you saved your own life? That feeling of being reborn, without weakness, without conscience, without consequence, as if you were a god walking the earth? That's what women kept seeing in Jacques, kept believing they were going to get to share. That kind of belief in yourself is like a narcotic to other people. You know that, Omah; look at the men who were seduced by your power. Most women will trade the physical aspect of a man just to cozy up to that vastness of the unlimited self and the fortune it accumulates around itself.

Maddie Shut: How do you explain the mystery of my Da? Why didn't he want me to marry and have a child?

JA: Read the journals, Maddie. He loved you. He hated betrayal more than anything, and he never forgave it after Annie Lark, his first wife. He loathed the weakness in himself that led him to marry Laura, his one great mistake. He was afraid that Laura's blood was tainted by greed and selfishness—something he couldn't stand in other people, by the way. He was trying to control the future with the codicil. He didn't want his hard-earned money going to someone like Laura. Basically, I'm sorry to say, he didn't trust you to find someone like L. O. Swan who would bring the best out of you and help create a person of fine character. Your Da was in his dotage, Maddie, gone slightly mad with having seen and done too many bad things, and lived too long. He came to believe that the world was a violent, hopeless place, and he didn't want all he had worked to build to fall. He was wrong, of course, as most of us are when we try to plan for the future based on the unchanging present we perceive.

RHRC: Okay, okay, it's about time we chimed in before you all get out of hand. Surely this could go on forever! Jonis, may we ask what it is about the New Madrid earthquake that you found so compelling?

JA: Growing up in the Midwest where we were always watching the sky for the tornado that was coming to tear our world apart, I developed a kind of fatal attraction for natural disasters. The New Madrid quake was the largest ever to occur in North America; it lasted for a whole year with over two thousand quakes and aftershocks, and it made the mighty Mississippi River run backwards at one point. More important, there are eyewitness accounts that give a personal view of the terror of those early days of the quake. The town of New Madrid is emptied and eventually taken by the river changing course because of the quake. As I was reading the early accounts of the quake, I came upon the haunting story of a young girl who was trapped and abandoned by her family the night of the first quake. In a way, *The River Wife* grew out of that one story and my need to save her life. I simply couldn't stand the idea that she was left to die by the people who loved her. She became Annie Lark, and Jacques Ducharme was one of the French fur trappers who were dug into the banks of the river that night, and who reportedly somehow survived.

RHRC: Very interesting indeed. In writing historical fiction around that kind of event, what delighted you the most—and what did you find most dangerous?

JA: It's wonderful to see a world come alive through historical details. Audubon was riding his horse in Kentucky during one of the big quakes, and there is an account of him beating his horse when it stopped, terrified. When Audubon jumped off the animal, figuring it was dying, he discovered the earthquake. It was exciting to have Audubon come into the novel, a natural place for him, since he was traveling and exploring for new species in the region. The day he appeared on Jacques and Annie's doorstep, I immediately begin to read his diaries, letters, and biography for more information to make him come alive. What I like most is the discovery of things I didn't know, and being able to include them in the fiction. The danger lies in the balancing act between historical detail and facts and character and plot. The people must always come first so they can stay realistic, alive, despite the clothing they wear. I had a lot of information about building log houses of the time, including research I'd done on tools used in that period—fascinating stuff, really—but I ended up cutting a lot of that detail because it was taking much too long to put up the first inn at Jacques' Landing. We needed to move along with the people to discover what they were going to do next.

RHRC: How did you research all of this?

JA: I began my research with histories of the New Madrid quake, the state of Missouri, the War Between the States, the geology, weather, plant and animal species there, and as I moved through each era, I focused on more specific subjects, such as early French settlements and cooking, river travel, clothing, slavery, battles fought in the region, logging, cotton farming, Hot Springs, Reelfoot Lake, and so on. There were always details that needed to be added, and I grew to love that process of discovering—what kind of pistol Laura would carry with her to Hot Springs, for instance.

RHRC: Now, there seem to be a number of ghosts haunting the house and land at Jacques' Landing. Can you lend a bit of insight as to whether you intend this to be a ghost story, and if so, why?

JA: I wanted to write a novel about a particular place, a patch of land along a river that was in constant motion, and tell the story of everyone and everything that passed through that place and left a piece of themselves, however slight, like a reminder to us that we are not the first, and we will not be the last. I love old houses because they bear evidence of all the lives that have been lived there, in the layers of wallpaper and paint, nicks in the woodwork and scratches on the window glass. Even the earth surrounding an old house constantly yields up evidence in the form of marbles, pieces of old hinges, coins, and combs. Last week I found a lead ball from an old rifle used when the military first set up on the bluff overlooking the river valley where I live. This was Ponca tribal land, and I keep wondering what that gun was shooting at. Ghosts are everywhere.

RHRC: Okay, here's a question whose answer I think we're all dying to know: Why does Jacques stop loving, or seem to stop loving, Annie Lark? It couldn't just be Audubon and the suspected affair, could it?

JA: Annie and Jacques suffer the worst kind of loss when their baby is killed. The aftershocks continue for the rest of their life together, as they often will. Annie registers her grief by withdrawing for a time into madness, then by going up the tree to observe the world. They are never really together after the loss of the baby. Jacques registers his grief by throwing himself into another kind of madness: the building of a vast empire beginning with the house he is constructing. When they argue, it's as if they are trying to push away the blame for the baby's death. They each blame themselves, as well as each other. Although there is almost no way for their pain to be healed, at the very end of Annie's life, Jacques discards the past and realizes that he still loves her. He has made a pact with the devil, however; now he can't save her and must live forever with this new loss of the one person with whom he shared a fully realized love.

RHRC: How powerful—and after Chabot dies, Jacques seems to change for the worse, and life at the Landing degenerates rapidly. Why?

JA: Chabot was the one male friend Jacques had, the person who knew him in the beginning and saw him in love with Annie, helped birth his child, knew him as a new father, full of all that potential for family. With Chabot gone, there is no one who is an equal to Jacques, and the dark force of his desires are free to couple with the strength of his personality to make him ruthless and heartless, at times. Chabot had the power of balancing Jacques, helping him control his impulses, such as when he helps the slaves escape rather than selling them downriver, as Jacques planned to do. There is more than money to life for Chabot, and he helps Jacques realize that while alive.

RHRC: Was Clement just a bad man, or did he originally love Hedie? Why did Hedie stay with him?

JA: Clement loves Hedie as best he can when they get together. He does marry her when she gets pregnant with his child, and he does try to be a good husband, although the kind of life he's leading eventually takes him away from her in every way. Again, the devastating loss of a child pulls them apart, although not as ferociously as it does earlier with Jacques and Annie. Clement is a more diluted version of Jacques, softer, less violent and certain of things. He isn't the builder or dreamer that Jacques is;

everything is a bit diminished in Clement's scale of living, although to him it seems large. Clement probably never had the strength of character to remain faithful for very long, but he would always intend to do so. He does appreciate Hedie as the woman who keeps his home, which is in large part a refuge from the illegal acts he is commiting in the larger world. He likes having a wife who can nurse him to health and make him comfortable.

Hedie is a seventeen-year-old girl with no family, no job skills, no money, during the Great Depression. She has no possible options except to stay with Clement or starve or worse. She makes the best of things, trying to salvage her marriage and build something that will endure for both of them so he doesn't have to keep leaving. She knows, after Hot Springs, that he is capable of infidelity on a serial or constant basis, but she is trying to make the best of things. She is more like Little Maddie and Annie Lark than she knows. She has strength and vision that she has to learn to use, and by the end of the novel, she does, although the cost has been great. Eventually, she embraces the family belief in preserving the land, the inheritance.

RHRC: Why don't Little Maddie, and later Hedie, bring Jacques' fortune above ground and use it?

JA: There is so much destruction and mayhem tied to that accumulation of jewels, coin, furniture, etc., that both women understand the enormous cost to the soul it represents. Neither is willing to take that burden on unless it becomes a matter of losing Jacques' Landing. By the time Hedie has read the journal narratives, she knows where the fortune is, but like Little Maddie, she intends to develop and use her own powers to maintain the family legacy so she doesn't have to share in Jacques' terrible demise. Successive generations all work to pay reparations, if you will, for Jacques' crimes, which continue to haunt the house at Jacques' Landing.

RHRC: Well, thank you, everyone, for being here. We've learned a lot, and hope you have, too.

QUESTIONS AND TOPICS
FOR DISCUSSION

1. The house Jacques Ducharme builds for Annie Lark is present throughout the novel. What is its significance? Why are Annie and later her ghost always seen outside the house, never inside?

2. The New Madrid earthquake profoundly changed not only the physical character of the landscape but also the human characters of the region. How would you describe the effects on the people in the novel?

3. Who is the "river wife"? Are all the women in the novel wives? Why and how are they attracted to these men?

4. What is the meaning of the circumstances of Jacques' death?

5. Why does Omah join Jacques as a pirate, and why does she stay with the family later? How is Omah like and unlike the other women?

6. Why does old Maddie stay to take care of Jacques and Laura's baby? Doesn't she realize that Jacques has been instrumental in the deaths of her two children?

7. Jacques Ducharme is a powerful figure throughout the novel—even in death. What is the source of his power? What did Annie Lark and Little Maddie find to love in him?

8. Does Annie really envision having an affair with Audubon? What are his intentions?·

9. Why isn't Laura satisfied with her marriage and prospect of wealth with Jacques? What is driving her to align herself with Major Stark? Does she get what she deserves?

10. Why does L. O. Swan give up his dream of returning home to stay with Little Maddie? Is it fair that Little Maddie asks this of him?

11. How is each of the characters both similar to Jacques and different from him?

12. *The River Wife* grapples with the secrets that plague families through generations, growing more hidden and deadly as they undermine the house. Would it have been possible to change this legacy? What would become of Hedie then?

13. Although their lives are filled with loss, what do the women and men of this novel gain through their marriages and relationships? What makes them continue to struggle with each other, with the land, with the ghosts that haunt their lives?

PHOTO: © STEVE KOWALSKI

JONIS AGEE is an award-winning author whose novels include the *New York Times* Notable Books *Sweet Eyes* and
Strange Angels, and most recently, *The Weight of Dreams.* A
native of Nebraska, Agee spent most of her childhood
summers in Missouri near Lake of the Ozarks. She taught
for many years at the College of Saint Catherine in St.
Paul, Minnesota, and the University of Michigan in Ann
Arbor. After a long absence, she returned to Nebraska,
where she lives north of Omaha on an acreage along the
Missouri River and teaches at the University of Nebraska–
Lincoln.

ABOUT THE TYPE

The text of this book was set in Janson, a typeface designed in about 1690 by Nicholas Kis, a Hungarian living in Amsterdam, and for many years mistakenly attributed to the Dutch printer Anton Janson. In 1919 the matrices became the property of the Stempel Foundry in Frankfurt. It is an old-style book face of excellent clarity and sharpness. Janson serifs are concave and splayed; the contrast between thick and thin strokes is marked.

Join the Random House Reader's Circle to enhance your book club or personal reading experience.

Our FREE monthly e-newsletter gives you:

- Sneak-peek excerpts from our newest titles

- Exclusive interviews with your favorite authors

- Special offers and promotions giving you access to advance copies of books, our free "Book Club Companion" quarterly magazine, and much more

- Fun ideas to spice up your book club meetings: creative activities, outings, and discussion topics

- Opportunities to invite an author to your next book club meeting

- Anecdotes and pearls of wisdom from other book group members . . . and the opportunity to share your own!

To sign up, visit our website at
www.randomhousereaderscircle.com

 When you see this seal on the outside, there's a great book club read inside.